ETTA MisPLACEd

ETTA MisPLACEd

The Story of Etta Place
The Woman Who Was Much More Than The Sundance Kid's Girlfriend

Honor Lee

AuthorHouse™ LLC
1663 Liberty Drive
Bloomington, IN 47403
www.authorhouse.com
Phone: 1-800-839-8640

Published by AuthorHouse 09/09/2013

ISBN: 978-1-4817-7853-4 (sc)
ISBN: 978-1-4817-7851-0 (hc)

Library of Congress Control Number: 2013913035

This book is printed on acid-free paper.

Thanks beyond words to my son
for the many ways he encouraged
the writing of this story

PROLOGUE

Foothills of the Sierra Nevada 1952

"It's a time gone by, gone forever, thought of as the old days, more than half a century ago, Merritt; even longer from when I first met Mabel and Etta."

"Well, hell, Pete, really, is it more than fifty years gone by?" "Yep, summer of '96 was when I met Mabel; met her sister Etta in '97 when she finally arrived in San Diego."

"Pete, that's about the same time I met Etta; winter of '96."

Peter reached for the whisky bottle lying on its side on the ground; he refilled Merritt's metal cup and then his own while Merritt added more wood on the campfire in the clearing just outside the old cabin. They both paused, quiet with their thoughts, staring at the snapping fire and listening to the chirping crickets.

Then Pete went on: "Hell it all really started in the spring of 1896 when the girls got on the train in Boston heading for their aunt's home in San Diego. Mabel making the full trip; Etta staying on awhile in Texas before she traveled around the west and began her place in history, just by the name Etta. No one, except us, ever knew who she really was; though now she's one of the most legendary women of the old west.

PART I

I

Raton, New Mexico Territory
Winter 1896

*

She first noticed him in the dining room; a good looking man of medium build, golden brown hair, light brown eyes, and sporting a sandy colored mustache. He was dressed informally yet had a clean well groomed appearance. He was handsome, in an unfussy way. She couldn't explain the intensity of her attraction to him, and couldn't help from staring. He seemed to be very amenable, talking with the mixed collections of society assembled at his table. The night before, he dined with men who appeared to be ranch hands and a boy who might be part Indian. This evening he was dining with the owner of the mercantile store and his wife, and another rather severe looking gentleman. They seemed to be lingering in conversation and exchanging books. She thought; I really must meet him.

Later, when she was in the lobby, she waited until the proprietor had no one in close proximity to him, to ask if he knew the gentleman seated at the table in the corner.

The gracious clerk came around to the front of his counter to take a look in the dining room and almost bumped into the man in question. Etta had no way of knowing that the handsome gentleman of her interest was approaching the lobby with hopes of meeting her, or to at least have the chance to look at her once more. The introductions were made.

After a tongue-tied moment by the gentleman, when he'd lost his breath and his mind looking at the pretty young woman standing before him, he at last focused on Etta speaking; she was saying that she was from Boston and was fascinated by the west . . . .

"From Boston! What brings you to New Mexico?" "Well, I didn't come here directly. I started out with my sister, on our way to San Diego, with plans to work as a governess or tutor for a family there. We made a stop and visited family friends in Fort Worth and I stayed on to learn more about the Texas way of life and see more of the west. Before I travel on to California, I wanted to learn more of the west, so I went to Denver and now here."

Fortunately, Harry Longabaugh did remember where he was from. "Sounds like me, my original plans got ambushed somewhere along the trail. I'm from Pennsylvania, but it's been awhile since I've been there."

"Do you live here in Raton?" "No, no, I've been on the trail heading south, coming down from Canada. I thought I'd come through here and see if they had work over the hill in Cimarron, at Springer's, the CS Ranch, but now I'm takin' a break from ranch work. Sometimes when work's slow, and I have ready money, (Harry had just recently been exceptionally lucky at the card tables) I like to spend some time cleaned up, away from that, and in a town where I can get a hold of some good books." "Oh, does this town have a library?" "I don't know, I haven't found one, but a lot of folks will let you borrow their books. Old George Pace owns a dry goods store just down the street and can try to order books or let you borrow one. I can introduce him to you if you're goin' to be in town for awhile." "Oh, I'd like to stay awhile; how long will you be in town?"

At Etta's question their eyes met and lingered in shared attraction. Etta blushed a very noticeable deep crimson. It wasn't just from a feeling of awkwardness, but also from enchantment. Each wanted the moment to continue and found it hard to break the spell. Finally, he spoke, "I'll be here for awhile. If you're goin' to be here tomorrow, I can take you around to see the town, if you haven't seen all of it already; you most likely have. Or, I can get a buggy, for a ride to see the territory around town." "Oh yes, yes, I'd like that. I hope it won't take you from your books, but it would be splendid for me." "Then it's settled. I'll meet you here when it warms up, about nine or ten?" "Ten would be best, let it warm up a bit. So enjoyable to have met you, Mr. Longabaugh; I look forward to hearing your stories of the west." "Please, just Harry, tomorrow at ten." "Good night . . . . Harry." "Good night . . . . Etta."

*

By ten the next morning the temperature hadn't warmed in any way noticeable. Harry hired a horse and buggy from the livery stable and it was now in front of the hotel. He was waiting in the lobby, sitting on a hard uncomfortable chair, though there couldn't be a chair anywhere that would make him feel at ease at the prospect of seeing Etta again. He just about didn't blink while watching the staircase, waiting for her to appear. When she approached him, coming from the dining room, he was at first startled, and then stunned again by her prettiness.

Etta had hardly slept, She was up early, dressed, and after pacing the floor in her room decided to go on down to the dining room. Though almost too excited to eat, she ordered a biscuit and tea. She could hardly hold herself together while she waited for the clock to strike ten. At exactly ten, Etta excused herself, leaped up from her chair and, summoning restraint, walked slowly to the lobby. Her smile was wide and her eyes full of pleasure when she saw him. Harry's smile showed his pleasure.

*

"We're going to need a cover for you to keep warm and protect your coat and dress. I'll ask the clerk for a blanket." "Thank you Harry." Etta waited in the vestibule enjoying the brightly colored stained glasswork in the skylight.

"We can start out with a walk in town; give it time to warm up if it's going to." Let's go down the next block, to Pace's store. You might like to see George's book collection, and then we can walk around town from there before our ride to see the surroundings, if that's alright with you?" "Oh yes, in fact I'd like to buy some postage stamps and then find a store that carries face powder." Harry laughed and said, "I could let you know where to find gun powder, but I'm completely flummoxed where face powder is concerned; we can try at George's store, or the department stores."

George Pace came home from the civil war in 1877. At first, he made some money operating a small store at the Willow Springs Ranch Station which was the center for the areas commerce when the coal mines started operations in 1879. He then went on to run a store in Otero, but when the railroad moved its headquarters to Raton, five miles north, the population in Otero dwindled rapidly. Coal mining was already a booming business when George moved, in 1882, to the new city of Raton where he built and opened his store. He received approval to be post master and got the rights to run the post office in his store.

When Harry and Etta stepped into the store, George was running around frantically as usual. While they looked around, they got into conversation with a couple of the clerks who told them about the time they tricked Mr. Pace. Mr. Pace was always in a hurry, and whenever the clerks had paperwork for him to sign, Mr. Pace would hastily sign each paper without bothering to read it. One morning, the clerks carefully drew up an official looking paper stating that George Pace was to be hung at sundown that day. When it was presented along with other papers, George scribbled his signature without even the slightest examination of the contents. Later, at the time of the store's closing, the clerks showed Mr. Pace what he had signed. George flushed bright red, and then agreed that he should slow down and take more time with the paperwork.

The morning vanished along with the clouds, and though the skies were clear, the temperature remained chilly. Harry took Etta out in the buggy around the hill just at the end of town. While he pointed out various volcanic features of the land and spotted the occasional creature, they talked about themselves, and the course the country seemed to be taking.

"Do you know New Mexico well . . . Harry?" "Pretty much, I travel this way now and then. Next, I'm heading southwest to a ranch to see if there's work. I don't commonly go much further south into New Mexico. It just seems like bad country, even with the Lincoln County wars being over, and Billy the Kid long dead, and the Apache Chief Geronimo and his bunch long ago surrendered to General Miles; there's still Apache out there that I wouldn't want to tangle with."

"Was that an Indian boy with you at dinner the night before we met?" "Yep, that's GoForth, but that's not his full, right name; it's long and unpronounceable. He's from Oklahoma, part Osage, I think. He's very smart; one of the brightest youngsters I've ever met. You know, he speaks English, Osage and Spanish; a genuine shame that his being part Indian holds him back from the chances he should have. An associate of mine took him in with our bunch of ranch hands the first of this year, and finds him work. In a couple of days he's goin' to ride over to a ranch in Alma, in the western part of the state, to see if there's work, and check if some of our friends are there. Don't ever worry about him on the trail; I swear he can make himself invisible. If you'll join me, he'll be dining with me this evening for an early supper, and you can meet him then."

Seeing Etta start to shiver, Harry nudged the horses on. At the hotel, he escorted her to the lobby. They assured each other they would meet in the dining room for supper. Harry was staying in a smaller, more humble hotel, a couple of blocks away.

*

GoForth was about thirteen or fourteen, and on his own, as many young boys were out on the great western frontier, during that era of the 1890's. Butch Cassidy, Harry's recent acquaintance, had taken notice of the bright youngster earlier that year. Wanting to give him a break and not wanting to see him starve, Butch found work for him; sometimes just as a runner, like now, riding to deliver messages. Also, GoForth had considerable knowledge and a sixth sense about horses.

"GoForth, stop staring at the lady." (Harry was having the same problem). "I'm sorry ma'am but gosh you're pretty." "Thank you for the compliment Goforth. Tell me more about your people on the reservation, and why you left." "That's just my trouble ma'am, the people on the reservation made fun of me, and the whites do too. I don't have people. My mama died when I was 12; my father was a white man who left before I was born. Reservation life wasn't getting me anywhere, so I headed out. I have met some bad people along my way and some good, like my friends Butch and Harry. First, a ranch lady in Utah, and then after that Harry, showed me how to read and write, and some arithmetic, so I'm doing better already. But, when I go up to folks looking for a job, they ask my name and if I'm an Indian, and that's the end of it."

"Goforth is a strong name. What if you used a white man's name just to get by, or, I'm sorry, does that idea bother you?" "No ma'am, that'd be alright, but I can not think of a name, and I can not rightly use the name of someone else." "I know of a good man with a strong name who wouldn't mind your using it. His name is Merritt; Merritt Barnes. He lives way down in San Antonio, Texas. He's a fine, decent family man who's well educated and a journalist; how would you feel about using that name?" "That would work alright, but I'd like to keep GoForth in there too. I could be called Merritt GoForth Barnes and just go by Merritt Barnes for white folks." Harry was smiling, "Well, my friend, taking on a new name calls for a celebration, I'll order champagne."

The next day promised once more to be downright wintry. Harry had let Etta know that he planned to get himself to the barber, and then meet a friend at the Home Ranch Saloon, (to play cards) He asked if he could see her in the evening at supper. Happy she'd be seeing Harry again, Etta used the day to write to Mabel, do some mending, and to start reading the book Mr. Pace had lent her. It would be an excellent topic for conversation, though it seemed there was so much to say by both, and their talk flowed effortlessly.

"Harry, where is young GoForth, no, I mean Merritt this evening?" "He's already had something from the kitchen; seems he went out hunting real early this morning and brought in a deer for the cook. One of these nights soon, it'll be offered on the menu. Besides your letter writing; did you get around to reading your book?" "Oh some. I've read many of Emily Dickenson's poems, now this book has even more, and I like her style of writing immensely. How about you, did you have time for reading; did you start your book?" "Oh yeah, George really came up with a dandy one this time. I've just barely got it started. Ol' Barnaby Rudge is such a dim witted funny guy, the whole story is interesting; but, what's remarkable is that the people Mr. Dickens wrote about half a century ago, are just like folks today, they just talk different. GoForth, Merritt, says he started the Mark Twain book; that means he'll be lost for awhile. Etta, it looks like tomorrow might be clear and sunny; would you care to go for a buggy ride to see more of the country around town?" "Oh yes! I'm so happy you asked, Harry, I'd like that very much. Could we get something from the store, or from the kitchen, for a picnic?" "We surely could, Etta."

They started out while the morning was still frosty, but the sun was strong and the day promised to be warm by afternoon. They rode along in the buggy in no particular hurry, not caring where they went. Bundled up and sitting close, they talked about themselves; each intent on sharing and learning more about each other.

"Etta, tell me about your upbringing and why you're headin' to California. You're so young. How old are you Etta?" "Harry, I was born in 1878, I'm now eighteen." "Gosh Etta, I'm older 'n you. I'm almost thirty. Please, go on."

"I'm the second of three children; my sister, Mabel is two years older, and Buddy, my younger brother, is fourteen. We were all born at our home in Boston. We were schooled at home also. My father was a Doctor. I think my father went into medicine just for the simple fact that his father had been a doctor. If he could have chosen his destiny freely, I think he would have been a frontiersman. He liked to take us children up to Maine, on camp out trips, much to my mother's horror. I thought it was the best fun."

"He died two years ago, in 1894 in the Tai Ping Shan area of Hong Kong, doing disease research and studying the bubonic plague. It may have been his way of proving his worth to himself by going there in the first place. His death devastated us all."

"My mother couldn't manage to handle us children or the household; so my sister, Mabel and I took over. Then our mother became more and more agitated with Mabel and me. After corresponding with my aunt and uncle in California; it was arranged for Mabel to be employed as governess for a family there in San Diego. Mabel is a bright, talented, lovely person, and with her excelling in her studies and music, she'll be exceptional as a governess. The original plan for me, I'm sure, was something much less glamorous in the Boston area. It was Mabel who suggested to mother that I should find a position as governess also, or teach music; my passion is the violin. Our uncle Stephen could oversee the household affairs; so, as it turned out, I could travel with Mabel.

Boston Spring
1896

Boston's new North Station was noisy, crowded, and full of the excitement of departing travelers, their well wishing friends, and anxious people greeting their arriving loved ones. In the spring of 1896, increasingly more people were going west, either to visit family, or to try their luck on the western frontier. The great drive west by the early pioneers in their covered wagons had come to an end. The train was now the most popular mode of transportation.

Rather than sit across from each other, the two attractive young ladies sat side by side on the plush seat in their train car. The youngest, with her gray-blue eyes wide with excitement, had already taken off her hat; her chestnut hair had come loose from its pins and made a soft frame about her delicate face. She was leaning across her sister to wave goodbye to their mother, their kid brother, Buddy, and their Aunt Charlotte and Uncle Stephen. Many years would pass before she would see any of them again.

Mabel, just twenty years old, was the older sister, fairer in complexion of the two, and with her bright blue eyes and soft light auburn hair, she reminded one of the silhouette on a cameo. While she waved along with her sister, Etta, she could scarcely believe they were on their way west. Both girls stood out; their beauty and loveliness were noticed.

"Oh Etta, Mother is behaving recklessly putting us on a train west unaccompanied, all the way to San Diego in California! She truly isn't herself. And taking the route to Fort Worth to visit Dr. Gardiner's family; it's just too wild." "Mabel, you know it's the best opportunity for us, and you've put in so much effort to see this all work, from the very start you've been as thrilled as I am, and I have you to thank that I can be on this train going with you. Please don't be uneasy; settle into enjoying the adventure and let's celebrate our exciting future. Our stay in Fort Worth will be the beginning of our adventures. Do you think there'll be a train robbery while were traveling through the west?"

For the girls, departing from the train in Fort Worth was truly stepping into a new world. They had witnessed the eastern greenery giving way to the Great Plains. This was a continuation of that landscape, but to be here, in it, was astonishing. The intention of the visit to Dr. Gardiner's family was to share news with the long time friend of their father, and to take a rest from the continual rocking of the train.

This was a different life and Etta blossomed in her new environment while Mabel was dubious. The family took the girls on a pleasure trip using both horse and buggy and a team led wagon to visit friends living on a cattle ranch northwest of Fort Worth. Etta was overjoyed and spent most of her time taking horseback rides to see the open scenery of the great state of Texas. Her guide was a handsome cowhand who couldn't take his eyes off her. For that reason Dr. Gardiner never let them be out alone but always prompted at least one of his five children to go along. Mabel wasn't as interested in riding.

Both girls were awe struck at the sight of Longhorn cattle. Since Fort Worth had become a major shipping point for cattle it truly lived up to the name "Cowtown." On another family outing they all went to see the Fort Worth Stockyards. The girls were overwhelmed by the activity and the sheer number of cattle, but glad they didn't linger and moved on without much delay. Being shown a map of Fort Worth, it was easy for them to appreciate that the city really was "the body of the spider", with the rail lines as its legs.

None were too surprised when Etta asked Dr. Gardiner if she could stay a while longer to learn more about Texas. The entire family was delighted at the prospect as Etta could help with the children and assist their oldest girl in learning violin. Etta played well while Mabel's talent was the piano.

Mabel, while happy that this would work out for Etta, felt some apprehension about traveling alone for the rest of the journey to San Diego. Dr. Gardiner assured her it was a brief distance by train, "Just some 1000 miles; the direct route to San Diego would go easily enough, though it would take about three days." He would send a wire to her aunt to say when to expect her.

Mabel enjoyed the scenery on the train ride to San Diego, though she was already missing her sister. She found her Aunt Betty and Uncle Frank gracious and entertaining, and delighted in the warm climate of southern California. The beaches were warm; the fresh produce delectable and abundant. Mabel liked the family and the home where she went to live as governess. She was content.

*

Etta assisted Dr. Gardiner's children with their education, taught the children piano or violin according to their interest, and helped with household tasks. She was loved and loved them in return. Toward the end of summer, Etta expressed a desire to see more of Texas and would like to travel further south perhaps towards San Antonio where she could see the old Alamo Mission site before continuing on to San Diego. Dr. Gardiner knew a well-to-do widow, Mrs. Kilchherr, who lived in San Antonio. She owned a large house on expansive grounds and would enjoy the company. Arrangements were made, and Etta was once again on to a new adventure.

*

San Antonio was exhilarating. Mrs. Kilchherr's house was in the elegant King Wilhelm district, not far from downtown on the south bank of the San Antonio River. The stately house was a bit neglected. Mrs. Kilchherr, its owner, an ageing woman of high spirits, was also somewhat in need of maintenance. Feeling a sense of freedom with her old age, Mrs. Kilchherr did what she wanted and wore her favorite clothes, not caring if they matched. She enjoyed Etta's companionship and was pleased that Etta enjoyed going out with her to pursue amusements, dining, and the theatre.

Etta was captivated not only with the eccentric layering of clothing worn by her hostess but also with the unique viewpoints she held on an extensive number of subjects. Mrs. Kilchherr was pleased with Etta's interest in the history of San Antonio, the last of Spain's outposts in Texas. With Mrs. Kilchherr's hired man taking them in her old carriage, they took several outings into town to visit the old Spanish missions along the San Antonio River, and Etta finally saw Fort Alamo. Whenever they went downtown they always stopped at the Menger Hotel for supper.

Politics and the law were favorite subjects for Mrs. Kilchherr. Merritt Barnes, a journalist who had previously practiced law in San Antonio, was a frequent visitor at the house, where he and Eva Kilchherr dissected and analyzed the law, the military, and

Texas politicians. Etta enjoyed his knowledge of the west, and his stories of bold frontier men and their daring exploits. Her favorable impression of this interesting and intelligent man would shape some of her future thoughts and actions.

In Etta's letter to Mabel early that November, she mentioned that she planned to be traveling to San Diego before the end of the year, and asked her to check with Aunt Betty to inquire if staying with them was still acceptable. Etta would write to her also. First, she planned on taking the train to Denver City, Colorado to see what the celebrated western city looked like. She felt that she should see more of the west while she had the chance; as she would be settling into work and her life in California soon enough.

*

The journey to Denver showed Etta a good deal of rugged, mountainous country. She could readily understand the lure and appeal of the west. The South Platt River Valley was an irresistible setting for the new western city with the majestic Rocky Mountains rising above it in the west.

Denver was an exciting busy city, full of activity and the reverberations of electric street cars clanging their way through the streets. The people were very diverse, from the rough frontiersman, to effete men long lost to indulgence. The more stylish of women could be compared with any from the big cities of the east coast, and they could be seen daily in the Grand Salon or the Atrium Lobby of the Brown Palace Hotel where Etta was staying. Looking up from the grand lobby, she could see the balconies with their decorative iron railings. Though it was built so recently in 1892, the hotel had the solid older feel of buildings built in the Italian Renaissance style. The wealth, from both the gold rush in the fifties and the silver boom in the eighties, was still very apparent.

Etta was thrilled to be invited to join some of the ladies who met for tea in the Grand Salon. They could all feel her excitement and were pleased to encourage her enthusiasm by telling her of their experiences in the west. She was most impressed with a woman of unusual vitality, Margaret "Maggie" Brown, though not affiliated with the hotel. Maggie and her husband were recently new to Denver. She was among the women who had plans on founding a Denver Woman's Club, whose mission was to be the improvement of women's lives through education. Etta found it stimulating to be in the company of such progressive women. Colorado was the second state in the nation to give women the right to vote in 1893; and in 1894 Colorado women voted in the first general election.

Etta considered staying on awhile, and then thought it best to be on her way. She wanted to see, and perhaps make stops, in other towns before arriving in San Diego. How could she possibly take in all there was to see, December was almost here.

*

"Harry, I've just been going on about myself; let me hear about you."

"Well alright, but you haven't told be anything about what you were like as a little girl; strong willed, I can bet. My upbringing wasn't anything near like yours. I'm from Pennsylvania, the last of five children. We didn't have much money. I was sent out to work and live on a farm when I was thirteen. After that my brother Harvey and I went to New York to find work. We didn't do so well and went back home where we felt like a burden on the family."

"In 1882, my brother Elwood got on a whaling ship heading around to San Francisco and further north, and after that I was lucky enough to go west to live with my cousin George and his family in Colorado. They raised horses and I worked with them, then I started working for other outfits and made my way on cattle ranches up in Wyoming, Montana, here in New Mexico, and Canada . . . ." Harry paused and took a deep breath while he remembered his time spent in the Sundance, Wyoming jail, in 1887, for stealing a horse and saddle; and his experience from the Great Northern train robbery outside Malta, Montana in 1892. He continued, "Then I went over to South Dakota and then came back, and kept making the rounds working on the ranches that were hiring and spent awhile around Calgary, up in Canada. Not an attractive life and I sure don't have much to show for myself."
"Harry, you've been living an adventurous life, one that I can

imagine includes hardships. You've learned how to make a living in the west. I find you to be an exceptionally intelligent and fine man." "Etta, thank you. I didn't know what you'd make of me."

Harry stopped the buggy, looked straight into Etta's eyes and found the courage to kiss her. She returned the kiss. Without thought of what they were doing; Harry helped Etta down from the buggy and started unpacking the picnic, but then found themselves leaning against each other under a tree while they kissed; then using the tree's trunk for support or each may have fallen in a swoon. Etta, did in fact, go completely weak in the knees and Harry helped her to sit down. They enjoyed their picnic, each very aware of the meaningful feelings they shared. There was no more kissing until the end of the day when they were just approaching town. Both knew it wouldn't be easy to not show their affection for one another in public.

*

They shared that evening's supper with three others, whose presence provided distraction and amusement which considerably lightened the tension they hoped didn't show. At the end of the meal, after the others had excused themselves, they were smiling, sharing the same fondness for each other.

"You know Etta, it may sound peculiar, we're probably completely opposite people from one another, but then we're a lot alike in our understanding. I like how you are with folks. I especially like the way you are with me. Tomorrow, I've got to see Doc Shuler; my head's congested. I suffer from catarrh, if you've noticed how I'm always clearin my throat. Sometimes I need to get something for it. By the way, young Merritt's ridin west day after tomorrow. He asked if he'd have the chance to see you and talk with you again."

"Please ask him to join me for breakfast, about eight or when he can. We can talk, and if he has time we can take a walk around town; I have some items to shop for. I feel very sisterly towards him and I'm exceptionally impressed with him." "Oh he'll have time alright if he can spend it with you! May I see you for supper tomorrow evening?"

*

Merritt was already waiting for Etta the next morning when she came to the lobby. At breakfast, she took pleasure in watching him eat; she had forgotten the appetite of growing boys. She was relaxed enough now to enjoy her breakfasts.

"Merritt, how are you feeling about being called a different name?" "It's kinda strange, but good too 'cause, I don't know if I am pretending or not, but I feel like a different person, kinda special." "Merritt, you have an exceptional way of expressing yourself. You're very honest in saying what you're feeling. I'm very pleased to know you." "Ma'am I have done things that were not honest in many ways." "Merritt, you did what you had to do to take care of yourself, the only way you could. Don't dwell on blame, just learn from those experiences, and try never to hurt anyone, including you. Would you walk with me now? I'd enjoy continuing our talk as I take care of some errands." "Yes ma'am!"

Etta couldn't help but think of her young brother, Buddy, who was about the same age as Merritt, and had every opportunity and privilege but wasn't half as bright or admirable as this young man.

*

Mr. and Mrs. Pace joined Harry and Etta at the supper table that evening. They talked about Merritt's new name and what a fine, bright lad he was. Two of their sons did errands and clerked at the store for them, along with two other young men. They didn't need extra help; otherwise they would have hired Merritt. George asked Harry if he had ever seen him count figures. "Harry, he's astonishing; he can count faster in his head than I can on paper. Where'd he learn that?"

Etta was concerned about what would become of Merritt. Merritt had told her of his desire to go west to California; to the gold country in the mountains. Etta considered the improbability of his going with her to San Diego. Merritt was leaving early the next morning, on the trail to the WS Ranch in Alma to see if any of the gang was there.

Parting at the same time as Mr. and Mrs. Pace were leaving, Harry and Etta didn't have the moment they wanted to make plans to see each other again. Etta spent an anxious night concerned that she wouldn't see Harry until the next evening at supper, and then was troubled with the thought that he may not be there even then.

After her breakfast, she went back to her room to get her great cape. Perhaps if she went for a walk she might see him in town. Then there was a gentle knock on her door . . . . . "Harry!" He would have apologized for his bad manners of coming to her room, if Etta hadn't reached for him, led him into the room, and kissed him, and kept on kissing him. They spent the morning in her room.

That afternoon, Harry left quietly by the back stairs. He hired a horse for Etta so they could go for an easy ride. Etta had mentioned to him that she had learned to ride as a girl at an uncle's farm. He was apprehensive at first, and then saw she could sit a saddle well enough, though a bit stiff. They enjoyed a carefree afternoon. Etta and Harry felt the strong bond between them but hadn't yet begun to think of how they would manage, or if they could continue to be with each other in the future. Harry was becoming shamefaced at his dishonesty for not yet telling Etta about his outlaw past.

*

They didn't meet for supper that evening; each needing to care for their own personal affairs. Their plan was to meet for breakfast, then go for a walk. Harry's intention was to tell all.

After walking through town, and stopping at Sperry's bicycle shop on 2nd Street, where Harry made a very wobbly attempt at riding a bicycle. Harry knew it was time to talk, "Let's go and walk a ways along the trail by that hill."

"Etta, I haven't been completely honest in speaking about myself. I've been reluctant to tell you, when I was twenty years old, I went to jail; the Crook County Jail in Sundance, Wyoming for stealing a horse, saddle, and bridle. I wasn't getting any work and stopped by the 3V's Ranch, on the Belle Fourche River, up in northeastern Wyoming, lookin for work, and that's where I stole the horse. I've done wrong, and I'm feeling shame to have to tell you. Some acquaintances have taken to calling me "The Sundance Kid" from that dreadful experience. Those were hard times. I knew of men who starved to death or froze out on the open range. I was feelin desperate. I know it would be hard to take that as an excuse. In those years, '86, '87, there was such harsh winters, thousands and thousands of cattle dyin' all over. They call that time, the big die up."

Etta was silent but kept walking with him. Harry tried to toughen his feelings believing the worst conclusion to his confession. How could Etta, such a fine, pretty lady, accept this news, especially telling her after their intimacy just yesterday. Since she still hadn't said anything, Harry presumed the worst and went on talking. "And, if the truth be told; there's something else. I was in on a bungled bank robbery up in Malta, Montana in '92, but didn't go to jail. There, I've told you my wrong doin's. I'm sorry, I am very sorry."

Etta stopped, gripped his arm tighter and looked up, right into his eyes, and said, "I'm just stunned!" Harry inhaled deeply, his head and heart pounding. "I'm so sorry." "No Harry, don't misunderstand my meaning. I'm taken aback by this news, certainly. What bewilders me is your confounded honesty. You and even young Merritt have shown me a different kind of man. More brave in your honesty than the usual. Of course I'm worried about you involved in such risky and dangerous, let alone unlawful, undertakings. It does frighten me. But, I'm going to tell you, I've met associates of my father, and men in Boston society who, though they may be pillars of the community, are in fact treacherous, dishonest men in their dealings. They would never, ever admit to their wrongdoings, too full of arrogance and self importance."

"Harry, I've read about the hardships of the west, and the hard times, the drought, and the brutal and severe winters of the late 80's, and the depression that was going on across the whole country. I had already wondered if you had, at some point, given way to some misdeeds, like cattle rustling." "Oh, I've done that too!" They both burst out in laughter, releasing the tension in both of them. "Etta, you're different than anyone I ever met!" Their holding each other was not so much an embrace, but much more a troubled clinging to each other. They parted at the end of the day, each bewildered with their own sorting out of this new development in their lives. Harry sorted out some of his thoughts at the Home Ranch Saloon before heading for his bed; Etta, by writing in the journal she'd been keeping since the beginning of her trip west. She had completely gone astray of the initial intent of her journey. Or had she?

*

THE WAYSIDE PRESS
March 12, 1887

HARRY LONGABAUGH ACCUSED OF HORSE THEFT

—

Charges were filed yesterday in Crook County and a warrant was issued for the arrest of Harry Longabaugh, who on February 27, stole a horse and saddle outfit from Alonzo Craven and a pistol from Jim Widner, both of the Three V ranch in Sundance, Wyoming. Widner filed the complaint with Sheriff James Ryan in Crook County Wyoming on behalf of himself and Craven.

THE WAYSIDE PRESS
April 11, 1887

LONGABAUGH ARRESTED THEN ESCAPES

Harry Longabaugh was taken into custody April 8, by Crook County Sheriff James Ryan who filed arrest papers on Harry Longabaugh in Miles City, Montana on April 8. Ryan traced Longabaugh to Miles City, where he was thought to have worked the previous year, found him and put him under arrest. Longabaugh is accused of horse theft from the Three V Ranch. On April 12, Ryan took the outlaw on the Northern Pacific train bound for St. Paul, Minnesota. While on the train, Longabaugh managed to free himself from his handcuffs and escaped by jumping from the train. He is being pursued by Deputy Eph K Davis and stock inspector W. Smith.

*

THE DAILY YELLOWSTONE JOURNAL
MILES CITY, MONTANA
Tuesday, June 7, 1887

—

How Deputy Sheriff E.K. Davis
Fooled a Fly Young Criminal
He Had in Charge

—

The Astonishing Record of Crime
Perpetuated by Harry Longabaugh
In Three Weeks

—

A Fly Kid
And the Way He was Caught Up
by Officers Davis and Smith

On Saturday Deputy Sheriff Davis, together with Stock Inspector smith, made a most important arrest. It will be remembered that about a month ago Harry Longabaugh, a criminal wanted in Sundance, and who was arrested here and turned over to Sheriff Ryan of Crook County, Wyoming, escaped from the sheriff by jumping from the train while in motion, in Minnesota. Sheriff Ryan being there in performance of his duty in taking him back to Wyoming soil. The Kid had not been heard of until very lately and was arrested as above stated by Deputy Davis near the N-Bar ranch on Powder River. After his escape from Sheriff Ryan he made his way back to Montana over the Canadian Pacific, and just before leaving Canadian soil stole seven head of horses from an operator on the new road and sold them near Benton. He came south stopped at Billings three days, and from there went to the Crow reservation, where he stole a pony, which is now in possession of Sheriff Irvine. He then perpetrated the robbery of the F U F ranch, which was detailed in these columns a few days ago, and from there proceeded to Beasley & Newman's sheep ranch and stole a horse from P.G. West. It was he who stole and cut the saddles at Kirwan & Langley's ranch on Tongue River, and he stole a horse from Geo. Liscom's ranch on the same river. He had planned to get away with a bunch of twelve mares belonging to Liscom, but he slipped up on that for some reason. The rest of his planned expeditions were nipped in the bud by his arrest. After Mr. Davis had made the arrest he took three six-shooters from the bold young criminal and shackled him and handcuffed him with some patent lock bracelets which were warranted to hold anything until unlocked by the key and which the manufacturers offered a premium if they could be opened otherwise. Eph Davis had heard of Longabaugh's prowess in effecting escape, and after taking all due precautions when night closed in upon them he lay down in one corner of a shack and Mr. Smith in another, the Kid between them. Smith was tired out and soon fell asleep and Davis played possum keeping an eye on the prisoner. Soon as he thought everyone was asleep the kid, shackled and manacled as he was, managed in five minutes with an old horseshoe nail to free himself and stealthily approached the window and raised it and was about to make a break for liberty when sly old Eph thought it was time for him to take a hand and raising on his elbow with a cocked six-shooter in his hand he said in a quiet tone of voice, "Kid, you're loose ain't you?" and then called to Smith. The Kid dropped back as though he was shot and it is needless to add the officers did not sleep at the same time during the rest of the night. Resolving not to loose his prisoner or reward this time Sheriff Irving had telegraphed Sheriff Ryan asking what he would give for the Kid laid down in Sundance. Talk about the James boys this fellow has all the necessary accomplishments to outshine them, and Tom Irvine considers him one of the most daring and desperate criminals he has ever had to deal with. The stretch of country he has covered in a short time and the success of all his planned robbery phenomenal. Deputy Davis and Inspector Smith did a mighty good job when they nailed the Kid without some blood being spilt. He acknowledged himself done up when he landed in this jail and expresses much admiration for our officers in the way they did business.

*

THE DAILY YELLOWSTONE JOURNAL
June 9, 1887

—

A Letter to the Editor From Harry A. Longabaugh

In your issue of the 7th inst. I read a very sensational and partly untrue article, which places me before the public not even second to the notorious Jesse James. Admitting that I have done wrong and expecting to be dealt with according to the law and not by false reports from parties who should blush with shame to make them, I ask a little of your space to set my case before the public in a true light. In the first place I have always worked for an honest living; was employed last summer by one of the best outfits in Montana and don't think they can say aught against me, but having got discharged last winter I went to the Black Hills to seek employment—which I could not get—and was forced to work for my board a month and a half, rather than to beg or steal. I finally started back to the vicinity of Miles City, as it was spring, to get employment on the range and was arrested at the above named place and charged with having stolen a horse at Sundance, where I was being taken by Sheriff Ryan, whom I escaped from by jumping from the cars, which I judged were running at 100 miles an hour.

After this my course of outlawry commenced, and I suffered terribly for the want of food in the hope of getting back south without being detected, where I would be looked upon as I always had been, and not as a criminal. Contrary to the statement in the Journal, I deny having stolen any horses in Canada and selling them near Benton, or anyplace else, up to the time I was captured, at which time I was riding a horse which I bought and paid for, nor had I the slightest idea of stealing any horses. I am aware that some of your readers will say my statement should be taken for what it is worth, on account of the hard name which has been forced upon me, nevertheless it is true. As for my recapture by Deputy Sheriff Davis, all I can say is that he did his work well and were it not for his 'playing possum' I would now be on my way south, where I had hoped to go and live a better life.—Harry Longabaugh

~

THE WAYSIDE PRESS
August 3, 1887

HORSE THIEF SENTENCED TO 18 MONTHS

—

Harry Longabaugh has been convicted on three counts of Grand Larceny on the charges of horse thievery and stealing a saddle and pistol. Longabaugh pleaded guilty to the thefts. Judge William L Maginnis sentenced Longabaugh to 18 months at hard labor in the Wyoming Territorial Prison. Due to his being a minor, Longabaugh will be allowed to serve his sentence in the Crook County Jail in Sundance. After Longabaugh stole the horse and outfit, he fled the area then was picked up by Sheriff James Ryan near Miles City. While being transported by train Longabaugh escaped from custody. Deputy sheriff Eph K. Davis and stock inspector W. Smith caught up with him on the N Bar ranch in Powderville, Montana. Again he attempted to escape but was stopped at gunpoint by Deputy Davis. Sheriff Ryan arrived and took possession of the prisoner on June 19. He brought the prisoner back to Sundance by stage arriving on June 22.

THE WAYSIDE PRESS
February 5, 1889

HORSE THIEF RELEASED AFTER SERVING SENTENCE

—

Harry Longabaugh has been released from the Crook County jail after being given a full pardon by Governor Thomas Moonlight one day before the completion of his sentence of 18 months, by Judge William L Maginnis. Longabaugh was convicted for horse theft and stealing a saddle and revolver. Longabaugh served hard time and was assigned to the work gangs involved in many of the improvements around Crook County.

*

$500 REWARD

The above reward will be paid by the Great Northern Express Company for the arrest and detention of Harry Longabaugh who in company with others held up and robbed the west bound train on the Great Northern Railway, near Malta, Montana, on the morning of November 29th, 1892.

DESCRIPTION—

Height, 5 feet 11 inches. Dark complexion, short dark hair. Age, about 25 years. Slender and erect, with a slight stoop in head and shoulders. Short upper lip, exposing teeth when talking. Teeth white and clean with small dark spot on upper tooth to right of center. Wore a medium size black soft hat. Dark double breasted sack coat. Dark close-fitting pants with blue overalls.

When last seen was riding bay horse branded Half Circle Cross on left shoulder.

Address communications to
B.F. O'Neal, Sheriff
Choteau County, Mont.

*

Their days, nights, suppers, and stolen moments together continued on for several more days, each wanting to share and learn more about each other. At least Harry could also share with her some of the better moments of his life and enjoyed telling Etta about his friend Ebb Johnson, and how he stood up for him, as best man at his wedding. He didn't tell her about saving more than one man's life over the years, and had been rescued from immediate peril himself, as that would just sound like boasting.

Raton's population in 1896 was about 2,500. Sixty trains came through town each day; a combination of freight and passenger. The booming coal town boasted twelve theatres, another dozen or so saloons, (with girls upstairs for the hard working miners). Department stores carried the latest fashionable attire and furnishings. Coal money was abundant and overflowing.

Harry invited Etta to accompany him to a theatre performance. He didn't buy new clothes but wore his best. He had his shoes shined and visited the barber for a shave and a haircut. Etta's trunks had gone along with Mabel to San Diego. In her luggage, she had one stylish dress with matching shoulder scarf, in a deep teal blue, which needed a new hat to complete the look. She set out shopping and was thrilled at the selections. She couldn't resist also purchasing a pair of long gloves and a beaded floral purse. At the theatre, neither of them paid as much attention to the performances as they did to each other.

On Christmas Eve, they dined at a different hotel, wearing the same outfits. This time enjoying sitting across from one another so they could look at each other continuously. They were invited to the house of the Pace family for New Years Eve; an evening as sparkling as the champagne. They were happy. Harry was wondering if he could keep Etta happy.

A couple of days later, Harry felt he needed to put forward to Etta his concern that there might be some that suspect their relationship. It wouldn't be right for her to be ill thought of. By that time they had talked of marriage in the future. Harry knowing he needed a different life if that was ever to work out. This was Etta's understanding also. Their uncertain future was a weight of concern which they both carried.

Harry mentioned to Etta that soon he needed to be in Las Vegas, further south in New Mexico Territory. Merritt would be meeting him there with any news of available ranch work, and let him know if any of the gang was in Alma or if he should head north to "the Roost." He asked Etta if she'd consider taking the train and joining him in Las Vegas. It was Etta's suggestion that they arrive there posing as a married couple.

They stopped in Whited's jewelry store. C. A. Whited owned the jewelry store and also fixed the railroad clocks for the trains that came through Raton. Harry bought a simple gold band for Etta. They both smiled at each other when he put it on her finger. Later, in Etta's room they spoke their words of love and devotion to one another.

Harry went ahead; his ride by horse would take much longer than the train. He found a pleasant rooming house where they would stay. His funds were low and The Plaza Hotel was too expensive.

It was already late January and Etta still hadn't made her way to San Diego, Mabel was more than worried, particularly now after receiving a letter about the handsome man Etta was keeping company with. Knowing Etta had very unconventional views concerning society's values; she feared for the worst.

Harry was waiting to meet her when the train screeched to a stop at the Las Vegas station. They were in each others arms before she touched the ground. Onlookers blushed at seeing the passionate couple.

Harry and Etta continued to enjoy their days together; their heads, always leaned towards each other as they took their strolls, and went on with their talks, constantly learning and sharing more. They were also discovering each other physically. Etta being new at these doings; Harry, though not a complete novice, became more skilled at pleasing Etta, exchanging clumsiness for finesse. A cowboy's life, in actual fact, doesn't give much opportunity for meeting and getting to know ladies.

Merritt arrived a few days later. Harry was to go to the Roost, there may be an opportunity presenting itself. Some of the gang were talking over future plans.

Three weeks into their stay in Las Vegas, Harry knew he should be getting back on the trail, and Etta, appreciating Mabel's concern, needed to continue on to San Diego.

Neither Etta nor Mabel had told the aunt and uncle, or their mother, of Etta's being on her own, during this last part of her travels.

At breakfast, before Etta was to board the train to Los Angeles, and then on to San Diego; Harry again told Etta he loved her and would try to figure a way for them to have a future together. Both were distraught at the thought of parting and her leaving was heart retching for them both. How could they know how long they would be apart? They had made uncertain plans to meet again in New Mexico Territory, but Harry thought it most likely wouldn't be until the next winter. When Etta had to let go of Harry to board the train, her held back tears gave way, spilling out in a rush, wetting her face right down to her collar. Harry's anguish was deepened by her sorrow. Only time could tell them what was yet to come.

*

II

San Diego
1896-1897

Mabel was thoroughly enjoying her more domestic life as governess for the Brakebill children, and was treated well. Her room in the home in Pacific Beach was clean and sunny but would be awfully plain if it weren't for Mabel's artistic talents of sewing and painting. In fact, the mistress of the home enjoyed visiting the room to view Mabel's brilliant drawings and colorful paintings. She asked Mabel to paint portraits of the children.

There were three children; at four, seven and nine. They were happy youngsters who loved their teacher. Though a strict martinet when it came to the children's studies, Mabel was fun, imaginative, and amusing during their outings, while playing games, or engaged in their artistic efforts. Love and warmth radiated from her.

Mabel had one day off each week to pursue her own interests. She continued with her painting, progressed in her proficiency at playing piano, and especially enjoyed the art museums and concerts available in San Diego.

In June of 1896, the neighbor's oldest son, Jonathon, returned home from New York where he attended law school. With him was his friend and classmate, Peter, who had accepted the offer to vacation in San Diego.

*

The morning sun was already warm in the garden where Mabel was cutting flowers intended for a bouquet in the dining room. She looked over, across the low hedge to see a fine-looking young man walking the neighbor's grounds. While she was looking at him, he looked up and saw her—an apparition in a flowing white summer dress! When Mabel saw him begin to walk towards her, she moved closer to the hedge to meet him. She liked his looks, with his well groomed dark hair and his shining brown eyes. Peter was dazzled by the bluest eyes he had ever seen.

Peter had one more year of law school, and then he was to join a law firm in New York. He was the older of two boys, and was expected to set an example for his younger brother, Thomas. His parents divorced when he was a young boy, not a well accepted custom of the period, and even more controversial as they had been Catholic. Both sides had money; it was a cold, yet well-mannered divorce. The boys were raised by their very strict and formidable mother whose father had been an attorney, and so it had been decided that Peter would follow this course also.

This next term would be Peter's final year at the New York Law School. The school was his mother's decision, as this was closer to home than the, perhaps more prestigious, Harvard School of Law in Cambridge, Massachusetts.

Mabel and Peter's relationship, which started with a talk in the garden, continued to blossom throughout the summer. Peter returned to New York in the heat of mid August to spend time with his family and then renew his studies.

Towards the end of his academic year, he braved bringing up the subject, to his mother, of his finding a position with a law firm on the west coast. This new idea didn't meet with his mother's approval, as he worried it might not. When Peter also mentioned that he had met the girl he intended to marry, and that she was a Protestant, his mother threatened to cut him off without the proverbial penny if he should persist and go through with this foolishness.

Peter finished the last of his exams, and then informed his mother that he'd be moving to California where he would marry his sweetheart and find a law firm who would employ him. His friend, Jonathan, in San Diego was going to help him find a placement. He hoped he could do this with his mother's blessing, but if not, then he would, in spite of everything, move and nevertheless marry Mabel.

*

Etta arrived at her Aunt Betty and Uncle Frank's home the last week of February, 1897. They were relieved to welcome her after the suspense of continued delays. At first, her Aunt seemed a bit stand-offish, until she realized this modern young woman was the same lively, sweet and spirited girl she remembered from their last visit to Boston so many years ago. Etta began instructing her cousins in playing the violin, and helped with their studies.

At Etta and Mabel's reunion, they had plenty to catch up on. Each talked excitedly about their new beau. "Oh when you meet him, you'll see what I mean Etta. He is entirely the man I want to marry. He'll be here next summer and you'll meet him then. We're to be married by the end of summer." "Mabel, I'm so pleased for you. You seem happier than I've ever seen you."

"My Harry is like no man I've met, or ever expected to meet. He's tall, has brown hair that has blonde on the top from being out in the sun a good deal. Because of our circumstances, his being a cowboy and working on ranches, and my being here in California, I have no way of knowing what the future holds for us. He and I will continue to exchange letters. I have an address at a ranch in Utah where I send him letters. They'll be picked up by Harry, or by a boy who does errands for him; a remarkable boy, whom I've met. Mabel, I miss Harry so terribly, as you must miss your Peter. I'm eager to meet your beau in June.

*

March 2, 1897

Dear Harry,

My darling, how are you? Did all work out, acquiring work at the ranch, as you had hoped?

The train ride here was uneventful, and though we did travel through picturesque country, it's all a hazy memory as my thoughts were preoccupied with you. I miss you enormously.

Mabel is doing well and has met a young man, from New York, whom she is very in love with. When he returns to San Diego this summer, they will be married and make San Diego their home.

I've started giving instruction on the violin to my niece and nephew. They already play piano. They humor me with their enthusiasm for learning. Soon, I will make a start at offering violin lessons publicly or find a position as governess, much like Mabel.

This is a pleasant life. I enjoy my aunt and uncle's company and I see Mabel once a week, on her day off, when we go downtown or to the ocean beach for walks. We behave like silly girls whenever we are together.

I hope you will have the chance to write before too long. I know it is so early to start thinking of when we might be together again; but please keep it in mind.

With all my love,
Your Etta

*

April 18, 1897

Dear Etta,

Your letters give me a much enjoyment and pleasure. I could never begin to return as many letters as you have written. Merritt asks for me to remember him to you and says thank you for his letter. Writing to him was very kind.

I should be heading towards South Dakota soon with a couple of associates. I hope to catch on to some profitable employment.

Since winter is always a tough time for getting on with ranch work, I have thoughts of meeting you at the end of the year and being with you for the winter. I miss you. Is there a chance that meeting then would work out with you? Would Raton or Las Vegas be alright?

I miss you my love.

Your devoted admirer,
Harry

*

May 1, 1897

Dearest Harry,

Today is May Day and the weather is superb, I spent the afternoon at the Brakebill's home with Mabel, and joined in with the family in merrymaking and partaking of all the tasty indulgences.

Is all well with you? I received your letter dated April 18. Have you remained in Wyoming, or have you gone on to South Dakota? You are so far away!

You tease me saying there might be a possibility of being together this winter. When you are sure, I will be there as soon as you say where.

You are missed so deeply! You are in my thoughts at all times. When I should be paying attention to conversation; I am thinking of you. I look forward to being with you and once again enjoying the western life.

It is now late and I must turn off the light. Please know that I love you beyond all doubt and I will always be—

Your Etta

*

Peter wasn't expecting such a large welcoming celebration when he returned to the Mitchell's house in San Diego, the summer of 1897. Jonathon, and his family, the entire Brakebill family, Etta, Aunt Betty and Uncle Frank, and of course, Mabel, were all there to cheer his arrival. Peter was staying with the Mitchell's while he looked into securing a position with a law firm, and made wedding plans with Mabel.

Peter told Mabel of his mother's stubbornness and seemingly intractable position. Mabel was aghast that anyone wouldn't find her suitable. Peter went on to tell her that his mother was always unpleasant when she didn't get her own way. He thought she might come around in her thinking after awhile; she'd softened a little when hearing that Mabel hailed from a well to do family.

Peter did find a placement with a small yet distinguished law firm in downtown San Diego. In August, he and Mabel were married in the Brakebill's garden where they had first met. Mabel had made her wedding gown, working on it all the past winter. Made of delicate pale ivory silk chiffon, with white silk lace inserted into the fitted bodice. The skirting was full and free flowing, just a bit longer in the back. Mabel had embroidered white flowers on the sleeves, down the front, and at the hem. White ribbons, meticulously sewn onto the embroidered flowers on the front, cascaded playfully down the dress.

Peter's mother did not attend; nor did Mabel's mother, but for the reason that she wasn't well, which had become a real concern. She did ship a magnificent grand piano to them in honor of the occasion and to promote Mabel's talent. She also sent a generous cash dowry. Peter and Mabel splurged on a two nights stay at the grand Hotel Del Coronado for their honeymoon.

Peter's mother, Gertrude, was true to her word, and did discontinue all financial support, as well as ceased all communication. Peter however, continued to write to her and his younger brother, knowing her curiosity would entice her to open and read his letters.

The couple found a small, yet suitable apartment conveniently located between Peter's workplace and the Brakebill's home. Mabel now rode a horse drawn jitney bus five days a week to continue to give educational instruction to her young charges. The children, being so fond of their teacher, had influenced their parents to agree to Mabel working only five days, in order to keep her with them.

*

November 9, 1897

Dearest Etta,

Please accept my apologies for not writing sooner. I've been in a real mess-up that came close to disaster. I will tell you about it when we meet. There are many plans I want to talk over with you. I hope you are free to meet me in Las Vegas in December. I am hoping that your feelings remain warm towards me.

I expect to take a room at the same rooming house, as I remember how we enjoyed the quiet of that place last winter.

I am heading that way and should be there towards the end of December. I'll use the same name as before on the register. If you are not coming, I will understand. Merritt will pick up any late letters waiting for me in Utah so I can catch up with your news, and to know if you will arrive.

All that keeps me going is getting to New Mexico Territory to be with you.

Affectionately yours,
Harry
P.S. Please bring your violin.

*

December 11, 1897

My dear Harry,

Yes. Yes. Yes. There is no way to know if you will receive this before I arrive in Las Vegas. I will leave here Tuesday, December 28 and take the train first to Los Angeles, then must change trains, and, if all goes well, the train to Las Vegas (and I) will be arriving Thursday, December 30. I long to see you and be with you. My feelings for you are as warm as ever.

We will be together soon.

All my love,
Etta

*

III

Las Vegas, New Mexico Territory Winter 1897-1898

"Has Mr. Alonzo arrived?" "Yes ma'am, but, he just went out." "Oh dear, has he gone to the station?" Yes, ma'am, he checks every train that comes in. You must be Mrs. Alonzo. Your Mister asked me to watch for you and show you to your rooms if he was out. Don't know how you missed him. Come with me, I'll show you to your room."

Etta had time to take off her hat and cape, freshen up and re-pin her uncontainable hair when Harry knocked once and then came in before she reached the door. They each gasped and just stared, and then they were in each others arms, needful of the prolonged embrace that could barely begin to fulfill their longings.

Harry had no intentions of deceiving Etta about his latest outlaw exploits, and had intended to do so before any intimacies took place. That plan was now forsaken by their shared craving and desire for each other.

Harry was amused at the fabricated story Etta and Mabel devised to tell their mother, and aunt and uncle. The story was told that Etta would be staying with a family in Las Vegas, whom she had previously met and was now to be employed as governess until spring. Mabel submitted that she had seen the letter requesting Etta be employed for at least the duration of the winter. Etta and Mabel were hugely relieved when they weren't asked to produce the letter that Etta was to have received while the aunt and uncle were out. It may have been a feeble story but, at least it worked. Etta did bring her violin and now told Harry she hoped to teach here in Las Vegas, if any were interested. It would make her feel somewhat vindicated from her lie.

Later that afternoon they walked along past the train depot, and watched the new hotel, La Castaneda, being built. Then they took the horse drawn streetcar to the town plaza to have their supper at the Plaza Hotel. They both noticed how the town had expanded this last year. Las Vegas was already a boom town, and now boasted an opera house, several new businesses and more persons of respectable society; it was getting away from its days of lawless brawling. 'Lions Park,' with its fountains, was the outstanding achievement of the Women's Christian Temperance Union. The idea of the large stone lion sculpture with fountains for drinking water was built to hopefully entice the saloon patrons to quench their thirst with water instead of strong drink. As Harry and Etta walked by, a dog was drinking from the fountains trough.

*

That evening, Harry knew he couldn't postpone it any longer. He told Etta of his involvement in the disastrous Butte County Bank robbery up in Belle Fourche, South Dakota, and how he and others were chased, captured in Wyoming, taken back to Belle Fourche and then on to Deadwood, South Dakota where they were put in jail and then they finally broke out. "Now I understand why you didn't write. You couldn't! Harry I thought your involvement in that kind of wrong doing was a thing of the past, when you were younger. Harry you just can't keep doing this. I don't want to know that you're involved in that kind of dangerous enterprise. Most of all because you could be killed or hurt, Oh Harry this is frightful news. I'm so shaken. Are they looking for you now?" "Yes they're looking, but look at this wanted poster; do I fit any of these descriptions? I hope not."

"Etta, I'm sad to offend and disappoint you. Etta, I'm havin a difficult time trying to figure out how to get out of the life I'm leading. Being a cowhand for ranchers who hire just in the good seasons isn't goin' to get me through life. How do I explain to you that being an outlaw isn't who I really am, but I've got nothin goin' for me. Or, maybe what I've done is who I am."

"No, Harry I think I understand who you are, and I'm aware that you aren't, by temperament, the outlaw you've let yourself become. I am confused on what you thought you'd gain from it."

"Money! Etta, I was willing to take a chance, to try and get a stake to start in on a new life. After the first time I went to jail when I was younger, I knew I'd made my bed. Heck, I'm called 'The Sundance Kid'. I have no idea how to alter my life now, or how I can change my circumstances. Etta, more than anything, I want a life with you, away from that past. I'd like a good start, to get out of that kinda life, probably most would. Maybe there's some that wouldn't—don't want out, and they'll stay with it 'till they die or die doin it. I know I'm goin to have to sort this out before we can ever have a future together."

*

WANTED

FOR BUTTE COUNTY BANK ROBBERY

$2500 REWARD

WILL BE PAID BY US FOR THE CAPTURE OF THE FOUR MEN HERINAFTER DESCRIBED. $625 REWARD WILL BE PAID FOR EACH MAN. THESE MEN ARE WANTED FOR ATTEMPTING TO ROB THIS BANK ON MONDAY, JUNE 28, 1897.

DESCRIPTION

Geo. Currie—About 5 ft 10 in., weight 175, age 27, light complexion, high cheek bones, flat forehead, flat pug nose, big hands and bones, stoops a little. Long light mustache, probably clean shaven.

Harvey Ray—About 5 ft 8 1-2 in., weight 185, age 42, dark complexion, round full faced, big headed, heavy long dirty brown mustache, might have heavy beard, dark grey eyes, hair quite gray above ears and inclined to curl, bow legged.

Roberts?—About 5 ft 7 1-2 in., age 39, rather small, weight about 140, very dark complexion, possibly quarter breed Indian. Formerly from Indian Territory.

Roberts?—Rather small man.? About 5 ft. 6 in., weight 130, age 28, very dark, probably quarter breed Indian, large upper teeth protruding from mouth.

$100 reward for information leading to their arrest. Please destroy former circulars.

BUTTE COUNTY BANK

Belle Fourche, S.D.

July 28, 1897

*

"We're both tired now Harry and I can't say that I have any answers. But dear, we're together right now, and we've got this winter to be together, we'll keep talking and we'll come up with a solution."

*

New Year's Eve was a wild and raucous event in town, though Harry and Etta spent the night in their room. They celebrated New Year's Day quietly, by going for a walk and enjoying another fine supper at the Plaza Hotel. They spent the next week, rediscovering each other, talking, going for walks, and getting to know the town. Etta had brought along a few books for the cold, snowy days when they would stretch out on the bed, propped up with pillows, and read; each pausing at moments to comment on an especially enjoyable passage from the book in hand.

When there was a morning that felt somewhat warmer, Harry hired a horse for Etta, at the stable where he boarded his horse. They took the day to ride out to the duck lake and watch the wide variety of seasonal water fowl. They returned at the end of the day tired, yet refreshed from the outing.

*

Early the next morning they woke to a tapping on the door, strange, not quite a knock. Etta was alarmed when Harry reached for his gun, his favorite Colt .45 that was setting on the bedside table, before he asked, "Who's there?" "It's me, Merritt." "Merritt!"

Harry opened the door enough to make arrangements for meeting him at the eatery on Lincoln Street. Etta called out that she'd like to join them. Merritt said "Mornin' ma'am," from behind the door.

Etta's reunion with Merritt was joyful and again they were happily talking with one another. Later that morning, Harry and Merritt went to check on their horses; at least that's all they told Etta. Merritt had news regarding the gang. Nothing was in the works at this time; the men were either living a thin existence at ranches or staying out of sight, up at Robber's Roost.

*

Etta did acquire two students for violin lessons, which she taught in their homes. It gave her a sense of belonging to the community as well as giving her a little extra cash for her own personal items. She didn't want to impose on Harry as she suspected he was short on funds, though he seemed to be skillful, or lucky, at playing cards. More times that not when he returned from a saloon, his pockets were full.

Etta told Harry about the trust her father had set up for herself, Mabel, and her brother, Buddy. She was to receive her full amount when she was twenty-one, in two years. She also had savings from a grandmother who had died and left all the grandchildren a modest inheritance. She had mentioned to him that perhaps that money could be a help in changing their situation. Harry would hear none of it. That money was hers! Nothing more on the subject was mentioned.

February 17, 1898

Dear Mabel,

How are you my dear sister? I trust your winter chest cold is over, and you are restored to health. How is Peter? Your last letter mentioned how well he was getting along at the law firm. He is a remarkable man!

I have an exciting adventure to tell you about. We, that is, Harry, young Merritt, and I, went camping (nothing at all like when we went with father and brought along absolutely every notion of comfort). We rode on horseback for most of the first day into the forested mountains north of Las Vegas. The trail went through stunning, yet rugged country; occasionally we would come out to an overlook where it was thrilling to look towards the southeast out on the lowlands.

In the early evening, the men set up the area for our camp and made a fire. They cooked a rabbit over the fire. We told stories and shared some of our own experiences while we enjoyed the light and warmth of the fire. To look up and see such a vast array of bright stars was astonishing beyond belief. We slept around the fire like cowboys in the stories. Though it was really just I that slept soundly, the men evidently stayed very watchful and the fire was kept going all night.

Early in the morning, Harry made coffee, then cooked bacon and warmed a can of beans in the same pan. Merritt made camp biscuits. My appetite had never been better! We poked around the hills all day and then we enjoyed nearly a repeat of the first evening. After breakfast the next morning, we headed home. I didn't want to go back to town so soon.

I had been asking Harry to show me what it would be like to camp out on the trail. He waited until we had a clearing and warming in the weather. I have now seen him in a completely different way. While being a capable and dashing man about town; he is also so extremely competent and confident in the out-of-doors, in a way that would greatly intimidate most town people.

I must confess, when we arrived home I needed a bath. We had, along with our own blankets, used the horse blankets to sleep on in the night. Phew! Thankfully, the Fung Kee laundry is nearby.

I continue to give lessons to my two students who are making progress. I never thought I'd say this, but I don't want winter to end.—At least, not this winter. In the morning, Harry and I will take a long walk to the Post Office to post this letter along with a copy of the Las Vegas Gazette that you and Peter may enjoy. On the way back Harry wants to stop at Houghton's hardware store for a metal buckle for repairing stirrups. We enjoy our leisurely walks together.

You must write and tell me absolutely everything about what is going on with you and more about your life with Peter.

Sending you all my love, and bouquets of kisses,

Your sister, Etta

P.S. Have you been successful in finding a larger apartment? Mother wasn't thinking when she sent that mammoth piano.

*

Etta was impressed by Merritt's desire to make more of his life. If only her father were still alive. He could have looked into a way the boy could be schooled or apprenticed in some position. Merritt was fantastically bright. Etta bought books for him to read, and taught him to play simple tunes on the violin. He was a young brother to her.

She wasn't sure where he made his camp in the evenings. During snowy weather, she heard he was allowed to stay in a store room in the back of the rooming house. Some weeks he was gone, on errands for Harry, or just on his own.

Occasionally, for an outing, Etta and Harry went for a ride to the hot springs by the Montezuma Hotel. They spent most of their time in each others company and enjoyed some evenings at the Plaza Hotel or the Exchange Hotel, either in the dining room or in the lobbies, enjoying being social with other towns people. Etta also had the families of her students that she enjoyed being with. Harry had the saloons for a more divergent pastime.

*

Winter passed unexpectedly soon. There were signs of spring, trees were in flower with white and pink blossoms, bulbs were shooting up their green spears with bright, vibrant colorful blooms. The grasses greened up around the town. Harry became restless. Merritt had returned from his last excursion, with word that George Curry and Harvey Logan wanted to get something started; some of the ranches were hiring; and also his newer acquaintance, Butch Cassidy, would like to meet up with him.

"Etta, it's time for the ranches to start hiring. I've got to head out and find work up north." "Is it possible to find work near here so I could be near you; is there a town near where you're going where I could stay?" "No Etta that would never work. It's a rough bunch that work the ranches, and I'm in a rough manner myself when I'm with them. I don't want you anywhere near that. I know we talked about me moving into a town and getting work or working a business, But, you know I'm not cut out for that." "Harry, I'm worried that you'll fall in to dangerous ways again."

"We never did figure out a real solution to that, with all our talk this winter, and I know I'm never going to get out ahead doing ranch work. It might be my only way, Etta, to get into something different." "No, Harry please don't mean that."

With nothing resolved regarding their future and not knowing when or if they would see each other again; they parted. Etta was once again getting on the train to go west to San Diego, and Harry riding north to "Hole in the Wall."

*

IV

San Diego Spring 1898 to December 1900

Now that Mabel and Peter had moved into a more spacious apartment, they wanted Etta to live with them. They had talked it over, and, if Etta was willing, it would be an enormous help. Peter put in long days at his work, commuting downtown by means of his horse and buggy. Mabel also spent an extended day away from home. She was fortunate that the horse driven jitney brought her to within three blocks of the Brakebill's home. Etta was delighted; Peter and Mabel lived a much more modern lifestyle compared to her aunt and uncle.

The apartment felt like a garden cottage, and even though it was the lower floor of a larger house, it received plenty of sunlight. They had access to the garden, which especially pleased Mabel since she could paint there. Mabel turned the sunny dining room with its French doors opening to the garden, into her painting studio. Peter had found a large table which needed repair; and now restored, it made a good enough dining table when it was covered with a tablecloth, and it also served as a first rate work table for Mabel's and Etta's projects.

Etta enjoyed cooking, and shopped for the meals at the nearby grocers. Too often she would buy overly much at one time and the boxes would have to be delivered by the grocery boy with his cart. She was careful to not buy more perishable foods than could fit in the icebox. The iceman came in the afternoon on Tuesdays. Early in the morning, Etta packed a lunch for Peter, except when he had a lunch meeting. Mabel ate her mid-day meal at the Brakebill's.

Etta needed her days to be occupied or she would otherwise become melancholy. So far she'd received only two letters from Harry. She suspected he was caught up in more unlawful ventures.

*

May 6, 1898

Dearest Harry,

Please write and tell me how you are doing. I'm concerned for your wellbeing. I will be straightforward and say I suspect you may be involved in the type of ventures you have told me about. I will never criticize you for your activities. As you know, I could not come up with any suggestions or answers to our dilemma, any more than you could. Just let me know that you are well.

As yet, I haven't found a position for myself. I feel I would be letting down Mabel and Peter, since I am managing their home while they are so busy at their employment. I will advertise in the San Diego Union and hopefully start giving violin lessons.

Though I enjoy my life here, I find it does not keep me busy enough to keep me from feeling dispirited at our situation. I feel so wretched without you. Perhaps soon I will break out of my gloom. Please write to me.

Last Sunday, we spent the day at the beach (Another May Day). We enjoyed a sandy picnic. The best meals I have eaten were with you and Merritt on our outing in the mountains north of Las Vegas. I look forward to the possibility of sharing that happiness with you again.

Harry, be well, and know that I love you!

Yours, with all my heart,
Etta

*

June 26, 1898

Dear Etta,

I hope this letter will get to you when you are feeling well and I hope not so sad. I just received three of your letters, April 22, May 6, and May 15. I am concerned about you. There is more strain and hurt in your words than I would ever want for you to feel. Do you realize the effect that has on me? I do love you Etta.

I can in no way feel right about causing you hurt. I am not going to lie to you and say that I am doing as you would have me do. To be honest and truthful with you, I am not. In fact the only way I figure on there ever being a chance in the future is to take a few chances now. I have confided in a friend of mine about the tight spot I'm in of wanting to make a life with you and having no assets. He and I both want out of this life.

We are not the desperados we might sound like. In spite of that, we hope to make enough money to get out of these doings and buy a ranch. We figure that to be safe, we will have to leave the country. I read where there are as many folks immigrating to South America as there are coming to the states.

Etta it would be a year or more to know if this plan would work out. I don't see how I can be with you in the meantime. I don't want you to be trapped into a life of worry about something that may never work out. You should find a life for yourself, there, where you are, and find happiness you can count on.

I will not write again unless it all works out. The pain it would cause us if this plan does not succeed is not bearable and it would be unreasonable to expect you to throw away your life waiting for what might only end up being bad news.

I do not write these words to be unkind. I love you except have no right to your affections.
Please enjoy a happy life my dearest Etta,

Love,
Harry

*

Etta continued to write, though less often. There were subsequently no letters from Harry. Etta went through the motions of her daily routines and did start teaching violin to four students. These obligations compelled her to keep functioning.

At one point, Mabel had to say something to help shake Etta out of her gloominess. "Etta, we make choices on what we do with our lives. Don't you think it best that you get on with yours?

Choose to find strength in your experiences; hold on to those good memories, of course, but now you must start a new life. You must look at the choices you've made, at your past choices with Harry and see . . . ." "No Mabel, I didn't choose to love Harry. We, somehow, always loved each other and then, fortunately, or unfortunately, we met." "What? Oh, Etta!"

*

$1,000 REWARD

€€

Southern Pacific Train No 1, leaving Humboldt, Nevada, 1:25 this morning, was held up and robbed about two miles east of that point by three or more men, supposed at present to be a negro and two white men. The express car was entered, the safe blown open, and the car demolished. Baggage and express packages badly damaged.

In addition to the standing reward of $300 offered by Wells, Fargo & Co., the Southern Pacific Co. and Wells, Fargo & Co. jointly offer a reward of $700, making a total of **ONE THOUSAND DOLLARS ($1,000)** for the arrest and conviction of each of the parties connected with said robbery.

Further information can be obtained from the undersigned, or from Mr. J. S. Noble, Supt., Southern Pacific Co., Ogden, Utah

J.A. FILLMORE, Manager Southern Pacific Co.
PACIFIC SYSTEM

L.F. ROWELL, Manager Wells, Fargo & Co.
SAN FRANCISCO, CAL.

July 14, 1898

*

In August, Mabel and Peter celebrated their first anniversary enjoying a weekend at the Hotel Del Coronado, where they had spent their honeymoon. Their concern for Etta was lessening as she seemed to be pulling out of her despair. While they were away, Etta wrote her last letter to Harry.

August 14, 1898

Dear Harry,

I have no idea if you are receiving my letters. I understand your feelings in closing off our relationship. I love you as deeply as ever, while now I realize that the circumstances of your being out on the western frontier, and my living here, is an extremely wearing position with no remedy in view.

You will continue to be always on my mind, and in my heart. My wish is that you be in good health and stay safe. In the future, if a day comes when you should feel disposed to write; I hope you will do just that—whatever the circumstances may be at the time.

I want you to know that I find you to be an especially worthwhile and compassionate man. You have had the most profound influence on my outlook and point of view. I will always love you.

Your Etta

*

Peter was becoming active in civic events and politics, and was already making a name for himself. It appeared that the partners would be inviting him to be a full partner before long.

It was a fortuitous occasion that December, when the firm handed Peter the account of Ammi Merchant Farnham, who had a minor legal matter to settle. Mr. Farnham was an artist of great reputation. Having studied in several countries abroad and winning the acclaim of art critics everywhere, he was an asset to the town of San Diego since moving there in 1888. While Peter and Ammi were enjoying their conversation, Peter brought up the subject of Mabel, saying that she was also an artist whom Peter couldn't praise highly enough. He asked Ammi if he would consider viewing Mabel's paintings. Ammi agreed to go to their house the following Saturday morning. He did make it clear that he didn't care to instruct women, as very few were serious enough about their art and viewed it as a hobby to pass the time between having babies.

Mabel was close to panic while arranging her paintings in the best light for viewing. She had heard of A.M. Farnham long before he became a client of Peter's firm. When he arrived, Mabel practically didn't breathe while Ammi looked at the paintings while murmuring only an occasional hmm-hmm. When he had finally completed his viewing, Peter offered beverages. They all sat down and Ammi began, what can only be described as, an interview.

"How many years have you been painting? How often do you paint? What are your future plans? Have you sold many paintings? What medium do you prefer? What do you think of your work? Why do you paint?" Mabel audibly gasped at this last question, construing this to possibly mean he thought her work trifling. Interpreting her reaction, he quickly continued. "Mabel you should leave your position as nanny. That is not going to provide what you need. You must paint! Paint as many days a week as your ambition dictates. I will be willing to have you join me one afternoon a week for instruction. Also, I would like to see the paintings that Mrs. Brakebill has purchased."

Later, when Ammi left, Mabel and Peter discussed the possibility of this becoming a reality and the effect it would have on their finances. They had been saving towards buying a house. Peter was adamant that Mabel pursue her passion for painting and all her artistic expressions. Mabel, wasn't sure at first, then gave way to the excitement that she could do this—and be a student of A.M. Farnham! Peter soothed her worries about their reduction of funds, saying, "Once Mrs. Brakebill tells her friends that A.M. Farnham is your mentor; you won't be able to paint canvases fast enough!" "Peter, I'll give notice of my leaving, to Mrs. Brakebill. It may take a couple of months before the transition is accomplished."

Etta was thrilled at the news. For one thing, she recognized Mabel's talent, and thought it all wrong that she hadn't been so encouraged before this; and the other thing was her own need to be occupied more fully, and now she might find additional employment in town.

*

That next April in 1899, Peter arrived home from the office wholly excited, Etta and Mabel wondered if this meant he may have received a promotion. "Yes, that and more! A partner in the firm is moving to his own office and would like for me to come in with him! He'll bring his secretary with him, and we'll need a second person for the keeping up of the paper work and the filing, and reception. What do you think, Etta?"

The women, who had been intently listening to Peter's announcement, just stared at him, then realized that that the plan was for Etta to work for him, not just to reply on what she thought of the plan. They burst into laugher, not at the news but at Peter who looked like an eager boy trying to impress them that his idea would work.

The idea did work out brilliantly for all. Etta was engrossed in her new occupation, and she continued to teach violin on Saturdays. Mabel made simple meals that didn't take much time away from painting. Her afternoons painting with Ammi, often meant her traveling to La Jolla, so on those evenings, Etta and Peter shared in preparing the evening meal.

On Saturday mornings, Peter fixed his specialty—pan sized pancakes made in the large iron skillet; afterward, he went grocery shopping using a list the women had prepared. Peter was becoming a recognizable figure around town and this outing gave him additional opportunity to make more acquaintances.

*

$12,000 REWARD

Office of United States Marshal,
Cheyenne, Wyoming,
June 3, 1899

To Whom It May Concern:

On Friday morning, June 2, 1899, a party of masked men, supposedly to be six in number, took possession of the United States Mail, near Wilcox station, Albany county, Wyoming, in the Union Pacific cars Numbers 1120 and 1190, by the use of dynamite and dangerous weapons. Warrants have been issued for their arrest under the provisions of Section 5472, Revised Statutes of the United States. Under Circular No. 532 of the Postmaster General of the United States a reward of ONE THOUSAND DOLLARS is offered for the arrest and conviction of each person violating the provisions of the said Section 5472 of the Revised Statutes of the United States.

By circular issued this date the UNION PACIFIC RAILWAY COMPANY offers the sum of ONE THOUSAND DOLLARS for the capture, dead or alive of each and every person proven to be the persons or either of then who held up the first section of train Number one, as above described, on the morning of June 2, 1899.

The following is a partial description of the robbers:

Leader of the party about fifty years old; five feet seven or eight inches tall; thin, round nose; large eyes with small eyeballs; wore slouch hat, light canvas coat; weight, about 160 pounds.

Second man: dark complexion; black, woolly hair; wore slouch hat, dark suit; about five feet nine or ten inches tall; weight, about 170 pounds.

Third man; about five feet, eight or nine inches tall; black suit; dark hair; weight about 160 to 170 pounds.

Fourth man: about five feet six inches tall; dark complexion; wore gray hat, pants inside boots; weight about 160 pounds.

Fifth man: about five feet six inches tall; weight about 145 pounds; wore cowboy white hat with drooping brim, black leather shoes; canvas leggings, brown overalls or corduroy pants, light, medium length overcoat; spoke with Texas twang; carried carbine with long wood on barrel reaching to within finches of end.

Sixth man: about five feet eight inches tall; weight about 150 pounds; stubby, sandy beard.

The robbers secured several thousand dollars in National Bank currency, in bills of the denomination of twenty and one hundred dollars, of the First national Bank of Portland Oregon, series 1553, and valueless because not signed by the officers of that bank.

Please communicate with any Sheriff, Deputy Marshal or other peace officer, or with me at Cheyenne, Wyoming, should you have or obtain any information of the above described persons.

FRANK A. HADSELL, U. S. Marshal
District of Wyoming

$18,000.00
REWARD

€€€

Union Pacific Railroad and Pacific Express Companies jointly will pay $2,000 per head, dead or alive, for the six robbers who held up Union Pacific mail and express train ten miles west of rock Creek Station, Albany County, Wyoming, on the morning of June 2, 1899.

The United States Government has also offered a reward of $1,000.00 per head, making in all $3,000.00 for each of these robbers.

Three of the gang described below, are now being pursued in northern Wyoming; the other three are not yet located, but doubtless soon will be.

DESCRIPTION: One man about 32 years of age; height, five feet, nine inches; weight 185 pounds; complexion and hair, light; eyes, light blue; peculiar nose, flattened at bridge and heavy at point; round, full, red face; bald forehead; walks slightly stooping; when last seen wore No.8 cow-boy boots.

Two men, look like brothers, complexion, hair and eyes, very dark; larger one, age about 30; height five feet, five inches; weight, 145 pounds; may have slight growth of whiskers; smaller one, age about 28; height, five feet, seven inches; weight 135 pounds; sometimes wears moustache.

Any information concerning these bandits should be promptly forwarded to Union Pacific Railroad Company and to the United States Marshall of Wyoming, at Cheyenne.

UNION PACIFIC RAILROAD COMPANY.
PACIFIC EXPRESS COMPANY.

Omaha, Nebraska, June 10th, 1899

*

$18,000.00 REWARD

THE UNION PACIFIC TRAIN ROBBERS

On Friday morning, June 2nd, 1899, a party of masked robbers held up the first section of train number one of Union Pacific railroad Company, almost ten miles west of Rock Creek Station, Albany County, Wyoming, and after dynamiting bridges, mail and express cars, and robbing the latter, disappeared. The second section of this train, being the overland Limited Passenger, following ten minutes behind, was fortunately stopped by the brakemen of the first section who escaped the robbers.

Three of the robbers went north mounted and were followed eight hours later by a posse. The robbers crossed the Platte river at Casper about three o'clock Sunday morning, and were followed from Casper by another posse from that point who overtook them about four o'clock in the afternoon about twenty-eight miles northwest of Casper, where a running fight occurred, the robbers shooting three of the horses of the pursuing party, and escaping to a point about fifteen miles further on, where they were again overtaken the following Monday morning by both posses, at which time sheriff Hazen of Converse county, was shot and killed from ambush. In the confusion which followed, the robbers eluded the posses and are supposed now to be somewhere in Johnson or big Horn Counties, and are being closely followed by the pursuing parties.

A description of these three robbers is as follows: One man about 31 or 32 years of age; bright, five feet eight or nine inches; weight 185 pounds; complexion and hair light; If moustache, likely to be long but not heavy; blue eyes; peculiar nose, flattened at bridge and heavy at point; round, full, red face; walks slightly stooping; may be slightly bow-legged; bald forehead; when last seen wore number 8 cow-boy high-heeled boots. Two men look like brothers; smaller, five feet seven inches; age about 26; weight 135 pounds. Largest, five feet five inches; about 30; weight 145 or 150; may have slight growth of whiskers; complexion of both very dark; one quarter Cherokee Indian; smaller man sometimes wears mustache; both have dark hair, indication Indian; eyes dark.

When overtaken about forty miles north-west of Casper where Sheriff Hazen was murdered, their horses were captured, described as follows:

An Arabian horse, weighing 1100 or 1200 pounds; strawberry roan in front, shading lighter to the rear; rump and back, white, with small black spots; has collar mark on right shoulder; short mane and tail; indistinct brand on right shoulder.

Second horse; dun color, or clay hank, with white mane and tail; weighs about 1100 pounds; is branded "spade or heart J" on left shoulder; has worked in harness.

Third horse; small sorrel, well shaped head; weighs about 950 pounds; white face and white hind legs; white ring around right fore-leg at knee joint; several indistinct brands on left shoulder, one resembling the letter "H", another resembling a "flying diamond"; also three perpendicular bars—long bar in center.

These horses are now in safe keeping at Cheyenne.

It is probably that these three robbers, when driven from their present hiding, will make for the north into adjoining states, or possibly British Columbia. Have not up to this time succeeded in locating the other three men, but it is probable will be able to do so soon.

In order to prevent the escape of these three robbers who are being pursued, it is important that posse be organized without delay in your state, and that they will be dispatched at once in the direction of the present supposed hiding place in northern Wyoming to capture them if they cross the line.

Union Pacific Railroad Company and Pacific Express Company have jointly offered two thousand dollars per head, dead or alive, for each of these men, and the United States Government has also offered a reward of one thousand dollars each, making three thousand per head for each of these men.

Any information concerning these bandits should be promptly forwarded to Union Pacific Railroad Company and the United States Marshall of Wyoming at Cheyenne.

UNION PACIFIC RAILROAD COMPANY

PACIFIC EXPRESS COMPANY

Omaha, Nebraska June 19th, 1899

*

Etta was astounded at all Peter would accomplish in a day at the office; meeting people, studying legal briefs, preparing for trials and court hearings. He often went out for lunches with people of influence. Etta met many of the prominent people of Southern California through Peter.

During this time Etta began to allow gentlemen to escort her to dinner, to the theatre, and to concerts. She was sought after for her good looks and her intellect. Mabel and Peter noticed that she never went out with any one man for more than two engagements; unfortunate for these fine gentlemen, so smitten with her. Never, ever, for reasons unknown to them, would she accept an invitation for a buggy ride out in the country.

Mabel and Etta became good friends with the wife of Peter's associate. They were often invited out to their impressive house. When the wife, Shirley, visited at Mabel's home, and saw Mabel's paintings, she was astounded at the quality and style, and bought two. In addition to the paintings in Peter's office, four more were now hanging in the reception area.

In late August of that year, Peter and Mabel took the train to Boston for the purpose of visiting Mabel's mother and younger brother. With no response from Peter's mother, they didn't plan on going to New York. Etta had been asked if she wanted to go with them, but she thought it was better for the couple to have time alone together, and besides, she wasn't ready for her mother's disapproval of still being single, as well as now being a career woman.

And, there was something else; the memories. When she thought about traveling by train and viewing the same scenery she associated with Harry, she trembled. No, she couldn't hold up to that, the wound was not yet healed, though she had long since given up hopes of ever hearing again from Harry.

*

So far, their Christmas celebrations had been modest. Now, with each of them doing well, they were ready to celebrate. They started with a Christmas Eve party, with their closest friends and associates invited for singing carols and enjoying "Tom and Jerry's". Next was the New Years Eve party, with as many people invited as could fit in their apartment. The celebration was complete with champagne, hors d'oeuvres, and Mabel's raved-over cheesecake. At the stroke of midnight, Mabel started playing Auld Lang Syne on the piano. All joined in this song of affection and remembrance. The year was now 1900!

The first year of a new century! It felt like the opening chapter of a book that held great promise. Peter maintained a very busy schedule; and in addition, he felt the responsibilities of being the head of his small family unit. He read a wide variety of newspapers, even though some were out of date, from the western states as well as the New York Times. Being a lawyer, he was in close association with law enforcement and read police and Pinkerton bulletins as well as a vast assortment of newspapers. He had noticed a name that came up too often. Harry Longabaugh! The name was linked with several train and bank robberies over the last two or more years. He wouldn't tell Etta about this unless she heard from him again, and that didn't seem likely as so much time had gone by with out any word. It looked like this man had chosen his path, and Etta had now stopped talking of the times she spent with him.

They each led active lives, making time for enjoyments, and attended the theatre regularly. On Sundays Peter and Mabel always spent the day together. They went for walks in the open space of the San Diego City Park that was slowly being developed into a botanical park. They enjoyed the ocean beaches, particularly La Jolla Cove Beach where Mabel also spent many of her painting instruction days. They were a romantic couple and enjoyed each others company.

Valentines Day was a gushy affair at their home. Mabel and Etta made Valentine decorations and cards for the Brakebill children and for Etta's violin students. Mabel made an elaborate Valentine card for Peter. Mabel asked Etta if she thought about finding a beau. Etta just said, she was enjoying her life and wasn't ready. Mabel fretted, but kept in mind that Etta would be only twenty two in October.

Occasionally on weekends, Mabel and Etta would play and sing songs for Peter, who cherished the moments of being the exclusive beneficiary of these performances. He infrequently took a turn at the piano.

That summer Mabel endured a miscarriage. Though in the early stages of pregnancy; the experience was devastating; the sense of loss was profoundly felt by both her and Peter. Etta stayed home from work for two weeks to care for her sister; mostly for emotional support. Mabel had a sensitive nature and now Peter was particularly concerned for her well being. Mabel spent more time painting at home. She enjoyed the gardens and since the owners of the house were abroad for the summer, it made a quiet and restoring sanctuary.

*

$4,000.00

REWARD

By Union Pacific Railroad Company.

Second Section Train No. 3 Held Up by Four Masked Men,
ABOUT TWO AND ONE HALF MILES WEST OF TIPTON,
SWEETWATER CO., WYO., AT 8:30 P.M.
AUGUST 29, 1900

$8,000 REWARD!

The PACIFIC EXPRESS COMPANY.

In ADDITION to the reward of $1,000 EACH offered by the Union Pacific Railroad Company for the capture of the men, dead or alive, who robbed the Union Pacific train No. 3 near Tipton, Wyo., on the evening of August 29, 1900, the Pacific Express company, on the same conditions, herby also offers a reward of $1,000.00 for each robber.

Green River, Wyo., September 1, 1900

Dear Sir:

Our money loss is $50.40, damage to our car safe and express freight will amount to $3000.00. Robbers used Kepauno Chemical Co., Giant Powder, dated September 15, 1899. Ashburn Mo. Works, forty percent.

Yours truly,
F. C. Gentach, Gen'l Supt.

Silver State Post
September 19, 1900

FIRST NATIONAL BANK ROBBED

Three desperadoes Loot It Secure Thousands of Dollars

Cashier and Assistants Forced to Hand Over the Money to the Robbers, who Afterward Escape with Their Booty

Three desperadoes entered the First National Bank at noon today, held up those who were in the building and perpetrated one of the most daring bank robberies on record.

They were in the building at the time cashier Nixon, assistant cashier McBride, bookkeeper Hill, stenographer Calhoun and W.S. Johnson, a horse buyer. Messrs Nixon and Johnson were in the cashier's office in the rear of the bank, the door between the rooms being closed.

The robbers came in at the Bridge Street entrance while the employees were busily at work and none of them at the time facing the door. The first intimation they received that anything was wrong was the quiet command of one of the robbers: "Gentlemen, throw up your hands, be quick about it and don't make any noise." the surprised clerks turned their heads and looked into the muzzles of two revolvers and the order was quickly obeyed. The third robber burst into the cashier's office where Messrs Nixon and Johnson were engaged in conversation. He had a Winchester rifle drawn on them before they could make a move and ordered them to throw up their hands under penalty of instant death. It is hardly necessary to state that this order was also obeyed. They were taken into the front room of the bank and, with a revolver held at his breast, cashier Nixon was forced to open the safe in the vault, the others being kept observed by the two remaining desperadoes. The leader of the gang threw three sacks of gold coin which were in the safe into an ore sack which he carried and then emptied into the sack of gold coins which was in the money drawer in the office, ignoring the silver and bank notes entirely. While this was going on a number of people passed along the sidewalk in front of the bank, but those inside could not give the alarm, and none of the passers-by took notice of the daring robbery which was being perpetrated.

Having accomplished the object of their visit the robbers marched the men through the back door of the bank building, lined them up against the wall with hands up and climbed over the fence into the alley. They ran down the alley to the rear of C. Robins and Co's store, where their horses were tied to a post, mounted the animals and escaped.

The first intimation people on the streets had of the robbery; cashier Nixon rushed from the front door of the bank and fired several shots in the air to give the alarm. By this time the robbers had turned into Second Street. A few men on the street who happened to be armed took snap shots at the robbers as they passed Bridge Street but without effect. The bandits returned the shots but fortunately no one was hit. At the Cross Creek Bridge on Second Street the robber who was carrying the coin sack dropped it and part of the contents rolled out. The man dismounted like a flash, picked up the money sack and handed it to a pal, he remounted and was off like the wind, leaving far behind the few men who had pursued them on foot.

The robbers took a straight course up the river towards Golconda. They were followed by a few scattering men on horseback, their idea being to keep the robbers in sight if possible until an armed posse could be organized for the pursuit.

As soon as the course of the robbers was ascertained, Deputy Sheriff Rose ran to the depot and started up the road on the switch engine. Near the Bliss ranch, fourteen miles from town, the robbers were overtaken riding along the road. The Deputy took several shots at them and is said to have wounded one of the horses. The robbers had horses waiting for them in the field on the Bliss ranch. They changed horses here and struck out again in a northwesterly direction. Deputy Sheriff Rose secured horses and accompanied by several men, started again in pursuit.

News of the robbery was telegraphed to Golconda and Constable Colwell started out from the place with a posse on a chase after the bandits.

Sheriff McDeid soon organized a posse here and started out accompanied by an Indian tracker. It seems almost an impossibility for the desperadoes to escape with their booty, but they are desperate and there is little likelihood of their being taken alive.

The amount of money taken by the robbers cannot be ascertained with a certainty at this writing. It is somewhere in the neighborhood of from $15,000 to $30,000. The bank offers a reward of $500 for any one of the robbers, dead or alive, and a like reward will be given by Sheriff McDeid.

The robbers wore no masks and their identification will be an easy matter in the event of their capture. The men have been noticed about town for a couple of days. they were dressed as vaqueros and there was nothing in their appearance to arouse suspicion.

The leader of the gang was a small man, not over 5 feet 7 inches in height. He has a light brown beard. The other men are about 5 feet 9 inches in height. One is smooth shaven while the other has a dark brown mustache. They are strangers hereabouts

The robbers are obviously old hands at the business from the manner in which they carried out a daring bank robbery.

At 3pm this afternoon word was received from Golconda that a posse was but a mile behind the robbers and was pressing them hard. They were then going through soldier's pass, a few miles south-east of Golconda. It sees that they left a change of horses at Silve's ranch and are heading for that place, but another posse has cut across the country and will prevent them from getting the horses.

Their pursuers being so close upon them, the robbers have not a shadow of a chance to escape, but when they are brought to bay there will be a fight which may result in the death or wounding of some of the pursuers. It is thought, that the desperadoes have only one rifle, and if this is the case their capture should not be such a difficult or dangerous matter.

*

Silver State Post
September 20, 1900

ROBBERS ARE HARD PRESSED

Last Reports Say Posse Was Not Far Behind

Desperadoes Are Heading for the Junipers country—News of a Fight Is Expected Hourly

Under cover of darkness the three desperadoes who looted the First National Bank of this place yesterday have escaped to the mountains in the north-eastern part of the country. An hour after the commission of the crime there seemed no possibility of the robbers making their escape. Now their capture depends upon the skilful trailing of the few remaining pursuers and the outcome of the battle which must inevitably follow when the robbers are brought to bay.

The story of the flight of these robbers and the tactics of their pursuers is best told by taking it from the beginning as there were several inaccuracies in the account published yesterday.

Leaving Winnemucca the robbers made their first change of horses in the upper field of the Sloan ranch, about eight miles from Winnemucca. There they left two animals and took in exchange a big black horse belonging to G.S. Nixon and another good horse belonging to the ranch. They then struck out for the northeast in the direction of Silve's ranch. Here mistake No.1 of the pursuers was made. Constable Colwell of Golconda had been notified of the robbery, and he and D.F. Abel accompanied by two Indians, started out. Through some misapprehension, instead of starting east to head off the robbers, which could easily have been done, the Golconda posse started down the river towards the Bliss ranch, and thus fell in behind the men they were after. They met the Winnemucca posse, consisting of Deputy Sheriff Rose, E.A. Ducker, Ernest Duvivier and several others, and the chase was taken up in earnest, the robbers having a lead of about three miles. This advantage they maintained until 3o'clock in the afternoon, when they arrived at Silve's ranch, about thirty miles northeast of Winnemucca. Here the robbers secured fresh horses, having left them several days before. They made the change hurriedly and when they left took all their horses with them, packing their effects on one of the animals. Before the robbers got away from Silve's the pursuing posse was in sight. One of the boys on the ranch asked the meaning of the body of men coming up the road and a robber said: "It's the Winnemucca Sheriff and a posse who are after us. We have robbed the Winnemucca bank."

Permitting the robbers to change horses at Silve's was the second serious mistake of the pursuit. The owner of the ranch was in Golconda at the time the news of the robbery was received: but he did not tell of men having left horses at his ranch until it was too late to prevent the robbers making the change which they had counted on as a part of their plan of escape. Had it been known at the time that the horses were at Silve's, a posse from Golconda could have reached the ranch ahead of the robbers and they would have fallen into a trap.

Leaving Silve's ranch the robbers headed for Squaw Valley. The two posses headed by Colwell and Rose kept on in pursuit, but their horses were so fagged that they were at a great disadvantage.

The intention of the robbers is evidently to reach the junipers country at the head of the Owyhee if possible. Once in those wilds it will be practically impossible to find them, and in any event they would have the advantage of choosing their own ground in case of a fight with their pursuers.

About the only chance of capturing the robbers is the possibility of the pursuing posses overtaking them before they reach the junipers. This is not unlikely as last reports showed that there was no great distance between the desperadoes and their pursuers. News of a battle may be received at any time.

This morning Abel returned to Golconda. He reported that he left Colwell and the other two Indians about 4 o'clock yesterday afternoon. They were then on the big flat about eight miles west of Silve's. W.L. Coulter, Marvin Hill and Mr. Brown returned to Winnemucca late this afternoon. They arrived at Silve's last evening, but some three hours behind the posse. they reported that Colwell, Rose and Duvivier, with Indian trailers, were only a short distance behind the robbers. The bandits left Silve's at 4 o'clock and turned south toward the river while the posse kept the upper road on the probability that the robbers turned south in order to avoid the fields at Noble's ranch, after which they would turn toward the gap leading to Squaw Valley.

Coulter and party remained at Silve's all night and this morning followed the tracks some distance and far enough to indicate their direction. Their horses being worn out they returned to Winnemucca this afternoon.

Another posse which is after the robbers consists of Constable Moore, W.J. Bell, Hugh Collins and J.T. Dunn of this place. They started out for Paradise Valley shortly after the robbery with the intention of securing more men and fresh horses at Paradise and then cutting across the mountains to head the robbers off. The plan is a good one and they may succeed in capturing the desperadoes.

Telegrams were sent to Tuscarora last night asking the officers to organize a posse and endeavour to cut the robbers off before they get into the junipers country. The Tuscaroarans would have an excellent chance of catching the robbers, but they are evidently not much given to chasing criminals. A reply was received this morning from Tuscarora that the men there would not start out unless their expenses were guaranteed. By this time it was too late for the Tuscaroarans to accomplish anything and they were advised to stay at home.

BIG REWARD OFFERED

Sheriff McDeid this morning issued the following circular:

Three Thousand Dollars Reward—Men Wanted for Bank Robbery—The First National Bank of Winnemucca, Nev. was robbed at noon September 19, by three unknown men of the following description:

One about thirty five to forty years of age, about five feet eight or nine inches in height; weight about one hundred and fifty pounds; dark mustache, weeks growth of beard; dark pants well worn, white hat.

One smooth faced, heavy set; about thirty years old; about five feet eight inches in height; dark hair; bluish grey suit, no vest, coat ripped under right arm; wore Congress shoes and white hat.

One with full beard—scraggy, sandy brown; about five feet nine inches in height; weight about one hundred fifty or sixty pounds. probably thirty years of age.

When last seen the men were headed for the junipers by way of the Squaw Valley. One thousand dollars will be paid for either of the parties, dead or alive, or three thousand dollars will be paid for the trio of robbers.

C.W. McDeid
Sheriff of Humboldt County
Winnemucca, Nev. Sept. 20, 1900

ROBBERS NEAR TUSCARORA

At 3:05 o'clock this afternoon Sheriff McDeid received the following dispatch from E.A. Duvivier, from Tuscarora.

Bank robbers are twelve miles from here. They are headed for White Rock and if all ranches north of here are notified they can be captured. Their horses are worn out. Ed Cavanaugh and Burns Colwell are with me.

This dispatch shows the correctness of the belief that the robbers were headed for Tuscarora. The dispatches sent to that town last night asked the officers to take a posse to White Rock where they could possibly intercept the robbers. If the Tuscaroarans had acted as they should have done the desperadoes would now be in custody.

NOTE OF THE ROBBERY

Sheriff McDeid sent telegrams to Boise City, Idaho; Silver City, Idaho; Burns, Oregon; Vale, Oregon; Ontario, Oregon; and also to Tuscarora from which place it was expected a posse could be promptly organized to intercept the robbers if they headed towards the junipers.

There is now much cleared wisdom exploited, which, under the excitement of the moment, could not have easily been utilized. However, commendable and prompt action was taken. From the reports now at hand it seems that the course taken indicates a determination to reach the junipers, an almost inaccessible region in southern Idaho and northern Nevada. If the robbers had relays properly arranged they could easily have reached the junipers by daylight.

Many conflicting reports by eye witnesses are now current. Sheriff McDeid was standing on the corner by the Reception Saloon and when the men passed one of them took a wing shot at the sheriff, who stepped back into the arch on the corner. Mr. Lane, hearing the noise, stepped to his door, which is opposite where the men dropped the sack of coin and they took a shot at him.

Directly after the robbery, Mr. Calhoun, the stenographer at the bank, took off towards the hospital and accidentally turned the corner where the men had dropped the sack and one of the robbers good naturedly took three shots at Mr. Calhoun, who promptly fell behind a fence.

Professor Kaye saw the latter part of the affair as the men were leaving the rear of the bank, but supposed that some hunters were departing and that the raised hands of bank officials was simply a parting salutation.

W.S. Johnson, the horse buyer, ran back into the bank, grabbed on one of the pumping guns, jumped the fence and drew a bead on one of the retreating robbers, but the gun wasn't loaded and Johnson threw the weapon away in disgust. It is said by a lady who witnesses this that had the gun been loaded Johnson would have got at least one of the men.

The robbers stole a valuable horse from loan's field belonging to Mr. Nixon and when they reached Silve's they took the animal along with them, evidently taking a fancy to the horse.

Silver State Post
September 21, 1900

CHASE OF THE ROBBERS
Were Near Tuscarora Last Night

STRONG POSSE IS PURSUING THEM

Last News Received Indicates the Capture of the Desperadoes

The scene of the chase after the bank robbers has shifted to Elko County and news of any new developments will be received from Tuscarora. Messrs Duvivier, Colwell and Cavanaugh, who were the leaders of the pursuit, arrived at Tuscarora about 1 o'clock yesterday afternoon and reported that the robbers were then about twelve miles from Tuscarora and headed for white Rock, a point about forty miles distant. At 4 o'clock a dispatch was received from George Miller at Tuscarora saying that Duvivier, Colwell and Cavanaugh, accompanied by four other men, had departed for white Rock. The party had fresh horses and divided taking different routes to white Rock, which they expected to reach early last evening. It was supposed then that the robbers were only ten miles away and that one or other of the two parties would cut them off somewhere in the vicinity of White Rock. This is the last news received from the scene of the chase up to 4 o'clock this afternoon.

News of a fight or capture of the robbers will come from Tuscarora and is expected hourly. At this writing the outlook is that the robbers have been cut off from reaching the junipers. Everything depends upon whether they were able to secure fresh horses last night. If they did not, the Tuscarora posse should have been able to either catch up with them or head them off.

Silver State Post
September 24, 1900

THE ROBBER HUNT

Posse Still following Them Through Wilds of Northern Elko

The bank robbers are flying from one place to another in their endeavor to escape from the Winnemucca and Golconda posse, which at last accounts was close on their heels in the Jack Creek Mountains in Elko County. The last news of the chase was received here last night, being a message sent by telephone from Johnson's, a station about thirty miles east of Tuscarora on the headwaters of the North Fork of the Humboldt. The dispatch said that the robbers were then near Rutherford's ranch, about six miles from Johnson's and were being closely followed by the Winnemucca and Golconda posse. It stated also that word had been sent to Sheriff Campbell of Elko, who, with a posse, was then on the North Fork and but a few miles away, and the two posses had joined forces in a final attempt to run the robbers down. This news, though few particulars are given, shows that the robber hunt is being skillfully conducted, with an excellent chance of the capture of the fugitives being made soon after the dispatch was sent.

Those who know the nature of the country through which the chase has been conducted are the only ones who can thoroughly appreciate the difficulties which the pursuers have had to contend with. It is one of the roughest sections imaginable and that the trail of the robbers has been kept at all is a matter for wonder.

It is stated on good authority that the identity of the robbers has been ascertained almost to a certainty and even if they should elude the pursuers for the present their ultimate capture is hardly to be doubted.

No further news of the chase had been received here up to 3 o'clock this afternoon.

Silver State Post
September 25, 1900

NO FURTHER NEWS OF ROBBERS

Up to the time of going to press no further news has been received of the chase of the bank robbers in Elko County. Yesterday's Elko Dependent contains the following:

Sheriff Campbell received word Saturday evening that the Winnemucca bank robbers were heading for North Fork. He and J.J.

Campbell left about 8 o'clock with the intention of heading them off if possible. A message was received from Johnson's this forenoon said that the sheriff ate breakfast there Sunday morning and left for the Mardis country. Word came from Tuscarora this morning that the bandits had robbed a sheep camp, about thirty miles from there, of ammunition and food and had broken a rifle. Posses are in hot pursuit and the robbers may yet be caught.

Silver State Post
September 28, 1900

ROBBERS STILL AT LARGE

Posses Still After them But There is No News of the Chase

Up to the time of going to press there is no news of importance in regard to the pursuit of the bank robbers. the posse which left Tuscarora Thursday afternoon returned that evening, having visited several sheep camps in the mountains without finding the men they were after. The posse again struck out Thursday evening for White Rock, which place they expected to reach by midnight. a letter received from Tuscarora says that Colwell, Duvivier and Cavanaugh are determined to run the robbers down and those who know Colwell and his companions best are satisfied that they will follow the desperadoes as long as there is a possibility of capturing them.

There are numberless rumours in circulation as to the identity of the robbers, but none of them seem to have any substantial foundation. One from Tuscarora is that the robbers answer the description of three men who have been working in a wood camp near that place; that one of the men was in Tuscarora Monday afternoon and that he was riding a grey horse. It will be remembered that one of the robbers rode a grey horse from Winnemucca.

Ed Ducker, Roy Trousdale and three Indian trailers returned last night. They went as far as Squaw Valley Wednesday night and took up the trail Thursday morning but were so far behind that they gave up the chase in the afternoon. they picked up one of the robbers horses in Squaw Valley. The Indians say the men turned all the horses loose except those they were riding before leaving Squaw Valley.

Messrs. Bell, Collins and Dunn returned last night from Paradise Valley. They turned their course homeward when the found the robbers had taken a different route and that they were too far behind to be of any assistance in the pursuit.

*

On an unseasonably warm October morning, Peter was attending to the Saturday grocery shopping while Mabel was outside in the garden, painting. After greeting the postman, Mabel stepped back inside through the glass French doors that had been left open to let in the fresh autumn air. "Etta, Etta, you have a letter." Walking over to Mabel, Etta was saying, "Oh good, I've been expecting to hear from Eva Kilchherr, or get a birthday card from Mother. Is it from Mother?" "**Etta!**" They both stared at the envelope. Tears started to flow from the eyes of both women. Etta was trembling.

October 4, 1900

Dearest Etta,

I hope you are well. There is no way for me to know if this letter will find you at the same address. It has been such a long time. I am sorry if this letter is unwelcome. There is no way of knowing if you would still want to hear from me. You may have met another and be married.

I am ready to start a new life. You do not want to know about my last years, but I can tell you that I am ready to settle down and buy a ranch, but it will have to be in Argentina – to find safety.

You are the only reason I have kept going, to get to this time when I could take care of you, and have a life with you, but it would mean you leaving your home.

Etta, I love you. Will you marry me?

If I can be with you, I promise you to never again be involved in the activities you would not approve of. Also, you should know that my good friend, Robert Cassidy, will be my partner in setting up and running a cattle operation. We will be ready to travel by the first part of next year.

May I come to San Diego to see you and talk this over with you? I can understand that this is a sudden surprise at hearing this news. Please think about it. I am going to Argentina, Etta. I have to go. I would like you with me.

I will write again soon with an address for sending a letter. I'm heading to Fort Worth to meet friends, and then I could take the train to see you, perhaps by the first of December.

Please think about this.

Eternally yours,
Harry

*

Mabel left the room to give time for Etta to read and take in what ever the news might be from Harry. She knew, no matter what, Etta's emotions would be much disrupted. After reading the letter, Etta couldn't remain indoors or face anyone, as she needed to collect her thoughts. She started walking. She walked aimlessly for a couple of hours, letter in hand. When she returned home she went to her bedroom and closed the door. Mabel could hear her crying. Peter arrived home and hearing the news, asked Mabel if she'd seen the contents of the letter. He hadn't told her about Harry's outlaw life. Mabel didn't know what was in the letter, but something must be done.

Finally, Peter knocked on the door and called out to Etta. She answered that she was alright and would be out in a moment. When she did come out, Peter asked to speak privately with her in the front room. He had just explained about Harry's unlawful activities to Mabel, so now Mabel was crying in their bedroom.

"Etta, dear sister, Mabel tells me you received a letter from your Harry this morning, and it seems to have caused you a great deal of distress." "I'm alright now Peter." "No, Etta, let me have my say. I haven't mentioned this to you before because I hoped there would be no need. I don't believe you're aware that Harry has been involved in unlawful conduct in the involvement of bank and train robberies and I don't know what else. I don't believe that you would ever have a secure future with him. He's wanted by the law; and with the railroads fixing the Pinkerton's on him, make no mistake in understanding that he will be caught or killed." "Peter, how do you know this?" "I read the papers, and the Police Gazette. Etta, I have an acquaintance with a Pinkerton operative who loves to talk. He doesn't know that, through you, I'm associated with Harry. Please open your eyes to the facts."

After a moment, Etta said, "Peter, when I met him, Harry told me that he'd done some things against the law. What he's done in the years since, he did for a future with me. He wanted to get the money to start a new life; to buy a ranch in Argentina where we'd be safe and we could be happy. Until now, I didn't know what he was doing all this time. Please don't judge too harshly. We've enjoyed a privileged life while he was on his own at an early age just trying to stay alive. I realize there's no excuse for breaking the law, except, maybe we can try to understand what it would be like when you have nothing to loose." "What does this mean Etta? Are you really thinking of going with him to Argentina? Etta, think of your sister, it would break her heart."

"No Peter, it wouldn't break my heart. I've been listening, and while I hear my sister's voice sounding strong and compassionate, I'm reminded of a conversation she and I had. I think you remember it Etta. Etta has always loved Harry, and loves him still . . . . she will have to see this through; this is her hearts course. How could she do otherwise? Peter, since they'll be moving to Argentina. They'll be safe from reprisal. We must give them our blessing."

Hearing these words, Peter remembered the stubbornness of his own mother and relinquished his arguments. Also, both women were crying again and holding each other; they wouldn't have heard him anyway.

*

Etta received another letter from Harry a few weeks later; this time Etta was first to retrieve the mail.

November 4, 1900

Dearest Etta,

Hopefully you have received my letter telling you about the plans to go to Argentina and that I would like to marry you. If you are free and willing to be with me, please write and let me know. I can be in San Diego, to see you and talk about this, by the first part of December.

I hope you; Mabel, and Peter (?) are well. I would like to meet your family. I would like for us to be married, and go with you on a honeymoon in San Francisco. You could meet my brother, who lives there.

Please write, and send the letter to the address on the card. I love you Etta.

Faithfully yours,
Harry

*

November 16, 1900

Dear Harry,

As you can see, I have received your letters. Much has happened to both of us since we last were with each other. I will get to the point. I would like to see you again. We will undoubtedly be unfamiliar to one another after all this time. If we still are good for each other, after meeting and talking; then, yes, I would want to be with you, marry you, and spend the future with you on a ranch in Argentina.

Mabel and Peter have given us their blessing and wish the best for us. Mabel wants a wedding here in her home, a garden apartment, which she has already started making decorations for. Would that be agreeable to you?

Please send a telegraph message to let us know when you will be arriving. We would like you to stay here with us.

Mabel has prepared the next page with our address, Peter's telephone number at his office and a very artful map showing how to find us in the event that Peter misses you at the train station. Peter plans to meet you. I don't think I could manage my emotions in public.

It has been a long while; and all that while, I've loved you.

Your Etta

*

Etta resigned her position at Peter's office, to have time for planning the long distance move and a wedding; so, she wasn't at the office when the call came.

"Yes, this is Peter" "Peter, I'm Harry Longabaugh; I believe Etta has told you about me." "Yes Harry, we've been expecting your call. When will you be arriving?"

"As soon as possible, I've just received Etta's letter. I could be on a train on December 2nd, and I think that'll get me into California and on to San Diego by Wednesday the 5th of December. Does that sound all right?" "That sounds real good Harry. When you have your ticket and know your schedule, either send a telegraph or use this telephone number again to let me know when to meet you. If I'm not here, you can leave a message with the secretary." "I will, either way. I'll get my ticket now, and then let you know." "We look forward to seeing you, Harry. Oh wait; I guess I should go ahead and give you my description. I'm almost 6 feet, I've got dark brown hair and, oh hell; I'll wear a red flower on my coat, or if it's raining I'll just stick it on my hat." "Ha, okay Peter, thank you." Peter was impressed by Harry's straightforward manner of speech and pleasing voice.

Etta and Mabel became girls again, not only did they have a wedding to plan for; (they both knew the reunion would work out just fine) they also wanted to decorate early for Christmas. Etta picked the date. They were to be married, at the apartment, on Saturday, December 8, at two o'clock. No sense waiting a day longer than necessary. The Justice of the Peace who would be performing the ceremony was a friend of Peter's.

Harry sent a telegram, and telephoned, to give Peter his arrival time. Before Peter left for the station, Mabel made Peter promise to be slow about putting the horse and buggy away when he returned with Harry. Her plan was for Harry to come in, then Mabel would go out and "check on Peter," giving Harry and Etta time alone together in the house.

*

The men knew each other right off. The large red rose pinned to Peter's coat wasn't necessary. When they reached the buggy, Peter noticed that Harry traveled light, with only two bags, and that Harry was dressed in a new suit and hat in the latest fashion; the man knew how to dress like a gentleman, spoke well, and was easy to converse with as they started towards home.

"Peter, I don't know what you think of me being absent for over two years. There were things I just had to finish. I don't know what Etta's told you." "Harry, please call me Pete. Etta mentioned you had a hard upbringing and that you were on your own early on. She also said you've done some things that, well, maybe you shouldn't have done, but you had been faced with some tough times."

There was a long pause and Peter could sense that Harry was struggling with what, or how much to say. Finally Peter broke the silence. "Harry, I realize circumstances like you may have found yourself in can break a man, but you've come through it well enough. To truly be friends and speak our minds openly with each other as friends, I must tell you that I'm aware of your activities against the law. I have no judgment about that. I've read newspaper and Pinkerton reports about the train and bank robberies. I can only say that your going to Argentina to start a new life, sounds very wise. The Pinkerton's are ruthless. I despise their way of doing business. Why they, themselves work outside the law with total impunity, especially when they're hired by the railroad magnates or the other tycoon industrialists. They hire known gunmen to track down whoever they're looking for. Charles Siringo, the man looking for you and your gang, is a well known gunman; hired to be a detective by the Pinkerton's."

Harry felt more relieved than defensive. Peter had presented himself in a straightforward and respectable way. "Pete, Etta will be safe with me in Argentina. The authorities don't know me by sight. I'm in a good position for a fresh start to live an honest life. We'll be raising horses and cattle in a safe place. A partner, a respectable friend of mine, will be there also."

"Harry, it'll be all right, and you have my word that I'll never tell a soul. I did tell Etta what I had found out, by the way, and to your credit, she already knew the story. Not much farther to go now; I see it's starting to rain. That's good; a fine excuse for a whisky when we get home."

*

Etta made a mess of Mabel's plan. She had been standing by the window for over an hour, watching and waiting for Peter's return with Harry. She was wearing the dress she had saved, somewhat out of fashion now, which she wore when she first met Harry in Raton, New Mexico in 1896. When she saw the buggy turn into the carriage house she ran out, through the drizzling rain, to meet Harry.

Peter now hurried, unhitching and minimally grooming the horse, so he could leave them alone. Meanwhile, Harry and Etta embraced, then stared at each other, and then again embraced, holding each other urgently close. Other than saying each others names, no added words had been spoken by the time Peter went inside, so he didn't have much to tell Mabel in answer to her questions, except for telling her he liked the man very much.

It took awhile, each now shy with the other, until they spoke. Harry saying, "It was you, Etta, only you, that kept me going." The vital significance of their conversation was how much they had missed each other.

Peter had the whiskey ready for Harry and himself. Mabel welcomed and hugged Harry like a long lost brother. All had shining moist eyes. Seeing Etta with Harry, Mabel felt this was meant to be. It had been years since she'd seen her sister so happy. She felt awkward about the cot set up in the front room for Harry.

The skies had cleared, and after a late supper, Etta and Harry took a slow leisurely walk. Harry was surprised at the mild winter weather in San Diego. In the same way as before, they had no difficulties talking candidly with each other. While walking, Etta noticed that Harry had a slight limp. He'd been trying to hide it, and now confessed to a bullet injury. He turned the conversation to their future in Argentina. Etta already told Harry she would like to marry him and make her life with him.

Peter had rearranged his schedule to take the day off on Thursday, to show Harry around town while the girls went shopping; again one of Mabel's ideas. She wanted Etta to have special things to wear on her honeymoon; also Etta needed a good warm coat for San Francisco and New York City. They all met late in the afternoon at the old Horton House Hotel on Broadway.

Later, after their supper, Mabel, in an exceptionally cheerful mood, started to play songs from the sheet music she'd recently been practicing on piano. She played the latest song by Scott Joplin; Maple Leaf Rag." Peter and Mabel sang as she played "The Sidewalks of New York." Even Harry knew the words to, "The Band Played On." They all had fun with that one. Etta played violin accompanying Mabel with, "After the Ball" and "Daisy, Daisy." Mabel finally found the sheet music for "Shenandoah" and after practicing, she played it and Harry joined in the singing, looking at Etta the entire time.

"Oh Shenandoah, I long to see you,. Away you rolling river.

Oh Shenandoah I long to see you, away; I'm bound away 'cross the wide Missouri.

Oh Shenandoah, I love your daughter. Away you rolling river.

For her I'd cross your roaming waters. Away, I'm bound away, 'cross the wide Missouri.

"Tis seven years since I've last seen you, and hear your rolling river, 'Tis seven years since I've last seen you, away we're bound away across the wide Missouri.

Oh Shenandoah, I long to see you, and hear your rolling river,

Oh Shenandoah, I long to see you, away, we're bound away across the wide Missouri,"

Peter got up to pour four Brandys, not because anyone would really like one, but to give him something to do while he cleared the lump from his throat. Etta was crying in Harry's arms, and Mabel sat at the piano, with her head bent and her eyes closed.

*

On Friday, Peter went to the office while Harry lost himself in a book, and the ladies were busy with baking the wedding cake which was lightly spiced and full of raisins, currants and finely chopped almonds; then they took up the hem of Mabel's wedding dress. Mabel was about an inch taller, at 5'6" than Etta, at almost 5'5". Some of the embroidery would be hidden but the overall effect would be as striking as when Mabel wore it.

In the evening Mabel and Etta prepared the house for the wedding the following day, Saturday, December 8, 1900. Peter and Harry had gone out to the carriage house to knock back a whisky or two. Peter set the mood of conversation, by asking Harry what he knew about the cattle wars of the early nineties.

"What can you tell me about the Johnson County War, in Wyoming? I heard it was the civil war of the west." "Oh yeah, the war on Powder River. What a shameless time. I wasn't in that area at the worst of it, but it went on for some time. I know the area and the ranches involved. It was a time of complete lawlessness on the open range. You learned to decide for yourself what rules you'd go by. You've got to remember there had been some harsh winters in '86 and '87. Very bad times, over three quarters of the stock died off."

"The war started out with a law against taking and branding the maverick calves found roaming in the open; something that had always been done. Supposedly, they were to be bid on. That was hard enough for the little ranches; hell, even the big ranchers got their start by finding unbranded calves. But then the big ranch's formed the Wyoming Stock Growers Association and with the help of some politicians, they got it so all unbranded calves went to the association." Peter nodded, "Yes, I've heard of the Maverick Law." "Pete, it used to be that rustlers were punished by the law, but then the big ranchers and their bought politicians and hired detectives and hired guns started taking the law into their own hands. The big ranchers bought up land with water and fenced it, cutting off the small outfits. Then they hired gun fighters to outright kill the owners of the small ranches, the cowboys who worked for them, and sometimes whole families."

"Outright stealing of cattle was a problem—on both sides. As I understand how it became the Johnson County War, was when the ranchers association hired over a hundred gun fighters, who all met up in Casper and then went to Buffalo and took over the courthouse. They took guns stored there, and set out to raid a couple of the troublesome smalltime ranches. A couple of cowboys got away from the KC ranch that had been attacked, and told the sheriff, who got up a small posse of small ranchers and townsfolk. They found the invaders at the TA ranch. They held them there in a stand off for two days."

"The invaders, working for the big outfits, had been supported by the senators and the governor of the state; so it took orders from President Harrison to send the 6th Cavalry from Fort McKinney. After they arrived the invaders dispersed. Charges were brought up, but, in the end, none of the hired killers were sentenced. And even after that, some cowboys accused of rustling, some guilty, some not, were hanged by vigilantes."

Peter was shaking his head, "I've read in the New York Times, where the courts dragged their feet for so long the witnesses had disappeared, the bought gunfighters were gone, and the court dismissed the case. Some points of the law and judicial system are unsavory and will never set right with me."

*

Very early on the wedding day, Mabel frosted the wedding cake with ornamental frosting; then she went out to the garden to find a handful of late fall flowers for Etta to hold. Etta had seen some in the garden the day before that she said would make a sweet bouquet. Mabel had bought two large bouquets that she put in quart jars, now emptied of their paintbrushes, and placed them on small tables on each side of where the judge would stand.

Peter had been up at dawn, as it fell to him to cook the turkey and make the dressing. The roasting pan barely fit into their small gas oven. The dinner would be a combination of wedding celebration and Christmas feast, as they wouldn't be together for the holidays. Etta and Harry, hand in hand, were taking an early morning stroll.

The Justice of the Peace, George Puterbaugh was a friend of Peter's. Judge Puterbaugh had been in the civil war as a young man. Peter was always interested in hearing about his experiences as he was forever bewildered at the magnitude of that war. As a favor to Peter, Judge Puterbaugh came out to their home to perform the ceremony.

The dining room was chosen as it was the sunniest room in the apartment. All traces of Mabel's studio-workshop had been cleaned out. The dining table stood folded against the side wall with a white linen cloth covering it. The champagne and glasses with white ribbons tied around the stems for the bride and groom were ready. White ribbons also streamed from the ceiling.

The wedding took place at 1:45 that afternoon. The old Judge stood in front of the French doors facing into the room. Etta and Harry faced him with Mabel and Peter on either side. Etta was beautiful in the wedding dress, as gorgeous as her sister had been when she wore it. Harry was strikingly handsome in his new suit. He had purchased it in Fort Worth before he and four other members of his outlaw gang had their photograph taken.

For a wedding ring, they used the gold band Harry bought for Etta in Raton, New Mexico; she had saved it all this time. At the end of the short ceremony, just as Harry reached for Etta, to kiss her, she added, "Harry, today I give you my hand, you've always had my heart. I love you." "I love you Etta." Their kiss was loving and tender. Just as the ceremony ended, bells rang from a neighboring church as if planned; perhaps Mabel had thought of that also.

After the champagne toasts, the cutting of the cake, and the signing of the marriage certificate, the judge left. Peter said he would have the document filed on Monday, but as Etta and Harry had not obtained a marriage license, he never did. Even though he and Harry thought it best that Harry use a different last name, to prevent even the most remote chance of Judge Puterbaugh recognizing his name; he wasn't taking any chances of bringing the law home. Harry had used his mother's maiden name, Place. Peter put the marriage certificate in his files.

Later in the afternoon, a professional photographer came to take wedding photographs. First he took a photo of the newly married couple. He started to arrange a chair for Harry to sit in, and have Etta stand at his side with her hand on his shoulder in a customary pose; then Mabel stepped in. "No, No! It is a wedding portrait! Either they both sit or they both stand, side by side; the way it was done for my and Peter's portrait." Then a group photo was taken with both couples uncontrollably smiling into the lens. The photographer frustrated from wanting a more dignified pose.

Peter turned out a mouth-watering, scrumptious turkey. It was decided then, that he would always be the one responsible for cooking the holiday turkeys. Mabel fixed the additional side dishes. The men praised Mabel and Etta for the delectable wedding cake. The dinner turned out to be a happy, laughing occasion; Peter commenting, “This may be the first dinner I’ve eaten in this apartment that wasn’t accompanied by the scent of turpentine and linseed oil.” While saying this, he was smiling at Mabel, then he raised his glass in another toast to the bride and groom. “To Harry and Etta. We are all family now, and have each other to watch out for, protect, and to love. To our family.” “To our family!”

*

They talked about the busy month ahead for Harry and Etta; San Francisco, San Antonio, Pennsylvania, New York and Boston all within about a month, and then the voyage to Argentina.

It was too late in the day for Harry and Etta to go to a hotel in town and Peter had put away the cot that morning. After the wedding feast, the newlyweds retreated to Etta’s bedroom. Etta had lit candles that were now glowing, giving the room a soft rosy glow. Mabel was at the piano, loudly playing Mozart. Harry and Etta were laughing and frolicking on her bed; then Etta put on the new lingerie Mabel had given her for a wedding present and it became very quiet in the bedroom.

Peter had hired a man with a team and wagon to take the newlyweds and their luggage to the train station for a late morning departure to San Francisco. Their parting was emotional and heartrending for all. While she hugged Harry, Mabel said to him, “Harry we’re at the beginning of a new century; keep in mind that all things are possible.” “Thank you Mabel. Thanks for everything.”

As they waved good-bye, Mabel buckled into Peter’s arms. Her dear sister was on her way to Argentina!

V

San Francisco
December 1900

"Oh Harry, look up at the glass roof, isn't this beautiful." The driver, who drove them and their luggage from the train station, had just maneuvered his team and carriage into the Grand Court of the exquisite Palace Hotel on the corner of Montgomery & Market Streets in San Francisco. Harry and Etta watched as others arrived and were stepping down from their stately carriages dressed impressively in fine clothes. Harry and Etta were also dressed well. Harry, wearing the top hat Peter had given him, was looking every inch the gentleman.

The day before they left, Peter had handed Harry a package saying it was a wedding present. Inside, Harry and Etta found that it contained a great deal of money, probably most of Peter and Mabel's savings, with a note saying that perhaps it could be used for a honeymoon week at the Palace Hotel; a hotel that had been recommended by a friend of Peter's.

They checked in as Mr. and Mrs. Harry Place, the same name Harry used for their marriage certificate. An attendant and a bell boy assisted them to their suite, taking the quiet hydraulic elevator, or 'lifting room' as some called it. The large bay window, in the room, looked out on Montgomery Street and allowed a breathtaking view across the San Francisco Bay. They could see numerous large ships in the harbor. They were shown the call button to use if they desired anything. Harry already knew what he wanted and asked the attendant for Champagne, some crackers, and a light meal. He knew Etta was fatigued from travel.

They took off their coats and shoes, and feeling weary, sat in chairs, resting and waiting for the bell boy's return. Then Etta, feeling restless, began getting a few things out of her two trunks to let them air. Harry then caught her up in his arms and they began kissing. The kissing heated up and they had to restrain themselves until the waiter with the champagne and food finally arrived.

They toasted each other with endearments while they drank the champagne. After their meal, Etta wanted to freshen up and announced she'd like a bath to wash off the dust and soot of train travel. She left the door open while she was in the tub and soon called out to Harry to please bring in a glass of champagne. He stood there immobilized, staring at her reclining in the tub. "You're beautiful!" She accepted the glass and asked him to sit and relax on the small bath chair and keep her company.

When she got out of the tub, he helped wrap her in a towel and thought of carrying her into the bedroom, but remembered he was none too fresh. Instead, he took off the rest of his clothes and got into the large tub, adding more hot water. Etta was now in a fixed stare admiring him. Before he reached for the soap, she climbed back into the tub with him. This was a shock for a simple cowboy like Harry, but he got over it fast enough as Etta crawled on top of him.

When they finally pulled the plug and left the tub, Harry wrapped a towel around his waist and then wrapped two towels around Etta while he kissed her cheek, mouth, neck and breasts. He then lifted her up and carried her to the bed, set her down and then picked up the top hat from the side table and putting it on, said, "The well dressed gentleman always wears a hat in San Francisco," and dropped his towel.

On the bed, still hungry for each other, they pulled each other closer. Harry had one hand in her wild hair and another moving down her hips. As he eased himself down on her, she felt the heat coming through him; their arms in a tight embrace; possessing each other completely.

They didn't leave their room until late afternoon the next day, when they took an elevator up to the seventh floor Conservatory where they enjoyed the statuary, the tropical plants, the expansive glass roof, and the view looking down to the Grand Court. They dined that evening in the hotel's American Dining Room, both a little overwhelmed at the vastness of the room and the amount of people.

*

They woke the next morning to a gray wall outside the window. A thick cold fog had come in during the night and had enveloped the hotel. After breakfast they put on coats and hats to go out for a walk, then stopped at the reception desk to ask where they could find a druggist, and then a telegraph station to wire Elwood, Harry's brother, to let him know they were in town. They were told the Western Union Telegraph Company was at Pine and Montgomery, or they could easily send a dispatch rider to deliver their message; which is what they did.

They headed up Market Street, to Kearney, where they stopped to look at Lotta's fountain. The plaque stated that it was donated by Lotta Crabtree in 1875. They had both heard of her, but neither had seen her. They lingered there to watch the scores of people walking by.

Walking up Geary Street to Grant Avenue, they discovered the City of Paris department store. Harry bought an overcoat as his wasn't warm enough for the chill wind off the bay, and he'd need it in New York. They were having fun and felt happy as they walked along looking at the splendid shops. Then they walked up Grant to Sutter Street, where they found the druggist. Harry needed something for his persistent catarrh.

They ate a light supper at an eatery on Bush Street. Then, back on Market Street, across from their hotel, Harry stopped in front of a jeweler's window and then beckoned Etta inside. He bought Etta a sparkling, diamond wedding ring which caused her to tremble when he put it on her finger. Then he bought a beautiful gold lapel watch and pinned it on her dress. She was filled with happiness and delight over these romantic gestures.

*

The next day they rested, read their books, and wrote letters. Etta wrote to Mabel and to her mother. Harry wrote to his sister, Savanna, in Pennsylvania, to let her know they'd be coming to visit in January. He was pleased that Etta would be meeting his family. He wanted her to see him as more than a drifting cowboy and outlaw.

Later, that afternoon, Elwood arrived at their door. He'd received their message the previous afternoon and now was just coming back from his work on the docks at Hunter's point. Harry used the call button for a waiter to bring supper to their suite. Etta noticed how different the brothers were from one another; Elwood being more opinionated and set in his ways, Harry with a broader view on the subjects under discussion. They made plans for an outing to the Cliff House on Sunday.

The fog cleared off early the next morning, so they decided to walk to the Ferry building at the end of Market Street. Now that Harry had a good warm coat they enjoyed the walk. After looking out at the bay and watching all the activity and hubbub of people coming and going east to Oakland or further on to Sacramento; they decided to take "The Creek Route" ferry, east to Oakland. While they stared back at San Francisco, they talked about their coming voyage and journey into Argentina, feeling both thrilled and anxious.

When they landed in Oakland, they walked and then enjoyed a trolley ride up the creek. Returning to San Francisco, they felt bushed, so they took the electric trolley car back to the hotel, and once again requested supper in their room.

*

On Sunday, Elwood left his flat on Julian Avenue, and walked to Market Street where he caught a trolley to the Hotel. He arrived early as planned. Elwood mentioned it was quite a ways out to the ocean and to the Cliff House, so they should get an early start. Harry hired a team and carriage for the excursion.

It was quite a stretch to go up Market Street, then west out on Fell Street and then ride all the way through the picturesque Golden Gate Park to the ocean. During the ride, Elwood told Harry that he'd read a newspaper article where Edward Harriman, one of the owners of the Union Pacific Railroad, had gone on a luxury cruise and science expedition to Alaska the year before. Harriman went to hunt for bear. He also told Harry, it was Harriman's idea to use posse cars to chase train robbers; and that the Pinkerton's were still looking for him.

By the time they arrived, they were hungry, though finding a hitching rack available was difficult as the Cliff House was a popular spot. They enjoyed the view of the ocean while they ate a hearty meal, and were greatly impressed by the opulence of the Cliff House, such a grand seven story Victorian Chateau on the cliffs. Outside, they huddled against the crisp breeze as they walked down the slope to the beach where people were walking, or riding in their carriages on the firm sand by the water. Harry was impressed with the sparkling Pacific Ocean. They spent a cheerful afternoon, and the brothers became reacquainted while talking about how the years had been for them since they'd last seen each other, when Elwood left home in 1882.

It was late in the day and the sky was darkening by the time they returned to the hotel, after leaving Elwood at his apartment. Nothing was planned for the next day as they needed to rest and make ready for traveling to San Antonio where Etta would meet Harry's friend, Butch Cassidy.

*

Harry and Butch became acquainted at "the Hole in the Wall" hideout, shortly after Butch was pardoned and released from the Wyoming State Penitentiary in January of 1896. Butch was arrested in 1894 when he and Al Hainer stole a herd of horses. Hainer was acquitted but Cassidy was found guilty. He was pardoned by Governor William A. Richards after serving a year and a half of his two year sentence in Wyoming State Penitentiary.

Butch was the brains and architect of one of the most successful, and notorious outlaw gangs in history, "The Hole in the Wall Gang." His core group included Harvey Logan, Elza Lay, George Currie, Will Carver, Camilla Hanks, Bob Meeks, Ben Kilpatrick, and Harry Longabaugh, who was known as the Sundance Kid, and a following of several other members; many of them had been part of the old Ketchum gang.

Butch was well liked for his pleasant, good humored and even-tempered personality. He wavered between going straight, with doing lawful ranch work, and the easy money of rustling livestock. He participated in his first bank robbery at the age of twenty-three in Telluride, Colorado. It was after his release from prison for horse theft, that he started his remarkable criminal career with a string of successful bank and train robberies.

Witnessing so many modern changes in communications and law enforcement, Butch realized his outlaw days were over. His good judgment, and Harry Longabaugh's desire to leave the country and start a new life with Etta, brought them together with the goal of getting enough money to go to South America to start their own cattle operation. They'd read that Argentina was a good place for raising cattle and horses.

San Antonio

After getting settled in their room on the second floor of the Menger Hotel; Harry left Etta, and hired a horse to go find Butch. He headed along San Antonio's Market Street, south to San Saba Street. Butch had told him he could ask at Fanny Porter's and she'd know where he could be found. Harry never was very keen on these houses of fallen doves, frequenting them only rarely out of sincere necessity. He preferred to have his own lady-friend. At the house, he asked to speak to Fanny.

Fanny Porter was a nice looking, solid built, no nonsense woman. She'd been married and was now a widow, running the house with just a handful of girls. When she came into the room, she gave Harry a good looking over and liked what she saw. Asking him what his pleasure was, he assured her he was just looking for his friend, "Butch Cassidy". When she doubted that was the only reason, he said, "Ma'am, I'm a married man." She laughed heartily and told him that half her clientele were married men.

Harry found Butch at the nearby saloon with Will Carver and Harvey Logan, and joined them in a round of drinks. Will had recently married his girlfriend, Callie May Hunt, so they gave a toast to the new wives. Butch had prints of the photograph they had taken in Fort Worth to give Harry. They were very pleased at how well it turned out.

After a while, Harry and Butch left to talk over their future plans. Butch also wanted to know about Etta. "Sundance, I just don't know about a woman comin' along, I know we talked about it before, but she sounds like a city lady, and I just can't see how that's goin' to work out." "Butch, meet her tomorrow and you'll see; she's alright."

Butch rode out to their hotel the next day and arrived just before the rain started. Harry was sitting, reading a paper in the lobby waiting for him, and for Etta, as she had gone for a walk around the square. Harry got up to greet Butch as he stepped inside. Harry told him that Etta would be along any minute. "Sundance, I don't know about this."

They were standing and talking by the front windows when Harry saw her across the street. He interrupted Butch, "There she is." Butch just stared, astounded at the pretty woman crossing the already muddy street in the rain. By the time she approached them, they had the door open for her. Butch was expecting complaints on the weather and mud. All he got was a big smile. "Butch, I'm so happy to meet you. Am I late?" "Pleased to meet you Ma'am; isn't the rain and mud awful!" "Oh, I've been wet and muddy before. Let me go upstairs to clean up and I'll join you two in the dining room in just a moment." "Sundance, I had no idea. Congratulations old friend."

They spent the afternoon talking and making plans for meeting in New York City where they'd make the arrangements for passage to Argentina. None of them were familiar with the country they were going to, or what they were going to find there. The men agreed with Etta when she said, "We'll just work with what we find when we get there."

*

The following day Harry and Etta traveled by buggy to pay a visit to Mrs. Kilchherr. They enjoyed the ride under the pecan and cypress trees on the avenues near her grand home. Etta was concerned when she saw her friend looking so unwell, and looking much more aged. Eva Kilchherr now had a nurse in the daytime, as well as her regular staff.

Harry enjoyed the stories Eva told of her experiences coming out to Texas in 1856. He thought Mrs. Kilchherr was a fascinating and interesting woman. Before leaving, they accepted an invitation for Christmas dinner. There would be a few more guests besides themselves.

They arrived early on Christmas day. Etta wanted to help with preparing the meal, and Harry was eager to hear more of Eva's stories. With a Christmas tree in the front parlor and the fireplace glowing there and in the dining room along with the brilliantly lit chandeliers; the setting was bright and festive. Having company gave Eva a lift and she looked much better that day. It was truly a joyous occasion and everyone sang songs after dinner. All were sad to part when it was time to say their goodbyes.

Harry and Etta stayed in San Antonio another three days, meeting with Butch again two more times. They went over the names they'd use in New York, and from then on. Harry would continue with using Harry A. Place. Etta, using her mother's first name, Ethel, would be Ethel Place. Harry didn't want to take any chances of her being found out and mixed up with his past. Butch would go by, James Ryan.

Butch became more and more impressed with Etta. He found her to be a pleasant person, and smart. She seemed to be quiet, with brevity of words, except when she really had something to say. He had been won over by her, and they were becoming friends.

*

New Orleans

On the last day of 1900, Etta and Harry were resting from so much time spent traveling on trains. New Orleans was town of entertainments; a good place for celebrating New Year's Eve. The day before, they had checked into the Hotel Bayou Metairie across from the St. Louis Cathedral; and that night they went to see a stage show on the Rue Bourbon that embarrassed Harry. Though he may be an outlaw, he could be a bit prudish.

In their room, before they went down to dinner and for the New Year's celebrations, Etta was sitting in a chair and telling Harry, "Last New Year's Eve, Mabel and Peter held a party. At midnight we all joined hands and sang 'Auld Lang Syne'. I thought of you, wondered where you were, what you were doing and if you were well—or alive. My private toast was to the 'us' that had been. I'm so happy to be with you now Harry." Harry came around to her side, bent over and sang softly in her ear, "For auld lang syne, my dear." Etta joined in, "for auld lang syne . . . .

They joined the rejoicing revelers in the noisy, raucous lobby. At midnight, when they heard church bells and gunfire, everyone held hands and sang;

"Should auld acquaintance be forgot,
And never brought to mind?
Should auld acquaintance be forgot,
And days of auld lang syne?

For auld lang syne, my dear,
For auld lang syne,
We'll take a cup o' kindness yet,
For auld lang syne!"

"Happy New Year Mrs. Place." "Happy New Year Mr. Place."

The next day, January 1, 1901, they took a walk around Jackson Square then up to Dauphine Street to ride on the electric streetcar, enjoying the old city, and marveling at the colorful buildings with the elaborately decorated balconies.

*

Phoenixville, Pennsylvania

"The depot kinda looks the same, but different. It's been about twenty years since I've been here. So it had to change some. Heck, I've changed some. I don't know exactly what to expect when we see my sister Samanna and her family." "Harry, first, let's get a driver and wagon to bring our things to the hotel. We can freshen up and then call on them."

After a quick clean-up, in their room in the Mansion House Hotel, they walked along Bridge Street and over the bridge across the Schuylkill River into Monte Clare. Jacobs Street, where Samanna lived, went by the railroad tracks; a good location for her husband, Oliver, who had his wrought iron business close to the house.

Harry couldn't get over that Samanna's children were fully grown. "That's what being away twenty years will do, I guess." Samanna wanted to hear all about what she had missed. Harry filled her in on some of the details of his life. He told her about the gunshot wound to his leg and that he was going to have it looked at when they were in New York City. Samanna was troubled by what she was hearing about her younger brother's outlaw life and made him promise to live an honest life in Argentina. She was happy to see that he'd married a pleasant and polite lady. Etta was listening intently to the conversation; there was a lot about Harry's past that she hadn't heard. Etta enjoyed the warm personalities of Samanna and her husband.

The following morning Harry and Etta rode to the Morris Cemetery in Phoenixville to visit the gravesites of Harry's parent's. His mother, Annie had died in 1887, his father in 1893. Etta walked away giving Harry time for himself, to pay his respects, and for time to reminisce and recollect his memories. They returned to Samanna's house that evening for supper. It had been a long time since Harry had felt like he had family, and with Etta sitting at his side, he now had a sense of fulfillment.

Two days later, Harry and Etta borrowed Oliver's team and wagon to go to Flour Town about twenty miles away, to visit his brother Harvey and his family. Harvey and Harry talked about the old times when they were just kids, and about when they went to New York trying to find work but were unsuccessful and ended up back home. The brothers gave each other an uncustomary hug when they parted two days later.

Parting with Samanna and Oliver wasn't easy as Harry had always felt close to them. Samanna had married before he left home twenty years ago, and at that time Harry had visited them frequently. They all promised to write to each other once Harry acquired an address in Argentina.

The next stop was Philadelphia, where Harry's sister Emma lived and had her dressmaking business, "McCandles and

Longabaugh." Harry was proud of Emma doing so well with her business; though Emma, on the other hand, didn't think so well of Harry. She did, however act more agreeable towards him after hearing he was no longer an outlaw and was planning on abiding by the law on a ranch in Argentina. Nevertheless, not willing to be associated with an outlaw, she later changed the spelling of her last name to Longabough.

"Harry, I can see that you're very loved by your family. Maybe your past actions aren't approved of, but still you're deeply loved." "How come Pete and Mabel can accept me for who I am? They didn't disapprove of me and they knew about me; so how come my family can't understand?" "Well, my sister and Pete met you as my friend and someone who wanted a fresh start, and also because we loved each other. Your family identifies with you. Being tied to you, and your being an outlaw, isn't what they want, because it isn't what they want for themselves. Give them time; they'll realize your merit when you have the ranch in Argentina and have a way to show them what a decent man you are. Still, remember that they've shown their deep love for you.

*

Buffalo, New York
Dr. Pierces Invalid Hotel

Finding out that they would have separate accommodations at the hospital distressed both Etta and Harry. Otherwise, the accommodations were designed with the intention of giving a home like atmosphere. The massive double entry doors with panels of stained glass above them, gave the appearance of a fine hotel.

Harry needed to have the gunshot wound in his leg looked at and treated. He also wanted to have his chronic catarrh treated and hoped it could be cured. He always feared it could be related to tuberculosis and wanted reassurance that it was not. Etta had complaints of fatigue and female ailments and menstrual disorders that she was concerned with. This was a good time to address those conditions.

Harry had read newspaper advertisements issued in the west, about Dr. Ray Vaughn Pierce's World Dispensary and Invalid Hotel at 653 Main Street in Buffalo, New York, and had been enthusiastic about getting treatment and be restored to good health.

While spending time in the gentlemen's reception room, Harry learned a little about what was going on in Buffalo and New York City. Buffalo was getting ready for the Pan-American Exposition that would open in May. He also got advice on where to stay, and was told that Taylor's Boarding House was thought to be respectable.

After a week, Harry did feel better. The Turkish baths seemed very helpful in breaking up his congestion. Minor surgery was required on his leg. Etta was diagnosed with anaemia and treated with a tonic. She was also given an elixir that she could tell contained a strong drug, probably laudanum. She stopped taking it.

*

Bliss Brother's Studio

While traveling by carriage from the train station to the Invalid Hospital, Harry and Etta noticed the Bliss Bro's Photography Studio three blocks away, at 365 Main Street. They thought they might like to have another professional photograph taken of them after their stay at the hospital. They expected prints of the photos taken at Mabel and Peter's, to arrive at Etta's mothers' house by the time they visited her in Boston; if not, they would have the new photos.

On the morning of their departure from the hospital, Harry and Etta put on their finest clothes for the photograph. Etta wore a high collared dark forest green dress with a roped belt at the waist and decorative rope decoration at the elbow and wrist with a lace inset in the front bodice. She pinned her gold lapel watch to her dress. Her chestnut hair, always clean and shining, though usually slipping from its knot, was pinned tight. Harry looked dashing in his frock coat and top hat. They walked arm in arm to the Bliss Brothers studio.

Frank Bliss arranged the couple in their poses, helping Harry find a comfortable position since Harry's leg was still mending. He suggested to Harry that he hold his top hat. Again, Etta stood by

Harry turned slightly towards him. The couple would have three poses to choose from.

Afterward they returned to the hospital, where Harry obtained a supply of Dr. Pierces cough remedy and a salve for his wounded leg. They checked out of the Invalid Hotel, pleased to have more time with each other again. Etta received a complimentary, "Ladies Notebook and Calendar."

They traveled north, on the New York Central Limited, to see the Niagara Falls they had each heard so much about. Standing at Prospect Point they viewed the grandeur of the falls, exclaiming that it was much wider than they realized. They were amazed at the power of the water going over the falls and the permanent cloud of mist at the base of the American Falls and the Horseshoe Falls.

A few days later, they returned to the Bliss Brothers Studio to pick up their portraits and bought all the photographs of each of the three poses. Their favorite was one that showed them slightly facing towards each other with their arms touching. They looked at the photographs as they traveled on the New York & Chicago Limited to New York City, while they talked over their future.

Harry sent one photograph, of their favorite pose to his friend David Gillespie from the Little Snake River Valley, near Baggs, Wyoming.

New York City

They found lodging at Catherine Taylor's stylish Boarding house on Twelfth Street. After remembering to sign the register with their new names, they were shown to their rooms on the second floor. They had explained to Catherine Taylor that Etta's brother, James Ryan, would be joining them in a few days. Harry immediately sent a telegram to Butch at Fanny Porter's, advising him of their address. Butch was on the next train to New York City.

Both Harry and Etta had been to New York City when they were in their teens, so they knew something of what to expect. New York City's population now reached almost three and a half million people, and Teddy Roosevelt was now the governor of the state.

On the day Butch arrived and reunited with Harry and Etta, who was now going by the name Ethel; he went to Tiffany's

Jewelers and bought a gold watch and a diamond stick pin. He'd already noticed well dressed men wearing wide cravats accented by fancy stickpins. Early that evening, they all went on a horse drawn carriage ride around Central Park. The driver took pleasure with the lively and spirited trio.

The following evening, Harry, Ethel, and James sought out a show at the Garrick Theatre on West 35th Street. The play, 'Captain Jinks of the Horse Marines', had just opened the night before. Watching the riotous comedy written by Clyde Fitch and starring Ethel Barrymore, they relaxed, laughed, and enjoyed themselves.

*

Boston

Later in the week, after feeling rested, Harry and Etta traveled by train to Boston to visit her mother. Traveling without Etta's two trunks made the trip much easier. Harry found a driver at Boston's North Station. "Where do we tell him we're going Etta?" "Just tell the driver to head towards Harvard College in Cambridge, Mother lives close by."

Ethel, Etta's mother, gave them a warm, congenial welcome. She had received Etta's letter telling all about her husband, the cattle rancher. She was never told about Harry's outlaw past. They found Ethel looking well. "Darling Etta, you look well, how have you been?" I'm very well mother. Harry and I spent a week at Dr. Pierce's Invalid Hotel recuperating from exhaustion from all the traveling, and for Harry's catarrh." "What? That quack! Surely you remember your father telling us about him. Pierce resigned from the Senate for reasons of poor health! Then he turned himself into a Doctor, though he may have gone to a medical school. He built up his empire, with his two brothers, selling mail order patent medicine. My lord, he uses alcohol and laudanum in his concoctions. Did he give either of you his "Golden Medical Discovery," or what's called his, "Favorite Prescription"?" Etta laughed and said, "Yes, I'm afraid he did, and I felt drugged so I stopped taking it." "Well, if you, or Harry, require any further treatment, go to see Dr. Weinstein in New York City."

Harry watched Etta skirt around conversations with her mother that were meant to make Etta feel she was not all that her mother would care for her to be. At the same time he could see her mother's genuine concern and love for her daughter. There was something to what Peter told him, about understanding Etta and Mabel better, after meeting their mother.

Overall, they enjoyed their stay. Harry met Etta's Aunt Charlotte and Uncle Stephen and her cousins. Everyone got along with each other favorably enough. Etta's brother, now called Bud, wasn't very social as he had just entered Harvard University, and was in his room studying most of the time.

Harry enjoyed wandering around the large house and looking at the furnishings. The older pieces were English and the newer and more massive furniture was from the trip Etta's father had taken to Hong Kong and had sent home. A large red desk, with its secret compartments, was Harry's favorite.

The photographs, taken in San Diego, arrived in time for Harry and Etta to see them. Ethel was very pleased and proudly showed them to her friends and family, along with her prints of the Bliss Brother's portraits.

*

Back in New York City

Harry made an appointment with Dr. Weinstein; he still had problems with his ears plugging up. Etta went with him to the Doctor's office on Second Street. The doctor sprayed Harry's throat and gave him a medicinal gargle to use twice a day and suggested that he gargle with warm salt water when the medicine was finished. He told Harry his sinuses were draining along his throat and contributing to the plugged ears. After hearing Harry's plans, he told Harry the dry climate in Central Argentina may be the best medicine for him Harry continued taking Dr. Pierce's medication until the bottles were empty, and still thought the steam baths had been a great help for his aches and pains.

Butch, now going by the name James, was glad to see them return. He liked their company and going out on the town with them. He was becoming very fond of Etta. That week they went to see another play, this time at Hoyt's Madison Square Theatre at Fifth and Madison. It was another comedy, "On the Quiet." The setting for it was in and around Yale University, and on a yacht. They laughed and guffawed and enjoyed the play enormously.

While waiting for their departure date on the British freighter, Herminius, on February 21st, they kept busy with entertainments and dining out in the fine restaurants that New York City had to offer. They enjoyed Delmonico's on South William Street, where Butch especially liked the Turkish coffee. Many days were spent just taking buggy rides around town, or taking walks and shopping for some of the things they might need in Argentina. Etta liked Larkin soap; she also bought bars of Bon Ami to use for laundering clothes. Harry noticed and remarked, "We're going to be clean in Argentina, if nothing else."

Some days were spent just relaxing, letter writing, and reading. One day when Butch seemed especially quiet, Etta commented, "Butch, you're awfully quiet and look so thoughtful. I hope you don't have second thoughts on going to Argentina." "Hell no, I didn't come all the way to New York City just to buy a watch."

On their excursions around the city, they always stopped to browse in Book Stores. Butch was flustered to find a paperback of Scott Marble's 1896 story, taken from his stage melodrama, "The Great Train Robbery." He mentioned that it was a lot like the real thing. The play had been immensely successful in Chicago and New York City in 1896.

Etta was unsuccessful in finding books about living on the open range or books with stories on life in Argentina. Some of the books she found to entertain her on the month long voyage were, 'Alice of Old Vincennes', thinking Harry might also like it for its historical setting. For the same reason, she chose 'When Knighthood Was in Flower', which told of Mary Tudor's political conflict with her older brother King Henry VIII. And another book; 'To Have and to Hold', which she chose for romance; and because it appeared to tell of piracy on the high seas, and Harry might like it also.

Harry's subjects of interest were on raising cattle, and anything he could find on Argentina, or South America in general. He was lucky and found a book on the geography of South America. He also found three books to send to Peter.

*

February 16, 1901
New York City

Dear Peter,

Thank you for your kindhearted welcome on my visit and stay at your home.

Your friendship makes our association one of goodwill. I have a sense of family bond with both you and Mabel.

How is Mabel bearing the fact that Etta is on her way to Argentina? I will send an address, where you can send letters to us, as soon as we are settled.

The books I am sending along caught my eye, remembering our conversation about your interest and dream, of some day owning a gold mine. "Getting Gold," also "Blasting: And the Use of Explosives," (I could help you out there), and: "Home Brewing," since you expressed an interest.

We visited Ethel, our mutual mother-in-law, and I see what you mean about her controlling ways, and I understand why Etta wants a different life. Mabel seems to have found her diversion through her talent of painting.

Our stay at the Palace Hotel in San Francisco was an appreciated extravagance. Etta was overjoyed. Our travels went from there to San Antonio, New Orleans, and on to Pennsylvania, to see my family; then New York City, Boston and then back here. We were feeling harried and are glad for being in one place this last week.

We will board the S.S. Herminius in four days, on February 20, then sail the next morning. It will take a full month to get to Buenos Aires, Argentina, and then we will learn where to go from there. We will write as soon as we land.

Best Regards,
Harry

PART II

VI

S.S. HERMINIUS 1901

"Harry, we're moving. Oh Harry, we're on our way! James, we're really going!" All three stood at the side railing watching the ship being towed out of the harbor, and then, under its own steam, enter the vast cold gray waters of the Atlantic. It was early morning and they were cold but they couldn't stop staring at the sight of the receding land.

Finally Etta feeling extremely chilled returned to their small plain cabin to finish organizing her things. The cramped space had two small built in berths to accommodate them. At least they were together. James was in a cabin of the same size with a gentleman who had been willing to share his space with him.

The men stayed on the deck somewhat disorientated in this new environment and trying to comprehend their unknown future. James finally asked, "Harry, can I be open with Etta, when we get there, and have more freedom to talk? Does she know about everything?" "Not everything, but she knows what's up. You can talk. She understands pretty much of what we've done, just not all the particulars. And if you notice, she never preaches; she has a good plain understanding of life and people. If you mean, can you trust her; I do, with my life. Let's go up top deck and look at those life boats, I'm feelin real uneasy out here on nothin but water, even though the ship looks real good, and it should, it was just built in '98.

The ship was a passenger/cargo vessel without much in the way of amenities. The small passenger dining area was just off the ships galley. At dinner that evening James introduced his cabin mate. "Senor Ernesto Maldonado, meet Harry and Ethel Place, my sister and her husband." Learning that Senor Maldonado spoke English and Spanish, and his destination was also Buenos Aires; Etta asked if he would teach them enough Spanish to get started.

Senor Maldonado was an inspector for the British & South American Steam Navigation Company that owned the ship. His position was to oversee the South American operations. Buenos Aires was his home, where he lived with his wife and family, though he was seldom home. He insisted his new friends call him Ernesto, and was happy to teach them Spanish and also have the opportunity to improve his English. He was also very pleased at the thought of spending time with Ethel.

They spent their days reading, walking the limited space on the decks, learning Spanish and learning more about each other. Harry, usually so quiet and absorbed in his own thoughts, told James and Etta about his visit to New York City when he traveled there with his brother Harvey when they were just youngsters. "It wasn't anything like what we just did. We were on the streets trying to find a job. We slept in flophouses and ate what we could. It was a lot like the bad winters with no work back in the northwest; I never want to have to live like that again. I've been wonderin' how it's goin to be where we're goin."

Butch had been thinking similar thoughts and told Harry, "We already talked this out Harry, and we both know what we're doin with cattle or probably any livestock, and I figure that we have enough money to have a goin concern in no time." Harry nodded, "It's goin to be rough to start up from nothing James, and you know that." "Hell yes, I know that. You don't hav'ta tell me that we're going to have problems . . . . I know that! Just tell me you're payin' attention and want to hear more about my plans." "Ha, ol' Bu . . . James, always makin' plans."

*

"James, would you like to see our studio portraits? Harry and I had photographs taken at my sister's home and we had these taken when we were in Buffalo." He noticed their photo was taken by the Bliss Bro's. "Harry, wasn't that George's last name? Wasn't it George Bliss, who owned the CS Ranch outside of Winnemucca?" "Yep, that's his name." "Et . . . um, Ethel, would you like to see the photograph of me 'n Harry and three of our friends? We had it taken in Fort Worth. I'll get it." Harry hadn't shown Etta his print.

She was impressed by the fine look of deportment of the men. “Don’t let that fool ya Ethel; those guys can be a rowdy bunch, except for Harry and me, of course.”

The men often sat at a table playing poker with a couple of their fellow travelers. During those times, Etta talked with Teresa, the only other woman onboard. It was good for her to have a woman to share the experience with. Teresa and her husband were returning home from a visit to Italy; they lived in Buenos Aires.

One evening during dinner with Harry and James, Etta turned the conversation to Merritt GoForth Barnes. “James, Harry told me how you befriended Merritt Goforth. Isn’t he an exceptional young man!” “Yes he is, and also an odd mix of qualities. He’s unusually smart and should be doing something more than cowboyin’. All the same, he’s one of the best horsemen I ever met.” “I’ve seen that in him James. We still exchange letters; I’ve been sending the letters to the ranch in Utah where he picks them up. I’ve been encouraging him to contact Peter, my brother-in-law. I’ve told Peter about Merritt and he promised to do something for him if Merritt would just contact him. Before we left I wrote, encouraging Merritt once again. I hope one day he’ll write to Peter.” “I hope so too, Ethel.”

“Say Ethel how did you and ol’ Harry meet? I don’t think he told me.” Harry interrupted with, “She got one look at me and chased down the street after me.” “Yes James, I suppose that’s the way it was.”

They kept their days busy; the men playing poker much of the time. On a restless day for everyone; Etta asked Harry and Butch to show her how to play poker. Being bored, they agreed. She caught on quick enough and had good luck. After winning the pot a couple of times, the men stopped being nice about their playing and started to play seriously. When Butch bluffed her into folding, holding three jacks, which in this instance would have won; she was disgusted and lost all interest in playing. How could she possibly read their blank faces, or stand a chance with these two seasoned players. The men started a game with two other men and Etta went out for a stroll and find Teresa to tell her about her foolishness. She didn’t find Teresa but came across Ernesto reading on the small side deck all bundled up in a blanket. She sat with him and tried speaking Spanish as much as she was able. She had been taught Latin at home and that seemed to be a great help in allowing her to catch on more quickly.

They were still sitting there when the poker game broke up, Ethel now wrapped in a blanket also. Harry wasn't so pleased to see them together. He disliked the way Ernesto looked at Ethel. Ernesto sensed this and stayed clear of Ethel in the future, except at meals or when they were all together for Spanish lessons. He didn't want to anger Senor Place, as just his look was too forbidding.

Harry and Etta found quiet moments to be together and enjoyed an exceptionally romantic moment one evening while looking out on the shining sea and up at the outsized full moon, and into each others eyes.

*

The ship made a stop in Belem, Brazil for dropping and picking up cargo, and for re-supply of provisions. The passengers noticed the waters change as they neared the mouth of the immense Rio Paro Amazonas which emptied its fresh waters for a hundred miles out to sea. The volume of water coming down the river was staggering. This was a river like none any of them had seen; twelve times the flow of the Mississippi. No wonder the locals called it the River-Sea.

The passengers were allowed to disembark and had time to go to the marketplace. All had trouble with vertigo now once again walking on land after the constant rocking motion of the ship. The variety of fresh fruits was overwhelming. They could see barges coming down the river's estuaries into Guajara Bay loaded with their cargoes of bananas, mahogany logs and crates of chickle.

They saw the colonial style buildings and tree filled squares. Mango trees were everywhere. All the bright colors of the marketplace were dazzling. The climate was warm and humid, raining without notice; a drastic change from the cold of New York. They were glad for the added excursion to this port, as they had come almost 60 miles up into the mouth of the Amazon.

Butch and Harry were a little confused as to why they were learning Spanish when all they had heard spoken in Brazil was Portuguese. Ernesto said, "Just wait until you are in Buenos Aires."

The ship left the bay, and once again put out into open waters. That night, Harry and James watched the initiation of a crew member crossing the equator for the first time. They thought it was a rough practice and more of a punishment than reward for the experience. The crew had told the husbands of the two women on board to keep them in their cabins. Etta wouldn't have liked seeing the crewmate beaten with boards and wet ropes. The ear piercing might have been painful but undeniably the least of it. The men retreated back to their cabins to avoid the same fate.

*

For the next few days, the few passengers all seemed quiet, perhaps thinking of where and what they had left, and where they were going or returning. When Etta noticed Harry and James looking especially glum, she got out her violin case that had, until now, been packed away with her clothes in a trunk. Harry picked up when he saw her take out the violin and rosin the bow. "Let's go to the sitting room Etta, everyone will want to hear the music. I'll find James."

James thought this might be like attending a recital and had some qualms, but when he heard Etta play one rousing tune full of fun and then another; and when the crew began to sing in three languages, he started to have fun. Markus, Teresa's husband, provided a bottle of whiskey and the fun really began. Ernesto got out his small squeeze box which added to the sounds of merriment. It was exactly what was needed.

*

When they put in at Rio de Janeiro, Etta wasn't feeling well and thought she'd like to stay aboard; but left the ship to practice walking on firm land right there on the wharf. The men stayed with her until she had evened out her walking skills and returned her to the ship; then they left to see the city.

The port of Rio de Janeiro was located on the west side of the Baia de Guanabara, The wharfs extended as far as they could see, harboring several ships. As they arrived, all could see Pao de

Acucar, the high point of land called Sugar Loaf; the calling card of the city.

Ernesto accompanied Harry and James. Harry felt better with this arrangement rather than Ernesto returning to the ship with Etta alone in the cabin. They got on a horse driven trolley just in time before being inundated by a heavy downpour that soaked everything in less than a minute.

Without Etta to guide them to cultural features of the city, and wanting to get out of the violent torrent, they stopped at a salao in a covered open court where they drank Cachaca, a clear colorless liquid that runs from 94 to 100 proof. It warmed them in a flash. Ernesto helped with the transaction as he spoke a little Portuguese. After a couple of these potent drinks, they returned to the ship, stopping first to buy flowers at a market.

Harry and James were proud of themselves for conducting this transaction, (they simply pointed and handed over a silver coin). Back onboard, they presented the large, intensely hued, floppy bouquet to Etta with wide grins on their faces. Of course she knew right then what they had been doing. Laughing and thanking them profusely, Etta was enjoying how pleased they were with themselves. She took one flower, tucked it behind James ear and sent him off to his cabin for a nap. Harry was in an amorous mood and Etta was enjoying the attention; however it wasn't long lived; Harry fell asleep mumbling, "I love you Etta."

*

"Don-dee es-ta el rest-our-ant-ey. Hell, Ernesto, I don't know what I'm sayin!" "Do not worry; it takes time to accustom oneself to a new language. Give yourself time Senor Place." Now you try Senor Ryan, say, I would like to start a bank account." "Me gust-our-eeya ab-rear oun-a quent-ah bank-kare-ee-ya. I don't know what I'm doin either." "Ha-ha, at least you gentlemen have Ethel to do the talking. By the way, when we get to Buenos Aires, I suggest the Hotel Europa, it is old but close to all. We can go there together if you like and I can help you there if you need to start business with a bank. If you like, I suggest the London & Platte River Bank. I can assist you to the bank next week when the bank is open; it will be closed the weekend when we arrive. I also have business there. I will introduce you to the officials at the bank who can advise for you who to talk with about land available in the country."

*

"Harry, ya know, I'm feelin' more and more free the farther away from the states that we get." "Know what you mean James, I've been easin' up, relaxing and feeling good; better'n I can remember feeling in a long, long while. I hear we've still got a little over a thousand miles before we're in Buenos Aires; that's where we'll begin to get it all started. I'll be glad to get the bank notes put away in a bank. Ha. Let's ask Etta to play her violin tonight. I feel like celebrating."

VII

BUENOS AIRES 1901

"Look at this James. I've been carrying this trade card. Look at the picture of Buenos Aires Harbor, hell it looks just like the picture." "Yeah, but a lot more ships; what's goin on?" Ernesto explained, "Senor Ryan, many peoples immigrate here; as much as are going to North America. Indeed, millions of people are coming to Argentina for the inexpensive grazing and farm land; high quality wheat is a most important export. Half of the people in this great city are from other places."

Automobiles merged with carriages on the wide tree lined boulevards of this imposing capital city; Buenos Aires; "the city of good airs." It appeared larger and more opulent than New York City. The harbor was indeed more impressive. The Hotel Europa was not far from the harbor and in a central location, at the corner of Calle Cangallo and Avenida 25 de Mayo. Senor Maldonado proved to be a tremendous asset. Even Etta, who had made great progress learning Spanish, was overwhelmed. People spoke much faster than Ernesto did while coaching them in their Spanish phrases.

They were shown to their small suite of rooms; two small bedrooms off either side of a salon. It felt somehow very European with its high ceilings and tall French windows. Much of the city had a strong French influence. Decorative spiked iron fences bordered the edge of buildings and parks; many buildings exhibited dark grey mansard style roofs. Iron shutters were at the fronts of the fashionable shops. It much more resembled Paris than New York City.

They rested the remainder of that day. On Sunday, their first full day in the city, they went out walking to discover the city around them. Very impressed with what they saw, and encouraged that they would find their way here in this vast and immeasurable country, Argentina. They celebrated that evening in the hotel dining room. Etta and Harry recalled other moments when they had celebrated with champagne while they enjoyed the marvelous local vintage.

On Monday Ernesto met them at the hotel to accompany them to the London and River Platte Bank. He knew the bank directors and felt confident they would help his new friends. The bank was incorporated in England back in the 1860's to operate in Buenos Aires and had since expanded to other South American countries. After the introductions were made with the bank directors, Ernesto excused himself. He made plans to see them again before he left for England next month.

The bank officials spoke some English and were very helpful with opening an account for Senor Ryan and Senor Place. Their deposit was $12,000 in gold notes. James and Harry agreed on not depositing all their money and decided to take the risk of keeping some of it with them. They would need ready cash for the purchase of supplies to set up a ranch and for the purchase of cattle and horses.

The bank officers suggested talking with the Director of Lands at the government offices to apply for land. They also suggested seeing Doctor George Newberry, an American immigrant from New York who now had his Dental office in Buenos Aires. Dr. Newberry owned land and a ranch house in the Chubut Province and could perhaps help them with advice on that part of the country. He and his brother Ralph Newberry were also honorary United States Vice Councils. After they were given the addresses and directions, they left with a feeling of good will; greatly impressed with the courtesy they were shown.

Etta found the Oficina de Correos, where she learned the postage required to post a letter to Mabel. She felt better, knowing that Mabel would be reassured at hearing of their safe arrival; though it would take weeks until Mabel would receive it.

They explored Buenos Aires, got lost and found their way again many times while learning the ways and places of this impressive city. At a mid afternoon meal they ordered a cheese and bread tray and an egg dish as it was the Lenten season and meat was not offered. They were tired and decided the land office could wait until the next day.

The next morning, at the government land office, they were again well received, and learned of the possibility of homesteading property. They were shown, on a map, an extensive area where they would find good land for cattle; though they were overwhelmed by the fact that they couldn't picture any of it, as they had no point of reference. They decided to arrange a meeting with Dr. Newberry and hear his thoughts on the subject.

Dr. Newberry was a very upright person with considerable charm. He was obliging in telling all he knew about the procedures for obtaining land and about the best places for raising cattle. He couldn't contain his enthusiasm for the Cholila Valley in Chubut Province, where he owned a ranch about one hundred thirty miles north of the small village of Cholila, near the border of Chile below the foothills of the Andes. He explained that the land wasn't as fertile as the land west of Buenos Aires that was better for farming, but it had excellent grass for cattle and was not as expensive. It was further into the country, more remote and wild, but very beautiful with many lakes and winding streams, and bright, colorful wild flowers. Astonishing forests were to the west, where one could view the rugged snow covered Andes Mountains. To get there they would need to take a steamer to Rawson and go inland about 400 miles, but well worth it.

After hearing this, James and Harry, now feeling once again more like "Butch and Sundance," felt that this sounded like the place for them. George told them he believed land was available there and that he understood there was a barraca, a simple ranch house that had been abandoned by Welsh immigrants, who left and moved to Canada, that may be available. The men could hardly contain their excitement. Etta remained quiet hoping that this would all work out. The men needed to find what they were looking for. She would be at home wherever Harry reconciled to live.

Dr. Newberry told them he would inquire into the availability of land and the ranch building in the area of District 16 de Octobre in Chubut Province. They could also go back to the Land Office to find out any information they could provide on that area.

Harry, Etta, and James had already found encouragement and happiness in their pursuit of their possible new opportunities. They met with Ernesto later that week, treating him to a meal at "The Cabana," and telling him about the support they felt from all the people they had met so far. Ernesto suggested they move to an apartment since their stay in Buenos Aires would be prolonged. He knew of a store owner who would rent the departamento above his store, just two blocks from the hotel where they were staying.

Ernesto surprised them by inviting them to his home for Easter celebration. It would be an informal event with many people invited on Sunday, 7 April. A few of his guests spoke limited English, so it would be an advantageous time for Harry, Etta and James to socialize. Until then, Ernesto hadn't spoken much about his wife or family.

Easter at the Maldonado's home was a lively, noisy affair where the threesome felt very comfortable and at ease, even when they couldn't figure out what was being said. Ernesto's wife, Celina, a strikingly beautiful woman with light brown hair and hazel eyes, hugged them like old friends. Ernesto kept the excellent Argentinean wine flowing and soon Ethel's cheeks were rosy and her eyes were shiny. Many of the dishes served were uniquely new to the three of them, but much enjoyed. At the end of the especially pleasurable evening, they took a carriage back to their apartment, feeling that life was good here in Argentina.

They visited the land office again and made inquiries about the land in the Chubut Province; then waited for them to look into its availability. They also had to give Dr. Newberry time for his scout to come back with information. It would take time. The eager trio needed to settle into life here for the time being.

A Tienda de Comestibles was located just a block from their apartment. They purchased food so they could have light meals at home. Though the custom was to dine late; it wasn't what any of them felt comfortable with; they went out for their main meal of the day in the mid afternoon. None of them had ever tasted such delicious, tender, sweet, juicy 'bif' steaks as they were enjoying now. They drank the wine tipica, a native red wine that went well with their steaks.

They were staying one block off the main Avenida in Buenos Aries, 25 de Mayo, commemorating the May Revolution of 1810, which was the beginning of the country's independence from Spain. The Plaza de Mayo was their point of reference with the May Pyramid as a beacon to guide them. They discovered many more Plazas throughout the city.

Interesting to them were the very wide Avenidas, sweeping boulevards with island parkways. Avenida Nueve de Julio—was the broadest street though short. Then, in contrast, the extremely narrow streets that were no more than alleyways. One street like this was Calle Florida that had become a shopping street in the late 1800's; a charming cobblestone lane with colorful awnings over the store windows. They found every kind of shop that one would expect to find in Europe and displays of the latest in European fashions.

Quite often, they stopped at one of the open courts where food and drink were served; where the men sometimes ordered Cana' another colorless spirit; being careful to just order one when they were with Etta. She felt protected and enjoyed the devotion from the two capable men: Harry, her husband, and James, her very good friend.

They would take long walks to view the new docklands and watch the ships; amazed at the bustle and excited activity of people arriving, and the dock workers loading and unloading cargo. Buenos Aires really was the hub of Argentina. The amount of people immigrating here was astonishing.

While they waited, none too patiently for news, the men grew restless. They decided to venture west to explore the pampas, the area west of the city known for its fertile soil, farms and ranches. They planed on being gone at least two weeks, maybe longer. They thought Etta should stay in town; this was not a pleasure trip but one where hard riding would be required to cover miles of ground everyday. April was autumn in South America and the chill could already be felt on the breeze.

Etta protested at first, wanting to be included. Then, understanding that the men needed escape from the trappings of town, and knowing they could cover more ground without her, she relented. Harry and James hired horses from the blacksmith at the stables. When Etta was told they might be gone as long as a month, she experienced some anxiety, but also understood the men's need for a sense of freedom. She could keep busy enough in this invigorating city.

*

Etta continued to explore the neighborhoods and Plazas around town. She took the trolley around by the northern end of Calle Florida to the Plaza San Martin where large mansions faced the Plaza. She would sit and gaze on the spectacular architecture of the Beaux Arts San Martin Palace, the Second Empire Palace, and the Neogothic Haedo Palace. Even more amazing to her, was the great Ombu tree; an unusually massive tree with branches a large as tree trunks.

Once a week, Etta bought a copy of 'La Prenza', the Buenos Aires newspaper. La Prenza was considered one of the most significant newspapers in the world, and already had a circulation of over 95,000 copies. It took her a full week struggling with the words, to comprehend the subject of the articles.

She often frequented a tea room on Calle Florida but was becoming increasingly lonely. She sent a message to Senora Maldonado, to inquire if she would join her for tea the next day. Celina Maldonado was glad to receive the invitation and happy to join her. They enjoyed a full afternoon together; first going to tea and then shopping. Celina knew how it felt to be lonely and benefited from the company also.

Celina showed Etta where she could get fabric. Etta wanted to make a blouse in the style she had seen on fashionable women on Calle Florida. Celina suggested they both work on it at her home, and so Etta started taking a trolley to Celina's home three days a week. It helped pass the time.

*

Saturday, 13 April 1901
Buenos Aires

Dear Mabel,

My thoughts are of you. How are you dear sister? And how is Peter?

Before we left New York, mother told us about your successful sale. That was an impressive sum for your garden painting! You are very talented and I am happy that you are now realizing just how talented! Many congratulations to you. I forgot to mention this in previous letters which I hope you have received by now. We must be patient with the mail.

Remind Peter to have patience with the new "girl Friday" at the office. I certainly didn't learn everything in just one week. They have a very complicated and involved business.

The temperature continues to drop, as it is autumn here. Harry and James are exploring the country to the west of Buenos Aires, though it seems we may be traveling further south and west to an area that sounds intriguing and may have possibilities. We are waiting for information on the availability of a section of land that may include a cabin. We should know soon. I am expecting their return by next week.

I spend three days each week at the home of Celina Maldonado, the wife of the shipping director we traveled with on the ship. She has become a good friend and as a result my Spanish vocabulary is much improved. Speaking is only one part of it. Now, I am learning to read and write it also. I feel like a schoolgirl. Even with all the immigrants and the large French and Italian population; the Spanish language dominates—of course.

Celina is helping me sew a blouse of the latest fashion, but one that will be practical in the country where we are going. The next project will be to sew a plain skirt. Her children are in their teen years and are such polite young people. I bring treats for them when I visit.

My dear sister, I miss you and Peter. Continue to use this address as we should be here for a while yet. This letter should go out on Monday on the mail steamship to Rio de Janeiro, then be transferred to a United States—Brazil mail steamship. Let me know when you receive it. Just think, it may be three months before I would get a reply. I will let you know immediately when we leave for the country.

All my love,
Etta

*

Etta, by nature was very calm and unflappable; but now after the end of three weeks, and the men not back, she became anxious for their return. Troubled with concern, her restlessness affected her sleep; when she did sleep, it was just for a short time then she would wake troubled. Celina was a great help, being accustomed to Ernesto being gone for long periods of time, some much longer than were expected. She had learned to cope by keeping busy and taking on new projects. Ethel's friendship was also a benefit for her. Talking with Celina made the wait easier for Etta, and relived some of her worry.

Etta found walking invigorating, and traveled over a wide area of the city, finding it very safe. She had no idea of the night life as she was always in her room by sunset. At times she enjoyed sitting at the Plaza de Mayo and watching all the people go by; always hoping she would see Harry.

On returning to the apartment, early on a cold afternoon, she gasped to find James in the sitting room. She screamed and ran to him giving him a big hug while saying, "Where's Harry?" "He just went down to find you!" "What, how could he possibly find me in this big city?" "Well, there's a note right here saying you're at the Plaza de Mayo down the street." "Oh yes, I forgot, I leave a note every time I go out. I'm going find him." "Watch out Etta or you'll both be lost. Aren't you happy to see me?" "Oh James, I'm thrilled to see you, but I've got to go find Harry."

Her feet barely touched the floor as she ran down the stairs. Then she ran to the Plaza, looking at all the men along the way as she ran, but couldn't find him. Then she went around the May Pyramid and there he was. She yelled his name. He turned towards her and shouted, "Etta, Etta," oblivious if anyone heard her name. They were in each others arms, completely unaware of anything but each other. They had both spent an agonized time being apart.

Harry and James traveled almost three hundred miles around the Pampas region. They spent the first and last weeks in wet rainy conditions. During the rest of their travels, the weather was mild, though the nights were cool. They saw the large estancias in areas used for grazing cattle, and they saw the fertile farming regions that were susceptible to flooding. The western region was appealing but it was more populated than they had imagined. While they were so far out to the west, they kept going, wanting to see the land to the south, towards Santa Rosa.

James enjoyed telling Etta about the Gauchos; the Argentinean cowboys. The wanderers of the Pampas, so much like the cowboys in the western states, but dressed a little too fancy in his way of thinking. He had also taken notice of the types of cattle they saw grazing by the thousands on the vast pampas; Short Horns, Herefords, Aberdeen's and Angus. They'd heard that cattle ranching also does very well further south.

*

They were hoping for news from the land office, and from George Newberry concerning land in the Patagonia region. By the end of the week they had good news from George; the land with the barraca was available. Next they were to give the map, that George's hired man had made of the property and its whereabouts, to the land office and learn the next step.

The land they sought was described on the Homestead contract as: "Four Square Leagues of Government Land, Province of Chubut, Colonia 16 de October; situated by the east bank of the Rio Blanco, in the Cholila Valley, near the foothills of the Andes, and the border of Chile. Butch and Harry were confused about the date indicated in the land description. The Chubut Province was given the date as its name, commemorating its formal acquisition of territorial status on 16 Octobre1884.

They made the application for the land grant to homestead, and raise livestock. They didn't need to wait any longer before heading out to their new home. It was understood they had time to view the property and start operating a ranch for livestock. The application could be finalized in one year when they were to show improvements to the land. There was a plain four room house, and out buildings. Drinking water from a creek was established to be on the property. The property had been taken back by the government's land company when the original settlers abandoned it.

They each had their concerns for getting ready for the rest of their journey. They were told they would find supplies in Rawson and Trelew. It was not known if the house had a woodstove and they had better get one as winter was steadily advancing.

Harry and Etta spent a day going to a few of the several bookshops to stock up for the winter. Both were content to spend cold winter days under blankets reading. They stopped at the Cabana for a meal and then walked back to the apartment while enjoying the jingling of a gaily painted milk wagon slowly making its way along the Avenida de Mayo; led by a shiny horse wearing an old straw hat. "Harry, if you like, I'll paint our wagon like that." "Sure, go ahead, but I won't be seen driving it. You'll need your own wagon for that."

Before they left, Etta visited Celina. They would miss each other, and the goodbye was a sad moment for both. She promised Celina she would write, and would visit whenever they were in Buenos Aires.

VIII

To Cholila

To get south to Trerawson, they first took a small steamer to Bahia Blanca, and then an even smaller steamer to Puerto Madryn, the deep water port north of Trerawson. From there they took the train to Trelew. The Central Chubut Railway from Puerto Madryn to Trelew was financed with English capitol and built back in 1888 by Welsh, Spanish, and Italian immigrants.

Immigrants from Wales, who left their own land to escape the tyranny of the English, settled in Trelew and in the nearby town they called Trerawson meaning Rawson's town; named after Dr. Guillermo Rawson, the Argentine Interior Minister at the time, who supported and aided the Welch settlement in Argentina.

As soon as they arrived, Etta wrote another letter to Mabel to let her know where they were and to confirm their new address. She was feeling anxious over it taking such a long time for the exchange of correspondence.

They stayed in the area four days obtaining supplies and information. James and Harry spoke some Spanish while on their trip exploring west of Buenos Aires; now they were confused because English was spoken here, but it could be difficult to understand. If they thought for a minute about what was just said, they could usually understand the words.

The Welsh towns were charming, although when the Welsh first arrived for settlement in the area of Trerawson they experienced floods and hardship. The Argentine government assisted them by providing food supplies during their first years. British and Scottish immigrants had also settled in the area.

It was a relief to have supplies available. Their first purchase was a large wagon. It took two days for James to find two sets of horses for the wagon, along with the reins and lines. Harry bought six horses for riding, which could also be used as pack horses; and found four saddles that would work well enough to start.

From the towns of Trerawson and Trelew, they were fortunate to obtain 50 pounds of flour, 40 pounds of sugar, salt, bakers yeast, numerous crates of canned goods, cinnamon, several bags of coffee and tea, a coffee pot, pounds and pounds of beans, corn meal, potatoes, a large cast iron skillet and Dutch oven, utensils, rope, tools, nails, fabric for window coverings, large and small needles and thread, a wood stove with vent pipes, lanterns, lamp oil, blankets, metal bowls and pitchers, and three metal tubs; two that would be used as water troughs for watering livestock, and one that would be used for laundry and baths. Though there was the town of Esquel not far from their destination; they didn't want to take any chances on poor availability of provisions. Etta also bought two fresh pumpkins that she thought should stay fresh until they arrived at their homestead where she would try to cook it with sugar and cinnamon for a treat.

Etta especially enjoyed the Welsh tea shops in both towns. In Trelew, she went to a tearoom built onto the front part of a house. The houses were all rectangular in shape, usually built of stone, with peaked roofs and had the look of English cottages. At the teashop, Etta easily fell into conversation with a pretty Welsh girl who served her tea and cake. The girl had a triangular shaped face, with the most beautiful blue eyes, and looked to be about thirteen years old. Her name was Anne, and she was completely delighted to talk with the beautiful woman from the states.

"Oh, you're from Boston! I would truly love to see Boston, and New York City, and California. I would love to see the whole world. I've never traveled anywhere. Could you tell me about it?" Etta told her about life in Boston and California while Anne sat wide eyed, listening. "Anne, do you have books to read, about North America and other places?" "Not many and I don't have much time for studies except in winter, or like now when the business is slow in the tea shop. My parent's don't have much time to teach me, and not enough money to send me to school; though my mother knows I would love to learn more about the world.

That night at the Inn, Etta didn't get much sleep. She was thinking about Anne. The girl reminded her of herself at that age. The next morning she decided to be courageous. She returned to the shop and once again engaged in conversation with Anne. She told Anne of their plans to go to their ranch in Cholila where they would raise cattle and horses and maybe sheep. Etta went on to say that she would need help cleaning and cooking for the men. "Would it be at all possible if you could come along with me and work for wages in the winter? I could instruct you with your lessons. Would you be interested in . . . . ." "Oh yes, ma'am, I would love to work for you on a ranch—anywhere, and learn more lessons, but I do not think I would be allowed." "May I ask your parents?" "Yes, you can try. I'll get my mother. My father will say no." "Anne, please, let me do the asking."

Etta waited so long, she started to worry that the girl had tried to ask and had been refused. Finally a pleasant looking woman appeared. At first Etta gently suggested the plan for Anne to earn wages, and then went on to say that she would see to the girl's education. The mother was interested in what wages were offered and how long Anne was expected to stay. The mother's questions led Etta to believe the idea was being considered. Anne could possibly spend the winter with them; in summer she was needed at the shop. She would have a definite answer the following morning.

Early the next morning, when the men were ready to head out on the road to Cholila, Etta asked them to stop for tea and let the parents see the men who Anne would be spending company with. Neither Harry nor James was enthusiastic about the idea; however Etta never asked for anything and seemed serious about her intentions. As soon as they stepped in the tea shop, Anne came running towards them. "My mother will have my older brother take me when he next goes to Trevelin. You must give us directions to your ranch." After finally being seated, they met the mother who confirmed what Anne had just told them. Anne would be brought out to the ranch by her brother in two weeks.

Etta noticed that the mother seemed happy for her daughter and wondered at the odd circumstances of this encounter and that there was no mention of Anne's father or his thoughts on Anne's leaving. Very relieved, Etta felt cheerful that morning as they started their journey across Argentina to their new home.

*

The previous evening Harry and James had covered and secured their provisions, added a barrel of water, and made a canopy over the driver's bench with the canvas. It might rain.

Etta and Harry rode horses. The four extra horses were tied with a lead to follow along with the wagon which James drove. He wanted to get a feel for the teams he had set in place. Etta thought horses were all the same for riding or pulling wagons until James explained to her why he took so much time inspecting the horses he chose. "There's horses bred for carryin weight, and horses bred for pullin weight. I picked the lead pair 'cause they're more aggressive and better leaders and evenly matched. The pair on the wheel are followers but must be strong; I'm not sure if they're matched as evenly. All of 'em picked for deftness and strength. They all know they have a job to do.

While riding, Harry told Etta about riding horses. "You notice these aren't as filled out as the wagon horses that have more muscle and more strength for pulling in their legs. I rode these and tested them, and saw they were even tempered and strong, they've got good endurance and they're built more for speed. Your horse there, Etta, is smaller at only fifteen hands, spirited but gentle. She looks to be seven or eight years old." "Harry, there's a lot to know that I've never thought of." "Well, Etta, we have to know what we're doin to be respected ranchers."

They had been advised to start out on the road along the north side of the Rio Chubut. The road would pass through a few small settlements on the way where they could find places to stay with folks who would provide bed and board. As they left town they saw the farms with fields now unplanted after the harvest; the potato fields were bare as were the fruit trees in the orchards. They passed by several berry fields. The Welsh had been industrious building a canal system for irrigation. This was a productive community.

James and Harry noticed the large flocks of sheep; the favored breeds seemed to be the Australian Merinos, Border Leicesters, and Romney Marshes. They saw more Angus and Hereford cattle which were sometimes crossed with local wild cattle to produce a very hearty breed. Dairy cattle were kept closer to the settlements;

the stock animals that none of them were interested in were hogs, though they did like the ham they had been served in town.

Harry, Etta, and James became quiet, immersed in their own thoughts, as they rode along. Finally James called out to Etta who was riding near the wagon. "Etta, I wondered what you were doin with invitin' that girl, Anne, to come out to be with us at the homestead; hell, we don't even know if we're going to have a roof over our heads that don't leak. But then I got to thinkin; Harry and I are goin to be real busy and even gone sometimes, looking for cattle and horses and even sheep to buy, and she would be good company for you. I hope that it's going to work for you. I gotta say that I don't know what on earth she's goin to do, cause I can't see where there's that much to keeping a up a plain ranch house. I do my own laundry, and I'll even be doin a lot of the cookin. Beef is best cooked over a fire. Ranch livin's not goin to be like New York or Buenos Aires."

"Oh James, I've been thinking the same way. What have I done? You men don't need another woman to worry about. But, like you, I've settled on the idea, and I think it'll work out alright. She and I will no doubt be busy with her studies; I enjoy teaching, and I hope she'll enjoy my instruction. At least, I won't be as ridicules as an instructor that my sister and I once had."

"When we were young, my sister and I had a tutor who would pace the floor while lecturing; back and forth in front of the room. Each time he turned, he would hike up his pants that would droop while he paced. We asked mother to get him a set of braces as a Christmas gift. But she thought that would be rude. So, Mabel and I continued to giggle. Mabel, as I've mentioned, is a talented artist, and even then she could draw hilarious pictures of him with his droopy drawers."

James laughed, "Etta it'll be okay; I'm thinkin about the times when Harry and I are gone. It'd be best if you're not alone. And I've heard there are reliable ranch workers around and we'll find a good foreman who can stay at the ranch for your protection. We might end up having a small community of our own; so it won't be just us anyway." Harry had been listening, and had to comment, "Oh no, Etta watch out whenever James starts talking about plans. He's a great one for plans."

That evening they camped just outside one of the small settlements along the Chubut Valley. Harry built a fire and James fixed up some grub. During the day they'd stopped for a snack of the cheese and bread Etta had brought along. There was no moon that evening which made the stars shine as bright as any of them had ever seen; but these were so close and brilliant, just a stone's throw away. She and Harry looked at the stars and talked until they fell asleep. They were tired and all slept well, though the men went to sleep with their guns ready; not expecting any trouble, just out of habit. They started wearing guns once again after leaving Trelew. They were up and back on the trail early the next morning.

In the morning, the men were amused at Etta's dismay at the scarcity of bushes or trees to hide behind while she took care of her personal business. James was smiling when she returned from her long walk away from camp. "You can just stop that grinning now, James." "Well now, I'd been wonderin how you were goin to get along with outhouses; I guess there won't be any problem with that after all." Harry and Etta exchanged a smiling glance at one another remembering Etta's awkwardness on their first pack trip with Merritt in the hills north of Las Vegas, New Mexico.

Harry was thinking now of how adaptable Etta was and how agreeable and cheerful. He would have to find time, after they arrived at their homestead, to do something very special for her and tell her how much she meant to him. In fact, he already thought of what he was going to do. He could hardly wait.

James continued to drive the wagon; he was working with the horses to further train them into a smoother ride. He told Etta and Harry that he'd sometimes be going off the path to work on turning with the teams, just so the horses would know how to work with him when that was needed. The path so far had just been meandering in a more or less straight direction.

"Etta, have you written to Merritt lately? "Yes, Sweetheart, I have, when we were in Buenos Aires; but I didn't have our new address at that time for him to send a letter to us. I encouraged him again to write to Peter, and I told him Peter is expecting to hear from him." "That's good Etta, keep writing to him, he's got to get away from the outlaw life and his association with some of the desperado's he hangs out with. Maybe he should come here with us. Keep writing to him Etta and I'll do the same."

Harry became very quiet the rest of the day. He could be moody at times, not temperamental, just real quiet, distant and withdrawn. He and Etta had been riding ahead of the wagon and after a while Etta dropped to a slower pace to ride by the side of the wagon. She asked James, "Has Harry always had his aloof, silent moments?"

"Yep, 'fraid so; in fact I've never known him to be as blabby as he's been on this trip. I probably learned more about him these last couple of months than I ever knew. Harry doesn't usually talk much. He's what you call a thinker. He's always riding me, about my always making plans, hell he does too, it's just that I talk about them. He just goes about it without making much noise."

"James, Harry told me that you're very smart and it was because of your well thought out, and skillful planning that kept you all safe when you were in dangerous situations. I want to thank you James." "My pleasure ma'am."

They were quiet for a while then James said, "Ya know, Harry's a better man now, maybe something to do with the bad days bein over. He shoulda never been an outlaw. As for me, maybe it's just the way I think that got me in trouble. Harry's doin better cause he's got you; someone who thinks real well of him and loves him, and 'cause now he can live honestly."

"James, I know you as either Butch or James; what is your given name?" "It's Robert Leroy Parker, born in '66, I'm the oldest of thirteen children from a fine Mormon family. My folks settled in Utah in the late 1850's. I changed my name to Cassidy; a name of an ol' friend of mine because I didn't want my family to know about my misdeeds or bad reputation; but then, they found out anyway. Ya know some of this country we're passing through, reminds me of Utah."

They made camp under the stars again that night. They figured on coming to a small settlement, they'd heard of, the next day. Each of them again quiet in their own thoughts as they traveled along at a good pace in a land they were seeing for the first time.

The next day Harry drove the wagon to get used to the teams. Etta sat with him and got a rest from the saddle. Harry had been showing her the finer points of riding and how to sit a saddle, and at the slow pace, traveling over gentle terrain, she had done alright but now she appreciated the rest.

Etta thought this time traveling would be well spent speaking Spanish with each other. James needed to practice with, "I would like to buy horses—and practiced with, Me gustaria comprar caballos." "Mi nombre es James Ryan." "Soy James Ryan." "Cuantos pesos?" "Bien."

"Yo vivo en un rancho en Cholila." "Muchas Gracias." They all had to be careful, if one of them mispronounced a word they would all follow.

Feeling very relieved that they were on course after first sighting a windmill from a couple of miles distance, and then the steeple of a church; the weary hopeful travelers arrived at dusk at a small Welsh settlement.

Though it was a very small outpost; it was part of the great Welsh immigration which began in 1865. Settlements began on the east coast of the Chubut Province, where they first settled in the area that became Rawson then extended west. Here also, the first years had been difficult. In the early years of the settlement, the local Tehuelche people helped the new settlers survive food shortages.

The greater Chubut Valley was called "Y Wladfa" by the Welsh settlers; meaning, The Colony. Later the colonists, with the permission of the governor of Chubut, Luis Jorge Fontana, extended their settlement further west into the fertile area they named "Cwm Hyfryd" (Pleasant Valley). This is where Harry, James and Etta were heading to find their home, in Cholila. The growing towns of Esquel and Trevelin had been founded in the area not far from where they would settle.

They inquired at a blacksmith shop for a place for their horses to water, feed, and rest; and where they might rest and eat. Again after struggling with the Welsh form of English; they found they could board the horses' right there, and the wagon could be brought inside to be kept safe from the weather. Mr. Williams, the blacksmith, took them up a small lane where they saw a few rectangular houses in rows. He found lodging for Etta and Harry at one home and lodging for James at another. They were to all join for supper in the home where Etta and Harry were staying. After their dinner they retired to their rooms and went to bed feeling very tired, never stirring the entire night.

In the morning they ate a delicious breakfast of coffee, eggs, ham, potatoes, green beans, canned peaches, and large portions of a scrumptious spiced yeast cake none of them had ever tasted anything like. They left generous compensations for the hospitality and then went to the blacksmith's stables. It took awhile for Mr. Williams, Harry and James to untangle some of the lead lines for the wagon teams. Mr. Williams's good nature and joviality made it a pleasant moment. They paid him handsomely for his work and his goodwill. Harry and James would remember his kind manner and looked forward to seeing him again.

*

Harry and Etta drove the wagon for the next few days. James had the horses now working as a good team. They took pleasure in each others company and conversation. "Etta, did you ever hear why the Rio de la Plata is called that, when there's no silver in the country? Was it for the color of the water?" "Ha, oh yes, or rather, no. Celina told me; the first people here thought there would be silver in the interior, and so when they arrived they named it the River of Silver. Even the name "Argentina" means "Silverland." "But Etta, you mean there didn't turn out to be any silver; hmm, peculiar." "Yes, no silver."

"Harry, James seems to talk, and be, a bit rougher than you. Why is that, what's his past?" "Yeah, well he was raised in the west, in Utah. He's been a cowboy all his life." "I tend to talk rougher when I'm not with you." "You're the odd cowboy Harry, good at it, but I wonder what you'd be doing if you'd stayed in Pennsylvania." "I was the odd one there too, Etta. Like Merritt Goforth, I've been looking for my place. But, you're an odd duck yourself, Etta. What's a girl from a proper Boston family doin out here in the open country of Argentina with a couple of cowboy-outlaws?" "Well because, as you already know, I love the wild beauty living out in the country, the sincere and straightforward life . . . . ." "Yeah, the wild beauty of it—maybe that's why you love me?" "Yes, maybe that's why I love you. This kind of life settles my conflicts of being in societies I don't respect; and maybe it's because you're so charming and handsome that I just didn't stand a chance." "That's it."

Each day went on, very much like the last. When they thought they were just a few days out from their destination, they took a morning to rest, for the horses and themselves, and to put the now jumbled wagon into some order. Enjoying the lazy morning, Harry fixed another pot of coffee. "I truly like this already roasted and ground coffee; that roasting the green beans in a skillet over the fire was a wasteful venture; too many times the beans got burned and were ruined."

"Harry, people name their ranches. Have you or James thought of a name?" "Hey, James, what do you want to name the homestead?" "Name the homestead?" "Yes, James, I was asking Harry what he thought. What about *Estancia de Esperanza*?" "What's that mean?" "It means, Ranch of Hope, it seems like hope's something we all have a lot of." "Well, that's fine with me, Esperanza Estancia, how about you Harry?" It's fine, just fine."

They were traveling through the Chubut Valley and could see the rugged and magnificent snow capped Andes Mountains as they headed west. "James, these parts look a lot like Wyoming." "Naw, more like Montana." 'You're full of worms, it looks like Wyoming." "Montana." "Boys, boys! It looks like Argentina to me! It's good that you feel this land is like places you know." James sighed, "Well, yeah, they are a lot alike."

*

Cholila

After traveling through miles of dry scrub brush, they arrived in the grassland. The tough festuca tussock-grass grew well and was resistant to the low rainfall and high winds. They could see lush forests in the distance, and above them the majestic snow capped rugged peaks of the Andes. They were getting close; traveling along a grove of willow trees along the east bank of the Rio Blanco. In the distance up ahead, they could make out a large, simple, split log building not far from the creek. Two smaller structures were next to it, also the remnants of a brush corral. It would be suitable. They had found their home.

On closer inspection, they saw that the large building had four rooms. The roof was in need of repair, but it would do. Riding around the property, they found natural spring fed ponds. Not far were forests of beech and cypress. There was plenty of land and the bunch grass would sustain livestock.

"Well, it's not hopeless. Estanchia de Esperanzo; the name's just right. What do you think Harry?" "Right James, it's a good name and we got lucky. All I ever asked for was a little luck." What do you think Etta?" Etta was smiling as she looked around the interior, so the men knew she was already making domestic plans.

Etta did have one request, that the floor be repaired where the boards were missing or rotted. Over all, they were very pleased with their home. They moved the supplies in to the main room in one big pile, and put their personal luggage in their bedrooms. Harry and Etta would have one room, James another, a room would be cleaned up for Anne, and they would have a common room where there was to be a table and chairs, the makeshift kitchen, and the woodstove. Etta hoped it wouldn't be too long before they got a real cook stove for the kitchen, then the small woodstove could be moved to Anne's room.

For the present, they would use crates to sit on and a barrel with boards on it for a table. The next day, Etta got out needle and thread, and started sewing sections of the wagon canvas tarpaulin to make mattress covers that they stuffed with dry hay Harry found in one of the sheds. After a morning of settling in, they saddled up for a ride to explore the limits of their land. Where there were lush grasslands, they saw running deer, boar, fox and skunk, small scurrying critters, hawks, and many strange birds.

A surprise was finding a group of native Araucanian-Maupuche people, living on the property. They had built shelters and were raising sheep and guanacos and kept a garden. The newcomers introduced themselves and established that they were the new owners. They told the people that they were welcome to stay on the land in exchange for work. Later there would be livestock to take care of, but right now they could use some firewood. James asked if they would help to provide some by the next day; and, if the women could help Etta clean up the cabin. It was an ideal arrangement for everyone.

As a gesture of friendship to welcome the new patrons, Juan, the spokesman of the group gave Etta two guanaco hides and a sheep's skin to help keep them warm during the winter. Etta tried talking with the women. One, whose name was Nora, spoke her native Araucanian, and also Spanish. She was very soft spoken and seemed to be well regarded by the other women.

A few men from the families were helpful finding straight trees that could be cut in sections to make a bed for Harry and Etta. To hold up the mattress, they used stripped branches and rope. James said he could wait for a bed, but was happy to have a straw mattress to cushion his sleep. Harry and Etta looked at their bed and decided they could make a better bed for Anne.

The days felt fresh, crisp, clean and cool. The evenings were cold; dropping to freezing temperatures. Precipitation wasn't as great on the east side of the Andes, in Patagonia, as it was on the West side in Chile; so there wasn't much snow on the ground, at least, not yet.

*

James wanted to check out the township of Esquel, so he set out to explore and find the way, and hopefully find more horses and perhaps cattle to buy. He found the town in a picturesque setting, by deep turquoise lakes and surrounded by mountains. He rode the surrounding region, meeting folks on the scattered ranches in the area. At the ranch nearest them, he met John Perry. Perry had previously been a sheriff in Texas. James decided to stay friendly, but not too close to him.

While James was gone, Harry thought it would be a good time for his surprise. All the way from Buenos Aires, he had kept a bottle of champagne hidden in his things which Etta never disturbed. Harry liked his things kept a certain way. At the end of the day, after they had eaten a simple meal; Harry mentioned to Etta that he'd like to celebrate, and that an initiation was required when a person moved to a new ranch in the wilderness. He asked Etta to take off her clothes. "What? It's cold this evening." "Etta you'll soon be warm enough." Harry's smile was so big she couldn't refuse, she thought his actions, though very enticing, were well out of the ordinary.

She went to the bedroom to take off her clothes. When she came back into the kitchen, there was Harry holding up a red flannel Union Suit, complete with button up flap in the rear. He helped Etta get into it. He handed her a metal cup of Champagne and said, "I love you Etta, thank you for everything. Remember, I promised to keep you warm this winter!" Etta had to control her laughter so she could sip some of the Champagne. They never finished buttoning all the buttons.

When James returned, Etta and Harry were outside grooming horses by the shelter of a tree. They both stopped what they were doing and stared; admiring the capable, dashing cowboy driving four horses towards the corral.

James told Harry he'd like to go back to Esquel with him; to a ranch where they could buy cattle for breeding. The weather turned cold and grey and it started to snow, so that trip had to wait. James was glad to be inside where he could make repairs on a saddle and a harness. He sat by the woodstove, on a crate covered with the sheep's skin. A stack of firewood was piled up along the wall.

Harry and Etta lay on their bed, knowing it wasn't the most comfortable bed but it would do for now. They were content to start reading their books. They were relieved that the pit for the new outhouse had been dug, and a make shift seat and shelter had been built out of old planks they found on the property. They also had a chamber-pot so Etta wouldn't have to go outside on a cold or snowy night.

"Harry, what about askin' the families to move their shelters closer to the house? We could help em, and even help them build better shelters. If we're gone buyin cattle or other business, we've got to have Etta safe. Juan's savvy, and on the alert, but he's too far away. Are you goin to show Etta how to use a rifle and a Colt?"

"Yep, I'm with you on your thinkin on both matters. Let's ride over and ask the folks in the morning; and when the weather clears up, I'll start teaching Etta." "And, we've gotta build a better shelter for the horses. We don't know what's comin."

The temperature never got much lower than the point of freezing. Harry and James were relieved. They didn't want to endure the bitter cold of their past winters. The elevation at the ranch wasn't that high at just over two thousand feet. That made the difference.

Etta liked to keep the small woodstove always fed. Her attempts at cooking on its small top surface didn't always work out. When she served burnt beans, and burnt biscuits, one supper, the men didn't comment. They'd eaten many bowls of burnt beans. When Etta apologized, the men both replied, "It's just the way we like it." Whenever a meal didn't come out right, they always said the same thing. They devoured her sweetened and spiced cooked pumpkin, they really did like it.

The Indian families shared lamb portions with them. Out on an open fire where James set up a cook site, he cooked down some mutton fat to use for cooking. Etta looked forward to fresh fruit and vegetables in the summer. The canned goods from Trelew were appreciated but they would need more.

The tough, down-to-earth men found a gentler side to themselves in Etta's presence. When Anne arrived they outdid themselves with politeness and helpfulness; though that evened out after a few days. Anne immediately called them Uncle James, and Uncle Harry. Anne's brother, Walter, a clear minded, enthusiastic young man, stayed for two days before continuing on to Trevelin. He was awestruck by these worldly wise cowboys and looked forward to spending more time with them on his return trip.

Anne arrived later than expected, but came prepared, bringing her own mattress and bedding. Her clothing was very suitable. When Etta noticed that she also brought along a doll; she thought, this girl wants comfort and someone to take care of. After looking around, Anne wondered what work there would be for her. "Mrs. Place, may I say that if you realize you don't need me here, I can return home when Walter returns from Trevelin." "Anne, dear, there isn't a lot to do, but I would like your company for the most part, and would enjoy helping with your lessons. I promised wages and so that will still be taken care of, and in spring, if you decide to stay until summer, I hope to plant a small garden with your help, and we can help with the horses. Please consider staying." Oh yes ma'am, I want to stay, but not be a bother." "No bother at all, only good fortune for me. You are a welcome companion. Please, just call me Ethel."

Anne remembered that she had packed a gift of seeds for spring planting. Etta was delighted and asked Anne about what she knew about gardening, as her experience was limited. Anne told Etta the seeds must be kept cool and dry until spring planting. The conversation then progressed to sewing. Etta and Anne were busy looking at the fabric Etta had bought for window coverings when the men came back inside. It was a family scene that answered a longing in both men.

Anne was a smart girl, shy at first, yet quick to learn the ways and personalities of her new friends. Giggling was something Harry and James got used to and came to enjoy. Anne took pleasure in watching the men work with the horses. After awhile James asked her if she was a good rider. "I'm a dreadfully awful rider, Uncle James. I'm always stuck in a buggy or on a wagon." "Well, I could show you." That started Anne's love of horses and riding. From then on, every afternoon, weather permitting she was riding or grooming the horses.

Walter returned and stayed almost a week, enjoying the company of the men. He would come by again in spring, on his way once again to Trevelin, where he visited relatives, and bought flour. At that time, he would bring Anne back home for the summer.

Often they would go for rides traveling around the countryside, discovering the lakes and the forests. Other times, when the weather was just too cold or snowing, they stayed inside, reading and telling each other stories. Anne showed Etta how to make pan bread by raising the Dutch oven on a couple of stones on top of the woodstove and thickly coating the bottom of the pan with corn meal. The aroma, while the bread baked, just about had them drooling. Often they ate the entire loaf as soon as it was baked.

Etta did practice with the colt pistol that Harry gave her. She learned to be skillful and capable though not expert. That August, with the ranch families' now living closer, and feeling that the women would be safe; Harry and James traveled to Esquel and on to Trevelin for more supplies and then stopped at the ranch where they bought twenty head of cattle. A small start but it would do until spring when they would hopefully buy at least twice that many calves. As much as they cared for them, Harry and James needed time away from the women, and enjoyed getting drunk one evening by their campfire while they talked of their old exploits.

While the men were gone, a rider came up to the house and asked, in Spanish, if he could have some food. Etta fixed a plate for him while Anne went to the native family's enclave and gestured to the man she worked along side of, while grooming the horses, to please come to the house. He understood her worry and stayed at the house until the rider went on his way. He returned in the evening and stayed in the shed to be closer should there be a problem with the rider returning. Morning came without any trouble. Anne and Etta made extra loafs of bread to bring to the families to thank them.

Anne liked the excuse to go to see the families, hoping she might see the good-looking young man, called Luis, who was always so willing to help Harry and James with any work that needed doing, and also helped her with the horses. Etta and Anne had a long talk about her attraction and what was best for Anne. Anne understood and said, "There is a young man in my town that I hope for a future with, though my father finds fault with him."

James was noticeably fond of one of the younger Indian women, but didn't want to have any problems arise from a relationship, so he went to the towns, or more accurately, just outside of the towns, to find agreeable women.

Winter was finally coming to an end. Signs of spring showed with the first blooming of lupine, even though the flowers would occasionally be dusted with snow. Etta and Harry started taking walks in the early evening along the willows, where they often stopped to kiss and enjoy an intimate embrace. Harry was never very demonstrative in front of the others.

Spring & Summer in Cholila (September to February)

The four very distinct personalities found a way to work with and enjoy each other. Anne had a lovely voice and some evenings she would sing Welsh songs. Etta would occasionally play the violin, James and Harry told tales, but never of their unlawful exploits in front of Anne.

The only time James would sing was during his Saturday night bath in the galvanized tub, used for bathing and washing clothes. Bath night could really be any night of the week, and was taken in the warm kitchen by the woodstove. When Etta bathed, Harry would add more hot water and take his bath right after her. It was an appreciated private and intimate time with each other. Anne and James would stay in their rooms, and then after Anne took her bath and more hot water was ready on the stove she would call out to James that his bath was ready then go to her room. Then all would have their ears at their doors to hear James bellowing away, singing songs whether he knew the right words or not, and filling in any nonsense word that would come to mind. "Yippee Ti Yi Yo, get along little lambses; good thing you're not pigs, cause then you'd be hamses. Yippee Ti Yi Yo, get along on the trail, cause if you don't you'll end up in jail. Yippy Tippy Ti Yi Yo, Yippy Ti Yi Yay." They had to be careful to muffle their laughter. It was one of their best entertainments.

*

Walter was never so eager to take his seasonal trip to Trevelin. He looked forward to his stop in Cholila, where he could talk with, James and Harry. The main reason for his traveling, two times a year was to stock up on flour and visit relatives. Trevelin's name came from Tre, meaning town, and Felin, for mill. He let his parents know he might be gone longer than usual as he might help do work for Mr. Place and Mr. Ryan. He made good time getting to the ranch. The days were warming to fifty degrees, while the nights were still freezing.

He was a welcome sight. Cabin fever had set in and spirits were low. His arrival, on a clear afternoon cheered them and put them all in a merry frame of mind. With the offer of help, the men started working on fencing and repairing the ranch house. Walter seemed to have brought hummingbirds with him as they were now always flying close to the small flowering bushes near the cabin.

Walter was a good hand, and skillful at every task. Harry had the idea to take Etta to Esquel and Trevelin to show her the towns and give her a chance to buy things she needed for herself as well as get some supplies for the ranch. Now was a good time with Anne's brother here. It was a fine idea with Walter; he could stay and get to talk with James.

*

Esquel was a little more than twenty miles from the ranch. They pushed the wagon team to make it there in one day. Etta's merriment was contagious and Harry was smiling, pleased that he was making Etta happy. They stayed at an Inn, in luxurious comfort compared to their bed at home. While they were in town they picked up supplies to build another, better bed.

The Esquel Creek streamed along on its course flowing by the village. Nestled in low hills, the charming valley town, with its activity and bustle was a real boost for Harry and Etta's spirits, inspiring them to meet the townsfolk. Etta met ladies she enjoyed talking with, while Harry talked to men at the stables and inquired about ranches that were selling calves.

They stayed two days then set out for Trevelin. Etta enjoyed wearing her better dresses and visiting the tea houses where the tasty breads, cakes and black pudding were absolutely heavenly. Etta, bought some of the delicious welsh cheese to take home.

After enjoying themselves and stocking the wagon with supplies, they headed back, again stopping at Esquel for a night. They took two days coming back from Esquel. The grasses were growing and greening the landscape; wild daisies had sprouted up everywhere. They saw lupine and low plants covered with many small multi-colored blossoms. They looked out on Futalaufquen Lake and caught sight of flamingoes, black necked swans, enormous flocks of geese and splendidly colored ducks.

They saw herds of guanaco, and the zorro, and deer. Birds were wonderfully abundant. They saw so many more hummingbirds and hawks, and wondered if the small, long tailed green birds they saw could be parakeets or parrots. Etta would have to mention this in her next letter to Mabel.

When they returned they were impressed to find the homestead looking so improved. Fencing had been repaired and added to, for the corral. Anne went on to Trevelin with Walter. On their return, they stopped to stay a night then were on their way home to Trelew where Anne would help her mother, during the summer, at their store and tea shop. Harry and James set out with the wagon to get lumber for building repairs and more wire for fencing; they used sturdy branches for fence posts. Then, they would head out again on horseback to buy calves.

*

Etta and her new friend, Nora from the ranch families, dug a garden plot near a spring where they could work the soil and create a channel for water to irrigate their plantings. Two more women from the family enclave came over to help them pointing at what they intended to show Etta, and also gave Etta seed potatoes to plant. Etta struggled in talking with them. They spoke their native Araucanian language and just a little Spanish. She would try to cultivate friendships as she guessed these women could share a great amount of knowledge.

Summer held many delights. Often, they would all go out to the lakes nearby for sun-up to sundown outings. They all came alive in the warm Argentina sun. Harry and James acquired more and more cattle, horses and sheep, and bulls, stallions, and rams for breeding. The native families helped out with all areas of the ranch work. Etta was learning the names of the local plants from Nora.

James and Harry traveled to Rawson that October to register their brands, “O<” for Harry, “R” for James, and a reversed P fronting an R for a joint brand. At that time, Etta received a letter from Mabel telling of their mothers failing health. Mabel asked if Etta and Harry could make a trip to Boston. Etta wrote to say they could be in New York in April and then would go on to Boston.

IX

Merritt

November 15, 1901

Dear Harry,

How are you and Etta and Butch?

This letter is to let you know that I am going to San Diego to meet Peter, who Etta told me about. She has been trying to get me to write to him. I finally did, and now I am going to meet him.

It is good that you and Butch left the United States. The cowboy is a sad figure now. It is dangerous for any one to try any of the old ways these days. This year has been full of wrong doings. Harvey Logan killed a man named Ollie Thorton in Texas. Will Carver was killed in Texas. I heard Black Jack Ketchum was hung in New Mexico. Harvey also killed the rancher Jim Winters in Landusky, Montana. He has got to get caught soon. Word is that he has really gone loco. I heard Ben Kilpatrick was arrested in Missouri, over robbing a bank.

So you can see that the time to change my ways and try to make something of myself is now or never. You and Etta have said Peter is a good man. I sure hope he will find some work for me.

Take good care of Etta and give my regards to Butch.

Merritt

*

November 25, 1901

Dear Etta,

Thank you for your encouragement. I finally found the courage to write to Peter. He and Mabel invited me to come to San Diego to meet. I guess the meeting went well as I am now staying with them. So far, I go to Peter's office and help there, and I help at their home. I wondered about feeling confined here, but with the amazing Pacific Ocean close by, I find a different kind of openness that is exciting.

Peter is a gentleman, and a man I can talk plainly with. Mabel amazes me by how she paints. I never have known an artist like her.

How do you like living on your ranch? Mabel says you are happy and are enjoying your life. Living with Harry and Butch might be a struggle some times. I know they sometimes get consumed by their plans. I am glad they have found a good life ranching in Argentina, away from the west that could only be trouble for them.

Mabel is bringing a gift for you to Boston, that I made. Have a fun time in New York City and Boston. I will help with things here while Pete and Mabel are in Boston. I hope your mother's health is better.

Your friend Merritt

*

November 29, 1901

Dear Harry,

Good to hear from you and read that your ranch is improving and your stock is growing. You have made good choices.

Young Merritt arrived last week, and Mabel and I are glad to have him here with us. I will see what I can do to find employment for him, something where he could learn a trade perhaps. In the meantime, he works for me doing everything from deliveries for the law office to helping put up new light fixtures in the apartment. He is living with us, using Etta's room. Mabel and I both see the extraordinary in him as do you and Etta.

He certainly enhanced the occasion of our Thanksgiving dinner yesterday. He is very polite, and Mabel adores him; his bright wit adds to conversation. I continue to be in charge of the turkey.

Please plan for the trip to Boston in spring (your fall). We should be meeting you at mother Ethel's in April. It will be good to see you. I look forward to more conversations with you and I know Mabel misses her sister.

All the best to you and Etta,
Peter

*

Sunday, December 3, 1901

Dear Sister,

Thank you for the gift of Merritt. He is a brilliant young man who has put us on our toes. Our conversations have really perked up since his arrival. He is interested in so many varied subjects and has us spell bound with his tales of adventure. I know he tells Peter much more than he shares with me, but that is alright. He is like a young brother, come home. He reads all the time; everything from Peter's law books to my cookbooks. He has even tried some recipes with me.

My painting and sales continue to go well. I enjoyed reading that you made a stain from the purple lupine to paint flowers on your wagon. Do the men really hate it that much?

It seems that mother is still weak. She continues to exasperate Uncle Stephen with her lack of interest in keeping up the maintenance on the house, but spending lavishly on inessentials.

We are looking forward to seeing you in Boston in April. Will you visit Harry's relatives first? Please telephone mother's *house when you arrive in New York to let us know when you will be in Boston.*

While we are away, Merritt will still help at Peter's office and also take care of things at home for us, He is a joy. Today he and Peter are building a new studio easel for me.

It has been a year since you were here. We do miss you so. I look forward to spending time with you when we can just talk and talk. We will celebrate a happy Christmas with Merritt. It seems we will all arrive too late for celebrating Easter together in Boston, so we will make our own holiday when we are together.

Take good care of yourselves. I realize it is such a long journey for you to come to the states, however I miss you so.

Your loving sister, Mabel

X

New York and Boston 1902

"Harry, do you mind? Will it be a problem?" "No Etta, in fact it works out real fine. James can travel with us to Buenos Aires to file our claim on the homestead. We'll leave the wagon in Trelew with Walter, and he can take care of the team until James returns, then we'll ask Walter to bring us back here with his wagon. James can come back with a wagon of supplies and we'll bring back more supplies with Walter. We'll be well stocked when we get back. But, hell, it'll almost be spring here by the time we get back. You know we better get ready. If we leave for Bahia Blanca before mid January, we can be in Buenos Aires by the end of February and maybe in New York the end of March or thereabouts. Glad we've now got Dan to call on to check with Juan on managing the stock, and show the men what needs doing. I'm looking forward to talking with Pete again, and I know you miss your sister."

In Buenos Aires, they stayed again at the Hotel Europa. Etta enjoyed the city and was thrilled to see her friend Celina. Ernesto was again traveling on business. During this visit, Etta's thoughts were on the ranch and what she was missing by not being there. She had enjoyed a happy summer. Her friend Nora would tend her small herb and vegetable gardens which included the many potato plants that would still need watering.

*

February 21, 1902, Buenos Aires, Argentina

Dearest Mabel.

It has been good to see this beautiful city again. We have just enough time to rest and visit friends before we leave.

We will be traveling to New York on the "Soldier Prince," leaving March 3, and should be arriving the first week of April, in New York. We will telephone to let you know when we will be in Boston.

I am grieved to hear of mother's continuing loss of health. The trip is long, but I feel it is necessary to spend time with mother. And you my dear sister; I miss you greatly. We have much to talk about. Letters do not convey all the feelings and experiences I'd much rather talk about with you beside me.

I must get this in the post so it will arrive at mothers' before we do. We will telephone mother's house as soon as we arrive. It should be mid April, about the same time as your arrival.

All my love,
Your loving sister Etta

*

On March 3, 1902, Harry and Etta set out for New York, on the S.S. Soldier Prince, leaving the crisp, cool weather of approaching fall in Argentina. With James, they had formally applied for their Four Square Leagues of Government Land in the Province of Chubut District 16 of II October, near Cholila. Their home, Estancia de Esperanza. On April 2 the application was officially accepted and James filed the homestead document with the Colonial Land Department. James stayed on for awhile celebrating in Buenos Aires. At the end of the month, he took the steamer to Bahia Blanca; then on to Rawson and Trelew where he picked up the wagon and team, loaded the wagon with supplies and headed home.

*

On April 3rd, Harry and Etta arrived at Bush Terminal in Brooklyn, New York. They found lodging at Mrs. Thompson's rooming house at 325 East Fourteenth Street, and used this location as a base. Then they went on to Boston to see Etta's mother and reunite with Mabel and Peter.

Mabel was too excited to wait for all the greetings to be done with, so she could give Etta the gift Merritt had made for her. He had brought the red-tailed hawk feathers with him when he first arrived in San Diego, with plans to make them into fans for Etta and Mabel. They were astonished at the fine workmanship. The feathers were joined together with silk thread that Mabel had given Merritt. The fan was a work of art.

Just before leaving Cholila, Etta and Harry heard about the assassination of President McKinley that had taken place the previous September in 1901, at the Pan-American Exposition in Buffalo, New York. Peter had a lot to say about the shooting of McKinley, and about their new president, Theodore Roosevelt. He was impressed with Roosevelt's address to Congress asking it to curb the power of large corporations.

Ethel seemed to be doing well, though she tired very easily. She appeared more annoyed with the disruption of her routine than she seemed to enjoy their company; so, at the end of the week, the two couples went to New York City and then to Coney Island for some fun. Mabel wanted to see the Statue of liberty, so they all took the ferry to Bedloe's Island and were astonished to see the immense size of the statue.

During their sightseeing, they paired off, with the men involved in their discussions. Peter asked Harry for a detailed description and map of how he and Mabel should travel, if they should ever have the opportunity to visit their ranch. It was more of a dream of Peter's, as he didn't think Mabel was cut out for that kind of adventure. As the women walked, they chatted and giggled, though sometimes their heads were close together in quiet and confidential conversation.

*

When Peter and Mabel returned to Boston, Peter met with Uncle Stephen to hear about the legal matters he wanted to discuss. Uncle Stephen was concerned about Ethel's estate and wanted advice.

Harry and Etta traveled by train to Pennsylvania, to visit Samanna and her family. Harry was astounded at how the boys, now young men, had grown up. He invited them to visit their ranch in Argentina and hoped some day they would. Harry enjoyed showing Etta the countryside, something they didn't do when they were here in the winter of 1901.

After returning to New York and resting, they traveled to New Jersey to see Harvey, Harry's brother, who had moved his family to the resort town of Atlantic City, where he now worked. The visit went well, though both brothers realized they had little in common.

Then, once again, they went to Buffalo, to Dr. Pierce's Invalid Hospital where Harry had his old wound looked at, and again took the steam baths that helped his catarrh. The Doctors mixed a medicine for him that helped also. While in Argentina, he was only mildly annoyed by this condition; but, on the east coast it set in again. Etta received a check-up and was told she was too thin. The doctor went on to say perhaps that was why she didn't get pregnant. She was told to eat more meat. That would certainly be easy enough to do.

*

Peter and Mabel returned to San Diego while Harry and Etta were in Buffalo, so their return visit with Ethel was very quiet. Ethel wanted to spend more time with Harry to listen to him tell her about running their cattle ranch. She asked Etta about her linens, china and glassware. Etta could only tell her that she lived a more rustic life, so she didn't have or need much. She did have some nice items, purchased from the Welsh, which were beautiful pieces of crystal and some china from Wales, Scotland and Ireland. Her mother insisted that she, at least, take some of her linens.

Back in New York they slowed their pace and spent the better part of their afternoons walking in Central Park. Etta was very taken with the bronze statue, the "Angel of the Waters", in Bethesda fountain. "Harry, look; it looks like she's just touched down. She's lovely." They sat on a bench leaning against each other, watching people walk by, and they talked about their families and themselves. They shopped for more books, and this time Etta found books on gardening and planting vegetables. She also picked out, "Silas Marner," to read on the ship while traveling back home. Harry found more books on cattle and horses.

Before departing, to return home to Argentina, they went to Tiffany's, to purchase a watch for Harry. He wanted to buy jewelry for Etta, but Etta said she'd rather have a larger bathtub. They laughed so loud; people turned to stare, and witnessed a very happy, handsome couple, smiling and enjoying each other immensely.

On July 10, Etta and Harry sailed aboard the freighter "Honorius," from New York to Buenos Aries. They had been in the United States for three months and they missed their home in Argentina.

XI

Return to Cholila 1902

They left New York in summer, arriving in Buenos Aires to Argentina's' early spring rainy season. They were homesick so didn't delay in Buenos Aires any longer than to book the next steamer to Bahia Blanca. While they waited, Harry withdrew the balance of their savings from the London and Rio Platte Bank. He and Butch had never liked being separated so far from their money.

Like Butch, from there they took a smaller steamer to Puerto Madryn; then went on to Rawson and Trelew where they stayed at the Del Globo Hotel. They met with Anne, her brother Walter, their mother, and this time also their father who seemed to be a sour, taciturn person.

They learned that James had been there to pick up their wagon and horses after returning from Buenos Aires in May. James had returned home feeling very lonely. Harry and Etta rode home on horses Harry bought at a bargain while Walter and Ann rode on the wagon, stocked with more supplies for the ranch. Anne was allowed to go to the ranch, but only to visit until Walter's return from Trevelin when she would need to come back to help in the tea room during the summer. Anne couldn't wait to hear all about Boston and New York City.

During the trip, Etta sometimes rested, riding on the wagon during the course of the journey, and slept under it some evenings for protection from the evening showers. While eating canned peaches and beans off metal plates, Harry and Etta laughed over the contrast of their lifestyles from city finery and manners, to the rough life and country clothes of the way they preferred to live

They arrived home in late September. James was coming out to greet them from a newly built bunkhouse, small but well built, near the native families dwellings. He had become closer friends with the men; and the women took care of him like an orphaned lamb. Even so, he was jubilant now that his family was home.

James had been lonely. He had been to Esquel and Trevelin on two trips, and purchased more cattle, horses and sheep in his boredom. It had been a plan of Harry and James for James to withdraw a substantial amount of their money from their account in Buenos Aires for this purpose. Harry withdrew what was left.

Etta was surprised to find the large cook stove sitting out in front of the cabin. James explained that in the hot summer months, the cabin would stay a lot cooler if they cooked outside. Etta enjoyed cooking outdoors with the convenience of a good stove. She now could bake breads and biscuits throughout the summer, and cook their meals without raising the temperature of their cabin. James and Harry continued to cook the meat for the meals over a campfire.

In his lonesomeness, James had also used his planning skills to build better gates for the horse corral. He showed Etta the work he'd done in the house to help keep them warm in winter, putting wood strips around the windows where the wind had previously blown through. Another project was his chicken coop, which amazed everyone; James wasn't known for being fond of chickens.

James was eager to show Harry and Etta the horses, and the mules, he'd bought and was training, as well as an Angus bull. He'd let it mix with the local wild cattle as they'd done before. Taking long rides around the property with Luis, counting and admiring the cattle, horses and sheep, had kept him occupied some of the time. He took rides alone to the mountains and to the lakes when the weather permitted. He was so relieved and cheerful now that his lonely days were over.

*

Home in Cholila 1902-1903

October 15, 1902

Dearest Mabel,

Being with you and Peter was splendid. We enjoyed a lovely time. You both look so well and happy. Peter and Harry get along so well; it is good to see them becoming good friends.

Mother seemed to be in a weakened condition from her former self; however seems to get along well enough otherwise. Have you heard from her recently?

Please accept my apology for not writing as soon as we arrived home. There is so much to catch up on and I wanted to work with the native families putting in our vegetable garden, (it is early spring here). So far, the garden consists of potatoes (more like a sweet potato), cebolla, ajo, corn, there's something like a carrot, and green beans and pumpkin squash, (seeds from our Welsh friends). And also herbs; Estafiate, good for the stomach ache, and others I am just learning about. The local families also have herb plants that grow year round. My friend, Nora, keeps encouraging me to try one that will help me to conceive. I am not sure at this point about using it myself, perhaps next year. Or, should I try it and then send some to you? I am not so sure yet about having children on this frontier; though the local children thrive and are quite healthy and beautiful.

Last Sunday, was Columbus Day, a holiday here also. We celebrated with the native families and our closest neighbors around Cholila. Everyone contributed their special dishes making a magnificent feast for all. I baked bread that I didn't burn, and a peach cobbler from canned peaches that we bought at Rawson. The men cooked lamb and beef. I am truly happy to be home.

Do write soon and tell me more about your paintings. If only I could see them. Peter is obviously very impressed and proud of you; as am I.

Your loving sister,
Etta

P.S. Remembering that this will not reach you until the holidays, I wish you and Peter the happiest Christmas. Thank you for the warm memories of Christmas at your home.

*

Dear brother Harry,

Thank you for the postcard from New York City, I hope I addressed the envelope for this letter correctly. It is hard to imagine that you will not get this letter for maybe two months.

I have a new address. It is 3012-1/2 16th St., San Francisco, California. If you remember the city, you know it is in a handy location between Valencia and Mission Streets.

I've been working at the shipyards again. It gets me by. Please give my regards to your fine wife.

Sincerely,
Elwood

*

Harry wanted to catch up on what was going on at the ranch and spent his days, from sunup to sundown, checking the livestock and working with James training horses. He needed to get back into the cowboy life after so much time in cities. When he and James rode out south towards Esquel, or north to Bariloche, to buy cattle or sheep, and were gone for weeks, Etta didn't feel at all nervous. She was close to the families now, and besides, her confidence was much stronger than it was when they first arrived.

Dusty, one of the ranch dogs was Etta's favorite. Dusty was a spaniel who wanted to be a cattle dog and help with rounding up livestock; though he usually gave up and was most often found by Etta's side. Their reunion had been touching. The men knew Dusty was Etta's baby though she treated old Blackie very well also.

Harry realized that Etta was the heart of the ranch. She worked with the other women in the garden. She sang as she washed clothes. She rode the horses to exercise them and herself, and helped in roundups. Etta was Harry's personal delight and a joy to all as a good companion. Her smile was even more pleasing than her cooking, and no one ever hesitated to come running at the dinner signal. He thought she might like to take a trip to Esquel or Bariloche.

At first she said yes, and then though it over and said no; she'd like to go camping at the lakes to the north, and spend time just with him. They could go to Esquel for a longer stay in the fall, in March or April, when Walter would be here when he brought Anne. Harry thought it was good idea. He did the packing for the trip, and planned on doing the cooking as well.

Setting out at sunrise, they rode their horses and led two supply horses. The weather was warm enough for a comfortable ride. They arrived at the lake mid afternoon riding through a field of lupine by the waters edge where they dismounted. Etta wanted to set up camp but Harry warned her that as soon as shadows started to spread, there would be mosquitoes. They could spend the afternoon there, but then make their camp higher, about half an hour ride from the lake. They relieved the horses of some of their burdens, tethered them to the trees and let them graze while they spread a blanket and took off their outer clothing to bathe in the sun.

They tried going in the water but found it too cold to enjoy, so they sat by the shore with their bare feet in the cold water until their feet turned blue. Back on the blanket, they enjoyed a meal that Harry had packed, cooked lamb, bread, and canned tomatoes which they ate right out of the can, and then drank the juice.

They reminisced over their first picnic in Raton, and in the course of remembering the passion that was held in check at the time; they now indulged in each other wholly, completely, and entirely. Etta took off all her clothes, and Harry was actually shocked at her abandon as she teased him by wriggling away and enticed him to chase her. He caught her too easily and carried her back to the blanket. There was no reason now to deny each other any of their desires.

*

Warm spring winds cut into the last of the winter chill and the grasses grew with enthusiasm. Juan and James cut a section of the pasturing grass to stack by the stable and corral for the horses and cattle that needed extra watching and were kept close, either because they were hurt or looked ill. When they had achieved a tall stack, James took a run and jumped right in the middle of it, then got up and had a good laugh.

Etta saw him and thought it looked like fun. She called to Harry asking him to join her jumping into the haystack. He said no, so she went ahead and jumped anyway. Then she jumped out as fast as she could, and the men who had started to laugh—stopped.

Something was wrong, she looked panicked and looked like she was trying to cough but couldn't. Etta looked at them wild eyed motioning to her throat. She could only mouth the words, I can't breathe. She was struggling to breathe but nothing was happening. James grabbed her, one arm under her back and another around her abdomen, and swung her up in his arms. As he did her head hung back and her airway opened just enough to let a little air suck into her lungs. He kept holding her in this inclined position, as slowly her airway opened and she could breathe fully. James then set her down on the ground holding her to help her sit up. She was exhausted and now started coughing from the dust and grass particles that had caused the shock to her throat. Juan offered water, which she sipped slowly, afraid of choking.

Harry had come over to the group when he heard the excited voices of the men. He rushed to Etta, and the men told him what had happened. "Thank you James." "Well I don't know what I did, and I didn't even know what I was gonna do when I picked her up that way." James eyes went moist, and he turned, and walked over to the horses.

Harry held Etta and felt stunned. He couldn't imagine losing her. Etta started to cry remembering a thought she had during her struggle to breathe—that she couldn't bear leaving Harry, not even in death.

*

By November, Etta realized she made a mistake in choosing the lake trip instead of going to Esquel. She had no gift to give Harry for Christmas! She fretted for days until she noticed the woven hatbands on the native men's hats. She asked Nora if she would teach her how to make one. After trying a few times she finally succeeded in making a very suitable woven hatband for Harry that she was proud of. She then made a narrow woven belt for James, not sure if he would wear it or use it for tying up something.

As the holidays came near, Etta asked the men if they would like to invite some of their closest neighbors, as well as their ranch families, and Dan, their closest friend, for a New Year's celebration; leaving Christmas to just themselves. They were all for it and spread the word.

Christmas gave Etta a surprise. Who would have thought the men would have remembered to think of Christmas on their last trip to Esquel. Harry gave her a large, high backed bathtub—exactly what she wanted. He also gave her a pair of kid gloves that fit her small hands just right. Butch gave her new pots and pans. They had hidden them all this time, just to surprise her. She tried not to cry, she was so happy. Her gifts to them were accepted with great appreciation; the men were impressed that she'd given them something that she'd learned how to do, just for them.

For the New Year's party, they dressed in their best ranch clothes and again, the food was prepared by the women, with Harry and James roasting a lamb for the occasion. Etta noted the contrast of the warm, pleasant summer weather here in December, to the cold, snowy holidays of her childhood in Boston.

That night, most of their guests stayed at the ranch house; two women used James room, two more in Anne's. The men never did sleep but played cards all night in the kitchen at the table James and Harry made. Ethel, Etta's mother, would have been aghast at her fine tablecloth being used on a card table.

*

Harry, James and Etta didn't have any notion that Pinkerton agents knew that they were in Argentina. After the photograph was taken of Harry, Butch, Ben Kilpatrick, Harvey Logan, and Will Carver, in Fort Worth; the photographer put a print of it in his display window. A law officer saw the portrait and realized he knew some of their faces. They all could now be identified. Copies of the photo of the "Fort Worth Five" were now in the hands of the Pinkerton's. Also, the Pinkerton's had spies at the Post Office in Monte Clare, Pennsylvania, where Harry's sister, Samanna, lived; they were reading her incoming and outgoing mail. Frank Dimaio, a Pinkerton agent, had already been in Buenos Aires making inquires. Wanted posters were posted in Buenos Aires and along the port towns.

The Pinkerton agents had been doing their work, and had the names Harry and Etta used signing the register at Mrs. Taylor's boarding house in New York, where they had lodged in 1901. They knew the names Harry and Etta used for travel. Harry and Etta's photo, taken in Buffalo, New York, was discovered after Harry had sent a copy to a friend in Wyoming. After discovering it; the Pinkerton agents located the return address at 234 West Twelfth Street, Mrs. Taylor's boarding house in New York City. The Pinkerton detective had copies made at DeYoung's Photography studio on Broadway, to use on Wanted Posters. Etta, known as Ethel by the Pinkerton's, was now "wanted" and accused of "Wild Bunch" crimes. The Pinkerton's were on an intense, concentrated, and fierce manhunt.

*

Cholila Winter 1903 (March to September)

Anne arrived once again, in the cooling weather of March, with her brother, Walter, who was again anxious to spend time with the rugged, knowledgeable cowboys. They were welcome wholeheartedly. The first day Anne helped Etta harvest vegetables. The next day Etta and Harry left for Esquel and Trevelin. Anne got her things settled in her room and resumed caring for the house, garden, and horses. Walter was jubilant over staying the few extra days and working again with James.

Harry and Etta enjoyed going to Esquel and Trevelin; they'd now been there several times, and had made friends there. Harry encountered David and his wife, Emilita, in Trevelin; they looked extremely despondent. Harry had met David at a ranch near Esquel when he and James were on a horse buying trip, and was impressed with his knowledge of horses.

David had been told his services were no longer needed when the ranch he'd worked for changed hands. "Their foolishness is to our advantage Dave. James, Etta, and I, will be honored to have you work for us. We're going back to Esquel tomorrow, be there for a day, and then we're returning to the ranch. You can ride along with us, or go on ahead." Dave and Emilita had their own horses and traveled to the ranch along with them. Emilita was strong and could drive the wagon team; so much of the trip she and Etta sat on the wagon bench, talked and became friends while the men rode and talked about horses and ranch life.

James new bunkhouse was converted into lodging for Dave and Emilita. Anne said she didn't need the woodstove that was in her room, so it was set up in their cabin. Estancia de Esperanzo was becoming colonized. Meals were now more communal in nature. James took the wagon to Rawson to buy a new woodstove for Anne's room. He looked forward to the trip to the big town, and to have some time along the way, to talk with his friend, Paul Williams, the blacksmith who had been so considerate back in 1901, on their first journey to their ranch and again when they traveled in 1902.

*

April 9, 1903

Dearest Etta,

All sounds well with you. You do indeed, sound very happy.

I have thrilling news. Peter and I are planning on going to the exciting St. Louis World's Fair next summer, in 1904 (North America summer, your winter). We are hoping that you and Harry will join us. The first stop will be at mothers.

I realize this is a long journey for you to take again, but it would be winter there, and what a fine time we could all have together.

Because of it taking such a long time for exchanging correspondence, we have made definite plans. We will be at mothers the second week of July. She is still holding on though in poor health. We could meet there and then go on to St. Louis. For this trip we feel we must spend more time with mother as she is not faring well. She doesn't write; we hear about her frailties from Uncle Stephen.

We will have almost two months to vacation in Boston and St. Louis. Please tell us that you and Harry will join us.

Etta, I must confide that I am distraught over not having children. Two incomplete pregnancies have left me desperate. I am very willing to try the herbs that your native women use. Please send the herbs and compleat directions on the amounts for a dose and how it is to be taken. I am very sincere in this request.

Beatrix Potter, an English author, has written a book, "The Tales of Peter Rabbit," it is so dear. I want to read it to my own child.

Merritt now has his own apartment, a small studio with a Murphy bed. I've gave him all the linens he could possibly use (many were gifts to us from mother), and helped him set up housekeeping. I miss him; he is always busy; involved in work for Peter. It seems he is a good detective and adds ideas helpful to Peter. He will come here to spend the weekend with us and be wonderful company on Easter Sunday. Peter is now in charge of cooking all holiday meats. He has ordered leg of lamb from the butcher's, so I am looking up recipes for mint sauce.

I miss you dear sister. Please write and say you and Harry will be going with us to the St. Louis fair.

Your loving sister,
Mabel

*

Winter was setting in early. Etta, Anne, and Emilita, canned some of the vegetables; the rest they stored in the new root cellar. Etta had never done any canning and was pleased with herself and thankful for Anne and Emilita's help. The men were unusually busy checking the herds, securing the corrals and checking the buildings to see if they needed repair. Their first snowstorm was a novelty and not very severe; however the next had been unusually fierce.

Some evenings, Harry, James, and Dave would play cards. Etta, Anne and Emilita, would sit in chairs around the woodstove and sew, share stories and talk about plans for the ranch. On clear days

Etta would go for a ride with Anne, or take walks with Nora and Emilita. Etta had improved her Spanish significantly, though Nora frequently interjected Indian words that often confused her.

After Etta received Mabel's letter, she asked Nora for an amount of the herb that her sister should take, and how she should use it. With Emilita's help, she translated the directions to write down for Mabel. She wondered if Peter would approve, or if he would even be told. Nora gave her plenty, so that Mabel would have an ample amount. She hoped Etta would try it, saying it would be good for the handsome couple to have a fine beautiful child.

On the days and evenings when just the family of Harry, Etta, James and Anne were together, they read stories aloud, or invented games. 'Name the can' was one game Harry and James remembered from long sieges of not working in winters and when they were holding out, at "Roostville". They would all read can labels, and then one person would be asked to fully describe what picture and wording was on a certain can, say, Tomatoes. Or, another version was for the person to guess what the product in a can was, by description of the decoration on the can and some of the wording, not giving away the product. Harry and James seemed to love reminiscing over this game and always had stories they would share of times when they were bored, back in their "ranch hand" days.

James really showed his colorful personality and love of fun at game nights. He would drag out a large bulging and clanging burlap bag and set it down in a corner. When someone would win at a game; he would reach in the bag of jumble, for a 'prize'. The prizes were usually useless items he'd found in rides around the country side; a scrap of cloth, a dried up boot, a pot with a hole in it, a rusted can, strips of leather, crusty hats (probably blown off someone's head while riding). A very small picture of the mountains, painted on wood was a prize that Harry won and then gave to Etta, who loved the faded image, and hung it up in the kitchen.

James Saturday night baths continued to be an amusement with his dreadful versions of popular cowboy songs. "*I woke up one dusty ol morning on the ol cattle trail, Rope in one han an a cow by its messy tail. Come a ti yi youpy, yippee, yuppee, do de day, come ti yi yappy doody day. Oh, it's beans and beans most ever' day, I'd soon as be eatin meadow biscuits, or the hay. Come a tidy iedy, iedy doody yippy, yappy aye, Come a ti yi doody yoody yea."*

That winter was frosty and cold. Though they didn't always get a lot of snow, this winter proved the exception. Other winters were wet and disagreeable though not as cold. As it neared spring, a warm wind came through occasionally. Harry and James wondered what the winds were called here. The warm winds in Montana and Colorado were called Chinooks, and in Utah, they were the foehn winds. Here, the warm winds were always followed by a return of the cold, and a wind that cut to the bone. It gave James deep, lonesome feelings.

*

September 27, 1903

Dear Harry,

We were happy to receive Etta's letter affirming you will join us in Boston and St. Louis. I appreciate the long journey you must make to come to the states.

Very pleased to hear your ranch is a promising enterprise. I would like to visit someday, perhaps in 1905.

Merritt is now indispensable to me and is learning law, though it's not his true love. He has an outstanding intellect and applies himself wholeheartedly. We've had much advancement in some cases because of his good mind. He now owns a horse that he boards not too far from his apartment. He enjoys his time riding in the hills.

The law practice has improved, and, I must admit, so have I. I've learned much more by being in the game and realizing how it all really works. Much is to do with politics. But, still; it is the game I love.

Recently, I had the opportunity to speak with a retired senator; as you know I have a fascination for the cause of wars and how they are fought. We talked about the Spanish-American War. At the start of that war; I was all for it. I based my beliefs on the accounts of the situation as

I had read in the newspapers. I was ignorant of the facts, and like most Americans, grossly mislead.

I have now learned that after Spain sank the battleship, Maine, in Havana harbor in April of '98, the United States set a list of terms for Spain to meet. Spain backed down and met all of the terms. Their queen had already ordered hostilities ended on Spain's part. Our government, and president McKinley, must have wanted to flex its muscles. It was ready to wage a war, so they went ahead and blockaded Spain's harbors. Only then did Spain declare war. Then, of course, the U.S. declared war on Spain.

Our government's interest in Cuba was understood to be about helping Cuba win independence from Spain. But, in fact our government wants to be an Empire, like the European powers that have expanded into Asia and Africa, and taken over Cuba.

The war ended not so much from any victory, but from a devastating Yellow Fever outbreak. By the time of the signing, of the 'Treaty of Paris', December 10, 1898; 3,000 lives of U.S. men were lost. Ninety percent died of Yellow Fever, Typhoid fever and other infectious diseases.

It was an all volunteer Army and Navy, with about 17,000 serving in the war. The cost was an outrageous 250 million dollars. Did you know that "The Pennsylvania Volunteers" was the largest contributor of men?

It seems I am being summoned to Sunday supper, and Mabel, who knows me too well, is telling me to not go on and on writing about war. It just strikes me as all wrong that we are misled into war by feelings of patriotism and not told the truth. We lost boys who believed that they, and their families, were contributing and sacrificing themselves to a just cause for a great nation. I do not know what to believe anymore.

As you know, Cuba did gain independence from Spain in 1902.

See you in Boston in July.

Best regards,
Peter

When Harry received the letter, he showed it to James, who cried out, "We were willing to fight in that war! I feel like a fool!" "That makes both of us, James."

*

Spring to Summer 1903-1904 (Argentina, September to March)

Walter's arrival in mid September was their first real sign of spring. Once again Etta and Harry enjoyed a weeks holiday in Trevelin and Esquel. They took their time, lingering by the picturesque Lago Fatalaufquen, stopping the wagon to get out and stretch and to admire the stunning country.

After their return, as in previous years, Anne went with Walter to Trevelin to visit their relatives and then returned with Walter to Trelew for the summer. During the last couple of years, Etta realized Anne had a deep yearning to do more with her life though she also loved her time at Estancia de Esperanza. Etta had given a lot of thought to Anne's future and was working out a plan she hoped might work.

Early in December, Harry and Etta took time out again to go off on their own, on a camp trip in the lakes area, this time around Lake Lezama, about three miles from the town of Bariloche. Etta especially enjoyed the sandy shore and pine trees.

Harry had been in a reflective, thoughtful mood and, while riding, began talking about his doubts, something he rarely did. "Would you rather have married a man who would've given you a nice house in a city in the states?" "What! You know me Harry. You know I love my—our, life here!" "Well, I was wonderin. If my life had gone another way and I didn't have to leave the country, we would have lived differently." Etta stopped her horse, and Harry did also. She nudged her horse in closer and leaned to face him. "Yes, we would have lived differently. We would have loved each other and got along alright. But, Harry, this life is better. We live a good life here; I think it suits our natures. Harry, I have you to thank for my happiness. I'm living a fine, happy, splendid life!" Harry smiled at Etta and kissed her tenderly.

Etta paused from kissing, to ask, "Do you miss any part of it; the excitement of a train or bank robbery? Do you miss being the Sundance Kid?" "Hell no! Pardon, but that activity was done at first because I had nothing going for myself, and then later from pure desperation. It's no wonder they call outlaws, "Desperados." That was a dangerous business. Every time you put a gun in your hand, you know that if you have to use it someone's going to get hurt or killed, and very likely, it could be you."

*

The summer passed with everyone at the ranch feeling a sense of accomplishment for the work they had done that season. There had also been many lazy days of enjoying each others company, sharing meals and laughter.

James had been unsettled about something for a few days and finally told Harry. "I suspect someone's rustlin' some of our cattle." "Rustlin' from us!" "Yep, a few of the cattle I always notice on the far end of the pasturing area are gone. Let's get Davy and Juan to go out with us when it's dark and keep a look out.

It was all calm until after midnight when they heard two riders on horseback come in from the west on the far side of the pasture where Juan was hiding. They heard Juan shouting and then heard gunfire. James came riding up on the rustlers. He shot at them through the dark moonless night. Not knowing if he'd hit them, he turned back to check on Juan. Harry was already with him. Juan had been shot in the arm. They took him back to Nora. Luckily the bullet had passed right through the fatty part of his arm. Nora poured some 'Cana' on Juan's arm after giving him some to drink. She told Harry and James that Juan would be alright; she would make a poultice to dress his wounds.

They set out again to get Davy who'd stayed out in case there was any chance of another attempt on the cattle. They told him to come on in because there shouldn't be any more trouble. For a few more evenings they kept watch, riding around the pastures in the evenings. They never saw anyone again and never knew who it had been. Etta was relieved; the episode had frightened and worried her.

*

Harry, Dave, and Juan, left the beginning of March to drive several head of cattle to sell at a ranch outside Trevelin; they then headed north to the lakes country. They crossed the Rio Puelo and set eyes on the pristine waters of Lake Puelo. Still traveling north they went on past Bariloche and then back, west along the Rio Manso to inspect the trailhead that went over the Andes leading towards Cochamo, Chile, that would go on to Puerto Montt. Then, heading home they stopped at a ranch near El Bolson, where they bought a large bull.

James stayed back at the ranch; he wasn't feeling so well. Lately he was complaining about his stomach. Etta told him to talk with Nora, who would tell him how to use the Estafiate. Nora gave him good advice on his eating habits; and_told him to make a strong tea of estafiate, and to add a great handful of the herb in a warm bath to bathe in. Etta visited Emilita while James took his bath. After his bath, he slept soundly through the night; very unlike James. When he woke, he felt better and wished he had gone along with the other men.

The men rode home with the bull, and a brace of ducks they had shot. While on the trail, they ate fish that they caught in the lakes. At home, for the evening's supper, they all enjoyed roasted duck that the men cooked over a crackling campfire. Etta thought Harry looked thinner; while on the trail he got by mostly on strong black coffee; he didn't eat as well as he did at home.

A letter arrived, in early March, from Harry's sister, Samanna. Everything was fine at home. She mentioned her suspicion that her mail was being opened and suggested that he didn't write again in case the letters could be traced back to him. She asked him to telephone whenever he was in the states.

*

Word had spread that the territorial governor, Dr. Julio Lezana, was making an excursion through Chabut province. When it was learned that he would pass through Cholila, by the estancia of the Senor's Ryan and Place, many of the neighbors in the Cholila area, gathered there. The women brought food to impress the governor. James grilled prime cuts of beef. When the governor arrived, he was greeted with great enthusiasm. Etta played the violin, adding to the festive spirit. The governor was very much impressed by his gracious hosts

XII

Boston
1904

"Harry!" "Pete!" "Sister!" "Mabel!" The greetings and hugs in the entry of Ethel's house went on for some time. Finally, they heard Ethel call out softly, "Come here." In the sunny parlor, Etta kneeled down by her mother's high cane-backed wheelchair, hugged her and put her head in her mother's lap. "There now child, let me take a look at you."

"You look radiant Etta, and have you noticed that Mabel is also looking resplendent. My girls have been well looked after. Harry, come closer." Harry offered her his hand which Ethel held in both of hers. "Bring a chair over and sit next to me Harry. Tell me everything about life on your ranch, and what you and Etta do there with cows and sheep and such." Mabel and Etta fixed refreshments while Peter and Ethel sat listening, delighted to hear Harry's tales of life in Argentina.

They spent the better part of the week resting and spending as much time with Ethel as her energy allowed. Ethel needed rest as her health was continually declining. On Sunday, Uncle Stephen and Aunt Charlotte came for dinner. Stephen and Peter began to quietly discuss Ethel's estate, and then made a date to take a deeper look into her affairs.

Etta finally found the opportunity to speak with Aunt Charlotte about Anne. Her hope was that her aunt would hire Anne as a maid or kitchen helper. She knew Anne would prefer kitchen work, but those details could be worked out later. Charlotte was skeptical at first, then as Etta kept talking about Anne's competence, her qualifications, and her bright disposition; Charlotte became interested and asked if Anne would need the permission of her parents to immigrate to the Untied States. Etta asked Aunt Charlotte if she would write a letter stating, that should Anne wish to work for her and travel to the states, she would be guaranteed a position.

When that was accomplished, Etta was jubilant. Etta knew Anne would be treated well and be given new opportunities. She gave Aunt Charlotte the biggest hug.

Uncle Stephen asked Peter to drive him and Charlotte home, so the young couples could use his 1903 Cadillac touring car to travel around and sightsee the next week. Peter recently bought an Oldsmobile Brougham automobile in San Diego, and enjoyed driving. While the girls were getting ready, Harry drove around the neighborhood, and was surprised at how much he enjoyed it.

A drive through Cambridge and Harvard Square was on the list of what they wanted to do. Peter wanted to drive over to look at the Harvard campus. They walked around the grounds and were enormously impressed. Harry was somewhat in awe of the idea, of what kind of money and privilege it would take, to be a part of this academic world.

They took a day to stay at the house to rest, just be with each other, and prepare for a drive to Lexington the next day. Peter, with his fascination with battles and war, intended to see the Lexington Green where the Minutemen stood to fight off the British at the first battle of the American Revolutionary War, April 19, 1775. He thought it curious that it wasn't known who fired the first shot of the battle; however it was known as the, "Shot heard 'round the world."

They spent the night at an Inn on Massachusetts Avenue. Peter had everyone up and at em, early the next morning, as there was so much to see. They went by the Buckman Tavern, which had been a central point of the skirmish. They walked on, to see the Hancock-Clarke house, and then the Monroe Tavern, which the British had briefly occupied. They traveled on to the old cemetery where Mabel was impressed in the types and decorations of the headstones. Harry mentioned to Etta that he was enjoying this excursion. Peter's enthusiasm for history was contagious. Many years had gone by since Etta and Mabel had been to Lexington.

They stayed close to home the next day, taking walks around Cambridge. Mabel suggested they should all see the historic sites in Boston. So they were off again, to see the inner Harbor, the main port of Boston and on to Faneuil Hall near the waterfront. Mabel commented that at one time sheep were kept in the Hall. They walked around the Custom House and the State house on McKinley Square; then drove to north Boston to see the Old North church on Salem Street. Harry had to exclaim, "Look at that steeple, Pete; "One if by land, two if by sea." While they were driving along Beacon Street, Etta repeated a newly popular poem that Uncle Stephen had shared; "And this is good old Boston, the land of the bean and the cod; where the Lowell's talk only to Cabot's, and Cabot's talk only to God."

*

The ladies wanted more time to shop, so the next day, they took the streetcar downtown. Etta needed a new dress for dining out in Boston, and for living it up in St. Louis. Peter took advantage of the opportunity to suggest a walk, to have time to talk with Harry. He waited, to say what he needed to say, until they found a pub with a private table. "Harry, I am distressed to say; you've been found out. The Pinkerton's know you're in Argentina." Harry sunk down, put his hand to his head and said. "No, no; I thought so." "Harry, evidently there've been wanted posters placed throughout the western states, and I believe in New York. I've heard there are posters along the South American ports." It seems they got a hold of one of your wedding portraits. Did you send a photo to anyone? They also have a print of you with your gang, that was taken in Fort Worth. They've traced you from New York and have Etta's name as Ethel. Their search has evidently been widespread and very extensive."

"Pete, when Etta and I were at the passenger terminal in Buenos Aires, I saw posters for myself, James and, unbelievably, Etta. They're including her too. I didn't wait around to read it all; I needed to get away from the poster as fast as I could, to not be recognized, and I didn't want Etta to see it. When I went back to where Etta was sitting, she commented that I looked pale. Before we left the ranch, James said he had a feeling something was wrong and he'd be sleeping away from the cabin while we were gone. I hope he's alright. And to answer your question; I did send a photo to a friend up in Baggs, Wyoming. Damn, those Pinkerton's aren't fooling around."

"Harry, if they knew exactly where you were in Argentina; they would have been there. Mabel doesn't know, but I'm going to have to tell her something after we leave Ethel's; because, I don't think you should go back to Argentina."

"I have to go Pete; my partner's there and there are people I'm responsible for. But Etta shouldn't go back; could she stay with you and Mabel?" "Of course, and I agree, she shouldn't go back. We can't mention any of this while we're at Ethel's. When we get settled in St. Louis, and after the girls have had some fun at the Fair, we'll tell them. With all the crowds there, you'll be alright; besides, now you look different than in the pictures on the posters.'

That evening, while Mabel played piano for their entertainment, Etta noticed Harry was looking very glum. Peter was withdrawn also. What had they been talking about? The last thing she heard Pete telling Harry, was that Panama had declared independence from Columbia, and now construction had begun on a Panama Canal. But, this wasn't about Pete's politics!

*

The Louisiana Purchase Expedition, World's Fair and 1904 Summer Olympics

The next Monday afternoon, Uncle Stephen drove them to Boston's South Station to take the evening train to Chicago, where they would stay one night, then take the Illinois Central, "Chicago to St. Louis Special," and arrive at the St. Louis Union Station by Thursday morning. The St. Louis station had been expanded to accommodate all the visitors to this year's World's Fair. It was to be a very grand affair. St. Louis was experiencing a building boom, very evident in the central west end and along the north-south artery of Euclid Avenue.

Peter made arrangements for a furnished guest cottage with two bedrooms. Linen service was included. It had a fully equipped kitchen where they could prepare most of their meals. Peter thought this would be better for privacy. He was concerned with exposure for Harry and Etta, in public places. Even though the fair would be overrun with great hoards of people, he thought they'd be safe in the crowd.

As it had become their custom, they rested the day they arrived; dining out at a small eatery close by. The next morning they took streetcar rides around town to get their bearings and spent their time sight seeing in the city. The following day, they were up early and excited for their first day at the fair.

The Louisiana Purchase Exposition, Worlds Fair, and 1904 Summer Olympics; what grand events! Exhibits were staged by 62 foreign nations as well as 43, of the then 45, states. The buildings were grand neo-classical palaces. Mabel had read about the Palace of Fine Art, and was so anxious to see what it contained. There were over 1,500 buildings connected by seventy-five total miles of roads and walkways. It would take several days to even begin to get a quick look.

Etta tasted "Fairy Fluff" for the first time: another vendor called it "Cotton Candy." They all enjoyed ice cream on waffle cones. Hot dogs and hamburgers were popular with everyone, as well as the iced tea. They had never heard of Dr. Pepper before they tasted the beverage at the fair.

Festival Hall housed the world's largest organ in the world. In the music hall, they listened to an inconceivable phonograph that played music from a flat disk. The centerpiece of one of the many German exhibits was a bronze eagle featured hundreds of hand-forged bronze feathers. Mabel studied it for a very long time wondering at its workmanship and considering whether she could do sculpture. They spent a full day and were exhausted by the time they arrived back at the cottage late that evening.

They slept in, except for Peter who had been to the grocery store and returned with food for breakfast; bacon, eggs, canned apricots, bread for toast, butter, and a jar of his favorite strawberry jam. After a hearty breakfast, they took time to write postcards to send to family and friends; then they took a streetcar to the Anheuser Brewery on the waterfront.

In 1860, Eberhard Anheuser purchased a struggling brewery in St. Louis. After becoming partners with his son in law, Adolphus Busch, they introduced "Budweiser" in 1876; the first beer to be distributed nationally by rail. By 1901 the company was turning tons of hops into over a million barrels of beer each year. The couples toured the brewery, and bought a few bottles to take back to the cottage to enjoy with their dinners.

Then it was back to the fair, with another early start to again enjoy a full day. The summer day was especially hot and humid and everyone looked and felt a bit wilted. They sat and enjoyed the ragtime music of Scott Joplin, which had been recorded and was now being played on a phonograph.

Etta was extremely distressed seeing 'Geronimo', the famous former war chief of the Apache. He was on display in a teepee, selling his autograph in the Ethnology Exhibit. But the main draw was the Philippine exhibit. The United States had made the Philippine campaign the centrepoint of the Worlds Fair.

Exhausted, they sat in a large open pavilion and talked about the exhibits. Mabel looked peaked, so Peter found the nearest food concession, and then led them to tables where they recouped and ate a good meal. Later, when they were somewhat revived, they went on to the Palace of Agriculture, the grounds of which covered some 20 acres. They spent the remainder of the afternoon engrossed by the modern, scientific methods of farming and raising stock.

At the cottage that evening they were content with a small snack. The next day, Peter and Harry planned on going to an athletic event. This was the first year the Olympics were held in the United States. One of the most remarkable athletes was an American gymnast, George Eyser, who was winning an astonishing amount of medals, even though his left leg was made of wood.

The ladies rested that morning, enjoying each other's company. Mabel confided to Etta that she had missed her monthly time. "I really think I'm pregnant, so I'm going tell Peter; I wanted to be sure." "Mabel, how fabulous for you!" "Are you ready for children Etta?" "I think so dear sister. Harry and I talked about it just before this trip. I'm almost twenty-six. When we get back home, I'll take Nora's herbs."

Later that afternoon, the sisters enjoyed looking in the stores downtown. They arrived at the cottage just shortly after Peter and Harry. Etta saw, once again, that they looked worried, or troubled about something. What was it?

Harry opened a bottle of beer and poured four small glasses. He and Peter looked at each other and nodded; they couldn't put off the bad news any longer. When they were all sitting, Harry began by saying. "There just isn't a good way to tell bad news, and I'm afraid I have some. Detectives have traced our whereabouts to Argentina and are bent on finding us. They have our names and photos, including Etta's. That's why Etta can't return to Argentina."

Etta went white. There was absolute silence in the room. Peter then added. You must come home with us Etta." "No, what about Harry. We'll go someplace safe together." "Etta, dear, there isn't anywhere safe for you and me. If they've found us in South America, they'll find us anywhere. You have to go with Mabel and Peter. I have to return to tell James and then . . . . we'll see. At least no one knows who your family is, or where you come from. They think your name is Ethel." "No Harry, I'm staying with you." "Etta, there are wanted posters out, saying we're wanted, dead or alive! They've already traced us to New York, when we were there with James." "No, no, I'm going home with you, we'll find a different country to live. I don't want to live without you."

Peter was holding Mabel, who was nearly in a faint, clinging to Peter, trying to find comfort from this devastating news. Etta and Harry were looking at each other in silence with tears in their eyes. They sat talking it over just a short while longer before retiring to their rooms. It was the saddest night.

Early the next morning Peter excused himself, with the explanation of visiting an old schoolmate. He did know a former classmate who now lived in St. Louis, but his primary reason for the visit was to use the phone. After a short visit, he was given an empty office to place his call.

*

"Hello, Merritt, this is Pete. We're in St. Louis. How's everything there? Good, good. Remember the conversation we had about our friend? Yeah, well, you're going to need to go to their ranch to bring her home after all. She's reluctant, like we thought she might be. Her husband is going to talk her, but it'll take some doing. You know where the large envelope is in the safe. Take the entire envelope. In it, there's plenty of money and the map to their place. Get on the next train east, a soon as you can. You'll be on your own finding transport from New York City to Buenos Aires, and on to their ranch. Book any kind of passage that you can. The rest of the directions are in the envelope. We won't be leaving here for another week. If you get a good start, you should arrive at their place right about the same time as them. That's right. Bring her home Merritt. Good luck Merritt and thank you, thank you."

*

The fair was now merely a distraction from their worries. They still enjoyed many of the exhibits but not with the same enthusiasm. They also managed to go to the St. Louis Zoo and to an art museum that Mabel was interested in.

Before parting, Harry gave Pete a map that he'd been working on. "Pete, this map shows where some loot is buried, close by the Musselshell River, outside of Lavina, Montana. I'd like Etta to have the money. See here, where the river goes by, west of town; from that point, I'd say walk north about half a mile to where you see an opening in the rocks where there's a seasonal waterfall that drops about twenty feet. You'll see a tree on the east side. The loot's buried three feet south of the tree. Send Merritt with this map. He can find anything."

*

Etta and Harry left the day before Mabel and Peter, to be on their way again to Boston and then New York. They hoped to get on a freighter and not be noticed. Mabel fixed Etta's hair in a different way that included short bangs which looked awful, but did effectively change her appearance. Harry let his beard grow, though he didn't like the look or the feel of it.

Though they had enjoyed themselves and were happy for the time spent with Mabel, Peter, and Ethel, they returned home very saddened. Harry had gone to the port in New York alone to arrange for travel on a freighter. They boarded without any trouble and spent much of the time, on the voyage to Buenos Aires, in their room lying on the small bed, holding each other. They knew the good days, and any chance of living their lives in peace, were over.

XIII

Goodbye Argentina

Harry and Etta arrived back at Cholila three months after leaving St. Louis. They made the trip without any hindrance and stayed only briefly in Buenos Aires to wait for a steamer to Bahia Blanca. When they'd reached Trelew, they were apprehensive. However, Walter and Anne seemed to be in their usual dispositions; neither Harry nor Etta felt any change.

When Etta mentioned to Anne that coming to the ranch in March, next fall, wouldn't work out that year, Anne was greatly distressed at the news. Then Etta told Anne of her plan for Anne to have the opportunity to go to the states, and have a good home with her aunt and uncle in Boston, in exchange for helping with kitchen work. Her travel expenses and travel lodgings would be paid for. Anne cried with joy and asked how soon she could go. This was her dream come true. "Even though my father would not allow it, I must go!" Etta told her that it may not be until she wrote a letter, and the letter was received by her aunt; so she would know to expect Anne. She gave Anne the letter that affirmed that she had a position in Boston, which included Charlotte and Stephen's names, address, and telephone number. Etta told her to keep it safe until the arrangements were made. Anne kept thanking her and crying; it was difficult for Etta to leave her. Walter had their horses ready. He, Anne, and their mother bid them a good journey.

Harry planned a route just off the main roads and trails which led them to the ranch coming in more from the southwest. Sighting the ranch, Harry thought everything looked alright, but James was nowhere in sight. They inquired at the native enclave and were told that Senor Ryan was staying at his camp, just to the northwest, in the willows. Though they were tired, they rode to find James. Harry knew where James would make his camp. James most likely had seen them coming.

James had taken a hasty trip to Bahia Blanca to garner any information that might be circulating. As usual, his hunch was accurate. He found posters with, not just his and Harry's names and photos, but Etta's also, which made him extremely angry. When he rode back to the ranch, he was in a haze of thought; wondering if his friends had been caught. He was greatly relieved, and very pleased, to see them riding to his camp.

James made coffee; they talked over the situation and the need to make new plans. They discussed which of their neighbors could be trusted. James and Harry felt strongly that Davy, Dan, and Juan could be trusted; but not Perry, or his gossiping wife, not Wenceslao, Newberry, or any of the other ranchers in the area.

The matter of Etta's safety didn't come up until the men were walking alone, the next morning, when James said, "Harry this is goin to sound mean, but Etta can't stay with us; she could get killed." "I know it! Pete and I tried to get her to stay back in the states, and go home with them, but she wouldn't do it. But she's got to go back, there's no future here for any of us." "You're right; it's over here, for all of us. I'd say go back with her, but she's safer away from you. Tell her you're goin with her, if you have to, if that's what it takes to get her on a ship." "I get what you're saying, James, keep in mind, she can't go to the eastern ports; she'd be too exposed. The wanted posters are up all along the eastern ports of South America. Pete called Merritt to have him come here and take her home. If he gets here, he'll have to take her over the pass to Puerto Montt, then over to the coast of Chile, and get a ship there.

Harry was finally letting out how angry he was. "It's the Pinkerton's, and those guys are professional killers. They'll kill us. Remember, their story, about always getting who they look for." "Harry, why couldn't they have just forgotten about us? We don't rob trains, or banks anymore, and we're not even in the same country. Is it for money?" "James, I need to say something right here. I'm not going back to prison, and I know you feel the same way." "I understand what you're saying Harry, we'll have to keep each other from that."

Over the next couple of days, James and Harry removed what they needed from the house along with the things Etta asked for, including the journals she'd kept during her years at the ranch. They didn't explain to the families why they were living at the camp, other than it being a lot cooler in summer, under the trees. They told Davy that some old trouble had come back to them.

Harry and James were both talking to Etta, insisting that, for her safety, she had to leave. It offended her that they didn't understand; she felt the same as they about having nothing to go back to. Disconsolate, living with the tension of being found, or possibly ambushed; there was now strain between Etta and Harry over her leaving. At the camp, the atmosphere of defeat was disheartening.

Etta overheard a conversation between the men, when James was saying, "Once you've crossed the line, you're on the outside; outside the law, and outside society. You're not wanted back, you're not allowed back, and you don't want to go back. We've been livin outside the lines for a long spell. "Yep, maybe we've lost something, but like Etta understands, you gain something too, because you're outside the restraints of society's control, and its own deceitful and dishonest ways." "Hell, we came all the way down here to the Argentine Republic and all the way out here to Cholila, and they're still coming after us; ain't there no place left on this earth where'd we be safe?" "I guess that question's been answered James."

*

James was the first to notice a single rider heading for the ranch house. Harry and Etta kept low while James circled around behind the willows, coming out from east of the ranch. He made a decision right then to go up to the rider, and if the outcome was the worst, he'd at least, draw fire away from Etta and Harry. Their horses were hidden, but ready.

The man riding the horse didn't look familiar, yet he was riding at his ease up to the ranch. James saw him get off the horse and begin to look around. James rode in closer, his gun in his hand. He heard the man call out, "Butch, Harry." Just as James was closing in, he felt there was something familiar about the man after all. The man turned to face him. "Butch, is that you? It's me Merritt!" "Merritt! Dear boy! But you're no longer a boy!" James signaled to Harry by waving his arms in a fashion he'd used in their holdups and escapes, meaning, all's well; then he and Merritt rode out to meet Etta and Harry.

Harry and James knew the purpose of Merritt's visit. Etta didn't get it yet, but she would have to, and soon. She hugged Merritt and cried, and hugged him again. James and Harry shook hands with Merritt, and hugged him, though indeed, Merritt was now a man. Though he was only twenty three, he stood straight and showed the confidence of an older, experienced man.

Later that night when Etta had bedded down in the shelter, the men talked. Merritt told them what he'd heard or read of the old bunch. "I think you already know that Flatnose Currie was killed in Utah by Sheriff Jesse Tyler in 1900. Will Carver was shot and killed in Sonora, Texas, in '01; he was wanted on suspicion of murder. Ben Kilpatrick went to prison in'01 for passing money from a train robbery in Montana; Harvey too, but he escaped, and just last year was killed in Tennessee, while he was escaping from the Knoxville jail. Harry, did Pete tell you that the photograph that was made in Fort Worth was what got you all identified? Someone, with the law, saw it at the photographer's studio and from that they were able to identify everyone. You're the only ones left out. That reminds me; I found wanted posters for all three of you along the different ports in South America. They were written in Spanish. I took a couple of 'em down and tore 'em up. What's the plan for getting Etta home?"

*

"How can you say we have to part?" "Etta it's very likely we could be killed. James and I might have a chance, hiding out somewhere in South America. That's no life for you; and it's dangerous for you to be with us. You know that I can't ever go back to the states, Etta." "Harry, with different names and changing our looks, we could go somewhere. I heard that conversation you and James had. You'd rather die than go back to prison. Harry, I'd rather die than go back without you." "No, Etta. No. If I can figure out any other way, I can write to Pete and let you know. Meanwhile you have to be safe. I love you Etta." "Harry, no!" "Etta, you're not understanding me this time. I chose my own rope. You didn't! I'm gonna take a walk."

"Hey Harry!" "James, sorry if you heard that." "Yeah, I did hear, and kept listenin and heard her voice breaking. Harry, in all the situations Etta's ever been in with us, she's never broken—ever, never acted anyway but calm and steady. I figure she must be hurtin pretty deep. I'd say go with her someplace, but we had that conversation. Make it easy on her till she's safely gone. Tell her you'll be joining her, if you have to. But we can't tell anyone that she's leaving over the pass to Chile; we want her long gone before anyone even knows she left. Maybe spread it around that you're goin someplace with her, someplace different.

*

Etta stopped her protests when she realized how much her leaving was also hurting Harry. The circumstances were just as unbearable for him. She accepted that it was over; Harry, the ranch, James, Anne, her friends that had all become her family, and the pleasant way they lived. She went to Harry, who was sitting alone away from the camp. "I'll leave with Merritt as soon as he's ready." Harry just nodded.

Merritt didn't waste any time preparing for the trip. He took three days making charqui, while also getting other provisions ready. Nora watched him, and offered him dried fruit for his trip. She enjoyed talking with Merritt and was sorry he'd be leaving. She didn't yet know Etta was leaving, and would never return.

Etta asked Harry if he'd like to read the journals that she'd kept during their years at the ranch, before she packed them. He had difficulty keeping his eyes dry enough to read. While reading her words, he was assured without a doubt, that she'd been very happy with him at the ranch, and that she'd always felt loved and fulfilled. He grieved for her anguish and the hell he was causing her; and he grieved for himself as he read:

October, 15, 1902

The glory of the early morning sky inspires me; the splendor and brilliance of colour is breathtaking to behold. Harry and James are already out working the horses. I will write to Mabel this morning and tell her how good it was to see her, (though I missed my adored ranch home). I love my life here. The men are at their finest. The air still holds a chill, though spring is fast approaching. I plan on enticing my darling Harry into taking a late afternoon ride to watch the sun set.

After Harry and Etta had a conversation about Anne's future, Harry promised to send Davy, after they'd sold some livestock, with enough money to insure Anne's comfortable travel to the states. Etta wrote to her aunt to say that Anne would be traveling to Boston, and could possibly be arriving at the ports of New York sometime in their summer.

Harry gave Etta a Colt pistol to take, and gave Merritt two pistols. Etta and Merritt would be traveling north, then west, over the Andes taking the Cochamo Pass to Cochamo, and from there get a boat to Puerto Montt, where they would take a ferry to the Chilean coast.

Harry helped pack provisions for the journey that should sustain them through the pass. Before then, they'd get food from the villagers on the way. Water should be plentiful, though James told Merritt there would be none available while going over the pass. They picked out five strong mules for the trip. Merritt and Etta would use two for riding, and each would lead the mules that would be packed with provisions; perhaps more mules and provisions than they needed, but Harry wasn't taking any chances of an injured animal leaving them in a difficult situation.

Harry had given Merritt a very specific map with directions to get to the pass. They would be traveling north toward El Bolson, and continuing north to the trail marker; taking the trail going northwest—then directly west through the Cochamo cut, that was marked, Paso Rio Manso. He was to watch for a wood sign pointing the way to the town of Cochamo, where they were sure to find a boat to Puerto Montt. They could rest there then take a ferry to the coast of Chile. Fortunately, Merritt spoke some Spanish.

There was no Christmas or New Year's celebrating this year. Etta and Merritt were ready to leave on New Years Day. Parting was an excruciatingly sorrowful, distressing, and heartwretching moment. Saying their goodbyes; Etta gave a hug to James, who couldn't keep the tears from his eyes. Etta and Harry's last hug and kiss wasn't prolonged, as that would have made their separation even more unbearable. Their tears told it all. Harry and James watched them until they were out of sight. Etta never turned for a look back; if she had, she couldn't have gone on.

Etta left her violin and most of her personal items, taking only the minimum of what she would need on the journey. The afternoon she left, not wanting anyone to get a hold of Etta's things or take any kind of advantage in using them, Harry made a fire and burnt it all; though he would always keep the things she had made for him and their photographs.

"That's the end of it, nothin left. Let's get the hell out of here. I'm through." "Harry, that's the worst end for two people I've ever known. Dyin' in a train wreck would be better." "Yep, you're right. It's over here, it's over for all of us." "Remember, we're just sayin to folks that Etta's gone to Trelew with Walter, for supplies and to visit Anne; that'll set anyone in the wrong direction. We want her to have plenty of time before anyone gets any ideas."

"What do ya say we start rounding up some of the cattle an' drive em down to Trevelin? Ol' Fredrick has been aching to get some of our stock. Then hell, let's get as far away from here as fast as we can. Let's ride to the very end of the country." "I'm with you James and I've been thinking, since everything's ended, even promises, let's take a weighty withdrawal from a bank, get some money to send to Etta, and for Anne's trip to the states." "What the hell, we've got nothin to lose."

*

By the first week of February, James and Harry made it to very nearly the southern tip of Argentina. In Rio Gallegos, they found a bank that, plain and simple, cried out to be robbed. In the habit of their old style, they had fresh horses hidden and ready when they robbed the Banco de Londres y Tarapaca on February 14, 1905.

While the men were away from the ranch, Davy and Juan were startled by two riders coming up to the ranch wearing the clothes of city men. They feared it was federales who might cause problems for their patrons. They were much relieved that the riders represented the new census being taken, which was to account for the Argentine population in 1905. They were happy to tell the officers that Senor Place and Senor Ryan were the estancieros who lived at the ranch, and that they were away selling cattle and maybe buying another bull.

*

Harry and James arrived back at the ranch by the end of April. Harry had already converted the pesos and sterling pounds to gold notes which he sent to Peter's office address, without any return name or address. He trusted a generous amount with Davy, to bring to Anne for her travel expenses, as he had promised Etta; and he gave a substantial amount to Davy for his help.

The two men immediately left again. They made arrangements for their stock to be sold to the Cochamo Land and Cattle Company, and then headed for Chile. They followed the trail that Etta and Merritt had taken so they could talk to the locals along the way and hear if there was any talk of recent mishaps or peculiar incidences along the trail.

They continued on, into Chile, eventually arriving in Valparaiso. By the end of June; Harry wrote a letter to his friend, Daniel Gibbon, who was a good friend and neighbor; instructing him to sell off anything that was left, keep the money for himself, and to give some to Davy. Harry didn't know that Dave and his wife left, just after him and James. He and his wife, Emilita were moving to Barranquilla, Colombia, where Emilita had relatives. The money Harry had given him had enabled them to make the move they'd dreamed about for some time.

Anne was relieved to have the company of Dave and Emilita and their support to help her leave home. Her mother was told of Anne's plan, but not her father, who would never have let her leave. Her brother, Walter, helped in her departure, saying he was bringing her to the ranch, but instead brought her to meet Dave and Emilita at the Trelew train station, where they took the train to Bahia Blanca.

Afraid that her father might look for her; Anne didn't want to stay alone for the week or more that it would take to board a ship from Buenos Aires going to New York. She felt safer continuing on with Dave and Emilita by the smaller ship to Columbia, where she rested at the home of Emilita's family before going on. Then she took a steamer the short distance to Colon, Panama, and from there she boarded a ship to New York without any delay. Panama's port was bustling with workers and supplies coming in on ships for the construction of the new canal.

While Anne traveled with Dave and Emilita, she posed as their daughter. Now, traveling alone, she used Etta's name, as she had first learned it, Mrs. Ethel Place. She stated her age as being twenty-four when she gave her information for registering to board the S.S. Seguranca, though she was now just eighteen, the same age as Etta when she first left Boston to go west. Anne wasn't aware of the possibility of extreme peril that she had put herself in by using Etta's name.

PART III

XIV

San Diego 1905-1908

"Tell me about the trip Merritt." "Pete, let's go out to the carriage house and have a whiskey, I've got a lot to tell." "Good, I'll tell Mabel; she's helping Etta wash up and get in bed. With Mabel due next month, we also have to be concerned with her. She's better now that you're both back; and I was greatly relieved when you phoned from the docks." Etta had completely broken down at the sight of Peter, and nearly collapsed. Merritt and Peter held on to her and almost carried her to the car.

"Pete; it was awful, just awful! First, Etta and Harry's parting was just too painful to witness. By the way, they had a nice ranch, a lot of good stock, and Etta made the ranch house real nice. Harry and Butch were leaving the place right after we left. What a shame. What a damn shame." Merritt slumped on the old wood chair.

"It's a bad deal all around. Are you sure you're alright Merritt, sure you don't need to rest and talk another time?" "No, no, Pete, I need to tell you about it. The first few days out was an easy ride; Etta and I each led pack mules. Etta didn't talk all day, barely ate; when she bedded down, she cried all night. The next few days, going over the pass was the same. She just gave the lead to her mule, which was exactly what worked—footing was uncertain and real hazardous, but we were on good mules. At one place I questioned our position. She said she didn't care if she was lost because it didn't matter where she was. She was getting real weak. I was afraid she'd fall off her mule. I'd forgotten there was some whiskey in a saddle pack; when I remembered, I asked her to drink some, and she did, and that night she ate a little. So I gave her some every night until it ran out; it helped her to eat."

"We made our way over the pass and down to a small village in Chile; then headed just a short ways south to Cochamo on the waterway where I sold the mules, and found a fishing boat that would take us to Puerto Montt. There, I found a place for Etta to rest a couple days. She was in bad shape. She finally slept and ate. Then we took a steamer, kind of a ferry, out to the coast. We stayed in the coast town of Ancud until I found a steamer going to Valparaiso. The voyage didn't do her any good."

"We stayed in Valparaiso for about a week, and she began eating more and got a little color back, but you can see how thin she is. There were freighters going to San Francisco on a regular route but I didn't think she could hold up to the trip back down to San Diego on the train. So, it took a couple of freighters, stopping once in Peru to find another ship to get us to San Diego. It took us several weeks to get here from Valparaiso. She stayed in the small cabin most of the time. I slept on deck. I made her walk to meals, and most often we took her food out on deck for her to eat."

After Valparaiso, when we were on the first freighter, she finally began talking about her life with Harry in Argentina. By the time we were on the second ship she was asking about you and Mabel, and I told her everything I could think of to help her start thinking about her future life here. I told her Mabel was expecting a child. I told her your father had been west for a visit, and that your mother still hadn't written. I didn't tell her that her mother was now in worse health.

"As we got closer to San Diego, Etta made a strong effort to rally. She started to ask about what I was doing, and wanted to know more about you and Mabel, and if Mabel was keeping up with her painting. I think her love for her sister and knowing she couldn't be a burden or a strain on Mabel, helped her pull out from her misery. Those were sorrowful days for Etta, but she's got a strong mind and will. She'll get through it, but, Pete, her spirit's deeply injured."

*

The sisters talked and rested for the next month. Mabel was very uncomfortable and hoping each day was the day; she was past her due date. Merritt did the cooking. Pete spent short days at the office. Everyone was waiting for the moment when they would meet the new member of the family. Peter picked the name, Joseph Thomas, for his boy. Mabel liked the name Ariel Florence, if she was a girl. Peter didn't like the name but wasn't worried because he was sure he had a boy.

"Etta, I've been talking with Merritt, and I need to bring up the subject of your safety. I really don't feel there is any worry with you here, as your background is unknown to the authorities. But, for a while, may we call you Laurie in public? As your full name is Lauretta, it's just another version of your name." "That's fine with me Peter, though it may take some getting used to, especially for Mabel; she's the one that began calling me Etta from the time I was born."

*

"Mabel, she's the most beautiful work of art you've ever created. Peter is so proud of you, and so am I. I'm in absolute wonder at what you've done. Peter's already so in love with her." "You know Etta, I was worried about if the baby was a girl, but Peter does love her and shows how proud he is. Etta, he doesn't like the name Ariel; I guess that isn't a good choice. What's a good name for her?" "How about Alma? There's a town in New Mexico named Alma; I've never been there, but isn't it a lovely name." "It is, I'll suggest it to Peter; Alma Florence. Remind Peter to call mother, will you Etta." "Oh Mabel, he's already called her twice to tell her about his beautiful and bright daughter; and he's written to his mother. Merritt can hardly wait for you to come home so he can meet "the new angel."

The baby's nursery was divided between Etta's bedroom and Mabel and Peter's. Mabel was very tired and had a difficult time recuperating. Many nights, when the baby was fussing, Etta would hold her, sitting in the rocking chair. Long after Alma stopped crying and was sleeping peacefully in her arms, Etta continued rocking and crying silently. When she finally laid the baby down and tried to get some sleep, she would often have nightmares. Even the times she woke from pleasant dreams of Harry, they caused her an aching sorrow.

The sisters had always been close and now it seemed even more so. They spent every part of the day together. Etta had arrived wearing a travel worn dress and had only travel-worn clothes in her pack. They looked forward to a shopping trip downtown as soon as they each felt up to it. Mabel looked in her closet trying to find more dresses that Etta would like. While they were looking over clothes and jewelry, Etta remembered her gold lapel watch that Harry had bought for her during their honeymoon in San Francisco, and went to her room to get it. She brought it in and showed Mabel. Mabel had admired it when she'd seen Etta wearing it during her trips to the states. "Mabel, would you keep this for me. I won't be wearing it again; and here's my wedding ring also. Please, just keep them tucked away in your jewelry case."

*

Both Mabel and Etta were regaining their strength and were enjoying walking out in the garden. Mabel was holding Alma and was trying to read a letter from Peter's brother. "Etta, listen to this; Peter's brother will come here for a visit the first week in July. Oh, that's splendid, we'll have a fourth of July picnic. You know, I think Peter's mother is getting curious now that she has a granddaughter. I wonder if we'll hear from her after Thomas visits us."

When Thomas arrived, he spent most of the first day staring at Alma; she was so pretty. He hadn't been around babies and certainly didn't see any on the campus of New York School of Law. He was following in Peter's footsteps, with his mother's plans that he join a law firm in New York City.

By the time Thomas arrived, Mabel and Etta were greatly recovered and enthusiastic about preparing a sumptuous feast for their holiday picnic. They finally decided on the San Diego City Park for their picnic. Up early; Peter packed his new car with what he said was a weeks worth of food, which just might be enough for Tom. They spent a quiet day; the women with the baby stayed close to the table and the blanket; Thomas and Peter took long walks.

Merritt didn't go along on the picnic, as he was taking a young lady out for a drive in his new automobile, actually Pete's old Oldsmobile. Peter gave it to Merritt when he returned with Etta. Peter's gratitude was immeasurable. Merritt was a well loved, and valued member of the family.

*

A letter from Peter's mother arrived not long after Thomas's return to New York. With no apologies, she announced that she was coming for a visit. Peter was noticeably emotional. Mabel was nervous until Peter read a letter from Thomas. Thomas wrote that he'd told their mother of Mabel's background and fine manners; also that she was an exceptionally gifted and highly regarded artist. Most of all, he'd told his mother about the beautiful baby, Alma. Thomas had also mentioned Mabel's sister Laurie; and that she was also a very pretty lady who was a great help to them. He told his mother that Peter was doing very well and looked better than ever. Gertrude had to see all this for herself.

Throughout Gertrude's visit, Etta boarded with a friend of Mabel's, who lived just two blocks away. As it turned out, Gertrude wasn't so formidable after all. Both Mabel and Etta admired Gertrude's elegant posture and stylish clothes. Alma was completely taken by her grandmother who unreservedly doted on her. They barely had a chance to hold the baby, as she was always in Gertrude's arms. She stayed two weeks and complimented Mabel several times on her paintings. Mabel gave Gertrude a painting of the ocean and cliffs she'd been admiring. Gertrude was also astonished at the fine dinners that Mabel served. Gertrude never cooked, and was rarely seen in her kitchen. Mabel was thankful for all the fine linens her mother had given her; they made a good impression.

At the end of her stay, she essentially pleaded with Mabel and Peter to come to New York to visit. She would hire a nurse for the baby while they were there. When they showed some hesitation of traveling with the baby; Gertrude invited herself for Christmas. The idea was well received by all. After his mother had been put on the train; Peter exclaimed, "There'll be no room in the apartment after Alma's Christmas presents arrive."

*

Mabel and Etta's younger brother, Buddy, was now attending Stanford University in Palo Alto. This summer he didn't return home to Boston; instead he continued with his studies and explored California. Ethel was now getting dreadfully weak and didn't want him to see her in her infirmity, so she had encouraged him to stay in California. Buddy arrived just a week after Gertrude left. He, like the others, was amazed and taken with the beautiful baby; his sister's daughter.

Bud spent a lot of time with Peter; going with him to his office and walking around downtown San Diego. When he met Merritt, he found him fascinating and wanted to learn all about him and listen to him talk about the ways of the west.

*

Etta often wondered if Anne had been helped, and would be traveling to Boston. All this time, her aunt hadn't received any word of her coming. Finally, in late August, Etta had a telephone call from Aunt Charlotte saying Anne had arrived, but not after a very difficult passage. Anne had telephoned her from New York City, before taking the train to Boston where Uncle Stephen retrieved her at Boston's North Station.

The ship Anne arrived on had a Yellow Fever outbreak onboard, causing the passengers to be quarantined after their arrival in New York. The sickness had started in Panama with the canal workers who quartered in the second class berths. Fortunately, Anne spent her money on a first class compartment. Though grateful that she never contracted the disease, she'd felt like a prisoner in her cell while waiting to be released. She didn't complain, because she wouldn't want to bring the disease to her new employers' home.

Aunt Charlotte was very pleased to find such a wholesome girl, and was probably spoiling her by insisting that Anne rest for a week before starting her duties as kitchen helper and housekeeper. Hearing the news, Etta laughed and then cried with relief and joy for Anne.

14, September 1905

Dear Etta,

Thank you forever for helping me to find a way to improve myself. I was surprised to hear you are now in the

United States with your sister and her family. I hope you are well.

Your aunt is a kind and cheery lady who makes me feel at home here. I get lost when I'm out on errands. On my day off, I will explore and learn my way to make an improvement.

I traveled with Davy and Emilita to Columbia; they moved there to live with her sister. Davy will maybe get work in the building trade there. I arrived in the United States from Panama on a ship that had contact with yellow fever that made us be in quarantine for twenty days.

Many times, I knew I must be brave, and then I thought of you and how you always stayed strong in every situation. I have seen many places now. The world is wonderful. I am very happy, and I hope to meet you again.

Affectionately yours,
Anne

*

Christmas 1905 was the most festive Mabel and Peter had celebrated in the eight years they had been married. The Christmas of 1900 was on their minds and Etta was suffering with her memories. Gertrude, though a bit stiff, in her reserved style, proved to be a woman of many interests and was a fascinating conversationalist, which made for animated discussions and helped Etta get through the holidays.

Merritt joined in the New Year's celebrations. When he had a moment to talk with Etta; he toasted her with his glass of champagne, and reminded Etta of when they first met in Raton and Harry ordered champagne to celebrate his using the name Merritt. Etta lifted her glass and smiled. "Merritt GoForth Barnes, you were like a younger brother to me then, and now you're my big brother and protector. Thank you with all my heart Merritt."

Rather than being an occasion for hope in the future; the New Year, 1906, only reminded Etta of what she had left behind. Two envelopes had arrived at Peter's office last year, postmarked Chile. There was no note or return address, but they knew the money was from Harry. Merritt converted the gold notes to U.S. currency and deposited the money in Peter's office account. Etta would open an account so it could be transferred. Her trust money was still in a joint account with Mabel.

Mabel noticed that Etta seemed to be going through the motions of living, but wasn't the lively and vibrant person she'd been when she lived with them five years ago. Time was Mabel's only hope for Etta. Etta was a joyful aunt when she was with Alma, and Mabel was grateful, as Alma adored her aunt.

*

Peter answered the telephone very late one evening in March; it was Uncle Stephen. Ethel had passed away that evening. Just from looking at Peter, Mabel knew and surrendered to weeping. Peter held his wife while she cried on his shoulder.

They woke Etta with the news. She hugged and cried with Mabel, and worried about this being too much strain on Mabel. Peter fixed brandy toddies. They talked and decided that Etta would take a train to Boston, attend the funeral, and help Aunt Charlotte pack up the household. They would sell the house when that was done. Peter and Uncle Stephen were the executors of Ethel's estate, most of which had already been transferred to Mabel, Etta, and Bud.

It had been years since Etta had traveled by train through the west. She tried to find strength in memories while grieving for her losses. She never expected to hear from Harry again; she told herself over and over to let it go though she still loved him deeply.

Uncle Stephen picked up Etta at the train station and took her to their home. She surprised Anne when she walked into the kitchen. Charlotte gave Anne the day off to be Etta. The ladies hugged and cried. They had a lot to catch up on. With difficulty, Etta explained to Anne that the men had business dealings that caused problems for them in the states, which were now affecting them in Argentina.

Anne was Etta's only link to her life in Cholila. Charlotte, noticing that talking with Anne was helping Etta, suggested that Anne work at Ethel's house and help Etta with the packing. Etta had many pieces of her mother's furniture and fine things crated for train transport to San Diego. Some items were sold and some were stored at their aunt and uncle's. Uncle Stephen and Peter would work out the legal and business matters.

While she was in Boston, Etta heard the news of the devastating earthquake and fire in San Francisco. Much of the city's downtown was lost, including the magnificent Palace Hotel where she and Harry had stayed while on their honeymoon. More loss. Weeks later she read that the citizens of the city were already cleaning up and rebuilding, and the Palace Hotel would be rebuilt.

She was exhausted when she returned to San Diego; though it had been good to be busy. She decided to look for a job, and was hoping Peter knew of a law office needing a secretary, though her skills might be too rusty. She might look into part-time store work; that way she could still help with Alma who was now a year old. Etta was now twenty-eight.

*

1906 passed swiftly. There had been an earthquake in Valparaiso in August that was at least as terrible as the one in San Francisco in April. Etta wondered where Harry was. She knew he was no longer at the ranch. She had a deep ache for him that would not leave.

Gertrude had been back for a visit at Easter and again for Christmas. Mabel and Peter thought that perhaps they might travel to New York the next year. Mabel would love to see Gertrude's house; she'd been told of her fabulous painting and sculpture collection.

The next January, Harriet, Mabel's friend and neighbor, took care of Alma while Mabel, Peter, and Etta went to see the world's first feature film, "The Story of the Kelly Gang." They enjoyed it, though all through the film Mabel kept watching Etta, hoping she was all right. She knew there was no doubt that Etta was thinking of Harry.

There had been a short, twelve minute moving picture film that Etta hadn't seen, which Peter and Mabel went to see in 1903; it was Edison's "The Great Train Robbery." The 1903 film was originally advertised as "a faithful duplication of genuine 'Hold Ups' made famous by various outlaw bands in the west." The plot was inspired by a true event that occurred on August 29, 1900 when four members of Butch Cassidy's, "Hole in the Wall Gang" stopped the No. 3 train on the Union Pacific railroad tracks near Tipton, Wyoming; where the robbers forced the conductor to uncouple the passenger cars from the rest of the train and then blew-up the safe in the mail car, escaping with $55,000 in cash and gold coin.

In 1907, Gertrude came to visit mid March and stayed until after Easter. Mabel and Peter didn't make the trip east that year, and so Gertrude arrived again in December, just before Christmas, bringing the customary stockpile of presents for Alma. She and Mabel were becoming friends even though Gertrude would like to have more say in Alma's future education. She wanted a private school education for Alma, while Mabel thought the public school would give her a more normal life.

*

By chance, Etta started working in a piano store. While the piano tuner was at the apartment, tuning Mabel's piano, he and Etta started a conversation. He needed someone to help at the store while he was out on his appointments tuning pianos; a person who could play piano adequately. Perfect! Etta showed him her basic skills and was hired, using the name Laurie. Merritt drove her to and from her work, three days a week. On her days off, Etta watched over Alma while Mabel would paint. Aunt and niece enjoyed their slow walks to the neighborhood park.

*

Peter and Mabel were now ready to buy a house; they all needed more room. They talked about where to live. Fate had brought them to San Diego. Should they stay? Peter was constantly reading about commerce and trade in San Francisco; in 1908, it was still the financial center of the west. They decided that Peter should go and see what the city looked like, meet with bankers and find out about house prices.

Peter left for San Francisco the end of September. The weather was perfect, though there was usually an impenetrable dense fog lolling on the ocean and bay in the mornings. Introducing himself to bankers and getting to know them was incentive enough for Peter to move to this city. He really liked their savvy outlook for the future.

Mabel wanted a house in a nice neighborhood away from downtown. Peter found just the house in the Pacific Heights area. It was everything Mabel hoped for, and there was a large sunny room that would be an excellent studio for her painting. He telephoned Mabel and described the house. "It's away from downtown, but very easy to get to; transportation's close by. It has a large yard with a balcony and a terrace in back. In front there's a large covered entrance. There are some steps up to the front door. The house is a crisp gray, with white trim; a very attractive two story house. It's on Scott Street, in a sunny neighborhood. Across the street is an open, wide expanse that takes up over four square blocks and it's now being turned into a spacious park, and the house has wonderful views of the city and across the bay.

After Mabel heard the details of the house, she wanted Peter to tell Etta, and ask her if she knew about the neighborhood. Etta had been to the area but didn't recognize the street name. She was aware that it was a very good neighborhood. Peter's excitement was contagious, the ladies were thrilled.

Peter's law partner had referred him to William Crocker, the owner of the Crocker Bank on Montgomery Street; the son of Charles Crocker, a financier of the Central Pacific Railroad. Crocker Bank had withstood the Panic of 1907, and Crocker had been an advocate of the Aldrich-Vreeland Act that established the National Monetary Commission to investigate the panic and to propose legislation to regulate banking.

Peter was pleased to meet the civic minded man. When much of the city was destroyed by the fire in 1906, William Crocker and his bank were major forces in financing the reconstruction. Crocker and his wife had sponsored a relief camp at Union Square. Peter secured a loan for the purchase of the house through William and knew he'd met a future friend.

Peter returned home with the news that they could move the first of the year. The apartment immediately became full of activity; packing their belongings and crating Mabel's paintings. Alma was enjoying the boxes to climb on and play in. Etta was doing better now that she was so busy with work, and helping with Alma, though she still had nightmares.

"Etta, I've expected you." "Harry, darling, you're here with me. This is our camp, at the lake, isn't it! How is it we're here?" "You know I love you Etta, and I'm sorry for giving you grief." "Harry let's go home. Why can't I open the door? It's not locked, but I don't have the strength to push it open. Harry what's the matter?" "Etta, our love has always been strong; now I need to tell you that Butch and I are gone. We ended our lives." "No, no, Harry, no! But, can we stay here together?" "No Etta, you have a life ahead. I've come to say goodbye. I'm going, but my love will always be with you. I love you Etta." "Wait Harry, don't go. Harry, I love you! Harry! Harry! Harry!

"Etta, Etta, wake up. You've had another nightmare. You were calling for Harry." "No Mabel, not a nightmare, or maybe a nightmare, yes." She couldn't go back to sleep, so she got up to go to the front parlor. As she passed the grandfather clock in the hallway, the one her father had bought in Hong Kong and had sent home to Boston, she looked to see the time, and saw that the date on the clocks' calendar read, November 6, 1908.

XV

San Francisco 1909-1910

Mabel and Peter, along with Alma, Merritt, and Etta, watched the Oldsmobile and Ford automobiles being loaded on the flatcar of the freight train that would also take their furniture and household goods to San Francisco. Once aboard the passenger train, and on their way, Peter enjoyed pointing out scenery and points of interest while they traveled to their new home in northern California.

Peter made arrangements for them to stay the first week at the Fairmont Hotel on Nob Hill, not too far from their new house. While they waited for their things to be delivered and the furniture to be set up, they toured the city. Much had changed from 1900 when Etta and Harry spent their honeymoon there.

Mabel and Etta could not believe the grandeur of the new Victorian chateaux. The house had been built by a banker in 1907 whose finances had since failed. It had been put up for sale shortly before the time of Peter's visit. William Crocker had suggested the property.

The rebuilt Palace Hotel was nearing completion. Mabel could hardly wait for it to open to see the new16 foot long painting, "The Pied Piper of Hamlin." Maxfield Parrish had been paid a whopping fee of six thousand dollars for the work. Etta wanted to see the Garden Court restaurant that was being built where the horse-and-carriage entrance had once been. The City of Paris department store was being rebuilt. Lotta's fountain was still there. To Etta, it looked like a new city. She sensed that San Franciscan's felt the same pangs of loss and desire as she.

Finally, their crates, boxes, and furniture were delivered and Peter and Merritt collected their cars at the station. The stored furniture at Aunt Charlotte's had been sent out which included two tall Chinese chests, a Chinese desk, an enormous mahogany dining table and the side buffet with its enormous mirror, a china cabinet, crates of silver flatware, linens, and heavy crystal pieces that could now adorn their new home. They had plenty of room now to enjoy these beautiful furnishings.

Merritt found a studio apartment on Stockton Street, in the north beach district. He and Pete scouted for an office to rent. They found one in the Flood Building on Market and Powell Streets, though it was perhaps too large for just one Attorney.

Peter telephoned William Crocker to set an appointment for when they might talk. They met for lunch at Tadich's near the bank, and talked about the city's future. Peter realized he'd need to quickly learn the ways of the city. He told William about the suite of offices he'd found in the Flood Building, and his worry that it may be too expensive if he didn't find an associate to share it with him. William helped him out again by suggesting Frank O'Brien, a young, up and coming attorney, much like Peter.

*

After lunch Peter invited William to view his new house. Mabel was aghast, she had a scarf covering her hair, Alma was a mess, and the household was in a state of pandemonium from the unpacking. William however, was charmed and quite taken with Mabel. He told her that the new Alta Plaza Park that was being built up across the street, was originally a rock quarry, and that the area had been used as a camp for refugees of the '06 earthquake and fire.

Before William left, he noticed the crates of paintings. Seeing a few of them open, he exclaimed to Peter, "Ahh, you're a collector of fine Artwork, I see." "A collector of Mabel's artwork, William." "Let me have a look. They're good, they're truly magnificent! My wife would love to see these! She is a patron of French Impressionist artists." "Give Mabel a little time to put the house together and we'll certainly enjoy welcoming you both for dinner, and for viewing Mabel's paintings."

*

Peter was establishing himself in San Francisco. His law practice was now concentrated on estate and probate law, as well as real estate law. He worked closely with William Crocker, whose friendship he greatly enjoyed. William introduced Peter to James Phelan, another banker, who had been mayor of the city from 1897 to 1902; another progressive thinker and steward of the city.

The Crocker's did come for dinner, and thereafter came often to visit. Ethel Crocker was astonished to find Mabel's paintings of such high caliber. She bought two paintings right off the walls of their home. She encouraged Mabel to join the San Francisco Institute of Art; certainly not because she needed instruction, but to enjoy the camaraderie of the other artists and instructors. Mabel did enroll and was asked to teach. She declined. Students still learned a good deal by watching her paint; and she was often joined at the park across the street from her home by students and new friends from the school.

Etta loved the city; she walked over the hills to the north beach district or rode a trolley downtown; sometimes she walked straight down Scott Street to the marina by the bay. She talked with fishermen at the wharfs. She would take a ferry to Oakland and look over at the Alcatraz Island, where the Lighthouse had been torn down to build a military prison. Occasionally she would go to the Cliff house. She watched the rebuilding of the Palace Hotel and the development of San Francisco as it became a very grand and cosmopolitan city. Etta often felt a wistful longing while seeing familiar sights, and recalling her honeymoon with Harry.

Etta continued to have struggles with her memories and requested more of Merritt's time, asking him to tell her about Harry and his robberies, during the years before they went to Argentina. Her days passed more easily when she was working. Peter, and his associate Frank, occasionally had more work than their secretary could handle. Etta would help out during those times, which were becoming more and more frequent. She also loved teaching and playing with Alma, who at age four could say and write the alphabet and was learning to read. Alma also showed an inherent talent for drawing.

Part of his time, Merritt was busy tracking down details and information for Peter. Many records had been lost or destroyed in the 1906 fire, so some clients had difficulty, even now, in proving their claims to property. Merritt was helpful in locating people who might help support these claims. Another interest of Merritt's was fixing automobiles. He had taken apart and rebuilt his car, and fixed Peter's on several occasions. He was now renting an area in a livery that had room for him to fix automobiles for the public.

There was still a mix of horses and automobiles on the streets. He was a good mechanic, and was developing steady customers. His only advertisement was "word of mouth" and it was paying off profitably.

*

In late spring of 1909, Peter read an account in the newspaper, that the outlaws, Butch Cassidy and the Sundance Kid, were dead from a shoot-out in San Vicente, Bolivia the previous year in November. Found with the men was the Aramayo Mine Company payroll and a stolen company mule. There had been an identification of the bodies; however the information seemed vague. He felt unsettled about the news and grieved that his friend had met with such a bad end. Harry would be just forty-one years old.

In the privacy of his office, he told Merritt the news. Merritt was extremely distressed at this and it took awhile before he could speak. "Do you think it's really them?" "It appears to be so. I've been reading the bulletins and it seems the Pinkerton's never stopped looking for them, and still had wanted posters out for them." "Are you going to tell Etta?" "Yes, Merritt I think so. Maybe now she'll let go, and her nightmares will stop."

The next morning, Peter and Etta were sitting in the breakfast room, and Mabel was gathering her art supplies, getting ready to go to the Art Institute when Merritt arrived at the house. "Would you like me to take you, with all your art stuff, Mabel?" "No, Merritt, Marianne, from the institute, is coming by to get me any minute now. Bye-bye all. See you at dinner; you too Merritt."

Peter got right to the point. "Etta, please stay at the table, I have some bad news. I've read in the papers that Butch and Harry have been killed. Evidently, it was in Bolivia, after robbing a mining company payroll." Etta just sat there, eyes wide. Neither of the men knew what to say. Finally, she said, "Yes, Peter, I know, though I didn't want to believe it was true." "What? You know? How do you know?" "Harry came to me, I guess you'd say in a dream, and told me; but that was back in November, last year." Peter rushed over to where his stack of newspapers was kept and found the article. "Yes it says it was last November." "The evening of the sixth?" "The article states the seventh, but how did . . . . ?" Then Merritt asked her if she was alright, and if he could bring her anything. Etta said she just needed to be quiet awhile, and then planned on taking Alma for a walk to visit a neighbor later in the afternoon. She just sat there; this agonizing news made Harry's death undeniably true.

That afternoon, at the livery, Merritt was surprised by a visit from Peter. "Merritt, you read that article; do you think it really happened that way?" "I've been thinking about it too Pete and I'd like to know if it's really true and if it was really them. I'm thinking, what you're probably thinking; what really happened; I want to find out." "Merritt, your business is just building up; you don't want to leave it." "No, but it'll be here when I get back. I can move out of my studio, and store my things in your basement." "Merritt, I would have never asked you, but it sure as hell would clear my doubts. Harry was a friend of us both. I'll finance your trip. You'll have it easier and more comfortable this time—not being on the run. I think it's them, but we have to know. I looked it up; you'll have to go to Tupiza, Bolivia to the mining company offices. See if anyone knows anything there and then go to San Vicente, Bolivia. If there was any way of Harry's being alive, and you could find him, bring him here." "Are you going to tell Etta? Or Mabel? We can say I'm going on a long trip to visit my people in Oklahoma." "Merritt, that's what we'll say."

*

Before he left, Merritt finished building a combination climbing and swing set for Alma for the backyard. Mabel was overjoyed to announce that another child was on the way. Peter, on hearing the news, hired a young woman to come in weekdays to help with the housework and some cooking, explaining, "Mabel must take it easy, and Etta shouldn't have to do all the work. This way Mabel will have more time to paint and to be with Alma."

The family spent a quiet enjoyable summer. Mabel stopped hauling her outdoor easel and paints around town at Peter's request. She enjoyed painting in Golden Gate Park on Sundays while on picnics with Peter and Alma and Etta. The sisters were slowly meeting the neighbors and still acquainting themselves with San Francisco's history. Peter helped Etta plant the gardens in the back yard. Mabel had designed brick walkways winding through sections of flowers and lawn. There was a place for growing vegetables, and vegetables grew among the flowers. Pansies were Mabel's favorite. Etta enjoyed her time working in the garden, though there was the pain of remembering her garden in Argentina.

On a day when Etta was working at Peter's office, Peter invited her to join him for lunch with William Crocker and the mayor, Edward Taylor. Etta's quick intelligence and beauty charmed the mayor. Mayor Taylor was the oldest mayor on record in the city. He had been a lawyer and was also a poet; he promised to give a book of his sonnets to Etta. The next day he was at Peter's office with a booklet for her.

That September, E.H. Harriman, president of the Union Pacific Railroad, died. Peter had followed his career and knew it was Harriman who was responsible for the intense manhunt for Butch Cassidy and the Sundance Kid; employing the Pinkerton's to track them down and end their train robbery career one way or the other. The idea of Posse cars on the trains was Harriman's idea. A smart one; it made train robbery an even more risky and dangerous game. After Wells Fargo Bank fell under Harriman's control; he merged it with Nevada Bank and moved its headquarters to New York City. Peter had no doubts that Harriman knew the story of the deaths of Butch and Harry.

There had been one letter from Merritt, sent to Peter's office address, saying he had arrived in Bolivia and would wait until he was back home to tell Pete what he had learned. He planned to be home by Christmas.

*

On December 8th, Etta went to the newly opened Palace Hotel to see the changes that were made in restoring the hotel. The dining room was a splendid as ever. What had been the Grand Court was now enclosed. It was now the Garden Court, an enormous space with marble columns and a towering glass ceiling. Etta ordered a cup of tea, and sat for a long while, partly reminiscing and part hoping Harry would walk in and they would then go upstairs to their room. Before she left the table, she said softly, "Happy Anniversary darling Harry. I love you."

Gertrude wasn't sure if she should come at Christmas, with Mabel so close to her due date, or wait until after the new baby arrived. Peter, knowing Mabel would like a very quiet home at the time of the baby's arrival, consulted with her, and then encouraged his mother to come for Christmas. Besides, Alma would miss her grandmother if she wasn't there for the holidays. Their decorations were kept simple this year so Mabel would not over-do.

Now, the New Year had arrived though Merritt still had not. Mabel was worried. "Surely he would have written if he was delayed in Oklahoma." Etta suspected that he wasn't in Okalahoma at all. Finally in mid February, Merritt telephoned Peter from the ferry dock. When Pete went to get him, Merritt briefly told Peter that, yes, Butch and Harry were dead. Arriving at the house, he hugged everyone, even the very round Mabel, and then he starred at Etta. Now she knew for sure where he had been, though she didn't say anything. She'd talk with him later. So would Peter.

Merritt's full story would have to wait, as that night Mabel went in labor. Early the next morning, Joseph Thomas, a son, was born. Everyone cried with joy and relief that mother and child were doing well. Peter received many telegrams at his office including one from the mayor congratulating him on his son. He brought them to Mabel. Mabel commented that somehow men seemed to forget the woman's part in this accomplishment. Peter went to Shreve's Jewelers and bought a gold bracelet for Mabel with two gold charms; one for each child, with their names and birthdates engraved on the backs.

*

Etta talked with Peter two days later, asking him if he and Merritt had talked about the trip to South America. Peter looked directly at her for a moment and then simply said, "No, Merritt seems to be avoiding the discussion. He says to wait until the time of celebrating Joseph's birth is quieted down. Are you sure you would want to hear what ever the news may be?" "Yes Peter, I must." "Etta, I can tell you that Harry is dead."

The accommodations for Merritt's journey were better and easier than when he and Etta had to escape from South America in 1905. He arrived in Antofagasta, Chile in August; bought a horse and began the long ride to Tupiza, and then on to San Vicente, Bolivia.

Merritt told them the story: "I got completely different information from the local folks than from the police. The police wondered why I was asking. I told them I thought they might be men I knew from Valparaiso, Chile, or maybe not. I asked them if many Norte Americano's come through that way. After I'd talked with the townspeople, and got their version, that I'll get to in a minute; I asked the police if it was true that the banditos who stole the Aramayo Mine payroll, also were known to be men who committed crimes in the United States. They told me; yes, they were wanted in the states for robberies of trains and banks. They showed me the wanted poster with their photos. I was told that the two dead men had been identified two or three days after the shoot out by an official. I don't know who that was. The police said the banditos were buried at the cemetery."

"But, that's not what I heard from the townspeople. They said the bodies were buried, then dug up later for the officials to identify. It was an order from the Colonel of the Army. The Colonel already knew to look for them, and if captured, to keep them for identification."

"Etta, sit down. It's too difficult to talk with you standing. Are you alright?" "I'll sit. Just go on Merritt; tell what happened."

"My Spanish isn't that good and I had a difficult time understanding every word. The local people told me that when the officials saw the condition of men, they said it looked as though they had been badly wounded, and then one shot the other in the head, and then shot himself in the head. The townspeople also said that after the bodies were identified, their bodies were removed and not reburied in the cemetery. During the shoot-out, Butch and Harry had killed a policeman who was from the village and the family didn't want them buried next to their loved ones, so they were taken away from the town, and, here's where there's some difficulty in understanding. I was told by two local men that they were buried on a small hill about a half mile out of town."

"I rode out to that dry parched hill, and walked slowly around the area to find the gravesites. I walked around for a couple of hours until I saw ground that looked as though, at one time, it may have been disturbed. Etta, sit down!"

"Then, the awfulness of what I found. I saw the remains of human bones. If they had even been buried, it must have been a very shallow grave that was afterward dug up by animals. They were not old bones. I've drawn a map of the site, Pete, here it is. I spent many days there, going out to the hill, grieving over the whole story of their lives, and remembering their good days. I buried all the bones and moved a large stone to cover and mark the grave. I carved "H.L" and "R.P" into the stone."

"It took me more time that it sounds. First, I stayed in San Vicente just taking my time, saying I was passing through, and stopping to rest. Then slowly I started talking about the big shootout there in November. I had some trust of the local people by then." "I'm forgetting some things. I'll remember more, but not now." Merritt gave way to sobs. Etta and Peter were so slumped over, in collapse, they barely noticed. Finally, Peter got up and poured three whiskeys. They hugged and cried, then gave a toast for their departed and grieved for friends. Etta was very quiet and withdrawn the next week.

XVI

San Francisco 1911-1913

Merritt found a studio apartment on Union Street, again in the north beach district, not far from his old apartment. Everything was as he left it at the livery on Broadway, not far from Pete and Mabel's house. His car was parked inside and it didn't take Merritt very long to get it running again. He hung out his shingle, and also a banner which read, "Back in Business." Within a week his customers were back, making appointments to get their cars fixed.

Etta enjoyed helping Mabel with the children. Alma was now six years old. Her governess came weekday mornings for her lessons. Mabel said Alma would go to a public school next year. Joseph wasn't as serious a child as his older sister. His favorite toys were the ones with wheels and movement.

They all were enjoying a lazy summer. For a break they went to Santa Cruz for a week, where they rented a cabin by the beach and enjoyed lazy days at the shore. Peter and Mabel were getting concerned that Etta didn't seem to get involved in anything, though Etta did read an abundant number of books. Mabel was concerned of what was to become of her. It appeared that Etta thought her life had already been lived, and was just living through the days left to her.

Peter had a plan. He invited a contemporary in law, whom he knew to be a bachelor and a person of great ambition, to dinner one Saturday evening. He already told Mabel that he hoped he and Etta would get on well.

The night of the dinner, Gerald Morgan arrived late, and with too many excuses. He was extremely overdressed. He fussed over Mabel and Etta in a way that made Peter uncomfortable, but not in a jealous way. The man reminded him of Mabel's hairdresser who loved to gossip with her and who would gossip about her, if he had any juicy tidbit to tell. Peter didn't care for that sort of behavior. Gerald didn't seem to get the humor of any of Etta's funny stories. As a result, that encouraged Etta to tell stories increasingly more and more bizarre and out of the ordinary. Everyone was relieved when Gerald finally left. While getting ready for bed, Mabel asked Peter what he could have possibly been thinking. "I don't know, Mabel. What a disaster. My god, the man must sit to pee. What a fusspot."

*

Mabel was impressed with the guest instructor at the art institute when she resumed classes in September. His name was Charles LeBesque. Originally from Lyon, France, Charles had arrived in San Francisco that summer after living in New York City for two years. He had a bohemian personality, and was an extremely talented artist. Mabel liked how he saw and described the world around him. She liked his cheerful manner, and thought his light brown eyes were gorgeous. One Saturday morning, Charles joined the group who gathered at Alta Plaza Park with Mabel. He stopped what he was doing to stare at Etta when he saw her come out of the house. Etta was bringing Alma to visit a neighbor who had a child the same age. Mabel noticed, and instantly knew, that if anyone had a chance to get close to Etta, Charles would be that person.

"Etta, tomorrow, after my morning art class, would you meet me at the institute for some shopping downtown?" "Yes, good, you know I'm not much for long shopping trips, but I need some things too, and I could use your help in choosing a new dress." Mabel was happy that the first part of her plan was in place.

Etta was on time. Mabel introduced her sister, "Laurie," to Charles. Mabel took her time gathering her things while she listened to their conversation. It was apparent that they liked each other. They talked freely and the conversation progressed effortlessly. She thought there was coquettishness to Etta that she hadn't seen in a very long while. Charles was unabashedly enamored with her. When Mabel couldn't stall any longer she joined them.

Charles mentioned the new art exhibit starting the next weekend which would show two of Mabel's paintings. Etta turned to Mabel and asked. "Are you planning on going to the opening

Mabel?" Mabel hadn't made definite plans, but answered quickly, "Oh yes, you'll be there too won't you Charles?" His response was a question. "Are you going Laurie?" "Yes, I'll be with Mabel."

At home, Mabel told Peter all about the meeting and informed him he would need to take them to the opening Saturday evening. Merritt, or Mrs. Tibidoe, their neighbor, a widow who had raised four children, could watch the children for a couple of hours.

Wearing their new dresses, Etta and Mabel were dazzling and received a tremendous amount of attention at the opening. When Charles finally got through the crowd to them, Mabel introduced him to Peter. Even while talking with Peter, Charles could not keep his eyes off Laurie. Finally he had Laurie to himself and kept her, to her enjoyment, with him for the rest of the evening. At their goodbyes, Charles asked Laurie if she would like to go for a walk with him the next day. She said, yes.

He arrived at the house at 11 a.m. Sunday morning; where he enjoyed a cup of tea with Laurie, Mabel and Peter, and met Alma and Joseph. Peter, true to his nature, asked Charles if he had become a U.S. citizen. "Of course; when my brother and I arrived in New York, we saw to that right away." Then Peter had to ask, "What do you think of our government?" Peter, this is still a new country with fresh ideas. I hope it continues to be progressive." "Yes, but it may not with our current president. Though I admire Taft for his appreciation of the law; his lack of imagination is holding the country back. It looks like we'll have a Democrat in office after the next election." "Maybe so Pete, I'll go ahead and tell you, though I'm not very political; it's the people who will make and keep the country strong. If they're weak, our government will be weak." "Right you are, Charles."

They set out on their walk to North Beach, the district where Charles lived. They stopped at a watering hole on Van Ness Avenue for a sparkling soda, where they sat and talked for an hour, and then continued on to Washington Park.

They were sharing with each other the essentials of their lives; Etta being careful to omit the years in Argentina. Charles told her about moving from France to New York City with his brother, where he'd enjoyed painting but couldn't get work teaching or work in his family's trade as meat grocer. His brother was doing alright there working in a grocery store. Here in San Francisco

Charles found work at a grocery and butcher's mart, and also as a visiting instructor at the art institute. He was happy to tell Etta that he had already sold seven paintings.

Charles suggested they get something to eat at a small café on Green Street. What a surprise finding Merritt there, then again, he did live in the neighborhood. And even more of a surprise for Etta to learn that Merritt and Charles knew each other; they'd already had many good discussions over the meat counter at Charles workplace. They joined Merritt and enjoyed a good meal with plenty of sourdough French bread and a bottle of good red wine.

When they finally got up to go outside and stretch; Charles invited them to see his paintings at his apartment, just a couple of blocks away on Greenwich Street. Merritt and Etta appreciated fine art from their association with Mabel, and were overcome with admiration of Charles Paintings. Rather than the soft impressionist style of Mabel's work, these paintings were so real you could feel the life in them. They breathed!

Etta felt very at home in the apartment that served as Charles art studio. After a cup of coffee and more pleasant conversation, Etta felt she should be returning home. It was now evening so Merritt offered to drive her. Charles went with them. They saw Etta to the door; then Merritt returned Charles to his apartment, just five blocks away from where he lived,

During the next month, Charles and Laurie took more walks, and enjoyed picnics on the beaches near the north beach area. They borrowed Merritt's car and went for rides through Golden Gate Park. They enjoyed going to movie shows. Other than a good-night kiss, nothing more romantic than that was happening.

By Thanksgiving Day, it was expected that Charles would come for dinner. Peter was again cooking the bird. Mabel and Etta cooked too many side dishes, to everyone's delight. Charles was a hit with Alma and Joseph and he and Merritt were already becoming good friends. Peter liked Charles very much, but held back a little. He couldn't stand it if Etta was hurt again. His brotherly feelings had given way to fatherly concerns for her well being. Mabel knew that it was Charles off beat personality, and his being of his own society, that made it possible for Etta to be interested in him. He reminded her of no one else.

Charles traveled to New York City for the Christmas holidays to be with his brother who was now married. Before leaving he gave Laurie a present. A small, stone sculpture of her standing with Alma, holding hands; just the way he had seen her the first time, from across the street at the park.

Gertrude, and Peter's brother Thomas, arrived for Christmas in plenty of time to help with decorations. And for the first time, Gertrude helped make Christmas cookies in the kitchen. She had never enjoyed herself so much. Alma, by her side and Joseph in his high-chair, would squeal every time their grandmother laughed. Mabel and Etta's brother, Buddy, came for Christmas this year with even more presents for Alma and Joseph. The joined families made each of them feel confident in the security of family.

Charles returned on New Year's Eve. He and Etta embraced like they had never done before. Gertrude fairly interrogated Charles. She had grown very fond of Etta and saw in her a bright woman who would require a man of strong character to impress her. Gertrude was curious about this man. There was now a painting of his in the front room, which showed he possessed extraordinary talent. He showed himself to be intelligent and passionate about life, and he was obviously in love with Laurie.

At their New Year's Eve party, Mabel and Peter entertained a varied and eclectic assemblage of guests; artists, neighbors, attorneys, bankers, politicians, and the automobile merchants, who were friends of Merritt. At midnight, as was her custom, Mabel played "Auld Lang Syne." Etta cried; this time with Charles holding her. The party went on long into the night. In the early hours of the morning, Merritt gave Charles a ride home. It was now 1911.

*

The morning after the party, Etta quietly got up, dressed and went for a walk. She left a note saying she needed exercise. It was a long walk to north beach. She didn't hesitate when she knocked resolutely on Charles door. She found comfort in his bright smile, his brown gleaming eyes and his passionate kiss and embrace. She let herself be loved and loved him in return.

Charles cooked a very healthy breakfast of a small steak, and potatoes fried with green beans and onions. After they ate, he ran down the stairs and out to the bakery on the corner, to get sweet rolls to have with their coffee. Then he sliced apples and oranges. Etta felt very cared for. During their conversation, Etta told him she had been married, and her husband had died. Charles had suspected she was getting over a tragic sadness. Charles had also been married; in fact still was, by law. His wife had left him, when he still lived in France, for a man with much more money than he, and had gone off to Italy; he didn't know where. Shortly after, he left his home town of Lyon, and he and his brother went to New York City.

When Etta wasn't working at Peter's office, or taking care of Alma, and Joseph, she was at Charles apartment. He had such a different way of living; so simple and casual. Etta enjoyed being there when Charles came home. He painted a portrait of her, sitting in front of the bay windows, which made her gasp when she saw it finished. If Charles saw her that way; he must love her very much. The painting presented her as a stunning beauty.

By March, Etta was living with Charles. Neither of them wanted a marriage ceremony, each for their own reasons. Charles had heard Mabel and Pete, slip so many times and call her Etta, he was now calling her Etta also. Etta explained that her name, Lauretta, could be shortened either way.

Mabel, though very moral and conventional, thought their living together was eccentric, yet the best direction for them both. Etta and Charles were a good match and obviously loved each other. She trusted Charles, and liked his robust yen for living. She could finally exhale.

*

"Charles, this is unbelievable; Maggie Brown is listed as one of the survivors of the Titanic that sank last week. I met her when I visited Denver. She belonged to the Denver Women's Group that invited me to join them for tea." "When were you in Denver?" "During the time I was seeing the west. After Mabel and I stayed with Dr. Gardiner's family in Texas, I went on my own to Denver and through New Mexico before finally going to San Diego."

"It says here that she helped others board the lifeboats, and then was finally convinced to board a lifeboat herself. Protesting to the leader and people in lifeboat six to go back to search the water for survivors, but it was too late when they returned to search. She's considered a heroine. They're calling her "The Unsinkable Molly Brown." I liked her very much when I met her; she's such a forthright person, and always was a fighter for women's education."

Before leaving for work, Charles kissed her soundly and gave her a warm embrace, then told Etta he would meet her later, at her sister's house, where they were expected for dinner.

Etta had an appointment to keep that afternoon before going to see Mabel. When Etta arrived at Mabel's house, she couldn't wait to tell Mabel the news. "Mabel, I have startling news." "Etta, I too have miraculous news . . . . . Oh Etta, could we possibly have the same news? I'm expecting a child next year, the end of February." "Mabel! I'm expecting the first of March." "Etta, oh dear Etta!"

Peter came home to find the women laughing and crying. "What now?" "Peter, we'll have another child." "Mabel, darling, are you sure?" "Yes, Peter, and our family will welcome yet another child also. Etta is expecting." "Etta is this true?" "Yes, Peter. I just found out. I'll tell Charles when he arrives."

Before the front door closed, Charles knew something was going on. Pete and Mabel left the room in a hurry after saying their hellos. "What is it Etta?" "Charles, Mabel just shared the news with me today that she's expecting a child in February." "That's wonderful, but what . . . . ." "Charlie, I'm expecting our child in March." "Etta! Our child! Etta!"

At dinner, Peter watered the wine in Mabel's and Etta's glasses by more than half. Charles talked about the women eating more fresh vegetables and said he would select very healthy beef liver, which he would cook with onions for them to eat once a week, just as his father had done for his mother. He had hoped for a child, and now was more in love with Etta than ever; if that was possible.

Happy as she was, Etta was troubled; she had wished she'd had a child with Harry. She couldn't stop grieving for him. She hadn't told Charles about her past with Harry, "The Sundance Kid," or about her life in Argentina. How could she tell him? She, Mabel, and Peter had kept this secret all these years for her safety. And, in turn, she worried for their safety if she should be found out.

*

On February 28, 1912, Mabel delivered a lively and beautiful daughter, Mary Louise. Peter added another gold charm to Mabel's bracelet. Two weeks later, on March 11, Etta delivered a hale and hearty boy, Edouard Paul. Charles made a cradle for his son; he'd been working on it all winter. Both fathers were swollen with pride.

Charles brought Etta to Mabel's home where Peter had hired a nurse for the first month to help care for the mothers and the babies. Alma loved being a big sister, and an Aunt. At age two, Joseph wasn't so sure this was a good idea. He was the baby; not this new sister. And there was the other boy baby who got a lot of attention too.

Charles was becoming recognized for his talent, and was selling his paintings. He bought an automobile that Merritt had picked up cheap and then fixed to be in top running order. After his workday, Charles didn't waste any time rushing to "the House of Babies," as Peter now proudly called his home.

Etta asked Peter to tell Charles about her past. Now that they shared a child, she wanted to be honest with him and she knew she could trust him. Peter agreed. Peter found a moment to speak with Charles privately. "Charles, I want to say how much I respect you for taking such good care of Etta and being such a good father. I'm honored to know you. As you know, I came into this family long ago, sixteen years ago, and Mabel is the love of my life. I've grown to love and be very protective of her family." "I realize that Pete, and I appreciate your devotion." "Charles, let's have a brandy and celebrate our family. There's something I want to talk about with you."

Peter took his time, starting at the beginning; telling Charles about Harry, how Etta met him, and about the years when Etta waited to hear from him. He told Charles about Harry's past, their moving to Argentina, and the home they had there. He told him that he had met Harry on several occasions, and liked the man very much. He told Charles the circumstances of how he came to meet Merritt, and that it was Merritt who went to Argentina to bring Etta home. And, he told Charles that Etta had to bear the news of the deaths of Harry and her friend James, Harry's partner.

When Charles cried, Peter thought it may be because of his disappointment in Etta; then Charles said, "My dear Etta, what she's gone through. The home and the love she's lost." Right then, Peter couldn't help but choke up, and say, "Thank you Charles." Characteristic of his usual need of diversion from emotional moments, Peter suggested another brandy.

Etta and Edouard made the return to their apartment with Charles driving as though he was transporting nitro. Merritt followed in his car, with all of Edouard's furnishings and boxes of baby supplies. The bedroom in the apartment became the baby's room. Charles and Etta slept on their bed in the front studio among the paints, easels, and canvasses. During their quiet first week together, Charles painted a portrait of Etta and their son that was certainly his finest work.

*

Once a week, at Pete's house, Charles resumed cooking liver with onions for everyone. He made delicious meaty soups, and always brought large pots to Mabel and Pete. Merritt was at their apartment several nights of the week for dinner and conversation.

Charles was teaching Etta to speak French. Her early education had included French lessons but she had forgotten most of it. Edouard was learning French from his father and English from his mother. Mabel's children were taught French by their governess and also benefited from Charles speaking with them.

Etta and Charles continued to enjoy long walks, with Eddy in his perambulator. They spent a lot of time at the fisherman's wharf. Charles knew most of the fishermen who were for the most part Italians. He bought their fresh fish for the butcher mart where he was now half owner. They took drives out to the "Sutros Baths and Museum of Oddities." The life-size figure of a Japanese man in a tall glass case fascinated Eddy. Etta liked the Egyptian art.

Charles found a vacant storefront for rent on Powell Street near their apartment. He painted the walls white and hung his and Mabel's paintings. He put out a sign which read; "Galerie d'Art." He sent out invitations for the opening to all of his acquaintances. Mabel sent invitations to her friends and neighbors. Then, they waited to see if anyone would come. They did.

Three of Charles, and four of Mabel's, paintings were sold that night. Because her paintings were priced more reasonably, Charles earned more from the sales. Soon they would have to part with a larger percentage of their income when, in 1913, the 16th amendment to the constitution would make income tax a permanent fixture in the U.S. tax system.

Etta now took care of the gallery, opening it in the afternoons, Wednesday through Saturday. Eddy would take his nap on a cot behind the counter that Merritt built. They were all flourishing. Etta's vigor had been restored; she started to play violin again. Years had gone by when she just simply had no interest.

Mabel didn't return to the art institute for the next couple of years. She spent more time at home with the three children. On Saturdays, Peter would take Alma and Joseph with him while he did the grocery shopping; always stopping first to visit a friend or bringing the children someplace fun or interesting. Their favorite was the playground at Golden Gate Park. Mabel would spend most of the day on Saturday painting, as well as afternoons during the week. When Lillie Tibidoe could watch the children, Mabel would go to the gallery and paint at an easel by the large front window. She painted the neighborhood from that vantage point. Those paintings sold quickly.

XVII

1914-1918

Charles came in the gallery looking pale and distraught. "Etta, we must close the gallery. Etta, I've just received a telegram from my brother. My father is ill and dying. I need to return to Lyon to be with him. Will you go with me?" "Charles, I'm so sorry. I realize you're worried and upset. Of course you must go, but Charles, I don't know if I can get on a ship without being found out." "Etta you'll travel as my wife. That worry should be behind you now."

"I just don't know Charles; travel would be hard on Eddy. I think you should go. You could travel faster without us. You could be on a train this afternoon. Are you worried that you'll be in time?" "Yes, oh yes. Etta, someday we'll travel together to France. But you're right it would take too long to prepare for all of us to leave. Oh darling, I'll miss you. You can stay with Mabel and Peter if you think the apartment will be too lonely."

Charles left, to take the ferry to Oakland and to be on the next train to Chicago, and there he'd get a train to New York and be on the next passenger freighter to France. Etta didn't move in with Mabel and Peter. She liked their apartment and their neighborhood. She and Eddy would spend at least one day every week at Mabel's; it was a day of rest for them both. Mabel was becoming something of a socialite through Peter's contacts, and the demands on her time were sometimes a strain.

Etta was just locking up the gallery when Peter came by with a gentleman he introduced as Mr. James Rolph—the current mayor. Mr. Rolph founded the Mission Savings Bank and the Rolph Shipbuilding Company, as well as serving as director of the Ship Owners & Merchant Tugboats Company. He chose one of Charles paintings, and one of Mabel's, to purchase for his home. While he lingered in conversation with Etta, introduced to him as Laurie, he found himself telling her about tugboats. When she showed enthusiasm in the subject, he offered for one of his tugboat captains to take her, Peter and Mabel and the older children out for a tour of the bay. How odd that she should still worry about being exposed, when she saw public officials almost everyday.

Mabel's neighbor, Lillie Tibidoe took care of Eddy and Mary Louise, while the rest of the family went on a tugboat tour of the bay. They started out in the fog, and then sun broke through to reveal a bright morning. Thomas, who was only four, was the most impressed and said he wanted to be a tugboat captain.

*

Peter was anxious for Charles return; he'd learned that in June the Archduke Francis Ferdinand, heir to the Austria-Hungary throne and his wife were assassinated by a Serbian nationalist in Sarejevo. The Kaiser was supporting Austria against Serbia. In August, while Charles was still on his way to France, Germany declared war on Russia and France. Emperor Franz Joseph of Austria-Hungary declared war on Serbia and Russia. Japan had declared war on Germany. More and more countries were becoming involved. Thousands of French soldiers were killed in an offensive push to the east of Paris. The battle of Marne ended in a French victory, halting the German advance towards Paris. Britain declared war on Germany and Austria-Hungary. Canada joined the war while President Wilson continued to declare a policy of American neutrality.

*

Etta wasn't sleeping well and was missing Charles. She was sitting in a comfy chair dozing one evening when she had another dream of Harry. These dreams happened only occasionally now and always left her feeling melancholy. This time Harry was with her, right there in the apartment. He was saying; *"Don't be afraid to live, Etta. Be happy; enjoy your child and family. My love for you is for your happiness, not for you to feel pain."* And then he was gone. She realized the date; it was December 7, 1914. Tomorrow would be their anniversary; fourteen years from the day they were married.

Etta had been going to the Palace Hotel every year on December 8th. Peter and Mabel accompanied her this year. While they were having lunch, she looked up to see a man at the far end, walking out of the dining room; he looked like Harry. Mabel and Peter saw him also. Peter left the table to get a closer look. The man was not to be found. Peter returned to the table saying, "From a distance it did look like Harry, but in the lobby, no one looked like him, even a man who was dressed as we saw. And, besides, the man looked to be in his thirties, as we remember Harry."

*

In February 1915, the city of San Francisco invited the world to the Panama—Pacific International Exposition, honoring the 1914 opening of the Panama Canal and celebrating the city's own rise from the ashes of the earthquake and fire of '06. The mud flats at the northern end of the city were filled in to make a marina for the 635 acre fair. The tallest building was the tower of Jewels. The grandest building was the Palace of Fine Arts.

At first, Etta had no interest in going to the fair; there were too many memories of the 1904 Worlds Fair in St. Louis and the distress that followed. Finally, Mabel and Peter encouraged her to go with them. Etta did enjoy the fair and took pleasure in explaining many of the foreign exhibits to the children. She hoped that when she returned to the apartment, Charles would be there. She was becoming more distressed that Charles had been away for so long, with no word from him.

Charles finally returned after being gone for over seven months. His father had died during his visit. Charles and his brother had immediately sold their father's house and land for much less than its worth, so they could make a fast sale. Their father's grocers shop had long since been sold. They would have liked to return earlier, but trains were sometimes not running, and ships were crowded. They easily avoided Paris and shipped out from Marseille to Lisbon, and from there boarded a freighter to New York. The brothers were glad they carried their U.S. citizenship papers. Both had been desperate to return home to their families. War was at their heels.

Charles was ecstatic when he walked in the apartment and saw Etta with Eddie, who was busy talking away about something. It was a great pleasure for him that Eddy greeted him speaking French, welcoming his papa home. Charles hugged him and Etta, feeling so relieved they hadn't gone with him to the county of his birth, that was now so ravaged by war, and so grateful that he was now home with them.

With the money Charles had from his inheritance, he wanted to buy a house. As it turned out, he found a large piece of property that encompassed four lots, on upper Castro in the Noe Valley district. Charles was friends with two fishermen, whom he'd, helped with building their homes in the North Beach area. With them, he and Merritt built a two bedroom shingled cottage with a large window that looked across the city to the bay. They also built a chicken coop. He had received a loan from Crocker Bank. Charles asked Peter to draw up his will, so the house would go to Etta without fail, in the event of his death.

Etta was delighted with the house and enjoyed having so much land and such a striking view of the city. She did have a quiet reflective moment when she saw the shiny new claw-foot bath tub being installed in the spacious bathroom. She wiped her tears after remembering the great surprise that Christmas when she received her new bath tub at the Cholila ranch, and how happy the men were to give it to her.

Charles taught Etta how to drive the car. They were living farther from Pete and Mabel, and from the gallery, and he wanted Etta to have an easier way to travel around the city with Eddy, rather than transferring on several streetcars. Eddy was just three years old. Etta loved driving and was a skillful driver. She remembered the few times when she'd driven a wagon with a four horse team.

With plenty of land to enjoy, Charles asked Etta if she'd like to have a dog. He'd been to see a litter of Airedales at a neighbor's house. Etta loved the idea, requesting that an area be fenced, and a large doghouse be built, so at times she could leave him safely outside if she didn't take him with her. Charles asked Peter if he could give a puppy to his children. Peter was hesitant, but after bringing his family to see Eddy's new puppy, and witnessing his children's delight, he was won over. At first, Peter insisted that the dog be kept outside in the backyard, but then he was the one to bring in the pup on the very first night, saying it was too cold; the pup could stay outside when the weather improved, and when it was full grown. Merritt was busy building doghouses.

*

Peter had been grumbling about the inevitable war America was sure to get into. The British ocean liner, "The Lusitania," was sunk last May by a German U-boat with a loss of almost 2,000 civilians, including 128 American lives, creating a U.S.—German crisis. Before the sinking, fear for the safety of the Lusitania and other great liners was high. Germany had declared the seas around the British Isles a war zone: starting in February; stating that allied ships in the area would be sunk without warning. The German Embassy in Washington had issued a warning to travelers who intended to embark on the Atlantic voyage as a reminder that a state of war existed between Germany and her allies against Great Britain and her allies, and that the zone of war included the waters adjacent to the British Isles.

*

That summer, Peter heard of a mining claim and property that had come up for sale; it helped take his mind off war. The mine owner had died and his family didn't want the property. Peter was so keyed up and eager to take a look. He had continued to read about gold mining, and still had the books Harry had given him. He and Merritt took off for the Sierras to check it out. They put the car on a Ferry to Oakland, drove south to Hayward and then southeast across the state, and up into the hills just east of Sonora, in the foothills of the Sierra Nevada. Merritt's knowledge of automobiles came in handy. He carried spare parts and two spare tires and an extra tank for gasoline.

They found the property and the land agent. There was only a crude shelter on the property. They hiked to the opening of the hard rock mine shaft and looked inside. The mine shaft needed shoring up but they saw good signs for gold, including a thread of a gold vein at the end where the tunnel was last worked. Peter had received information from the Sonora assayer's office that the previous owner repeatedly came to town with gold nuggets to sell.

They drove on to Twain Harte, to stay for the next couple of nights. Pete and Merritt talked about their dreams. This was Peter's greatest dream; to be the owner of a gold mine. Merritt talked to Pete about the realities of needing someone to watch over the mine and work the claim. Merritt went on to say that he'd been meaning to get out of city life and back to the ways he loved as a boy.

Both were realizing exactly what they wanted to do. Merritt would close his shop, move to the property in the Sierra's, and build a cabin with help from men in town. They chose a site for the house well away from the concealed miné shaft. With the help of William Crocker, Peter ordered a solid safe door for the entrance to the mine.

The framing and roof were up on the new cabin before the cold weather set in. Merritt worked hard to finish the outer walls by the first snowfall. The woodstove was already in place. By spring, the house would be ready for the family to visit. Merritt had just begun building better truss supports for the mine shaft.

*

Peter and Mabel took their children on a train trip to New York City that winter to celebrate Christmas with Peter's mother and his newly married brother. Peter needed a rest from his involvements in the city. Mabel would finally get to see his mother's home. She hoped the children would behave and not break anything. The visit went well. They returned after seeing in the New Year at a party given by a friend of Gertrude's. Time was on the move, it was now 1916.

During the last year, Japan made twenty one demands on China. There was a German zeppelin air-raid, and a submarine blockade on Great Britain. American citizens died when the passenger liner, Falaba, was sunk.

*

Finally, in spring, Peter crowded his family, in among mining supplies, into the car to bring them to the property to see their new cabin in the Sierra's. Merritt put in enough food to last at least the week of their stay. When they arrived, the children first hugged Merritt and then took off running to explore. Mabel was worried about bears and other animals until Merritt told her that wasn't a bear brave enough to come anywhere near that pack of wild kids.; besides, Alma and Joseph watched over Mary Louise and didn't go far from the cabin.

Merritt did all the cooking. Mabel didn't know the first thing about rustic living. She enjoyed walking with Peter, though the outhouse was a timorous experience. She looked at the mine once, and that was enough. She made several sketches and wished she'd brought her paints. Merritt had stacks of books to choose from and the week passed quickly. Before they left, Merritt asked Pete and Mabel to encourage Charles to bring Etta for a visit; he knew she'd love it there. And, he promised Pete that the next time he came out, there'd be gold for him; he'd been doing a little pick-axe work already.

*

Peter was stunned at the news following their return. Before they left, President Wilson had been on a nationwide whistle-stop campaign to generate support for Preparedness and for the Continental Army. Pancho Villa had raided into New Mexico. The French passenger ship, Sussex, had been torpedoed, and there was much more talk of the U.S. getting into the war in Europe.

By 1917, it was clear that the U.S. would get into the war. Germany was employing unrestricted warfare. By March, President Wilson's war cabinet voted unanimously in favor of declaring war on Germany. On April 4th, President Wilson delivered his war address to congress and asked the House of Representatives to declare war on Germany. On April 6th Congress made the declaration of war. The war was now called "The Great War," and sometimes, "The World War," or "The War to End All Wars."

Merritt was thirty-four years old, so he didn't register for the draft until the third and final registration date on September 12, 1918 when ages were extended from eighteen to forty-five. At that time Peter registered also; he was forty-three. The armistice was signed on November 11, 1918, and Peter and Merritt were never called for duty.

Mabel and Etta thought the world had gone mad. While they all gathered together for a Saturday dinner at the Castro Street house, Mabel asked Peter if he thought the war would come here. "That's exactly the fear we're put in everyday."

"Charles, you mentioned closing the gallery for the duration of the war. That's probably a good idea. It seems we're faced with some hard times. It's good to see your vegetable garden looking bountiful, and your chickens so fat. How's the meat and grocery business?"

"Slow Peter, very slow. The war seems to help some industry's, but it hurts a lot of little businesses. Where's the U.S. getting the money for this war?" "From us; remember Charles, back in 1913, the 16th amendment to the constitution made income tax a permanent fixture in the U.S. tax system. Just in time for this war."

XVIII

1918
War and the Spanish Influenza

"Peter, please leave your office and come home. I've just received a call from Aunt Charlotte; Uncle Stephen died of the influenza that's taken over Boston." "Is she alright; are you alright?" "Yes, Peter she's going to sell her house and move in with her sister's family." "Mabel, we'll talk more about this when I get home. I'm on my way."

The first outbreak was thought to be from a military Fort in Kansas; it was called the Spanish Influenza because Spain, though not involved in the war, was the first to report extensively on the influenza's impact. The influenza erupted during the final stages of the war, with the first wave of the virus resembling a typical flu. By the end of March, it had already spread to the east coast and Europe. By September, a more virulent strain had spread around the globe. People suffocated to death as their lungs filled with fluid.

When Etta heard the news, she telephoned Aunt Charlotte. "Etta dear, thank you for calling; yes it's a shock. I want to talk with you about Anne, I'm giving up my help, but Anne is like family, isn't she. Can she come live with you or Mabel? It seems Mabel has the larger household; perhaps Anne could work and live there. Would that be alright?" "Yes, oh yes, please make the train arrangements for her, and let me know when to meet her at the Oakland station. Aunt Charlotte, have you heard from Bud lately?" "Yes, he came for a visit last Christmas. His medical practice is going well and his wife is expecting their second child. He reminds me so much of your father. I wish he lived closer."

Peter immediately telephoned his mother. He was going to suggest that she go upstate to his cousin's house. His brother answered the phone. "Mother already left, and my wife and baby and I will be joining her at the country house tomorrow. I haven't even heard what the mortality rate is in New York, but in Philadelphia over 3,000 people died this last week. How is it there?" "It's just started here, Thomas, but so far, it doesn't seem as bad."

Anne arrived at the Oakland train station looking tired and perplexed until she sighted Etta, then a smile lit up her face. Etta wanted to give her a big hug, but Anne insisted on not letting her get close, saying she might have been contaminated on the train with so many people from the east on board. "Hundreds of people are dying each day and the military hospitals in Boston are overflowing with soldiers dying of the influenza. Please, I don't want to bring the influenza to your family. Is there somewhere I could stay to be quarantined, just like when I first arrived in New York?" "I don't know if that's necessary Anne." "Yes it is."

When they arrived home, Anne insisted on staying outside on the sheltered sun porch at the front of the house, while Etta fixed a meal for her. Charles arrived and said that if Anne insisted on a quarantine, he'd put up the large tent he'd purchased to use at Pete's mountain property. He set up the tent by the side door of the house, and put in a cot, plenty of blankets, a small table and chair, a lantern, and books. He then made quick outhouse arrangements.

Anne appreciated Charles wonderful soups, and all the meals that he brought out to her. Eddy was impatient to meet the pretty young lady. Anne spent her time reading in the tent, and wandering around their large section of land.

"Charles, do you mind Anne being here? I mean here with us. You know she's a link to my life and my memories of Argentina." "No Etta, how could I mind? Would you mind if my brother moved here? He shares memories of my past. No, she's like a sister to you, I don't mind."

Anne showed no signs of illness at the end of the week and finally joined the family inside. Mabel could hardly wait to see her again; she met Anne briefly when they visited in 1916. When Mabel arrived she was again impressed by the well spoken young lady. She asked Anne if she'd like to come live and work in her house, and help with the three children. Eddy was disappointed; he liked sharing his room with Anne and didn't want her to leave.

In July a record of seventeen war vessels were launched from the San Francisco bay area, regardless of the outbreak, and were on their way to the war. By the end of October, there was no denying that the influenza was in the city. 4,000 cases had already been reported. Schools, theatres, churches, and places of public gatherings were closed. People were discouraged to assemble, even for patriotic rallies. Most people who were infected with the virus recovered within a week following bed rest. Others died within twenty-four hours of being infected.

Peter was going to his office just two days a week, conducting business by phone as much as possible. At the market where Charles worked, they asked customers to set their orders outside, then they were filled and were handed out to them. Charles now slept in the tent being careful not to bring any contagion home.

The two families gathered to talk about what was happening. Peter had been reading statistics; one third of the world was infected. Hundreds of thousands were dying in the United States, Europe, Japan, France, the Dutch West Indies and Canada. Entire villages perished in Alaska. In Tahiti, fourteen percent of the population died in two months; in Samoa, twenty percent of the population died.

Peter and Charles insisted that the women and children go to the cabin in the Sierra's. Merritt arrived to help with the transport to the cabin. But they were too late to avoid the contagion. The night before they were to leave, Eddy showed signs of the infection. He ran a high fever with chills and already had a heavy cough. The next morning, it looked like Mary Lou showed symptoms. Mabel called Etta to ask how Eddy was doing and mentioned Mary Lou had some symptoms. Etta suggested that Peter bring Mary Lou over to her, so the other children wouldn't be infected.

Anne took over the care of Alma and Joseph, while the mothers took care of their sick children, doing everything they could think of; making sure they drank lots of liquids and gave them iced fruit juice and mashed fruit. They were thankful for aspirin which seemed to help reduce the fever. They remembered their father telling them that the new drug could be overdone and cause poisoning if too much was taken. Doctors were hard to find, as so many people were requiring their assistance. Eddy seemed to pull through the worst of it, while at the same time Mary Lou succumbed into pneumonia. That night they feared the most horrible conclusion a mother can face. Mabel broke down with her worry and terrible grief. They continually used damp cloths to sponge bathe Mary Lou, and kept her propped up on firm pillows to help her breathe.

Charles told Etta to make garlic tea, and to have Mary Lou drink it as often as she could. It seemed to work as well as anything so far. Mabel and Etta tried to clear their minds and remember what their father would have done. They talked about a mustard plaster, and then decided Mary Lou was too young; it might make her worse. Then they remembered the cough syrup that was made for them when they were children. Etta made it with thyme, boiled down to a very strong tea, and then she added honey. They helped Mary Lou slowly drink half of a small glass. Mary Lou was exhausted and weak from coughing. After watching Mary Lou's prolonged suffering, Etta suggested adding whiskey in the cough syrup; at least it should relieve some of the pain. All through the long night, the women administered to Mary Lou, continuing with the sponge baths.

Finally, by morning, the fever went down; not to normal, but improved. By afternoon Mary Lou could talk and her cough was producing some results. Her lungs were clearing. The women kept up their vigilance for the next few days and then finally relaxed. Mary Lou would be alright. Mabel helped Eddy telephone his cousins to tell them Mary Lou would be well.

Both Etta and Mabel succumbed to the influenza, but each felt they had a mild form after witnessing Mary Lou's struggle. They took care of each other until they were well. At the end of another week, Peter came and took Mabel and Mary Lou home, bundling them in blankets. He had been in agony, worried for them both.

The door opened and Harry walked into the cabin. Etta rushed to him and they embraced. Etta couldn't get enough of his kisses and held him close. Then, they were on the wagon seat on their way to Cholila, riding along by the Chubut River. The ranch house was just up ahead. There was Butch waving at them. Etta was thrilled to be home. She turned to look at Harry. He was gone. She woke up at the sound of her own voice saying, "No! Let me stay!"

Charles was still spending his evenings in the tent. Merritt felt helpless while worrying about the children, and Etta and Mabel. He cheered up Pete by giving him a small sack filled with gold nuggets, and a jar of gold flakes. It would help; as Peter's business had been in serious decline since the influenza outbreak.

*

The children thought that since the schools were closed, it was to be a holiday; so they were extremely cross when Anne gathered them for lessons. Once a week, Anne had each child instruct the others in a subject they were most interested in. Alma, being the oldest at thirteen, almost the age Anne had been when she studied her lessons with Etta at the ranch in Argentina, was very serious about teaching the children good grammar and anything to do with science, especially biology. Joseph liked talking about anything mechanical, and liked to take apart clocks and old radios to show the others how they worked. The six year olds had their turn also. Mary Lou's favorite lesson was to show how to make embroidery stitches in cloth; and Eddy, very proud of himself, taught French.

Mabel had been completely engrossed with the children since returning home and hadn't kept up with the news. "Peter, have you heard any more on the influenza, or the war?" "The influenza seems to be clearing out, though reports say that almost 200,000 Americans have died from it. As far as the war goes, The Germans launched their final desperate offensive on the western front, which, of course was designed to defeat the French and British. But, they were defeated, and forced to seek an Armistice, which put an end to the fighting. After the Armistice, on November 11th, thousands of people, here in the city, went out to the streets to celebrate; didn't you hear? President Wilson attended the Peace conference in France and signed the Treaty of Versailles."

"The law was still in effect for wearing face masks, but just two weeks later, the sirens went on all over the city, signaling that it was safe and legal to remove our masks. Didn't you hear them, Mabel?" "Peter, I just don't remember." "Well everyone thought it was over, but now, thousands of new cases are being reported, though this last phase of the virus is said to be much milder." "Oh Peter, that's a relief." "Mabel, I've read that it's estimated that over nine million have died on the battlefield, and nearly that many more on the home fronts in Europe, from food shortages, genocide, ground combat and the influenza. Did you hear that San Francisco celebrated the return home of her soldiers with a Victory Parade down Market Street?" "No Peter; and right now I just want to feel safe with my family, here at home."

Merritt stayed in town since it would soon be Christmas. He read stories to the children and showed them how to make toys. On clear days they went outside in the back yard where he showed them how to climb a tree. Mabel showed them how to paint with watercolors. Still, they all had cabin fever from being kept in. Etta suggested they make Christmas cards for each other. It kept them busy until it was time to start baking Christmas cookies.

XIX

The Roaring Twenties

From information he'd learned from James Phelan, who was now a U.S. Senator, since entering office in 1915; Peter had stocked his basement with pre-war wines and several cases of brandy and whisky. During the war, the Senate proposed the Eighteenth Amendment, but even before the Act went into effect, Congress passed the temporary Wartime Prohibition Act going into effect in June of 1919, which banned the sale of beverages having an alcohol content of greater than 2.75%.

Over President Wilson's veto, Congress passed the Volstead Act, prohibiting the sale, consumption, and transportation of all alcohol, which went into effect on January 17, 1920.

"Peter, what a shame there'll be no wine with dinner, to go with that nice roast. I suppose we wouldn't dare bring up a bottle or two with Mayor Rolph coming." "Take it easy Mabel, just put wine glasses on the table along with pitchers of water; if he doesn't bring wine himself, he may ask for some.

Charles and Etta arrived early; they wondered if wine would be served. Arriving with them were Henry and Violet Little, a couple Mabel and Peter had become good friends with ever since Peter worked on a real estate settlement with Henry. Henry was a pharmacist, and also a friend of the Mayor. The problem of whether or not to serve wine was solved when Henry brought six bottles of "medicinal wine." "Good for the cough, you know." Henry's wine was discreetly exchanged with Peter's non-medicinal and better tasting wine.

After dinner the men gathered in the front room for brandies, while the women remained at the table discussing art, literature, and the new fashions. Violet talked about what she'd read about Coco Chanel, "She's one of the first women to wear trousers in public, cut her hair, and stop wearing a corset!"

The straight-line chemise and the bobbed hairdo became the uniform of the day. Hemlines were rising to the knee. Social customs and morals were more relaxed since the war. Optimism soared along with the booming of the stock market.

The nationwide prohibition on alcohol was ignored by many. Enterprising grape farmers produced semi-solid grape concentrates, called "wine bricks" or "wine blocks." The grape concentrate was sold with a warning: "After dissolving the brick in a gallon of water, do not place the liquid in a jug away in the cupboard for twenty days, because it would turn into wine." Several varieties were available. California grape growers increased their land under cultivation by about seven hundred percent.

The opulent Granada Theatre, on Market Street, opened in 1921, and the Golden Gate Theatre, on Taylor, opened in 1922 with much fanfare, including long lines that wrapped around the block. Etta and Mabel wore formal gowns; Charles and Peter wore new suits and top hats to the opening shows. Etta and Mabel were crazy for the movies. They adored Douglas Fairbanks in "The Son of Zorro," Tom Mix in "My Own Pal," Glenn Hunter in "The Little Giant," Mary Pickford in "Sparrows," and Rudolph Valentino in "The Son of a Sheik."

*

Etta and Charles reopened the gallery, which this time was a complete success. Mabel and Charles became the neighborhood celebrity artists. Charles was the better portrait artist, and was kept busy painting portraits of many of San Francisco's distinguished matrons.

In the summer of 1925, Etta and Charles brought Eddy and Joseph to the cabin in the Sierra's for a vacation. They had been going there every summer enjoying the rugged pine covered mountains. Eddy, now thirteen, and Joseph, fifteen, were fascinated with the mining of gold. Every morning, Etta rode one of Merritt's horses. She always came back refreshed and excited about new terrain she had covered. She picked and hung up wildflowers to dry for Mabel to see on her next visit. She hated leaving at the end of the week.

More reluctant to leave were Joseph and Eddy. They asked if they could stay with Merritt and return home the next time Merritt came to the city. The idea was fine with Merritt, who asked if it would be alright if they went with him to Sonora on the weekends. He usually went into town on Saturday's, to see a widow woman who ran a dry goods store, and he usually stayed the night. This time, he'd get himself, and the boys, rooms at a local Inn. Charles hugged the boys and smiled at them, knowing this kind of outdoor experience was a rite of passage for a boy. Merritt would teach them skills of survival and test their fortitude.

Merritt brought the boys home a month later. Proud of looking like Indians; they were as brown as berries, their hair had grown longer and they appeared to be very satisfied with themselves. They had gone wild in the mountains and improved their riding skills. Merritt said they acted very respectably in town on Saturdays. The boys talked about the widow Clark's "good grub."

*

Charles and Peter went with Merritt to the Levi-Strauss store on Sacramento Street, where Merritt bought a pair of Levi's denim pants, a pair of blanket lined pants, and a blanket lined denim coat. He could have used them last winter. Charles bought a pair of denim jeans for the days when he was out painting landscapes, and seascapes. Peter thought, what the hell, he also could use a pair for wearing at the cabin.

After their shopping, Peter suggested going to a "Ham and Egger." Merritt said, "No, Pete, how about a place that serves a real good meal." "You don't get the meaning, Merritt. A "Ham and Egger" is a speakeasy that serves eggs up front. Let's go to 'Coffee Dan's" on Mason. You can take the rickety slide to the basement or take the stairs. The stairs are steep, so unless you're wearing a dress the slide's the way to go.

They sat at a table and were served glasses of surprisingly good whiskey. None of them were hard drinkers, so after two drinks, they were feeling very loosened up. Charles asked Merritt an unexpected question; "Do you think Etta is still hurting over her loss in Argentina; is she happy with me, Merritt?" "What? Are you kidding? You and Eddy are what keeps her going. I'll tell you something right from my heart; after she had to leave Harry and her home, I didn't think she'd make it. The years before she met you, she was just going through the motions of living. She loves you Charles, as much as she loved Harry. As much, but different, she met him when she was young, and lived an extraordinary life with him—as she does here with you. That's another thing about you, you're a strong person and you have your own style that can't be matched. And your latest paintings show you're in a different world; she likes that." "Thank you Merritt." "My pleasure, I'm honored to call you a friend."

Peter listened and watched the men as they talked. He loved these friends; men who truly had no equal. He had loved Harry also, and wished somehow he could've been with them today. After all these years, he was still missed.

*

Peter and Mabel felt honored to be invited, for a weekend, to the country estate of the now former Senator, James Phelan, in Saratoga. The Mediterranean style mansion, "Villa Montalvo," sat on 160 acres nestled in the Santa Cruz Mountains. The mansion boasted nineteen rooms in two stories. Marble sculptures embellished the gardens and beyond the formal gardens were acres of untouched natural areas.

Helen Wills was a frequent guest at the estate. Mabel was so pleased to find her there. She had heard of Helen, the famous tennis player. Mabel knew her to also be a painter who exhibited her paintings and etchings in New York City. Mabel liked the young woman who seemed lonely for all her fame. While talking with her, Mabel learned that Helen also wrote poetry. After dinner, Helen read one of her pieces, "The Awakening." Mabel was astonished at the accomplishments of this woman, just twenty-one years old.

Among the other guests were Ralph Stackpole and his wife. Mabel knew him from the Art Institute, which was now called the California School of Fine Arts. He had returned from France and New York, to sculpt many of the architectural features for the Panama-Pacific International Exposition. He was a friend of Helen's and admired her paintings.

Dorothea Lange, an accomplished photographer was there also. She was well known for her portrait photography. Mabel had seen her at the School of Fine Arts a couple of times, but before now had never met her. Mabel had never enjoyed a social get together as much as she did that weekend. She'd been worried that it would all be about politics.

*

The World Series of 1926 created a hullabaloo of excitement. On October 10, most folks had their radio dials set on the local stations that carried the game. Peter was rooting for the New York Yankees and Babe Ruth; Etta, for the St. Louis Cardinals. St. Louis won, 3-2.

The twenties were years of entertainments and distractions. In every district in the city, there were amusement parks. The families went to Croop's Glen Park to ride on the roller coasters, and hike in the hills. They went to the Sutro's Baths and Museum, and the Cliff House to listen to the barking seal lions. They spent spring days in Golden Gate Park and enjoyed the fortune cookies at the Japanese Tea Garden.

Many summer days were spent at Ocean Beach, and at the "Bug House," the fun house at Playland at the Beach. They loved "Laffing Sal," the mechanical laughing character at the entrance; then the maze of mirrors, and squeezing between the large spinning tops. The kids enjoyed the Joy Wheel and the Barrel of laughs, though Joseph was the only one who could walk through the large rotating wood barrel without falling. The moving bridges and the rocking horses on the moving platforms were a sensation. Mabel didn't like the air jets that blew her skirt up, or the rocking staircases. They all made the three story climb to the top of "the longest, bumpiest indoor slide in the world."

Alma was home for the summer; she now attended Radcliffe College in Cambridge, Massachusetts and lived, during the school year, with her Great Aunt Charlotte at her cousin's home near the school. She was studying chemistry and physics, and hoping to continue her studies to become a doctor of medicine.

Joseph began his general college studies at Stanford University in September 1928. He planned to go on to law school. He still was fascinated by all things mechanical, but much more, he admired his father and respected what he had made of his life. He hoped to be as respected when he began his career. Peter and Mabel made several weekend visits to Palo Alto to visit Joseph. Joseph always enjoyed, and benefited from talks with his father.

Anne had met and fallen in love with a young man when she lived in Boston. Before she left for San Francisco, he promised to join her as soon as he was able. He kept his promise. George arrived in 1919. He had been a tailor's apprentice. As soon as he found a position at a clothiers that made custom suits for men, he proposed. He and Anne were married in Mabel's home. The children loved Anne and needed to be reassured that she would still be there for them on weekdays. Anne continued with helping at Mabel's home, including the additions of her own two boys until Mabel's children were grown.

Anne continued to meet with Etta and Mabel for tea and long talks. Anne became a woman very involved in community affairs. Mabel had introduced her to women who shared the same enthusiasms.

*

Etta surprised everyone by getting her hair "bobbed." With her new look; wearing the new straight line chemise dresses or the low-waisted dresses with fullness at the hemline, she looked ready to kick up her heels. She was a striking sight. Mabel followed her lead. They looked every bit as stunning as when they first got on that train in Boston over thirty years ago. Etta enjoyed making "fascinator's," the feathered head decorations that were replacing hats. She made them with beads and feathers, and sometimes flowers. While she worked, she thought of when she made the woven hatband for Harry. Memories could still crush her.

*

"Mabel, would you like to go to a party at a speakeasy?" "Oh! I don't know Peter, could you risk it?" "Sweetheart, the most notable, prominent, and illustrious will be there; and, you might like to know, I've heard that movie stars will most likely be present; and besides, we're going to one of the finest hotels in the city, not some dive" Oh Peter, Etta and Charles must come with us."

When they entered the lobby of the new Sir Francis Drake Hotel, Peter ushered them to the elevator; car No. 2—the only car with an "M" button that would take them to the speakeasy, on the mezzanine level, that was located between the lobby and the second floor. They entered the crowded, bright, and dazzling room, filled with people just as bright and dazzling. The band was playing a Charleston, and the dancing was wild. "Mabel, do you see any movie stars?" "Well, I can't tell, everyone here looks like a movie star. Charles, how does the hotel smuggle all the hooch in here?" "In hard sided luggage; and by the way, everyone looking at you and Etta must think you're movie stars! Mabel, do you realize tonight you look exactly like Billie Burke."

In 1929 San Franciscan's attended the gala opening of the new Fox Theatre, on Market Street, which premiered, "Behind the Curtain," with Charlie Chaplin. Etta, Charles, Mabel, and Peter attended the opening. They all looked radiant. Etta was now 51, and Mabel 53.

*

Throughout the twenties the stock market had been on a run that saw stocks soaring. On September 3, 1929, the day after Labor Day, the Dow reached an all time high. These were high flying, reckless times. A lot of money was borrowed to invest in the market. It was a sure thing. A sizeable return on an investment was expected.

Most people weren't aware of what was happening until the stock market began to collapse. Panic selling started on a sunny morning in October, "Black Thursday." Five banks invested about twenty million each, to buy stock to restore confidence in the market. It seemed to work; on Friday the market was calm. However, on October 28th, "Black Monday," the panic selling resumed. By the next day, October 29th, "Black Tuesday," it was official; the stock market had crashed. The banks started calling in loans. An estimated 30 billion dollars in stock values disappeared by mid November.

XX

The Great Depression 1930's

Mabel walked into Peter's study and found him sitting in a wood chair slumped over with his elbows on his knees, his hands clasped together, just staring down at the rug. "Peter, what is it?" "Mabel, the stock market has crashed, our stocks are worth nothing." "But, we own stock in just two companies, did we loose a lot?" "Enough to make me worry about the future, and continuing to pay for Alma and Joseph's college education; and Mary Lou will want college in another year or so." "Peter, if that's the worst case, they'll understand. But you still have your clients, and Merritt's bringing us more and more gold." "That's right Mabel, the gold's bringing in a good price, and we don't owe anyone anything; maybe it'll be alright."

*

"Charles, we need to talk, you've been in the dumps with worry." "Sorry Etta, but I am worried; already people are buying a lot less meat at the grocery. Their worried faces make me sad. And, how can paintings sell in a time when people have nothing? You said yourself that no one even walked into the gallery this week. We'll close it again. I still owe the bank for the building supplies for the house." "Charlie, that's what I want to talk about; and it isn't just you that owed the bank; we're in this together. That's why I paid off the loan this morning with part of the savings from my inheritance from Mother." "No, Etta, that's yours. I should be providing for you!" "Nonsense, it's ours. What's that money for, if not for our family and home? How do you think Mabel and Peter bought such a large house back when we first moved here? Their down-payment was made with Mabel's inheritance. And, with any luck, we still should have enough for Eddy to go to college."

*

More than three million people, in the United States, were unemployed by March of 1930. Banks failed, and bank robberies became more common. Cotton prices plummeted. Even with President Hoover saying the worst will pass within sixty days, people were despondent; a feeling of hopelessness prevailed among the downhearted struggling populace of bewildered and frightened people.

In August, James Phelan died; Peter and Mabel attended the services. They followed in the long procession to Holy Cross Cemetery in Colma, just a few miles south of San Francisco. Peter was inconsolable for days. Peter was now fifty-six years old; a gray haired man, who was becoming somewhat world-weary.

Peter's brother, Thomas, phoned early, on a crisp October morning, before Peter left for the office. Peter couldn't make any sense of what he was saying. Then it came out; their mother was dying; her age was against her and she was failing. Peter was on a train that afternoon. He arrived in enough time for his mother to tell him what joy he, Mabel, and his children, had brought her. Peter stayed for the services, and spent a few days helping Thomas sort through the affairs of their mother's estate.

While he was in New York, Peter went to see Mabel's brother, Bud, who now had his medical practice there. It wasn't entirely a social call. During the train ride east, Peter felt tiredness in his body that gave him concern. After a long consultation, and examination, Bud told him he appeared to be in excellent health, but the sad news of his friend's, and his mother's recent death, was affecting him and he should rest.

Peter went on to Boston to see Alma who was still attending Radcliff College in Cambridge. Alma was shocked to see her father looking so old and sad. She spent as much time with him as she could. He stayed for three days. While he waited for Alma to be finished with her daily courses, he rested in his room at the Parker House Hotel. His grieving would need to take its course. He tried not to show Alma just how despondent he was. He benefited from Alma's kind manner. Then it was time to return home.

*

Ralph Stackpole taught at the School of Fine Art, where Mabel occasionally attended painting workshops. She liked keeping up with current styles of painting and enjoyed the association of other artists. She found Mr. Stackpole to have a deprecating manner toward women artists; though he was good friends with Helen Wills and the photographer, Dorothea Lange. Stackpole was also a friend of architect, Timothy Phlueger who invited the Mexican painter, Diego Rivera to paint a mural for the Lunch Club at the San Francisco Stock Exchange.

In November 1930, Diego Rivera, and his artist wife, Frida Kahlo, came to San Francisco and stayed at Stackpole's San Francisco art studio while Diego started painting the two-story mural, "The Allegory of California." It was at the studio that Diego met Helen Wills Moody, the famous tennis player. Diego sketched Helen and asked her to model for the main female figure of "California" for the 30-foot-high mural. She was delighted and consented.

Mabel, Peter, Charles, and Etta attended a reception for Mr. Rivera. Peter found his usual cronies to talk with, while Charles and Mabel gathered around Diego to listen to him talk about his paintings. Etta sought out Frida. Frida was as accomplished a painter as Diego but had not yet reached his level of fame.

Etta and Frida got along well. Frida was only twenty three and had been through a great deal of suffering. At six she had contracted polio, leaving her spine and one leg damaged. Then, a trolley car accident, when she was eighteen, left her with a very broken body.

Etta talked with Frida in Spanish, which made Frida feel much more at ease. Frida talked with Etta about her desire to have a child; and Etta talked openly with the troubled woman saying she too had a time of wanting a child but not conceiving. Frida told Etta about her childhood during the Mexican Revolution when she and her sister were told to hide in a large walnut chest, while their mother would cook for the soldiers who came by.

Later that week, while Diego was working on the mural; Etta, Mabel and Frida went to the California Palace of the Legion of Honor at Lincoln Park. Alma Spreckles, the sugar heiress, had seen to the impressive museum being built, and donated over seventy Rodin sculptures, as well as a large portion of her collection of French furniture, silver, ceramics, and antiquities to the museum.

That evening, during dinner at Mabel's house, Mabel mentioned to Etta, "Frida is the most tormented woman I've ever met." Frida had talked with the women about her problems with Diego's infidelities. Mabel went on to say, "Of course, I completely agreed when Frida said that historically, women artists have always been considered amateurs. She said, she paints for herself; as it should be."

They all met again, at a party for Diego, when he finished a second mural for the School of Fine Arts, "Making of a Fresco." The mural depicted the rebuilding of the city. Diego painted himself in the center of the scene.

*

"Charles, did you hear the good news, Mayor Rolph won the governorship; he'll be resigning as mayor as soon as he's inaugurated." "Pete, I thought you were a Democrat." "Well now, I just don't know, it's the man that counts and what he stands for. I've always liked James Rolph." "He's got some tough years ahead; this state's in trouble, like all the rest. Looks like hard times are here for awhile longer." "Did Etta get students for violin lessons?" "Hard to believe, but yes, two students."

"Is there anything growing in your vegetable garden?" "Not now, the season's over, but Etta and Anne canned everything they could, and stored squash and potatoes in covered wire crates, under the house. They said it worked in Argentina. Bring Mabel and Mary Lou over tonight for another one of my hearty and meaty soup dinners. Etta's making some of that wonderful bread she bakes, the kind Anne taught her to make. Pete, are you letting your kids know that you're doing without so they can continue school?" "No reason for them to know. It makes me feel good to know they're continuing to move ahead. My mother would be proud to know her money is going to their future, though a lot of her money was lost to bank failures." "How's Mabel holding up; I know she feels the strain." "She's alright but, just as you say, she does feel the strain. I'd really like for us to go to the cabin, to get away for awhile."

Mabel and Peter had recently been in an argument that started when Mabel came home from shopping with an expensive new dress. "Mabel we can't afford new clothes right now." Well, how do you expect me to look when we go out with your friends and their wives are wearing expensive dresses?" "Mabel, I'll bet, if you look close, the dresses aren't new. Maybe they're refashioned, like you've done with some of your clothes. I've been careful with the food budget when I'm out shopping for the groceries. I'm worried everyday that, if times get worse, we'll be in a real fix." "I'm sorry Peter, I'll return the dress. Etta recently asked me if we could work together on re fashioning some of our dresses; we'll do that this week." "I'm sorry Mabel; I'd like you to have what you deserve." "It's no fault of yours Peter. I've been spoiled. What about the dinner for your colleagues that you mentioned?" "Mabel, I know that will be an extravagance we shouldn't be spending on; but these men have been very helpful to me. Charles said he would provide a good roast for the dinner and lots of potatoes."

The depression years were just getting started. In New York City; the street corners were now crowded with nearly six thousand people selling apples for five cents apiece. Food riots broke out in several cities across the states. At the closing of 1931, New York's "Bank of the United States" collapsed. The bank had over $200 million in deposits, making it the largest single bank failure in the nation's history. In 1932, the stock market bottomed out with an eighty nine percent drop from its pre-crash high.

More and more San Franciscan's, like those in so many other cities, depended on city relief. Across the nation, industrial production was down 56 percent from 1929, and over thirteen million people, a third of the work force, were out of work. Farmers were going broke. With the extremely low prices offered by the brokers, they couldn't afford to bring their goods to market.

*

"Charles, look at this news article, it says; Charles Lindbergh's 20 month old son, who was kidnapped from their home almost two weeks ago, was found dead in the woods not two miles from their home. Oh, the sick people who did this!" "Etta, calm down; though

I understand how you feel. What a heartbreaking tragedy for them. It seems this world is changing, and I'm afraid it's not for the better. I'm glad Eddy's grown now and taking a healthy direction for his future, though I don't know what our president is doing."

In November of 1932, Franklin Delano Roosevelt was elected President in a landslide victory over Herbert Hoover. After his inauguration in March of 1933, FDR announced a four day bank holiday saying that during that time Congress would work on a plan to save the failing bank industry.

FDR's plan was to nationalize gold. In 1933 much of the world was on the Gold Standard; paper money could be exchanged for its value in gold. To stop the run on the banks, from people who now didn't trust paper money and wanted to exchange it for gold, Congress passed the Emergency Banking Act which made it illegal for Americans to possess gold coins or bullion, and took away the right of Americans to be able to exchange paper money for gold. Within a year the government owned most of the gold in the country. In 1934 Roosevelt used the authority given to him by Congress to unilaterally raise the price of gold. Now the treasury had the money Roosevelt needed. Roosevelt was planning a number of expensive social and economic programs and he needed money to finance them.

Prohibition was a failure. Many of the groups of women, who had at one time advocated Prohibition, now saw its repeal as a way to lower crime and help the struggling economy. The reality of the Volstead Act was that it led to appalling social conditions, greatly increased crime rates, and established a black market dominated by organized criminals. Most of America was disenchanted with the prohibition, especially after the Valentine's Day massacre in 1929. The 21st amendment was fully ratified on December 5, 1933, which repealed the 18th amendment; ending the "Noble Experiment."

*

The Longshoreman's strike in San Francisco, in1934, lasted from May to the end of July. It started with a march down the Embarcadero; the Pacific coast longshoremen and seamen had shut down the waterfront. There were several battles between the strikers and the Waterfront Employers Association who employed local and private police to break the strike.

At Pier 38, on the morning of July 5, "Bloody Thursday" the strike turned deadly. Strikebreakers moved trucks, with the help of the police, through the picket lines which started a war. Seven hundred policemen, ready and armed with tear gas and riot guns were organized into an assault force. When the violence stopped, over a hundred workers had been seriously injured; two men had been shot dead.

A meeting of representatives from 115 Bay Area unions was held at the Labor temple and a motion for a general strike was passed. 127,000 workers stayed home from Monday July 16, to the end of the week. Then, after a tumultuous debate and an acceptance of government arbitration, twelve thousand longshoremen and thirteen thousand seamen and marine workers returned to work.

The federal mediation board announced a settlement that implemented better wages, overtime payments, and a five-day work week. It was less than a complete victory but better working conditions had been achieved.

Etta wondered if Harry's brother, Elwood, had been involved, if he was still alive. But, he'd be about seventy now. She hoped he'd stayed home. She'd looked up his name in the phone book once, years back, but never dared to contact him. Peter had told her the Pinkerton's knew where Harry's family lived.

*

In a period of three years, Roosevelt signed legislation creating the Civilian Conservation Corps, the Civil Works Administration, and the Works Progress Administration; all were aimed at employing thousands of people to build roads, bridges, schools, parks and airports, and in improving the National Parks and Forests. Artists were employed in various art projects throughout the states.

The Social Security Act of 1935 was signed into law. Peter joined those who found arguments with the Act. Among the most controversial stipulations of the act was that Social Security would be financed through a payroll tax.

Photographer Dorothea Lange took photographs of migrant workers in the San Joaquin Valley, and the San Francisco News ran a story with the photos. Shortly after, government food was delivered to help the starving migrants, most of whom had fled the Oklahoma dust-bowl. Then the newspaper published a series of articles written by John Steinbeck called, "The Harvest of the Gypsies." Steinbeck told of the hardships of the people living and working in the migrant labor camps.

*

Alma continued on with her medical studies at the "Woman's Medical College of Pennsylvania," the world's first woman's medical school. She would soon take her final exams. She was always under strain, yet doing very well in her courses. Alma would serve her residency at Boston's Woman's Hospital, where she'd be working under close scrutiny and prejudice from the men graduates of Harvard Medical School. Women still faced serious opposition from the male medical establishment. She called home often to talk with her parents and get a boost of support. Peter and Mabel were exceedingly proud of her.

After finishing his studies at Stanford, Joseph applied to Harvard School of Law, where he was accepted. Peter and Mabel visited Joseph his first year there. Mabel showed him the house where she had grown up, and her favorite places. Joseph showed them the more modern attractions. Though Aunt Charlotte had passed away, Joseph had cousins in Boston to visit. Alma would join him on the odd occasion when she took a break from her studies.

Eddy, an enthusiast of nature ever since his childhood, spending summers in the Sierras, had hopes of being a park ranger in the new National Parks Service. Having excellent marks in his studies and with Peter's pull and having family that had previously attended Stanford, he was accepted. He started his studies in Earth Sciences. He could talk for hours about the earth's natural resources.

Secretarial School was Mary Lou's dream come true. Over the years, she'd seen the fashionable secretaries in her father's office, and in the offices of his friends. A secretarial career seemed absolutely glamorous. She was thrilled when she received a new Underwood typewriter for her birthday. Peter was relieved that she was serious about learning skills, all the while knowing she would, without a doubt, attract a husband before long. She was a striking beauty like her mother.

Anne's husband, George, hadn't done well through the hard times. He, Anne and their boys returned to Boston, to live with George's parents while he went back to work at the same Tailor shop where he had apprenticed. Mabel wanted them to stay with her and Peter. Anne had to tell her that George would feel better being with his family.

*

Many jobs were created in the construction of the Bay Bridge that would reach from San Francisco to Oakland, and with the building of the Golden Gate Bridge, that was to cross the span to Marin County. It helped boost the dismal economic conditions in the city. The Bay Bridge was completed in 1936.

There was the shocking news in May of '37, of the disastrous crash of the "Hindenburg," and the spectacular news coverage and the newsreels at the movie houses. It added to the feeling that these were luckless, disastrous times.

In late May, San Franciscans celebrated the opening dedication of the Golden Gate Bridge. On the first day, only pedestrians were allowed to cross. 200,000 people walked or roller-skated across the longest main span suspension bridge in the world. Etta and Charles, with Mabel and Peter, walked across the bridge going half way to the middle, enjoyed the view and the festive atmosphere, and then turned back.

The following day, the bridge was open to automobile traffic, so the couples, in Charles 1928 Dodge, toured across the bridge to Sausalito, spent the afternoon there, and then enjoyed another trip across the bridge, back to San Francisco. Mary Lou waved to them from her boyfriends open top car. The festivities went on for a week.

*

Times continued to be lean and volatile. Back in December of 1936 there had been a strike of the United Auto workers in Detroit that turned violent. Then, ten people were killed and dozens more wounded in the "Memorial Day Massacre" at Republic Steel's South Chicago plant, when workers and their families tried to combine a picnic, in an open field near the plant, with a rally and demonstration. People fighting for better working conditions were met with hostilities in all areas of industry.

Peter was concerned with recent developments in the world. Since 1935, Adolph Hitler had gained tremendous influence over Germany after being appointed Chancellor, and then assumed dictatorial power. The Nazi party was declared the official party of Germany and all other parties were banned. Hitler denounced the disarmament clause of the Versailles Treaty, and introduced compulsory military service.

Spanish Civil War broke out in 1936. In 1937, Japan withdrew from the Washington Conference Treaty that had previously limited the size of its Navy. By 1938, Hitler ordered a plan for the military occupation of Austria, and a directive for the occupation of Czechoslovakia. Hitler gave the German press the task of preparing the German people for war.

"Peter, it says in this article that Amelia Earhart disappeared on July 2nd, over the Central Pacific Ocean, near Howland Island. It was during her attempt to make a circumnavigational flight around the globe. How could she, and her plane, just disappear?" "They'll be looking for her, Mabel. But I wonder if she was over Japanese territory when she went down."

Desiring that peaceful times would resume, Peter hadn't made much of the war when talking with Mabel. But now, how could he not face it, while the world seemed to be getting ready for a continuation of the hostilities from the Great War. Peter, like so many people around the globe, was losing faith in mankind's ability for peace.

Peter's mood of sadness declined further, in September, when he heard of the death of his friend, William Crocker. After attending the services and returning home, he retreated to his study and spent the rest of the day, and most of the night, alone in his despair. After Mabel persuaded him to come to bed, he walked up the stairs feeling very old.

*

Mary Lou worked in the Russ Building, in the financial district downtown. It was San Francisco's tallest and most beautiful building and known as "The Center of Western Progress." She had realized her goal and was the executive secretary for a large law firm. She was still living at home, and was twenty six when she and her boyfriend of four years asked Peter for his blessing of their engagement to be married. Mabel was delighted; she and Peter had met the young man on several occasions and he had been a regular guest on all holidays. Mary Lou met Kevin when he walked into the reception area of her office, when she was new to the firm, and asked her for information about the architectural design of the building. Actually, he had seen her through the glass doors while on an architectural tour of the building with his class, and had to meet her.

Though Joseph had announced his engagement to a Boston girl, months earlier; Mary Lou, the youngest, would be the first to get married. Mary Lou was astonished at the invitation list and realized, not for the first time, what an important man her father was. She insisted that Merritt had to be at her wedding. He was her very dear uncle. She would miss the evening talks with her father and mother, but at least she'd still be living in the city.

Joseph with his fiancé Carol, and Alma, and Eddy, arrived home in June of 1938 for Mary Lou's wedding. It was the first time they'd all been together since Alma finished her residency in Boston; where they had all met for the celebration. They had caused somewhat of a stir in bean town, everywhere they went.

After the wedding, Peter, Mabel, Charles, Etta, and Merritt gathered at Peter's; to enjoy a bottle of champagne and talk about all the years, and all the transformations, that had led to this moment. Their peace was interrupted by Alma, Eddy, Joseph, Carol, and even the newlyweds who were staying at the Fairmont Hotel for their honeymoon. They all wanted to be together for as long as they could make the weekend last.

Eddy still sought out Joseph to talk with; Joseph had never stopped being Eddy's idol. He thought Joseph's girlfriend was beautiful, and hoped to find someone like her for himself; though there were few women interested in the Park Service, and he spent most of his free time out on camping trips. He still went to the cabin in the Sierras whenever he could. He was now enlisted as a ranger in the National Park Service.

They were in the sunny dining room of Mabel and Peter's apartment. White ribbons were streaming from the ceiling; there were fresh flowers in Mabel's paint jars. Champagne glasses were setting on the side table with a bottle of champagne. The judge stood in front of the French doors facing them. Etta had just said "I do." Harry held her, kissed her and said, "I do. I love you Etta." Butch was standing at Harry's side. He was reaching up with his pistol, pointing it at Harry. There was a deafening Bang. Harry fell down dead. "No Harry, no, don't die. No!" "Wake up Etta, Wake up. You've had another nightmare. Dear, you're shaking.

Joseph and Carol decided not to wait any longer for their wedding, and were married early that September. It meant another vacation in Boston for the family. Joseph and Carol's wedding was very traditional as were Carol's parents. Mabel wondered what they thought of her bohemian family. Joseph's Uncle Bud with his wife and two sons, traveled from New York to attend the wedding. Etta had more time to spend with Anne this trip, and was relieved to see she was getting by very well.

While they were in Boston, Alma took them on a tour of the hospital. She looked to Etta to see if she was as impressed as she hoped. Etta noticed this and told her how distinguished she looked in her white coat and that she'd observed how much respect her colleagues showed her. Alma beamed at this compliment. Alma's aunt held a significant place in her affections. Etta had raised and nurtured her through her childhood, right along with her mother.

Etta reminded her that Alma's grandfather had been a doctor; a fine, gentle man, who would've been very proud of his granddaughter.

Alma introduced them to Alan, a handsome surgeon she had been seeing for over a year. Later that evening, Alma and Alan met with her parents to get their blessing. They planned to be married next year in Boston. Alma told her father not to worry; she didn't want a big wedding like Mary Lou's. She wanted just the families to attend.

*

Mabel and Peter didn't know what hit them when Joseph and Carol moved in temporarily while they looked for an apartment. Joseph found a placement with a large San Francisco firm which Peter recommended. Joseph was in high spirits being home again, and enjoyed showing Carol all the sights of San Francisco.

Eddy came home and stayed for two weeks with his parents, before he was to start his assignment in Yellowstone National Park. At the two houses, the much missed pandemonium resumed. Joseph and Eddy talking so fast about their interests, their ideas and the world; no one could keep up with them.

When Eddy left, everyone was in tears, including Merritt who had come to town to see him before he left for Wyoming. He had watched Eddy grow up, and knew his heart. Eddy loved the wilderness and every critter in it. They watched Eddy drive away in Charles newly acquired, but not brand new, 1936 Chevrolet. Charles was once again driving the old beat up '28 Dodge he'd previously given to Eddy. Merritt took care of the needed repairs.

*

October 28, 1938

Dear Family,

I Trust that everyone is well. The drive here to Yellowstone was breathtaking. What an awe inspiring country. I'm housed in old Cavalry barracks in the Mammoth Hot Springs geyser area. The Cavalry was here taking care of the park, before us Park Rangers.

I've already seen herds of elk, antelope, moose, some black bears and grizzlies, but only a few bison. The mountain lion are very elusive. I've only seen one coming down from Duck Lake near the Old Faithful geyser area. There are beavers in ponds just up the hill from the Mammoth compound.

I love it here. We've already had a light snow. They say we'll get a lot of snow this winter. A team of rangers chopped down a lot of dead pine trees in the forest just outside the Montana border of the park (Montana is only a few miles north of Mammoth), so we'll be warm this winter.

I guess we'll need snowshoes for getting around. Thanks to Merritt for showing me ways to get around and stay warm in the cold and snow. Thanks to you, father, for showing me how to make a good soup; I've already impressed my fellow rangers with my cooking skills. Mother, thank you for always encouraging me to follow my dreams!

I was given a uniform, and pair of boots that are too big, but will be fine when I line them with felt for the winter. I will not be home for Christmas. But I will be sending a gift of some examples of rocks, horns and antlers.

Love to you all,
Ed

*

In January of 1939, Peter, Mabel, Mary Lou, Merritt, Etta and Charles traveled, by train to Boston for Alma's wedding. Joseph and Carol followed the next day, staying for a short visit at Carol's parents after the wedding and reception, and then had to return home for Joe's work and Carol's classes. Mary Lou returned with them, anxious to get home to Kevin. Being new to the architectural firm, and with a new building on the drawing board, Kevin hadn't been able to leave his work. Uncle Bud attended the wedding alone. He and his wife had separated.

By her smiles, and hugs and kisses, it was apparent that Alma was pleased that her brother and sister were able to come to her wedding. She hugged Merritt for a long time. Anne, and her husband, George were there also. Mabel and Etta cried at how lovely Alma looked in her beautiful dress; a simple, yet very stylish gown. They felt distressed by the fact that they weren't there with Alma when she picked out her dress. Alan's mother had been there to help, and had arranged an elegant reception in the beautiful home where she and her husband had raised Alan.

*

Treasure Island, in San Francisco Bay, is a man made island, built by filling in an area of shoals by the Bay Bridge. Construction of the island included transplanting over four thousand trees. The first use of the island was for the 1939 Golden Gate International Exposition; which was also a celebration of the completion of both the Golden Gate and San Francisco-Oakland Bridges.

Etta enjoyed herself even more than she had at the 1915 Panama-Pacific Exposition, when her memories of the St Louis Fair, and the aftermath, were still raw; and when she was anxious for Charles return. She, with Charles, Mabel, Peter, Joseph and Carol, enjoyed two days at the fair. Its theme, the "Pageant of the Pacific," focused on the Pacific Rim cultures; many of the architectural structures reflected a sense of past civilizations.

Charles persuaded Etta to go on the rides in the amusement park area. They had fun and laughed together throughout the day. They sat hugging on a bench while looking up at the Phoenix that sat on top of the 'Tower of the Sun," which was designed to remind Treasure Island visitors of the 1906 earthquake and fire, and the rebuilding of the city.

They all enjoyed the "Cavalcade to the Golden West," and all the California Exhibits. Peter and Etta added a lot of information which added to the interest and enjoyment of the rest. Later Charles and Etta talked more about her personal experiences traveling in the west. Etta knew she could speak freely, as Charles was a person with a generous spirit and an understanding and loving nature.

Mabel's favorites were the Fine Arts displays. Peter and Joseph were captivated by the presentations in the Aviation Pavilion. They talked together about how the aviation industry was going to be a big part of the future. The Industrial Exhibits took up alot of everyone's time. Joseph also spent time just with Carol, taking in everything there was to see, and spent a good deal of time in the "Pacific Basin" exhibit grounds.

Carol had been sent to college by her parents who felt this would be the way she would meet a suitable husband. However, she was a bright young woman and had become engrossed in her anthropology and language studies. Joseph was impressed with her knowledge of the Incan, Mayan, Malaysian, and Cambodian cultures represented in the displays. Carol was continuing her studies at the University of California, across the Bay Bridge in Berkeley.

They concluded their second day at the fair watching Billy Rose's fabulous Aquacade. The swimmers formed astonishing patterns and synchronized arrangements in the water. Some were high divers, soaring from the high boards down into deep water. These displays featured Esther Williams, already recognized as a world champion swimmer, as Aquabelle Number One.

Mabel brought home a souvenir song book, "Songs of San Francisco." After dinner that evening she played Sterling Sherwin's, "Two Bridges that Bridged Two Hearts." Then Joseph took over the piano and played a couple of Scott Joplin's tunes, which really livened up the occasion.

*

In May, they decided to return to the fair to see it at night with all the colored lights, and to watch the light shows offered in the evenings. Mary Lou and Kevin were going with Joseph and Carol. Peter and Mabel were picking up Etta and Charles and would meet the kids in the Agricultural building.

Etta and Charles had put on their coats and hats, as the weather was still cool in May. Their house sat a ways up on the hill, so they walked down their path to the street to be ready when Pete drove up. Charles was walking in front of Etta when he fell. Etta rushed to assist him and realized that Charles was gasping for breath and clutching at his chest. He looked like he was in agony. He looked intently at Etta and murmured, "I love you." Then he slumped, falling away from her hold. "No! No! No Charles, don't!

Hold on. Here comes Peter. "Peter! Peter hurry, Charles has had a heart attack!" Peter looked at Charles and moved him to check his breathing and see if he could get a pulse, but there was nothing. "Etta, go to the phone and call the operator for an ambulance." While she did that, Peter went down to the car and told Mabel what had happened; that it appeared that Charles was dead, and there was an ambulance coming.

They waited by Charles until the ambulance came. Etta rode with him. They went to St. Luke's, the closest hospital. It was confirmed that it was a massive heart attack that had killed Charles. Etta was in a zombie like condition and collapsed on the floor. She needed to be hospitalized so the doctor could give her a strong sedative. Mabel wanted to stay with Etta, but Peter insisted she go home and rest. Etta would sleep, and they would return the next morning.

At home, the kids were all waiting at Mabel and Peter's house, wondering why no one had shown up at the fair. They were playing records on the Victrola phonograph player when Mabel and Peter finally arrived. When Peter told them the news, they all broke down in anguish and shock. Mabel hugged the children, one by one, and then went to sit in her bedroom, wondering how her sister could survive another painful and devastating loss.

In the morning, Peter called the emergency number where he could leave a message for Eddy. He didn't want him to receive a message informing him that his father died; so he said to tell Ed that his father was ill, and to please call Uncle Peter. Then Peter called Merritt's friend, Nadine Clark at her store in Sonora, and left a similar message for Merritt. Peter always called Merritt whenever there was any good news or misfortune; Merritt's friendship was better than gold.

Nadine closed her store and drove her car to Merritt's house, to give him the message. She had met Peter, and had taken many messages from him in the past, but had never heard him sounding so shattered. Fortunately Merritt was at the cabin, because she didn't have any idea where the mine was located. Merritt followed her back to the store in his car.

Merritt was the first to call back. When he heard the full news he sobbed so hard he couldn't talk. Then he asked if Eddy had heard the news. Peter said he was waiting for Eddy's call and hoped the roads would be clear for Eddy to travel home. Merritt told Peter he would be there the next day.

After bringing Mabel to the hospital to check on Etta, Peter drove over to Charles house hoping to find the phone number for Charles brother in New York. He found it by the telephone and dialed the number. Peter wasn't holding up well and began to cry while he told Jean about his brother's death. He mentioned what a shock it was; Charles seemed to be such a healthy man; for him to die so suddenly! Jean took the news hard, asking how it could be that his brother was gone. Then he told Peter that heart trouble ran in his family and that Charles knew he had heart problems. He asked if Charles had ever mentioned it. Peter said, no, Charles had never said anything. Jean would not be able to travel to San Francisco for the funeral. But would talk with Etta when she was ready, and send her a telegram of condolence right away. Peter said thank you, hung up the phone, and cried.

Eddy didn't get his message until that afternoon, then he called. "Hi Uncle Peter. How's my father?" "Eddy, your father had a heart attack last night . . . . Oh Eddy, I'm sorry; your father has died." "What? What are you saying? My father is dead? How did it happen?" Peter began, but had to stop while Eddy was sobbing. Peter told him the details. "We were going to the fair last night. Your mother and father were walking down the steps of your house to the street, where Mabel and I were going to pick them up."

"So it happened at there at home—did he suffer?" "No Eddy. It was over in seconds." "How's mother?" "Not good Eddy. This has been a shock; she's resting now." "Uncle Peter, before I left, my father told me a secret; it was that he had a bad heart. He told me so I would understand if anything happened to him. He worried about mother. I'm coming home. There's been a break in the weather. I'll go through Missoula, through Idaho, and then Oregon and over into California. I'll be home as soon as I can. It'll be a few days. Will I be in time for the funeral service?" "We'll wait for you; but Eddy, if the roads are bad you shouldn't travel. We can all gather together at another time when you can come safely home." "Thank you Uncle Peter, but mother will need for me to be there. I'll call along the way, if I can find a telephone. Tell mother I'm on my way." "I will Ed" "Thank you Uncle Peter. Take care of mother and Aunt Mabel." "I will Ed, you take care driving. Bye for now."

Then Peter called Alma, first at her house, hoping she had a day off from her work. When there was no answer, he called the number for the hospital. After telling the hospital operator he was Alma's father, he was connected with her office. He was relieved when she answered. Not knowing if she was in the middle of something, he began by asking her how everything was going with her; but she could hear the strain in his voice, and besides she wondered why he had called her at work. She quickly asked, "Father, are you alright? How is mother?" "We're alright Alma. It's Uncle Charles. I'm so sorry to tell you he died of a heart attack." "Oh father! No! How is mother? How is Aunt Etta?" "Not good Alma . . . ." "I'm coming home. I'll have to take care of some things here first and then I should be on a train by tomorrow. Have you told Eddy? "Yes, but Alma you don't have to come, I know you have your work." Nonsense, I'm coming home to be with my family. I'll call you and let you know when I'll be there. I love you Father." "I love you dear daughter."

Everyone was worried for Etta; and also for Eddy, traveling all this way with such a burden of grief. Etta was now at Mabel's home. Mabel never left her side; calling for Peter or Joseph whenever she needed help. Etta was drinking water but not eating much food. She was still shaky from the shock, and from the sedatives that were given her in the hospital.

Merritt arrived; said only a quick hello to everyone, and went right in to see Etta. She lifted herself to hug him and he rocked her gently in his arms. He began talking with her about how she had seen trouble before, and reminded her that he was her friend and they had both been through some real bad times before this. She cried for awhile in his arms then let go and rested again on her pillows. Merritt also talked with her about the good times they'd had in the past, both with Harry, and with Charles. After they talked, Etta seemed better. Merritt turned to Mabel and said he'd be right back, then went to get a glass of watered down whiskey for Etta. "Remember our old way, Etta; you have a glass of whiskey, and then eat a little something." Then he went to the kitchen to fix toast and applesauce for her.

Peter had also phoned Paul, Charles partner at the grocery store. Then Joseph drove to the store to talk with Paul about what happened. Paul closed the store; picked up two baskets and filled one with fruit, then sliced lunchmeats and cheeses; wrapped them, and put the packages in the other basket, along with loaves of French bread, then drove to Joseph's house. He'd been to the house a few times, mostly to deliver groceries for Mabel's society dinners. Joseph continued on to the Art Institute, to deliver a message from Mabel. He posted it on the bulletin board. It read:

Friends of Charles LeBesque

Our dear friend and teacher, Charles LeBesque,
passed away Monday night, May 8, 1939 at his home. His wife, son,
and family would like you to join them in a celebration of his life,
at a service
to be held at a time and place to be announced shortly.
In lieu of flowers—donations to
the Art Institute are welcome in his name.

Etta was on her feet when Eddy finally arrived. She wanted to be strong for him. Jasper, a fellow park ranger from Yellowstone, arrived with Ed. Jasper had done the driving. He'd been due for time off before the busy summer season started, and wouldn't let his friend drive all that way in the condition of despair that he was in. Jasper was welcome into the family fold like a returning hero. Eddy spent all his time with his mother.

"Eddy, I've been thinking; I plan on going to the cabin, once I take care of things here, and stay there for some time. I just need to be away from everything for awhile. Would it be alright with you, if I let Mary Lou and Kevin use the house? They can use the help, especially with a child on the way." "Good idea mother and the Sierra's are just what you need. I can stay until June, and then I have to return to the park, so stay here until I have to leave. Mother; father's really gone isn't he."

Alma kept a careful watch over Etta, and her mother, who seemed more than sad; she was clearly in a weakened condition. Mary Lou would have liked to be more of a help, but she was suffering from morning sickness. This was the most distressing event for the family since years ago when Joseph fell from a tree in the park and the rest of the children came running in the house, saying he was dead. A trip to the hospital to fix a broken arm, and rest from a bump on the head, was all that was required.

Besides making arrangements for the service, and placing a notice in the paper, Peter drove out to the cemeteries in Colma, to purchase a burial plot for Charles. He bought a dual plot; when the time came Etta could be buried beside him. He also bought a dual plot for himself and Mabel. It gave him the willies to be buying these burial plots, but he realized that he and Mabel were now in their sixties, and he didn't want to leave the job to his children. He didn't tell Mabel; that could wait for another time. On the way home, Peter stopped to buy wreaths with black bows; one to put on the front door of Charles house, with a note stating that the family would be at the Scott Street address, and the other for his front door.

Mabel was kept distracted by her many acquaintances from the Art Institute that came to give condolences to the family. Etta stayed in the bedroom and wasn't aware of the visitors. On the morning of the service, Etta entered the chapel and stood transfixed at the entrance, not really understanding at first, that all these people crowded into the large room were there to pay their respects to Charles.

The room was filled with family, customers from the store, artists and students, the people Charles met in the park, or met around town while he painted his canvases, politicians he'd met through Peter, and patrons who'd bought his paintings. He'd made a profound impression on them all. His sincere interest in everyone, his astonishing excitement for life, and especially his wide, happy smile, made each and every one he was with feel better about what ever they may be experiencing in their own lives.

Everyone gathered at Peter and Mabel's house after the service and the burial. Etta sat on the divan in the front room with Eddy and Merritt at her side. When she found a moment, at the end of the day to talk with Peter, she asked him to have the deed of the house transferred to Ed's name. Peter told her he'd take care of it right away, while Ed was still in town.

Mabel was asked by the director of the Art Institute, to send as many of Charles paintings that Etta would part with. The interest in Charles work had escalated overnight. After the Institute put out an announcement, eighteen of Charles paintings were sold in two weeks. However, the family portraits and other favorites that Charles had painted were never to be sold.

*

Before he left, Ed convinced his mother to take a walk with him; he remembered the walks he enjoyed with his parents during the years he was growing up. As they walked, they reminisced how Charles always talked with people along the way. They walked through Washington Park, and by their old apartment in North Beach where their small family had begun, then walked further on, up the steep hill to Coit Tower.

At the top of the hill they paused to catch their breath and took in the panoramic views. Inside they viewed the murals; painted when the tower was constructed in 1933. It was easy to see Diego Rivera's influence on the artists. They took the elevator to the top, where the startling spectacle of the city halted their conversation. As they looked out in every direction on the bright, electrifying city, they became absorbed in their own memories.

A week later, Eddy left, with Jasper, to drive back to Yellowstone Park. Etta packed her personal things, her city clothes, her journals, letters and photographs in locking trunks and had them stored in Mabel's basement; then she packed for her stay at the cabin. She showed Mary Lou and Kevin how to care for the chickens, and how the furnace worked. There was no dog now; he had passed away long ago.

Etta drove her old car the 150 miles to the cabin, with Peter and Mabel following in their car. Strapped on the back of the cars were the auxiliary gas tanks to get them through the long stretches where gasoline was unavailable. They made rest stops along the way and stopped in Sonora for food supplies and to visit Nadine, whom they had all grown very fond of.

*

Etta returned to San Francisco with Merritt and Nadine, to celebrate Christmas and the arrival of Mary Lou and Kevin's new baby, Michael Thomas Morrison. Etta stayed at the house with Mary Lou and Kevin and enjoyed helping Mary Lou with the baby.

Merritt and Nadine stayed with Peter and Mabel, which overjoyed Mabel. She took a lot of pleasure in telling Nadine about the days when Merritt first came to stay with them so many years ago. Merritt enjoyed showing Nadine the sights of San Francisco.

Though there was the remembrance of their loss, there was also new life to celebrate. The Christmas festivities brought some joy to the family. They enjoyed a quiet New Year's Eve celebration, and then on Tuesday, January 2, 1940, Etta returned, with Merritt and Nadine, to the cabin in the Sierras.

XXI

1940's

While the economy was getting back on its feet from the worst fiscal decade of the century, most Americans were feeling threatened by the approaching war. With abiding pessimism, they were already calling it World War Two.

German troops had invaded Czechoslovakia and Poland, and were now in Denmark, Norway, France, Belgium, Luxembourg, and the Netherlands. By June, Germany had taken Paris. The German Blitz against Britain had begun. Italy invaded Egypt, North Africa, and Greece. Every major world power was rushing headlong into the fight for global domination and a continuation of the plights and ills of the First World War.

Diego Rivera returned to San Francisco in June of 1940, to paint a ten-panel mural for the extended second year of the Golden Gate International Exposition. After the fair ended, his mural, "Pan-American Unity," was moved to the library at San Francisco's City College. Mabel and Peter went to the fair to watch Diego paint, and talk with him and Frida Kahlo. Peter had a difficult time understanding Diego's views on communism.

*

Alma and Alan were doing well in Boston, and now were each in private practice; Alma in general family health, and Alan in referred Surgery. Ed was living his dream at Yellowstone Park. Mary Lou, Kevin, and baby Michael, were living in Etta's house. Kevin was struggling to be recognized among San Francisco Architects. Mary Lou worked occasionally through a temporary placement service. Joseph was doing well as an associate in his law firm, and Carol continued to take classes part time at the University of California in Berkeley.

Frank O'Brien, Peter's partner, had retired the year before; now Peter closed his downtown office and worked from his office at home; keeping only the long time clients he'd helped over the years. Mabel still painted though she wasn't as productive as in the past. The house was lonely with Etta at the cabin, and the children out of the house; though Joseph and Carol, and Mary Lou and Kevin came over often. The delighted grandparents often took care of Michael, giving the young couple time for each other. Michael reminded them of Joseph, when he was a baby.

*

Nadine Clark was petite, attractive, and intelligent; she and Merritt were just right for each other. She sold her mercantile store and now lived comfortably in a small house on a hill just five blocks from the center of Sonora. Merritt continued to spend his Saturday evenings and Sundays with her, returning back to the cabin on Monday mornings. Nadine went out to the cabin occasionally, and now that Etta was there, she came out at times just to enjoy Etta's company. They'd ride the horses, or take walks, or just sit and talk. Sometimes Etta would stay at Nadine's house to give her time alone with Merritt at the cabin. Etta enjoyed the townspeople that Nadine had introduced.

Nadine had seen misfortune and suffering and understood some of what Etta was going through. She had lived in the hills with her husband back in the days when he was mining; through the ups and downs of sometimes being flush, and other times being broke. Finally they had enough money to buy the store in town and then her husband had been killed in a mining accident helping out at a friends mine.

Nadine was a very straightforward, down to earth person, and during one of the long walks in the mountains with Etta, Nadine finally said, "Etta, there's more to you than you reveal. I hope someday you'll tell me your story." "Yes, perhaps . . . . No, I'll tell you now. I was married when I was young, to a man who had done things against the law; so we left the country to live in Argentina with his partner. We had a good ranch where we raised cattle and lived a happy life. Then the Pinkerton's detectives, found out where we were. Merritt came down to bring me back home. I had to leave my home and my husband. My husband, Harry, and his partner, James, were found and killed a couple of years later, after they'd robbed a mining company payroll. Merritt went to South America again, to look into what had happened. I thought perhaps Merritt might have told you." "No, no, he mentioned once that he'd been in South America but never said why. Tell me, Etta, do you regret your life in Argentina?" "Oh, no, it was the happiest most thrilling time of my life; I learned so much and I enjoyed that life immensely." "Even though it ended so painfully for you?" "Yes, I took that chance when I went there, though I didn't believe it would end that way. I cherish the memories and the time I had with my Harry; though it's true that I still grieve for him."

"Etta, I recently read a book written by Isak Dinesen, a woman from Denmark, who went to Africa where she and her husband raised coffee beans. She enjoyed fantastic adventures and also extreme disappointments; her husband left her, to go with other women. Later she had an affair with an adventurer whom she deeply loved. When her coffee plantation failed, and then her lover died in an accident; she returned home to Denmark and wrote the book. In it, she said; Perhaps the earth was made round, so we would not see too far down the road. Isn't that just how it is." "Yes, Nadine, thank you. I'd like to read that book."

Etta now had a friend she could be open with. She'd enjoyed talking with Merritt about the past but sometimes kept guarded, not wanting to bring up the memory of the troubled journey home and cause him distress; she knew it had been awful for him. Merritt was always concerned about her well being, indeed he was her big brother.

Merritt's mining efforts were still paying off. Peter had always been generous with him in their arrangement, and had recently put Merritt's name on the deed making him half owner of the mining claim and the property.

*

In August, Etta joined Joseph and Carol on a vacation to Yellowstone Park. It had been over a year since they had seen Ed. None of them had any idea of the grandeur of the country that they now experienced. They went over rugged mountain passes and into

Montana, east to Livingston, and then turned south to the north entrance of the park. Once up the hill to the Mammoth compound, they saw the old Fort Yellowstone where Ed lived and worked. The old National Hotel had been torn down and the new Mammoth Hot Springs Hotel was being built. They were staying in the newly built cabins. After they got settled in their cabins, they went to find Ed. They found him in the second park service building. It seemed everyone knew they were coming, and Ed introduced his family to each one of the park rangers. Etta and Ed hugged for a long time. After dinner they found time for a long walk and talked with each other about what was going on in their lives, about their loss of Charles, and about Ed's future. Etta was pleased, seeing her son so happy; there couldn't be anyone better suited in his position.

Ed had planned for time off when his family arrived. Etta rested the next day while Ed, Joe and Carol went hiking to Ed's favorite beaver ponds. Along the way, Carol listened to Eddy and Joseph talk about the coming U.S. involvement in the war as though it was a certainty. Ed told Joseph that he'd heard there would be mandatory conscription coming up soon. Carol was horrified realizing that these young men talked as though they planned to join in the war when the U.S. was involved.

From Mammoth Hot springs they all took the Grand Loop tour of the park. They stayed at the Old Faithful Inn, the Lake Yellowstone Hotel, the Lodge at the Grand Canyon of the Yellowstone, and at the cabins at the Roosevelt Lodge at Tower Junction, seeing all the sights, geysers, bears, elk, bison, and wildflowers along the way. They spent two weeks enjoying the wonders of the park and being with Ed before they returned home.

On her return, Etta stayed for awhile with Mabel and Peter. Then she stayed with Mary Lou to take care of Michael while Mary Lou worked at a temporary job for two weeks. Mabel missed Etta and came over every day to talk with her while they watched over Michael. Sometimes Peter came also. They all were aware of the war and were distressed that their sons might be involved. Peter had already talked with a senator, about keeping Joseph, Ed, and Kevin away from the front lines. Mabel and Peter drove Etta back to the cabin and stayed a week. Peter wanted to talk with Merritt about the war and get his take on the outlook for the future.

President Roosevelt signed the Selective Service Act on September 16, 1940, beginning the first peacetime draft in the United States requiring men between the ages of twenty-one and forty-five to register. In November, FDR was elected to an unprecedented third term as president, which showed the nation's support for entering the war.

*

The following summer, Merritt and Nadine made the trip to Yellowstone to see Ed. There was so much Ed wanted to share with, and show Merritt. Ed and Merritt took a long overnight hike to the top of Electric Peak where Merritt's hair stood straight up from the static electricity. Nadine spent that time reading about the history of the park and taking walks around the hot springs. They spent two weeks touring and hiking in the park, and another two weeks exploring Wyoming and Montana.

Etta was living at the cabin. Her garden had done well that year. While Merritt and Nadine were traveling, friends from Sonora stopped by occasionally to see if she was alright. She liked this life, living in the mountains, in much the same way as she'd enjoyed living in Argentina. It had been Charles that brought her the joy of living in San Francisco.

Merritt and Nadine returned to the Sierras the last week of October and Merritt immediately went to work cutting and stocking firewood for the coming winter; the air was already icy. Nadine and Etta already made plans to try their hand at making fudge to give as Christmas presents.

On Monday morning, December 8, 1941, Peter telephoned Nadine and told her that yesterday, on Sunday, the Japanese had bombed Pearl Harbor in the Hawaiian Islands, and the United States and Britain had declared war on Japan. Fortunately Merritt was still at Nadine's house, lingering after a good breakfast and enjoying the cozy warmth of her home. Nadine seemed to be in shock over the news. She couldn't explain why she didn't want to be alone, so she went with Merritt to the cabin where he would have to tell Etta the news. Peter had asked for them to come to the city so they could all be together. Ed had called and said he was given leave from the park and was on his way home.

Germany and Italy had declared war on the United States, and the draft now required men from 18 to 65 to register, with those aged 18 to 45 being immediately liable for induction. Many of Ed's and Joseph's friends were already enlisting.

*

Everyone except Alma and Alan would be home for Christmas. Alan was considering enlisting in the Army to work as an army surgeon. He and Alma were discussing it while they spent time with his parents in Boston during the holidays.

Nadine and Merritt arrived in mid December and were staying with Mabel and Peter; they were there when Joseph arrived at the house to talk with his father. Across town, Carol arrived at Etta's house, wanting to speak with her. Etta was staying there and taking care of Michael who was now two years old, and adorable.

"Aunt Etta, Joseph is going to tell his father that he's enlisting in the Army. He's heard that he would go into officers training. I can't stand it, but there's nothing I can do about it." Oh Carol, I've been dreading this news but expecting it. Peter will oppose Joe's signing up, but I fear Joe will do it anyway, and then Ed will follow. Joseph has always been his champion. They both want to do what they think is right. I've heard Mary Lou and Kevin talking. Mary Lou is trying to convince Kevin to wait and see if he's drafted; but I don't think he'll wait. Oh hell!"

"I'd be lost without Joe. I remember when Uncle Charles died. I don't know if I could live if anything happened to Joe. How do you manage?" "Carol, you keep your mind very busy with the ordinary things of daily life and you just muddle through. Joseph will no doubt be given officers duty and hopefully won't be put in the middle of the conflict; that's what I'm hoping for Eddy." "Aunt Etta, how thoughtless of me, you have Eddy to worry about, while I'm talking about myself." "I'm glad you are; you have to be concerned for your own well being. When Joseph is away, learn or try something you've always wanted to do; then you'll have something to keep yourself busy, and can look forward to showing Joe, when he returns. Make him proud of you."

Aunt Etta, my studies did teach me one worthwhile thing; that in all cultures, young men have some sort of rite of passage; it's stupid that, in this culture, it has to be going to a war, but I do understand Joe's need to be a man among men. I'm quitting school and looking for a job; with all the men leaving, I've read there'll be a need for workers at home. I'll move in with Mabel and Peter. Oh, Aunt Etta." Etta held Carol until she finished crying.

*

"Joseph, I taught you to think for yourself. I hoped to arrange for you to not go overseas. You can help the war effort at home! Father, this is different." "How is it different?" "This maniac, Hitler, is a criminal with a wholesale license for killing. Our country can't let this go on!" "Joseph, there are other ways. At one time I was fascinated with the study of war, until I learned too much. Joseph, towards the end of the First World War, there was the outbreak of the Spanish Influenza. It devastated every country around the globe, and had a heavy impact in the fatalities on soldiers from every country. It's been thought that's why the fighting ended. It was only then that the governments went to the table and worked out their differences, and made the Treaty of Versailles. They could have done that in the first place. Now a new generation of cannon fodder has come up and the power hungry leaders are at it again. Joseph, when you were growing up; I taught you about settling your arguments with reason." "But father, we're living in an unreasonable world!" "All the more reason for you to stay away from it!" "Father, Ed feels the same way. He feels strongly about protecting the security of our country and also France, the country his father was raised in. He's heard the stories of Charles life there. He doesn't want to stand by and hear about more destruction."

Peter paused, trying to keep his emotions in check. He loved the fine man that Joseph had become. He knew Joseph was going to enlist and go to the war, and admitted to himself, that it was what he would have done under the same circumstances. There really was no possible way to keep his son from the more atrocious aspects of war. "Joseph, I realize you must do what you feel is right. Please seek a position as an officer and avoid being a hero. Will you do that?" "I'll try father." Peter gave his son a warm embrace, holding him very close, and then had to turn away to dry his tears. Merritt and Nadine heard the conversation from their room, and were holding each other.

*

It was not a cheerful Christmas at Peter's house. Mabel had sunk down into a deep sadness and despair, and could barely hold up for the Christmas Eve and Christmas Day celebrations. Peter cooked a delectable twenty pound turkey, and made his renowned dressing. Carol and Mary Lou fixed the side dishes. Etta made the pumpkin, and apple-cranberry pies. She wanted to stay busy and give Ed, Joseph, and Kevin a feeling of strength and support. Mary Lou and Carol were doing the same. Peter tried vigorously to be supportive of the young men. His New Year's toast was for their safe return.

By January; Joseph, Ed, and Kevin had been inducted and had received their classifications. Joseph entered specialized training, and would go on to Officer Candidate School with the Army Air Forces. Ed would also have specialized training, then Officer Candidate School, and would be going into the Army's Counterintelligence Corps. After talking it over with his father, Kevin entered the Navy, where he'd receive specialized training for the Navy's Civil Engineer Corps.

Being forty-two, Alan received stateside duty. He was in training with the Army Medical Corps, to be a Commissioned Medical Officer at the Valley Forge Hospital, which was to be opened in early 1943. Alma was enormously relieved. When she phoned home to tell everyone the news, she also spoke with Etta, telling her about Alan going to Phoenixville, Pennsylvania, to work in the new military hospital being built there. Etta gasped at the mention of the town where Harry's family lived.

Anne's sons were so young, only twenty and twenty two. They were drafted in the navy before they had time to enlist. Anne phoned to ask where Ed, Joe, and Kevin were going. She couldn't come to grips with parting from her boys and needed to talk with Etta and Mabel.

Etta was again staying with Mabel and Peter. Mabel never rallied from the news that the boys were going to war. Peter had called Dr. Morris, on the advice of Alma who had suggested there may be more to her mother's depression than Joe and the boys leaving. The diagnosis revealed a weak heart and a generally weakened physical condition; no doubt made worse by her recent worries. Mabel had evidently been suffering with this condition for sometime.

*

Carol found a job at the docks keeping records on harbor traffic. The war effort gave a big boost to U.S. Industry and effectively ended the Great Depression. After Carol moved in with Mabel and Peter; Etta went to live with Mary Lou and little Michael. She went to visit and check on Mabel every day. Peter again hired a woman to clean and to cook so Mabel wouldn't have any strenuous work. Peter was usually at home for the better part of each day. Mabel and Peter always enjoyed each others company and always found new subjects to talk about. Peter bought stacks of books for them all to read and keep their minds off the war.

Everyone was stunned when American citizens of Japanese descent were served warrants to report to the Civil Control Station to be evacuated. The Army transported the evacuees to the Manzanar Internment Camp located in California's Owen Valley. Bunkers were built on the bluffs and hills along the coast, and an anti-submarine net was stretched across the entrance to San Francisco Bay. The news kept getting worse; there was now information of the mass murder of Jewish people in Germany.

*

1943 passed with excessive sluggishness with every season feeling like winter. A withholding tax on wages was introduced. No more paying taxes just on the tax dates. The tax now came right out of earnings.

Letters from the men were waited for and looked for everyday, but were few and slow in coming. When a letter did arrive, it was passed around and read over and over. Receiving a letter from any one of the men meant that he was okay, and made everyone feel better. They continually wrote to the men; sending their letters to a military receiving office, hoping they'd be received and read before too long.

Kevin was stationed in the Pacific Islands, where his Construction Battalion was building airstrips, hospitals, bridges and roads. Joseph was a navigator for his Tactical Reconnaissance Squadron, securing information about the enemy, terrain, and weather for immediate use on the battlefield. His last letter indicated that he was somewhere in the Mediterranean

Ed was the least heard from. He'd scored very high on the Army General Classification Test, and with his knowledge of French and Spanish languages had been chosen for an exacting position in counterintelligence. Going by his last letter, which had as many blacked out sentences as not, the family thought he might also be in the Mediterranean area. He, like most CIC agents in the field, held a non-commissioned officer rank. He wore plain clothes with a U.S. collar insignia.

Alan, and his fellow surgeons at the hospital, felt like a clean-up crew. They were always exhausted; mentally, physically and emotionally. To see the great extreme of damages inflicted on these young men was at times unbearable; nevertheless the doctors kept at it day after day, month after month. The hospital had grown to be the largest military hospital in the United States, with over one hundred separate two-story buildings. Alma went to Phoenixville often, to be with Alan and give him encouragement.

*

The war continued on. Treasure Island, in San Francisco Bay, that had once been the site of the worlds fair, became a naval base. American forces joined Great Britain, and were conducting air attacks in Germany. War raged across the globe. Etta, Peter and Mabel went to the movies and watched newsreels of the fighting. Several people in the audiences cried, thinking of their loved one's in the fight.

Merritt registered for the draft but didn't enlist. He was never called up for duty. He was 58 years old and glad to be staying close to home. He and Nadine spent most of that winter with Peter and Mabel. Because of gas rationing, Etta and Peter used every one of their ration stamps so any extra gas could be siphoned into a large gas tank on the hill behind Etta's house, to be used for Merritt's trips to and from the cabin.

Etta still grew a large vegetable garden. During the depression she had invited neighbors to use a portion of the property to grow gardens also. There was always someone out working on the gardens when she or Mary Lou looked out the window. One of the neighbors was a young woman who Mary Lou had become good friends with. Her husband was also away in the war. When news came that her husband had been killed she came over to see Mary Lou and Etta. The women now understood, more than ever, what it was like to be at war.

Etta felt she should be contributing towards the war effort. She went to Letterman's Army Hospital, not knowing for sure how, or if, she could be of any help. Her age was now sixty-five. She looked and felt in good health, and she still held her good posture. It turned out she was a welcome asset from the first day she walked in and began talking with recuperating soldiers who were sitting in a reception area. From then on, four days of each week, she talked with the men, and wrote letters for them. She brought them goodies from her home, and listened to them tell the stories of their experiences in the war. At the end of those days, she would take the bus home and then cry.

*

All correspondence from the military, concerning Joseph, Ed and Kevin came to the Scott Street address. It was Peter's idea that no one should be alone if they received bad news. The afternoon the Western Union courier arrived, he was carrying two brown envelopes. Peter answered the door, received the telegrams, and stood there shaking with the unopened envelopes in his hand. How could there be two? Surely not two of the men could be dead; and certainly not at the same time.

Peter went to his office and sat staring at the envelopes in his hand. Now he understood. One was addressed to Carol, the other to himself and Mabel. He slumped over on his desk and cried. There was only one conclusion; his son, Joseph! He opened both envelopes. Joseph had been killed in action. His body could not be returned. A letter would follow to explain the details. He sat there crying for over an hour; then he called Mabel's' doctor and explained to him that he would be telling Mabel the news and needed him to come over to help Mabel.

Peter found Mabel reading, reclined on the chaise in her sunny studio. He didn't realize that he was still holding the telegrams. Mabel saw them and immediately started to cry. "No Peter, which one?" "Mabel; our son, Joseph." "No Peter, no, it's a mistake—No!" Mabel broke down; sobbing so hard that Peter was worried she'd stop breathing. After she calmed a little, she moaned, "Joseph, our boy. No Peter!" "I re-checked his service number. It's Joseph." "I can't, I don't know how to live through this Peter." Peter was sitting on the chaise with Mabel crumpled in his arms; both crying with grief too horrible to bear.

Dr. Morris arrived and gave Mabel a sedative. He left the bottle of pills in Peter's hands. "Don't let her take the pills on her own Pete, I've seen too many mothers and wives break down and give up. I'll leave additional pills for your daughter in law. When will she be home; should I stay?" "She'll be home in about an hour. Will you join me with a drink?" Thanks Pete, but I really should get back to the office. Call me for any concern. I'll stop by tomorrow and have that drink with you."

Peter called Mary Lou, told her the news, and asked her to come to the house as soon as Etta returned from the hospital. Mabel was lying in bed when Mary Lou and Etta arrived with Michael. Michael rushed over to climb on the bed with his grandma. Mabel held him and wept until Mary Lou saw that her mother was tiring and took Michael out of the room.

"Etta, I'm sorry. I had no real understanding of what it's like to lose someone you love." "Dear sister, you did understand, and were a great comfort. Right now you're in the worst possible suffering and agony. It's unthinkable and impossible to even imagine that Joseph is gone. It's not even believable. It'll take awhile to get used to even the thought of it. Sleep now, it helps." "No, I hear Carol, I told Peter to bring her to me right away, and we would tell her the news together. Help me take care of her Etta."

Peter phoned Alma to tell her the news. She would come home by the end of the week to be with her parents. Peter reminded her that, though she could tell Alan, neither of them could include this news in letters to Kevin and Ed.

When Merritt got the news, he and Nadine closed up her house, and the cabin, and planned to stay awhile with Mabel and Peter. He couldn't make many trips, now that tires were nearly impossible to find.

Michael was the focus of Christmas that year in 1944. Seeing the four year old so thrilled over his new toys made their hearts a little lighter. Merritt had spent many days in the basement making a wood train set for him. Mabel held Michael more than ever. Mary Lou knew her mother saw Joseph in him. Carol wasn't doing any better, and said she would be returning to Boston to live with her parents after the first of the year. That news felt like more loss for the family.

*

Another New Year began and the unrelenting war continued. Roosevelt, Churchill and Stalin met in conference in February, at Yalta, with no change to the war. Then, Soviet troops marched through Germany and liberated the concentration camp at Auschwitz; captured Danzig, and in late April made their final attack on Berlin. The Americans entered Nuremberg. Mussolini was captured and hung by Italian partisans. Hitler committed suicide, and then Germany and Italy surrendered. May 8th was the day of Victory in Europe.

Harry Truman became president, when President Roosevelt died in April. President Roosevelt had been working on his speech for the United Nations Conference of International Organization, which convened as scheduled that June in San Francisco. Representatives of fifty countries met to draw up the United Nations Charter. The Charter was signed in June and made official that October, in 1945.

At home, all were hopeful that the war would be completely over soon. On August 6th, the first atomic bomb was dropped on Hiroshima, Japan. The second atomic bomb was dropped three days later on Nagasaki; then the Japanese government signed a surrender agreement. Victory in Japan Day, August 15th, 1945, signaled the end of the war throughout the world.

Over sixty million people had lost their lives, and Europe and parts of Asia lay in ruins. It had been a time of doing without, much like the depression, but this time there were shortages in metal, rubber, steel; gasoline and foods that had been rationed since these were needed staples for the war effort. Milkmen had resorted to making their deliveries using horse-drawn wagons. There had been no new cars produced while the auto factories were manufacturing military vehicles.

*

Kevin returned home in October. He'd gone to Etta's house, his home before he left, and found Mary Lou hanging up the laundry in back of the house. He paused just to look at her and compose himself. He made a noise clearing his throat and she turned and saw him. Now, she just stared, not sure if her eyes were playing tricks; then Kevin said, "Mary Lou," and she was in his arms; each hugging and kissing and crying.

Then Kevin noticed a little boy come running across the hill. Was this Michael? The boy hid shyly behind his mother, not knowing who this man was. Kevin understood: when he'd left, this boy was a baby, and because at first, he didn't recognize his son, until he looked directly at him and saw himself as a boy.

After celebrating with their families, Mary Lou, Kevin, and Michael went to the cabin and stayed until mid December. Kevin had sustained a wound in his right leg that would, in time, completely heal; also shrapnel had made a mess of his right shoulder. His real difficulty was in not yet feeling like a part of American society. To make matters worse, his father had died two weeks before he arrived home. Kevin's mother had gone to live with his older sister. Taking it slow, being out in the country and talking with Merritt was helping him readjust.

Etta received word that Ed would be coming home by next spring. She hadn't received any correspondence for quite a while, so now felt somewhat relieved. She could relax completely when he was finally home.

Ed went to his house, hoping his mother would be there. He stopped at the front door and knocked; knowing she would be alarmed at someone just walking in. Etta opened the door; her eyes went wide and she flew out the door into Ed's strong arms. They went inside, bringing in Ed's large duffel bag. After she stopped crying, all she wanted to do was to look at him, her son. "Can you talk about where you were, and what you saw, Ed?" "I will, but not just yet. The main reason it took so long in coming home was all the paperwork; more for me because I was in counterintelligence; form after form. A lot of information is still considered classified, and until it's declassified, I can't talk about it. To tell you the truth, I need to sort it out in my thoughts anyway. Some of what I saw, I just can't come to terms with. Say, what about some food; do you have some good soup ready?"

After a big meal, Etta was pleased that Ed wanted to drive over to see Peter and Mabel. Peter greeted them at the door, and cried out, "Ed, my boy!" Once inside, Peter and Ed shook hands, then Ed reached out to his Uncle Peter and hugged him. Peter took at good look at Ed; there was no boy left in this man.

Mabel came in the room, and Ed took her in his arms and held her while they both cried. Then Etta and Mabel went to the kitchen to slice cake to celebrate Ed's return. Peter poured Ed and himself a whiskey, and sat down to talk.

"Uncle Peter, I heard about Joe. I knew before I came home. I was able to keep track of him; I was in Italy at the time he was shot down. I'm sorry Uncle Peter, so sorry. The war liberated millions from tyranny, but at a cost. Millions lost their lives and there are millions still homeless across the globe. So far, there's still not an end to the suffering from what people have endured. Even now, there's an atmosphere of uncertainty. It'll take time."

When Etta phoned Anne, as she often did, Anne cried in relief to hear that Ed was home. She had taken the news, about Joseph, very hard, and worried about Mabel and Peter. Anne had her own anguish. Her youngest son, Sean had one leg amputated at the knee. He'd be in a naval hospital for some time to come. They were teaching him to walk using an artificial prosthesis. Her oldest son had returned and offered the best support and encouragement for him.

*

Christmas of 1946 offered some happy and joyful moments. Merritt and Nadine had stayed in town since returning that fall. Mary Lou announced that she was pregnant. The men thought that was the perfect reason to celebrate with whiskey. Mabel made 'Tom and Jerry's" earlier, but that was all gone. Michael was now seven, and had never seen such rejoicing. Yet, there were several moments when they wept. Peter, Merritt, Ed and Kevin went into Peter's office after dinner to talk. The young men talked some more about their experiences in the war, Ed telling what he could. Peter asked them what they were looking forward to in the future. Both young men were silent. Finally, Kevin said, "I guess I still need a little time to figure that out." Ed followed with, "I guess that's the same for me."

Now that Kevin was home, Etta had moved back in with Mabel and Peter and Ed had done the same. Kevin finally went to the offices of his old employer. He didn't know what kind of reception he'd receive. When it turned out they were hoping he'd come by, because they wanted to rehire him, he relaxed. He'd start back to work the first week of March.

During the war, Alma's husband, Alan, suffered chronic exhaustion and felt used up. After the war he stayed on at the military hospital for another year, improving on the hasty field surgeries performed in the battlefields, hospital trains, and ships.

Ed spent a lot of time with Kevin; they walked everywhere, and found that talking about their experiences was easier while they were walking. When Kevin went back to work with the architectural firm, Ed started going on walks with Mabel and Peter, around Alta Plaza Park and the neighborhood. He noticed that talk also came easier walking with them. He and Joseph had played in the park as children. Mabel finally could talk a little about Joseph, and reminisce with Ed and Peter.

Most afternoons, Ed would meet his mother after her day at the hospital. He'd go into the rest and recreation room where she could usually be found. He was proud of her and noticed she didn't look away from unpleasant sights, but always faced the men, and looked directly at them in conversation.

When Alma came for a visit, Peter treated his entire family, which included Merritt and Nadine, and a few close friends, out to dinner to celebrate, as he put it, "the ending of world violence and chaos." They went to Fisherman's wharf, Grotto #9. The wine flowed, and the fresh fish dishes were scrumptious. Ed and Kevin talked about missing San Francisco's sourdough bread.

Before Merritt returned to the Sierras, Ed asked him if he could stay with him, at the cabin, for awhile. He was packing for his move when two Army officers arrived at Peter's front door. They were carrying a metal box. Ed showed the alarm he felt and the officers quickly explained that in the box were medals honoring Joseph. Ed called Peter and Mabel to the front room.

This was what was left of their son! This hit them as hard as the first news of Joe's death. After the officers left, Ed explained again what the medals represented: The Air Medal, for meritorious achievement, the Silver Star, for gallantry in action, the V for Valor medal . . . . . Mabel had to lie down; she'd have to hear the rest later.

Ed had been holding up for his family. At the cabin, his mental exhaustion showed. Merritt's calm views on life and the world helped him find peace in himself. Ed had been confused about whether to return to the Park Service, or perhaps seek another kind of employment.

After spending time in the majestic Sierra's, with Merritt pointing out the wonders of nature around them, Ed decided that he would try to get into the naturalist program offered by the National Park Service. In his way of thinking, the realities of nature were what he held dear, not society or government. Perhaps he inherited this sentiment from his mother.

In August, Mary Lou and Kevin's second child was born; a daughter, which surprised everyone. Every other couple seemed to have boys; the same phenomenon that occurred after the First World War. They named their daughter Hannah Louise.

The next December, Ed left the cabin before Nadine and Merritt, to return home for Christmas. First he wanted to see Yosemite Park. He had been there many times as a child, with his parents and on his own. He'd heard that the Navy had taken over the Park during the war, and the Ahwahnee Hotel had been used as a hospital for recovering Navy sailors and Marines. Now, once again, tea was served in the afternoons in the great lounge. He sat and talked with veterans who had come to the park with their families. He hiked to Mirror Lake, and sat by the shore looking at his reflection and tried to make sense of where he'd been, and he wondered what was yet to come.

XXII

Mabel
1951

Etta had been looking out the window of Mabel's sunny studio while Mabel rested on her chaise, when she suddenly turned to Peter and asked, "Peter, what do you think about taking a trip to Boston to see Alma and Alan, and Carol? I've been wondering how they are, and I'd like to see Anne. What do you think Mabel, would you feel up to it?" Yes Etta, I think so. I really miss them all." Peter was enthused; "Should we go by airplane? I keep reading the advertisements for Pan-Am, and the T&WA airline owned by Howard Hughes." "Peter, I don't think I could do that as yet; I'd rather take the train. We always have so much fun, and it's relaxing on the train. I've got oodles of new books to read and you always find men to talk with and play cards; Etta and I will reminisce about our long ago train trip west. Tell me, wasn't it a Howard Hughes film we all went to see it at its premier a couple of years ago?" Etta laughed. "Yes, the movie was, "The Outlaw," I remember noticing Mabel looking distressed for me; and Peter was enjoying looking at Jane Russell. Ed liked looking at Jane Russell also."

Ed had returned to the Park Service, and as he had hoped, was now stationed in Yosemite. There were changes being made, and expansions of park services. He hoped eventually to become a back country ranger. He'd been allowed to bring his own horse to the park. Merritt had given the horse to Ed after seeing him admire it. He visited Merritt often, and occasionally went in to Sonora to enjoy Nadine's "good grub."

Etta, Mabel and Peter took the train to Boston in the warm spring of 1949. Mabel was very sincere when she said she and Etta would reminisce about their first trip west. She was feeling exceptionally nostalgic and reflective. "Etta, are we so different now from the young girls we were then?" "Well, let's see, you were twenty, and I was eighteen. Now you're seventy-three and I'm seventy-one. No, I can't see how we could possibly be changed." The women laughed and leaned into each other giggling, just as they'd done fifty-three years earlier. "Mabel, don't you wish it was all before us and we were just starting out?" "Oh Etta, yes!" And they each reached for their handkerchiefs to dry their tears.

They stayed with Alma and Alan in their sparkling new, yet modest, house. Alan's practice had begun to build up again. He now shared a suite of offices with Alma. They saved money by employing just one receptionist. Alma thought her mother looked tired, but on the whole, satisfactory enough.

Carol was no longer living with her parents; she now shared a flat with a fellow teacher. She was teaching grade school; however she made more money while tutoring Latin to the sons of Boston's elite, who attended Boston's Latin school, where the Latin language was compulsory. She met Etta, Mabel and Peter at a restaurant for dinner, but, at that time, didn't mention that she had met a man she was planning to marry.

Though years had passed since Joseph's death, seeing his parents brought up memories for Carol, as seeing Carol did for Mabel and Peter. Over the weekend, when they visited Carol at her parents' house, Carol told Etta about her beau and asked if Mabel and Peter would be offended. Etta told her not at all; in fact they'd be relieved. They'd worried that she hadn't made a new life for herself. When Carol told them, they hugged her and told her they were delighted and happy for her, and would enjoy celebrating with her at her wedding.

Over the years Anne and Alma met often. Alma had been thirteen when Anne came to live with them as governess and help for Mabel. Anne was always thought of as part of the family. From the very first, Alma had imitated her, and tried to speak with Anne's lovely accent. In these recent years, they thought of themselves as sisters.

Anne and her husband, George, arrived at Alma's to a welcome of open arms, tears, and joy. The dinner was as spirited as those long ago at Scott Street. Anne's youngest son, Sean, who had been so seriously injured, was now working for Boston Bell as an operator. Their oldest was a high school athletics coach and also taught history. He was married and already had two children.

Etta and Anne met again for tea, and they talked about the past and how times had changed, and themselves as well. Anne had always written to her mother, telling her that she was doing well, and was very happy. Her parents were now both gone, and her brother, Walter, ran the store but had closed the teashop. Walter visited her once, before the war. He'd told her what he'd learned about Harry Place and James Ryan, and that they had been killed in Bolivia in 1908. Their outlaw past didn't matter, to Anne or to Walter; those men were among the finest they had met.

Anne and Etta hadn't talked much about their lives in Argentina; Anne always knew something must have gone very wrong for Etta to have left her home with Harry. On this visit, Anne finally asked Etta about Harry and told her what she had learned from Walter. Etta suggested they go for a walk to the commons so she could talk more freely. They walked arm in arm, Anne quiet, while Etta told the whole story of her life so many years ago.

*

Once home, Mabel seemed to fail. She lost her usual vitality and was tired and weak. Dr. Morris came out to the house to check on her. He told Peter that her heart function showed increased weakness and recommended bed rest. Perhaps after she was well rested, she could perform her usual tasks, but going out, even for walks, would have to be postponed until she showed improvement.

Within two weeks, Mabel was up and spending time in her studio sorting her collection of drawings; separating them in stacks. She made a list of her paintings stacked in the studio and on the walls of their home. Many of her paintings had already been given to Mary Lou and decorated Etta's house; more were at the cabin in the Sierra's. She listed whom she'd like the paintings to go to when she died. Peter was alarmed when he saw the list; Mabel was contemplating her demise. This couldn't happen.

Etta was again living with Mabel and Peter, and was there to watch that Mabel's spirits were kept up. Etta no longer went to Letterman's hospital; she needed to be home more often, and to always be in an optimistic frame of mind. A couple of Mabel's friends from the Art Institute still came by once a week for lunch. Violet Little, Mabel's closest friend, whose husband, Henry, had passed away last year, came one afternoon a week for tea and friendship.

Mabel read the newspapers and learned in that in June of 1950, the U.S. was at war again. It was now the Korean War. She was despondent over the prevailing state of mind in the world. "Peter, it seems there will always and continually be war now, ever since the First World War. What has mankind let itself become? As a species, we seem to be going backwards." "Let's see what President Truman can do, though his term is getting short." "Yes Peter, we'll see."

Mabel surprised herself and everyone by rallying and improving in health and strength. Peter started taking her on scenic drives around the city and down the coast, or across the Golden Gate Bridge to Sausalito, or up over Mount Tamalpais. Sometimes Etta would go with them. Once a month they'd take a longer drive for a couple nights stay in Guerneville at the Russian River, or to the wine growing country in Napa County. When Mabel was feeling very well, they went for a weeks stay at the cabin.

In the city, they sometimes went for walks in the Japanese Tea Garden in Golden Gate Park. Etta took Mabel to the De Young Museum, and to the Palace of the Legion of Honor, where they sat on benches and Mabel would tell Etta about the history and styles of the paintings and the artists.

Christmas was now a quiet celebration, though Mary Lou's children, Michael and Hannah, kept the festivities alive for them. Mabel looked back over the years and Christmas times of the past. Could the coming year really be 1951?

When Mabel was feeling much stronger, Peter brought her and Etta downtown for shopping. Mabel was looking for stylish shoes that would also be comfortable. Her legs and knees sometimes ached. She and Etta enjoyed their shopping excursion and their leisurely lunch at the Emporium's mezzanine cafeteria. Afterward, they thought they'd ride the cable car to North Beach. They planned on calling Peter, to have him join them at a restaurant there. Peter had said he'd meet them whenever they were ready.

They had just left Woolworth's, at the corner of Powell and Market Streets, where the cable cars are turned around. Mabel went to step up on the high steps of the cable car and found she couldn't. Etta held her, and a man who was standing next to them helped Etta bring Mabel into the Bank of America on the southwest corner. Etta wanted to call an ambulance, but Mabel insisted that she was alright now; something had just come over her. Etta called Peter, who then called Dr. Morris to ask him to come to the house, and then raced to get Mabel and Etta.

*

Dr. Morris was introduced to Peter many years ago by his friend Henry Little, the pharmacist who'd saved an important dinner party, back during prohibition, by bringing "prescription wine." Dr. Morris had been the family doctor ever since. After examining Mabel, he left her to rest with Etta at her side. He sat with Peter while he told him that Mabel's condition was now critical, her heart condition worsened, and she was in a much weakened state. She evidently had suffered a stroke.

Peter summoned all his resolve to be strong for Mabel and make her days as pleasant as possible. He bought a television set; something he'd been putting off until he felt the makers really knew what they were doing and the things were safe. In the past they enjoyed listening to radio shows like, "The Texaco Star Theater," "The Philco Radio show", "Burns and Allen," "The Lone Ranger," and "The Shadow." Now they took pleasure in watching the shows on TV. Mabel really liked "The Fireside Theatre," and "Your show of Shows." Etta liked, "Arthur Godfrey's Talent Scouts." They all thought the Sunday evening program; "Toast of the Town" with Ed Sullivan was wonderful. Merritt arrived and also enjoyed the new fangled picture box.

Anne arrived as soon as she heard the news of Mabel's poor health. She and her husband had just returned from a tour of Europe, which had been a dream come true for Anne. They were doing very well; George was now the owner of the tailor shop. With Anne and George, was their youngest son, Sean, who was now thirty-two. Sean remembered Peter and Mabel, and his trip to the cabin with the family, when he was about ten. He asked Peter and Merritt if he could go to the cabin to stay for awhile. He said he could use some hard work and country life. Peter and Merritt thought it was a good idea. Merritt was getting on in years; he was now sixty-seven. He could use the help at the cabin.

Mabel was very pleased that Sean would stay at the cabin. “I’m so happy Peter bought the cabin. Look at the times it’s been a refuge and a sanctuary for us all. It’s been good for you too, Etta. Etta, you’ve always been strong for me, and supportive and encouraging. I remember our years in San Diego. You helped me believe in myself. You helped me with Alma, my first child, when I was overwhelmed; and at that time it was you that needed my support.” “Mabel, being with you, in your home gave me support. I remember all the years I spent with you, at first, when you were a new bride, and then after Argentina, but didn’t mind me being there. I’m grateful to you for that.” “Etta, would you make the same choices again, knowing the outcome?” “Nadine asked me the same question not too long ago, and the answer is yes; yes I would. I’ve lived an eventful and full life, even with the losses. What if I never had those experiences? That would be worse.” “Yes, Etta, for me also, even with Joseph . . . . .oh I don’t know, he didn’t get to live his life. That part is too painful. Etta, encourage Peter to spend more time at the cabin, perhaps not in winter, but, you know, I think that’s the life he’s always dreamed of, and now he’s on in years but still has his dreams. I’d like Mary Lou and Kevin and their children to live here when I’m gone. Mary Lou would take good care of Peter. Would you live in your house again?” Yes, that’s a good idea; and I’d also like to spend more time at the cabin.” “Etta, isn’t it fantastic how so much worked out so well? I remember when Merritt came to live with us. We loved him immediately, such a bright young man.”

*

Mabel passed away early in March of 1951 when her favorite cherry trees were just beginning to blossom. Etta and Peter were at her side. The weight of their loss was tremendous. Peter couldn’t be persuaded to leave Mabel. Etta called Dr. Morris; then Mary Lou and Alma. She left a message for Ed. That was enough, and all she could do that day. The next day she called Mabel’s close friends. Peter was barely well enough to make arrangements for the service and call the newspaper to place the notice; it reminded him of when Charles died; and it reminded him of Joseph.

Mabel's brother, Bud arrived and stayed at the Fairmont Hotel. Alma, Ed, and Merritt and Nadine stayed at the house. They helped fix meals and offered whatever support they could. Though the house was busy with friends that came by, for the most part they talked among themselves. Peter and Etta were withdrawn and isolated in their sorrow.

After the service, the house on Scott Street filled with Mabel's friends; though it was eerily quiet. Everyone spoke in hushed voices, as though Mabel was still resting in her room. They felt the sadness and despair of realizing she was gone, and comprehended the actuality of no longer seeing her smile or enjoying her gentle conversation.

After everyone left, Etta and Peter talked with each other about Mabel's passing. "Etta, Mabel was my life, all the rest would have meant nothing without her. I remember when I first met her in the garden in San Diego. She always retained that fresh, clear eyed radiance. So lovely. So beautiful."

"Peter, you meant the same to her. I've rarely seen another couple who enjoyed each other as much as you and Mabel. I know you feel empty and alone without her. She's always been there for me too, always, my whole life; the one constant and unwavering influence. I feel blank and empty; a part of me is missing. We were always two sides of the same coin."

Peter asked Etta to go through Mabel's things and separate what she thought Mary Lou and Alma would like, divide her jewelry, and discard the rest. Etta phoned Mary Lou and asked if she would help. They looked through Mabel's clothes and furs, and then boxed up several of the finer garments to send to Alma. Peter spent the better part of his days looking at Mabel's paintings.

Etta and Mary Lou spent an entire afternoon looking at and admiring Mabel's jewelry. Mary Lou knew the pieces that Alma admired, and put them in a box with the other items to send to her. When Mary Lou saw the gold lapel watch in the back of Mabel's jewelry case, she shrieked with excitement. "Aunt Etta isn't this a beautiful piece!" Alma looked over and saw that her aunt was in tears. "Aunt Etta, what's the matter?" "Mary Lou, that was mine from many years ago; I asked your mother to put it away in this case. I'd like you to have it."

XXIII

Etta
1952

Mary Lou, Kevin and their children moved into the house on Scott Street, where Michael and Hannah helped to lift Peter's mood by always engaging him in their activities. Mabel's paintings adorned every wall of the home, and were a constant reminder to Peter of the times when Mabel created each painting.

Back at her house, Etta started to go through her own things. She had the trunks, which had previously been stored at Peter's, delivered back to her home. Going through the contents, she rediscovered the wedding photos of her and Harry. Their clothing styles looked so old fashioned, truly from another age; even when compared with the wedding photos of her and Charles. She especially liked the photos that were taken at Mabel and Peter's apartment in San Diego. There they were, smiling at her from the photo; Harry, Mabel, Peter, and a younger version of herself.

She removed the paper wrapping that covered the old saddlebag she'd used on her trip across the Andes with Merritt. She looked it over and smelled it, hoping for a scent to remind her of Argentina. There was nothing; just the smell of old dry leather.

She found the journals she'd kept during her years in Argentina. Reading them was almost more than she could bear. For three days, she read over the entries that told of a different time, and a different life. It was almost as though it had been the life of someone else; except that it wasn't. Etta had to keep drying her eyes as she read the passages which took her back into the memories of her life with Harry. Overwhelmed with feelings of despair and sadness, Etta put the wrapping back on the journals.

Then she unwrapped a small package that revealed the plain wedding band she and Harry had bought for their stay in Las Vegas, New Mexico, and the diamond ring Harry bought for her in San Francisco. She put them on.

*

Etta walked around the grounds of her property on the hill while she thought out her decision to suggest to Ed that they sell the house. She planned on living at the cabin. She wrote to Ed to ask if he wanted to keep it, or sell it. She heard back from him the following week. He said to go ahead and sell it, as he would always be living in National Parks or the backwoods somewhere; and there would always be a home in San Francisco, on Scott Street.

With Peter's help, the property sold quickly. Ed came to town, on a brief trip, to sign the papers. Etta sold most of the furnishings, except for a few pieces that she had delivered to the cabin along with a few of Mabel's paintings, and the old trunk that held her mementos.

Etta drove first to Yosemite to spend some time with Ed. He was happy and looked incredibly healthy and Etta benefited from his positive, cheerful outlook. She drove to the cabin, and discovered Sean, Anne's son, helping Merritt finish a second cabin. Sean was doing the majority of the work, with Merritt's supervision.

Etta settled into a comfortable routine of going for walks in the morning, reading in the afternoon, and fixing dinner in the early evening. Etta, at seventy-three, went out horseback riding with Merritt or Nadine only occasionally for short rides.

Christmas that year was different than any they had celebrated. Peter, Mary Lou, Kevin and the children drove to the cabin. Alma and Alan arrived for a weeks stay; Ed came for a few days. It was crowded but joyful. On Christmas Eve, Alma fixed "Tom and Jerry's" from Mabel's recipe. Etta and Nadine made six different kinds of cookies, with the help of Michael and Hannah. Alma told the children about their grandmother, Gertrude, and the times when she and Joseph, and the baby, Mary Lou, made the holiday cookies with her. They were all in a nostalgic mood and talked about their past holidays.

On Christmas Eve, Etta asked them each to hang a stocking on the fireplace mantle in the new cabin. The socks came right off their feet. What a sight; twelve odd sized, mismatched, discordant, and cheery socks. She filled them with wrapped hard candies and candy canes.

Merritt showed Peter, Kevin, Alan, and Ed, the improvements he and Sean had made at the mine. There was now a second shaft going into the mountain that was paying off. The children were given gold nuggets as a memento of the occasion.

Peter stayed on, after everyone left. He'd return with Merritt the next time Merritt was going to the city. Etta spent a couple of days in Sonora, with Nadine. They looked in the shops around town and enjoyed lunches at the new inn. Nadine noticed a sadness about Etta, and asked her how she was feeling after losing her sister last spring. Etta confessed that she felt empty and lost.

Sitting by the woodstove in the old cabin a week later, Peter started talking about Mabel's passing and reminded Merritt and Etta that, when the time came, he would be buried next to Mabel. Merritt said he'd prefer being buried there at the cabin property, but that could please wait awhile, and certainly not until after he was dead. Peter continued to reflect on the past, and then asked Etta what was the best time of her life; the time spent with Harry, or Charles. Etta was bewildered by the question. "They were such different times, Peter. My time with Harry was short; at the most knowing him just eight years. I had almost thirty years with Charles." "But, what life would you like to go back to, if you could?" "Well, it would have to be with Harry; because that time was so brief, and the end was so severe and cruel. Since then I've lived in the time of two world Wars, and organized violence. With all that chaos and killing, it's difficult to believe that this country was so intent on hunting down and killing three people minding our own business in South America." "Etta, don't forget the egos of the railroad owners, or the Pinkerton's."

"I feel so grateful that I have you, Peter, and you, Merritt. You've both been with me through it all. We've all enjoyed rich and full lives. Now I'm going to excuse myself, and go over to the new cabin to check on the fire in the fireplace, and get some sleep. Sean is probably still awake in his room, reading one of Merritt's books. I saw him reading the book on mining that Harry sent to Peter so many years ago. Sean is a fine man isn't he. He reminds me of Anne's brother, Walter."

When the crocus, that Mabel had planted, sprouted through the snow, their spirits were renewed. Peter had stayed at the cabin over the winter. He cried while he looked at the flowers. Etta felt spring to be the true beginning of the year. The flowers gave them the assurance of spring's promise of new life. She became preoccupied with writing letters; which she sent to Ed, Alma, Mary Lou, Anne, and her brother, Bud; very cheerful missives that described the joy of spring in the Sierras.

Nadine noticed that Etta seemed more at ease, but she worried because Etta had also become withdrawn. Etta asked Nadine if she would consider living at the cabin. "Oh, no, I like town, and visiting the cabin works out just fine; and being in town gives Merritt a reason to spend time in town and be sociable. Besides, as you know, Sean stays with us in town some weekends, to court the young ladies."

*

On a day when the men were working at the mine, Etta, got out the photos of her and Harry; she had been looking at them everyday. While sitting at her dressing table, she stared at a photo of herself and Harry at the ranch. She thought again about the way Harry and Butch died. She would have expected their end to come from being shot when they were living the outlaw life in the states; but all the while they were in Argentina, she would have never thought it possible. Her grief began to take over her daily thoughts and she was again absorbed in sorrow. There had been an article in Elks magazine, in 1930, about Butch Cassidy and the Sundance Kid, and there had also been some speculation whether it was really them that died in Bolivia. Etta knew it was. Harry would have contacted her if he'd found a safe way to live in the States. The landlords, at the apartment where Peter and Mabel lived in San Diego, had their address in San Francisco and Peter's phone number was in the San Francisco phone book.

She set the photo down on the dresser and then opened a drawer to get out three envelopes; one addressed to Peter, another addressed to Ed, and one for Merritt. She looked up, and saw the image of Harry reflected in the mirror. Though she knew this was an illusion, she felt comforted. "Do I have the strength to do this now? My dear Harry, how many nights have I sat here contemplating your fate and mine." She then lifted Harry's colt pistol from the drawer.

She was happy and smiling, as she looked out the window of the train, on her way to meet Harry. She felt an immense sensation of joy, an expectation of something brilliant and wonderful. Now there he was, in bright light. She felt weightless as he took her in his arms,

---

She was playing a rousing tune on the violin, "Whiskey before Breakfast," a song her father had taught her. Then Harry said that he wanted to dance with Etta, and James could sing a song for them to dance to . . . .

"Yep tonight we're havin a dance,
an if you're lucky you'll have a chance.
Lordy, the cows are gonna dance all night.
All the fancy dance hall dames
wanna dance with good 'ol James.
By Lordy, the cows are gonna dance all night.
I went n got all good n slicked up;
n got me some whiskey in my cup.
And Lordy, the cows are gonna dance all night.
I met a maiden who was quite a sight;
she was a fadin' n not too bright . . . . ."

Harry twirled Etta out the door and onto the snow. After a moment they stopped dancing and looked up at the stars, and then at each other. They didn't talk. The spell was broken when James came out singing his next chorus;

"Now you all listen to what I sings;
'cause that's the way it is, by jings.
And the cows are gonna dance all night."

"Harry, look at you, standing on a chair afraid of a mouse. You've never been afraid of mice." "But this one's vicious, look at him. He wants a fight." "Get down and help me sweep him out" "Sweep him out! Kill it!" "Just help me." "Ah, I'm surprised you don't want to keep it for a pet. Did I ever tell you the story about the mouse in the train car?" "Yes, and I don't want to hear it again."

"James, come for a ride with us; we're going fishing." "I don't know if they're biting this time of year." "That doesn't matter; we just want an excuse to ride to the lake . . . ." "Well, look at that, you caught a fish." "But Harry says I have to take it off the hook, and clean it myself. Oh, it's so wiggly, but I can do it. There! Oops I dropped it; look it's swimming away. Oh darn, I was really looking forward to cleaning it."

"Harry I'll race you to the tall tree at the far point. Are you ready, get set, go." Her horse seemed to know it was in a contest, and took off like it was already a winner. Etta didn't hold it back as they sped towards the tree. But even with her devious head start, Harry passed her and won the race. "What's my prize for winning? And what's your penalty for cheating?" "Hmmm, perhaps it's the same, and I win after all."

*

Dear Peter, my friend, Mabel's love,

I've lived an extraordinary life. There is nothing more that I care to do. I do not stop my life at this point because of old age, sadness, or despair; but for my peace, and the freedom of letting go. I'm happy; and I have grand memories.

Do not think I have lived a tragic life. Though life has had its painful moments, I was blessed with great love. ~ My family, Harry, Charles, and Ed.

Thank you for being so magnificently strong for me ~ for us all. Thank you for bringing incredible joy and love to Mabel.

Harry was always my hearts compass; Charles, my hearts anchor; you and Mabel, my hearts home.

Please make the news go smoothly for Ed. I have left a letter for him and a letter for Merritt. Please give Ed my journals, but have him read them here, at the cabin, with you and Merritt.

Take good care of the family, as you have always done.

With all my love,
Etta

*

Dear Merritt, my dearest friend,

Do you remember, many years ago, when we were both very young, of your telling me of the ways of your people in Oklahoma? That, when they were old, they would go off to die when they felt ready. Merritt GoForth, my friend ~ I'm ready.

I love the boy you were, and the man you are. I do not know how to convey the great love and appreciation I feel for you. I am immensely happy that you are a part of my family. What would we have done without you?

You were a friend to Harry, and understood my love for him, and you were a friend to Charles. We were both fortunate to share in their lives.

You are now my son's best friend. Please help Ed to understand. It is a fact of nature; we live and we die. I would like him to read the journals I kept while I lived in Argentina. Please be with him when he reads them. I would like you to read them also. Harry and I lived well and were happy during those years at the ranch.

Merritt, please bury my remains here on this property. Explain to Peter that I love Charles, but he is gone.

Be happy with Nadine.

Speaking from my heart, I love you Merritt.

Etta

*

My dear Son,

My darling Ed, I do not want you to feel any kind of remorse; I am content. Merritt and Uncle Peter may have explained my views on dying. I'm sorry to leave you, but it was an inevitable event in any case. I've lived a long and happy life. I love you Ed. You have been the finest joy and source of wonder in my life.

Your father and I experienced happiness, and an awe of you, from the moment you were born. I'm not sure what kind of parents we were; a bit unusual perhaps. You have grown into an exceptionally fine person, nevertheless.

I have one regret; that you had to go to war. No mother wants their child to see and know about the ugliness in the world.

You were told that I was married once, before knowing your father, and that my husband died. So that you may know about that and more of my life in Argentina, I have left the journals, that I kept from that time, for you to read along with the journals I kept in San Francisco.

You know that I met Merritt when he was a boy, while I traveled through the west. He also knew my first husband. He is a true friend. Ask Merritt and Uncle Peter anything you wish to know. You know they will always give a straight answer.

I leave you, knowing that your future will be rich with adventure. I hope you might visit Argentina at some point.

Be happy my dear son.

With much love, Mother

*

"Pete, don't we have to get a permit of some kind to bury Etta on our land?" "I don't know Merritt, but I do know that if we ask, and they say no, we've opened a can of worms that can't be closed. So, I say let's just do it and no one will be the wiser." "Why Pete, you've become an outlaw." "It's about time." They chose a place by an overlook that could be dug. Sean did the work of digging the grave, while crying and swearing. He had been shocked and stunned at Etta's death. He had seen too much death during the war.

Ed arrived and cried at the sight of the casket Merritt had made. Just Merritt, Peter, Sean, Nadine, and Ed were there for the burial. To keep it simple, Peter decided to let the rest of the family know after the fact. They all spoke a few words and then Merritt added, "Etta had greatness in her. She was never afraid to seek a new path. She lived well. Look at who she was for your father, Ed. She was his muse. It was just natural that the people in her life were attracted to her; she had an extra brightness."

Ed read her journals; sometimes stopping while he cried. He spent the week talking with Merritt and Peter about the details that he'd just learned. "She was remarkably brave wasn't she? From the time she left Boston with Aunt Mabel, when she was just a girl. I knew she'd lived in Argentina, but I had never, until now, realized what great courage she had. She always encouraged me to try whatever I dreamed of doing. Imagine, my mother, a refined, cultured woman, living a life with outlaws. But, she always loved people for the person they were, and didn't get sidetracked by their circumstances. I think they must have been fine men." Merritt and Peter agreed that they were.

Ed took walks with Merritt, talked with him, and learned more about his mother. Before he left, to return to his work in Yosemite, he put the journals in a box, wrapped it and tied it with string. He asked his Uncle Peter to give it to Mary Lou; as she had become the family historian who kept all the records.

Nadine was there the morning Ed left. She told him that his mother had confided her story to her, and that she admired Etta more than any woman she'd ever met. Ed gave her a big hug, then turned to Sean and told him to look after Merritt and Peter, take care of them, and see that they don't get into any mischief.

*

Now there were just the three men at the cabin; Sean, whose mother was a Welsh girl brought up in Argentina, who, with the help of Etta, had come to the states, hoping to see more of the world. Sean's slight Boston accent delighted the young ladies in the town of Sonora. He had found a happy life in the foothills of the Sierra's.

Merritt would have never guessed, back when he was a young boy on the Osage reservation in Oklahoma, that he would meet Butch Cassidy and the Sundance Kid, and hold horses for the gang during train robberies; or that he would have the pleasure of meeting Etta, his inspiration. And, how could he have known that he would go on to live in San Diego and then San Francisco, and now own a gold mine with an attorney, who was his best friend.

An interesting set of circumstances had led Peter to his life here; starting with a vacation in San Diego, and meeting his lovely Mabel. He had good memories of raising his children in the sparkling city of San Francisco, though his thoughts and memories of Joseph could still devastate him. But for now, he was living here in the Sierra's with his dear friends, and close by was his nephew, Etta's son.

*

The campfire was going out. The two old men got up slowly and went inside the cabin. There would be a few more campfires, when they would again reminisce over memories of years past.

Should old acquaintance be forgot,
And never brought to mind?
Should old acquaintance be forgot,
And auld lang syne

For auld lang syne, my dear,
For old lang syne,
We'll take a cup of kindness yet,
For auld lang syne.

CPSIA information can be obtained
at www.ICGtesting.com
Printed in the USA
LVHW091920181120
672046LV00006B/49